New York Times bestselling author **Sherrilyn Kenyon** lives a life of extraordinary danger . . . as does any woman with three sons, a husband, a menagerie of pets and a collection of swords that all of the above have a major fixation with.

Writing as Sherrilyn Kenyon and Kinley MacGregor, she is an international phenomenon with more than twelve million copies of her books in print, in twenty-eight countries. She's the author of several series including: The Dark-Hunters, The League, and Lords of Avalon. Her books always appear at the top of the *New York Times*, *Publishers Weekly* and *USA Today* lists.

Visit Sherrilyn Kenyon's new UK website www.sherrilynkenyon.co.uk

Dianna Love is the *New York Times* bestselling co-author of *Phantom in the Night*, *Whispered Lies*, and *Silent Truth*. She is a national speaker who started writing while working over a hundred feet in the air creating marketing projects for Fortune 500 companies. When not plotting out her latest action-adventure, she travels the country on a motorcycle to meet fans and research new locations. She and her husband live near Atlanta, Georgia.

Visit her website at www.authordiannalove.com.

BLOOD
TRINITY

SHERRILYN KENYON
AND
DIANNA LOVE

BOOK 1 IN THE BELADOR SERIES

piatkus

PIATKUS

First published in the US in 2010 by Pocket Books
A division of Simon & Schuster, Inc.
First published as a paperback original in 2010 by Piatkus

A CIP catalogue record for this book
is available from the British Library.

ISBN 978-0-7499-5458-1

Typeset in Garamond by M Rules
Printed in the UK by CPI Mackays, Chatham ME5 8TD

Papers used by Piatkus are natural, renewable and
recyclable products sourced from well-managed forests and certified
in accordance with the rules of the Forest Stewardship Council.

Mixed Sources
Product group from well-managed
forests and other controlled sources
www.fsc.org Cert no. SGS-COC-004081
© 1996 Forest Stewardship Council
FSC

Piatkus
An imprint of
Little, Brown Book Group
100 Victoria Embankment
London EC4Y 0DY

An Hachette UK Company
www.hachette.co.uk

www.piatkus.co.uk

We'd like to dedicate this book to
our mothers, who both left too soon and
will forever live in our hearts.

ACKNOWLEDGMENTS

FROM SHERRILYN

Thank you to my friends, family, and fans. I love you all and couldn't do this without you. You guys rock!

FROM DIANNA

A big thank-you to Sherrilyn for wanting to team up on a new series. I'm thrilled. Who wouldn't be ecstatic over the opportunity to collaborate with a paranormal romance publishing legend? I can never thank my amazing husband, Karl, enough for his constant support, and ensuring my world is stable and filled with love so that I can create. Author Mary Buckham helped as an early reader and in wild brainstorming moments, sometimes with a glass of wine involved. Cassondra Murray is the best assistant anyone could ask for, but having the benefit of her sharp eyes and understanding of story—for she is a talented writer as well—is priceless. Plus, her husband, Steve Doyle, is always ready to offer his former Special Forces expertise when needed. I also want to thank Barbara Vey for spending that impromptu day in Atlanta with me researching locations, and for what her informative and positive Beyond Her Book blog brings to the publishing industry. Thank you, as well, to Kim Newman, who once again shared her knowledge of the Spanish language and on short notice. I love hearing from fans and book clubs at dianna@authordiannalove.com.

We'd like to thank the entire Pocket team, with a special thanks to our terrific editor, Lauren McKenna, and outstanding publisher, Louise Burke. Everyone, from the marketing department to the art department to the copy editing department, worked hard to give us a wonderful presentation for our first Belador story. We'd also like to thank our amazing agent, Robert Gottlieb, who directed this project from the beginning and continues to show why he is an icon in our industry. Thanks also to the RBLs for always bringing joy like fairy dust when we see them.

Last, but never least, we want to thank you, the fans, for reading and coming out to share time with us when we tour. You are the reason we write.

TWO YEARS AGO
UTAH . . . BENEATH THE SALT FLATS

*U*phold *my vows and die.*
    Or break my vows and die?

Evalle Kincaid had faced death more than once in the past five years, but never with these odds. If she had a one percent chance, it would be a miracle.

A citric odor burned her lungs, confirming that Medb majik shrouded the rock walls, high ceiling and dirt floor of her underground prison. It was the stench of her worst enemies.

She still couldn't believe that one of her own, a Belador, had betrayed her.

Not just her.

Anger over the betrayal and being tricked into falling for this chewed at her insides. But she pushed it down, knowing it wouldn't do anything except weaken her more. And right now, she needed her full sense and bearings.

Peeking carefully from beneath lowered eyelashes so that no one would know she was awake, she took in the other two captives—male Beladors—also held upright by invisible constraints.

A human would be blind in this black hole, but her vision thrived on total darkness. Natural night vision that allowed her to see in a range of monochromatic blue-grays. One rare perk of being an Alterant, a half-breed Belador, unlike those two pure bloods with their backs against the glistening red-orange stone wall.

Did those men know each other?

Did she really care? They were either allies or enemies. And until she knew more about them, they were definitely enemies.

Similar in height and size, they were different as night and day in skin color and the way they dressed. The one with nothing on but jeans had been conscious when she'd regained her wits twenty minutes ago. Completely still, he hadn't made a sound since then—like a snake lying low until it saw an opportunity to strike. Arms outstretched and legs spread apart, his gaze now cut sideways at a rustle of movement.

The fair-haired guy on his left struggled to reach lucidity.

Being imprisoned with two Beladors would normally fill her with hope for escape because of their ability to link with each other and combine their powers. When that happened, Beladors fighting together were a force only the upper echelon of preternatural creatures could touch. They were damn near invincible.

But linking required unquestioned trust. And right now, she couldn't offer trust so easily. Not after a Belador's telepathic call for help had lured her into this hole—into the hands of Medb warlocks. Her tribe had fought this bunch for two thousand years.

Burn me once, shame on you. Burn me twice . . .

Die with pain.

Even so, could she refuse to help these two warriors—members of *her* tribe—if there was a chance to save them? Beladors were a secret race of Celtic people connected by powerful genetics and living in all parts of the world. She'd only met a few.

Never these two.

But every member of the tribe had sworn an oath to uphold a code of honor, to protect the innocent and any other Belador who needed help.

If a warrior broke that vow, every family member faced the same penalty as the warrior, even the penalty of death.

Evalle had no one who would be affected by her decisions. The only person she'd had was an aunt who'd died that Evalle didn't mourn. Not after what that woman had done to her.

But even without having someone to worry about she'd upheld her vows since the day she'd turned eighteen. Not because she had to, but because she wanted to. And—until now—she'd always supported her tribe without question.

If only she knew which side of the lake those two across from her swam on. Hers or the Medb's?

She had one chance to answer that question correctly.

Live or die . . .

What else was new?

"Anyone know who called for this delightful little meeting?" the fair-haired male grumbled in a smooth voice born of enhanced genetics and a hint of British influence. The sound matched the urbane angles of his European face, which could be Slovak or Russian. He straightened his shoulders as if that would smooth the creases in his overpriced suit, obviously tailored to fit that athletically cut body that James Bond would envy. She'd put him in his early thirties and at close to six foot three.

Bad, black and wicked next to him might be an inch shorter, but he balanced out the difference with a pound or two of extra kick-your-ass muscle.

"Introductions appear necessary . . . unless you two know each other." The blond guy looked in her direction, then at the other male, but she doubted he could see a thing in this blackness.

Then again, who knew what powers he had as a Belador? That thought sent another chill down her spine.

Evalle fought a smirk over pretty boy's dry tone and well-honed nonchalance. She'd never met a Belador male who wasn't alpha to the core. But she had no intention of jumping in first to answer after deceit had landed her here.

One of these two could very easily be a Medb surveillance plant.

Tonight's betrayal had put a serious damper on her "team" mentality, and it burned raw inside her.

"I suppose I shall have to open," pretty boy continued, undeterred by the rude silence. "I'm Quinn."

The other prisoner still hadn't twitched since being hauled into the cave by four Medb warlocks and slammed against the wall. He'd been the last one captured. Blood that had trickled earlier from gashes in his exposed chest had dried . . . and the gashes were gone. Rumors had surfaced that a few of the more powerful Belador warriors could self-heal some wounds overnight, but she'd never heard of one healing so quickly. Odd.

His head was completely bald, which added a lethal edge to his face. Ripped muscles curved along his arms. All that body flowed down to the narrow waist of his jeans. He cleared his throat, and even that sounded dangerous. "I'm Tzader."

"The Maistir?" Quinn's gaze walked up and down the other warrior, sizing him up.

"Yes."

Truth or lie? Evalle had never met Tzader Burke, commander of all the North American Beladors. If he was Maistir, that might explain why *he* was here. He would be a coup in any Medb's career.

She slashed a look at the self-appointed cave host, waiting on Quinn to make the next move.

He shifted his head in Evalle's direction. "I can see another faint aura glowing across from us. A woman, I presume from the look of it."

How come other Beladors could see auras, but not her? What had she done to tick off the aura fairy?

When she didn't pick up the conversation thread, Quinn asked, "You would be?"

"Pissed off." Evalle opened her eyes all the way.

He smirked. "Love the name, darling. Should I refer to you as simply Pissed?"

She ignored his sarcasm. "No offense, I'm going to need a little more information before I'm ready to buddy up to *anyone*. Especially two who could be lying to me."

First again to keep the ball rolling, Quinn nodded. "I had assumed only Beladors answered the call, but your aura is—"

"—not Belador," Tzader interjected.

Quinn's moment of hesitation spoke louder than his words. "I see."

Snubbed again. What else was new? Even though she'd heard the traitor's call for help telepathically just like this pair of full bloods had and felt the sizzle of their tribe's connection on her skin, they still didn't consider her one of them.

Raw fury roiled through her veins. What would she have to do to be considered one of the group? Too bad their hazing wasn't as simple as eating a few live goldfish. But then, why was she surprised or even hurt? Her own family had wanted nothing to do with her. Why should anyone else?

Still, she refused to be discounted so easily. "You two may be able to see *auras,* but I doubt that either of you *see* anything else in this pitch dark. Not like I can."

"That explains it." There was no missing the disgust in Tzader's tone.

"What precisely does that explain?" Quinn allowed his annoyance to come through that time. Not the happy cave host after all.

"She's an Alterant." Tzader stared her way, studying on something. "The only one *not* in VIPER protective custody."

Evalle released a sharp stream of air from between clenched teeth. "Right. *Protective custody* sounds so much more civilized than being *jailed,* which is what really happened to the other four Alterants. I'm not there because I don't deserve to be there and I refuse to live in a cage —just like you would if you were me. So deal with it." She'd been there, done that and burned the T-shirt reminder, and it would take more than the entire Belador race to put her back in one.

And she had no doubt how he'd vote if she shifted into a beast in front of him.

Thumbs down. Hang the Alterant.

Yeah, the pendulum was buried on the side of them being her enemies.

Tzader frowned. "You work for VIPER?"

VIPER—Vigilante International Protectors Elite Regiment—was a multinational coalition of all types of unusual beings and powerful entities created to protect the world from supernatural predators. Beladors made up the majority of VIPER's force, and if that really was Tzader Burke across from her, he'd know the only free Alterant worked with VIPER. Might as well cop to it. "I'm in the southwestern region."

Quinn cleared his throat. "I'm with VIPER as well and was on my way to investigate a Birrn demon sighting in Salt Lake City when I heard the call. What about you two?"

"Meeting an informant in Wendover," Tzader replied, mentioning the small gaming town at the Utah-Nevada border. "What were you doing in this area tonight, Alterant?"

Following a lead I have no intention of sharing with you . . . dickhead.

When she didn't answer, Tzader chuckled in a humorless way that brushed a ripple of unease across her skin. "Listen, sweetheart. We might have another couple hours, or we might only have a couple minutes. The Medb don't ransom. They trap, plunder minds, use bodies in hideous ways and toss the carcasses into a fire pit. I could reach Brina even this far below ground, but I can't get through the spell coating these walls. So there's not going to be a Belador cavalry charging in to save us. You either join up and help us find a way to escape, or prepare for the worst death you can imagine."

As if she didn't know the stakes. . .

And hadn't already lived through a fate worse than death. They had no idea who and what they were dealing with.

"I quite agree, love," Quinn added. "I can understand your resistance to trusting anyone after being caught in this trap. I, too, want that traitorous Belador's head as a hood ornament on my Bentley, but none of us will have any chance to discover his identity if we don't survive, and that endangers all our people."

Evalle would give him that, but hanging here manacled to a rock wall by majik didn't exactly instill a sense of camaraderie in her. More like, it brought back memories that made her seethe.

She held the key to possibly overpowering the Medb—a physical ability to shift into a more powerful form that might afford the three of them the combined energy to fight their way out of here. But using that ability would expose the secret she'd shielded for five years and give the Tribunal, the ruling body of VIPER, all the reason they'd need to lock her up.

Adult Alterants did not get a second chance for any infraction. The four male Alterants with unnaturally pale green eyes like Evalle's had shifted into hideous beasts over the past six years and killed humans—and Beladors—before being imprisoned.

When she'd turned eighteen and an old druid had appeared and informed Evalle of her destiny to be a Belador warrior, Evalle had explained how the dark sunglasses she wore constantly protected her ultrasensitive eyes. By the time the Beladors had realized her eyes were the pale green of an Alterant, she hadn't shifted or posed a danger. For that reason alone, the Belador warrior queen Brina had asked the Tribunal to allow her warriors to train Evalle with the understanding by all parties of what would happen if Evalle shifted.

They would cage the beast if it ever made its presence known.

These two Beladors in the cave with her had taken a vow to uphold the Belador Code of protecting humanity—which also meant reporting any Alterant who shifted.

Evalle had almost changed into a beast once.

Almost.

Even now, she didn't know if she could do it and maintain control. Which meant she could shift and the Medb could still kill her.

So her only real option for escape depended on trusting these two men enough to link so the three of them could use their cumulative natural abilities to defeat the Medb.

If not . . .

Casket time.

Her choices narrowed by the heartbeat, and Quinn had a valid point. She couldn't find the one who had betrayed her and make him pay if she died in this underground prison.

"I'm Evalle. My reason for being in this area tonight is personal." She shot her attention to the one who would clearly lead a charge against the Medb. "Got a plan, Master T?"

"Working on it. They must have used water from Loch Ryve to coat the walls and hold the spell. That's the only substance I've ever known of that can drain Belador powers. I don't know how long we've been down here, but it's probably been working on us for awhile—"

"Not my powers," she corrected, enjoying a moment of satisfaction over another unexpected difference between her and the pure bloods. "I'm at full strength."

Tzader paused for a moment, then nodded. "Good. That's one plus for us, but *we're* losing power, right, Quinn?"

"Correct. I'm probably at half strength, which is why we must strike soon while we're still capable of battling."

Evalle looked across at both men. "Either of you have an idea how many we have to fight to get out?"

"Best I could tell, there were five Medb warlocks and the one traitorous Belador." Tzader's deep voice hardened on the last word. He was either just as pissed off as her or a very convincing liar. "Didn't get a good look at the fifth Medb, but he wasn't big and wore a priest's robe. This is a war party of hunters. If they were taking us to someone higher, we'd be gone. They plan to torture information out of us or maybe use us to bait another trap. I want blood from that traitor, too, but I won't let the Medb hurt another Belador regardless of what that bastard did."

Tzader's immediate concern for his tribe struck a note of guilt in Evalle, making her realize she'd been more worried about getting out of here alive than protecting her tribe. She'd fought alongside Beladors until she was bloody and spent to defend the tribe . . .

And to prove she was worthy.

Refusing to help another Belador now would destroy what trust she'd gained from some and give voice to the ones murmuring that she was little better than a trained animal.

Quinn shifted. "I agree with Tzader."

Before she had a chance to say yea or nay, Tzader started strategizing. "Let's do a quick check of resources. Since she's wary of us, I'll start. I've got kinetic, telepathic and energy force, plus two sentient blades they stripped from me with my body armor. If I can get out of here, I'll call them to me."

Quinn went next. "Ditto on the kinetic, telepathic and energy force, plus I can mind lock."

Evalle had no idea what he was talking about. "What do you mean by mind lock?"

"I can reach into another mind remotely, lock into their brain waves and see through their eyes. I can guide them as well . . . if they don't realize I've invaded their mind and resist. Then I'd have a battle on my hands."

"I thought the spell coating the walls was blocking us from reaching anyone. How can you access someone's mind from here?" She hadn't lived this long by accepting anything at face value.

"I can't reach beyond this facility, but I feel air movement. The Medb must have air passages running between the caverns or we'd have already died of asphyxiation. I can access anyone in another space connected to this one by even a thin gap in the rocks."

Tzader perked up at that last bit. "Can you destroy their mind while you're inside a person's head?"

Whereas his question had been asked purely for battle strategy, Evalle wanted to hear the answer for another reason. Could Quinn tamper with her mind if they linked? She didn't like the thought of that at all.

Quinn's pause indicated he'd given Tzader's question some thought. "Yes, but I won't. Not without our warrior queen's approval."

On the other hand, Evalle had hoped he'd share something no one knew about him, a secret that would make Quinn as vulnerable as she was if she had to shift.

Fat chance either of these two men would make that mistake.

"Are you . . . dressed, Evalle?" Quinn asked that with sincere concern that surprised her. He thought they'd stripped her?

"Yes. I'm in jeans and a shirt." The dark brown cotton shirt hanging open over her T-shirt was one of the two changes of clothes she owned—she preferred to live her life unencumbered by anything, even wardrobe. She'd twisted her shoulder-length hair up beneath a frayed ball cap to spend a night of surveillance in Wend-over. Lost the cap when she was captured.

"What about your powers, Evalle?" Tzader clearly wanted all the weapons laid out so they could make a solid plan.

"I have exceptional vision, similar to infrared illuminated night-vision optics. I have kinetics, telepathy, energy force . . . and the Medb failed to remove my boots, which conceal blades." *And I might be empathic, but that was a recent surprise and is unimportant right now.*

Quinn gave a low laugh. "Can't wait to get a look at you."

"Your optics are another plus." Tzader's eyes stared her way. "The next step's gonna take some trust. You willing to link with us so we'll have your full power and night vision?"

Not if Quinn could overpower her mind.

11

"Evalle, I sense hesitation on your part after learning I have the capability to take control of your mind." Quinn's voice was smooth, as though he'd lifted her thoughts. Could he? "But do realize that I could have already done so and locked onto your vision if I'd so chosen."

He was right.

She considered her dwindling options and had no choice but to relent. "Linking is our only chance, but first I want an agreement from both of you."

"On what?" Suspicion filtered into Tzader's commanding voice.

"That no matter what we have to do to get out of here you vow that we keep any secrets shared between us. You swear on the life of our goddess Macha."

"You get a head injury when they caught you, woman?" Quinn lashed back, not sounding quite so cultured, as if he hid a less-than-polished background behind that suave voice. "Swearing on Macha's life's a good way to see the last of yours."

"You think that's any crazier than me making a leap of faith with you two after one of our tribe tricked me?"

"*Our* tribe?" Quinn asked.

"Yes." Evalle was tired of always being doubted. "I swore the same oath you did. I've put my life on the line many times for other Beladors, even though—" She bit off her last words, stopping before she finished with *even though I'm treated like some mutt with tainted blood.* Never let them know how much their biased stares and constant spying slid under her defenses.

Beladors might tolerate an Alterant, but any trust she'd received in the past had been an uneasy alliance in tense times. She'd admit that the tribe had reason to be suspicious of Alterants after the last male who'd shifted two months ago had killed nine Beladors trying to contain him. But she'd proven herself for five hard years and deserved respect.

Too bad they didn't see things the way she did.

"No deal." Tzader's unmerciful gaze arrowed through the dark in her direction with the intensity of a lightning bolt.

"I think not as well," Quinn concurred.

Now what was she going to do?

The stretch of curved wall on her left that ran between her and Tzader began to fade.

Evalle tensed. She had no offensive edge. Not until she either linked with the two men or was released from the shackles so that she could shift. Both options twisted her stomach into a sick knot of terror.

When the rock disappeared, leaving a hole big enough to drive a small automobile through, a diminutive Medb figure wearing a pale gray robe entered. Light glowed from inside the hood. Where were the four brutes who had hauled Tzader into this chamber?

"You shouldn't be here." Quinn's soft voice was full of tender feelings.

Evalle glanced at him. Was he talking to that warlock?

The person in the robe moved toward Quinn as though floating across the floor. Evalle debated the risk of linking with Quinn and had just about talked herself into helping him when the hood fell away from the Medb's head. Not a warlock but a stunning witch, with hair so bright it had to be the color of a flame in natural lighting.

Angling her chin at him, the witch stood a head shorter than Quinn. Without saying a word first, she lifted up on her toes and cupped his face with her hands, then kissed him sweetly on the mouth. Quinn didn't just let her kiss him: he joined in until she finally pulled away. "When my men described the three Beladors they'd caught I didn't want to believe what I heard. I had to see for myself. What are you doing here?"

"Protecting my tribe." Quinn's heavy sigh bulged with regret. "Leave before your men find you here."

"I don't know how to help you," she whispered desperately.

"You can't. If you do, they'll kill you for treason, regardless of your being a priestess."

"You shouldn't have been caught in this trap," she whispered. "They weren't looking for you—"

"*Who* do they want?" Quinn's tone sharpened.

The witch shook her head. "They'll take you last. I'll come up with a way to free you. I have to go." She turned to leave.

13

"Kizira."

When the witch turned around, Quinn softened his tone again. "Don't try to save me. I'm bound to my tribe and will die with these two if they can't also be saved."

"Ever the fool." She shook her head. "You should not have protected me that day."

"I must uphold my oath of honor in *all* situations."

Quinn's reply renewed Evalle's hope at gaining an ally in keeping secrets. If she had to shift to escape, would either of these two be willing to say she'd done so with honorable intent?

The Medb witch visiting Quinn lifted her hood back into place and started to leave, then hesitated. "Your time nears." She vanished, and the wall was solid again.

The tight muscles in Evalle's chest relaxed after that bizarre scene. Quinn was friends—more than friends—with a Medb priestess. Not kosher in the Belador world, but she couldn't fault him if he'd acted out of honor and spared an enemy rather than kill without thought as their bloodthirsty ancestors had. Their goddess would respect that, but Quinn had a secret to protect as vigorously as Evalle shielded hers.

Now, if only Tzader had something to hide.

But he was a warrior who would die before exposing any vulnerability. She'd bet he hadn't shared all his powers either.

"Want to explain that visit, Quinn?" Tzader asked.

"Sorry, chap. Rather not."

Evalle smiled. "Maybe you should both reconsider my offer to hold each other's confidence in order to escape."

Quinn gave a quick shake of his head. "I won't ask either of you to put yourself in jeopardy with Brina or Macha. Not for me."

Damn. Damn. Damn. What was with these two? Why couldn't they bend an inch? Evalle wouldn't admit defeat, but winning their freedom wasn't looking too promising either. The witch had said they were running out of time.

Quinn narrowed his eyes. "I'm roving mentally through the tunnels for a mind."

Evalle was starting to like this guy in spite of his being cozy with

14

a Medb. He knew his ass was in a sling if word of his association with a Medb made it to Brina, but he was still determined to help. Maybe she could trust *him*.

Tzader, on the other hand, had yet to get her vote.

"Got one . . . don't think he's the leader." Quinn's voice changed to a monotone. "He's listening to one of the other warlocks . . . they can't wait on the spell to drain the Beladors . . . Kizira arguing they should wait . . . Beladors dangerous even one at a time . . . leader says . . . " Quinn's head jerked back. His shocked eyes swung toward her. "You're the one they want, Evalle, and you don't want to know what they plan to do to you."

"Bring it," she said with more arrogance than she felt capable of backing at the moment.

Quinn's eyebrows tightened, his eyes staring at nothing as he concentrated. He sucked in a breath. "I hope you can take on four warlocks alone, because that's what's coming for you . . . Right now."

The warning in his voice spiked chill bumps along her arms.

"Link with us, Evalle. Now!" Tzader's tone brooked no argument or questions.

She had seconds to make up her mind. Tzader and Quinn couldn't link unless she lowered her mental shields. "How do I know you aren't lying just to trick me into linking?"

"You don't." Quinn shrugged. "Just like I don't know what I'm in for when I link with an Alterant, but I'm willing to trust you for a chance to escape."

The wall to her left started fading again, slowly widening as though to accommodate more people this time.

Grace be to Macha, it was time to decide if she'd live or die.

As the cave wall disintegrated under Medb majik, Evalle realized she only had to answer one question. Could she let even one Belador die after vowing to protect her tribe?

The answer was an unfortunate one for her . . .

No.

She sighed softly. "Let's do it."

Flexing her fingers quickly before the warlocks entered, she opened the channel to her mind for Tzader and Quinn.

The immediate synergy that shot between the three of them sparked the air with combined power. She flagged physically for a couple seconds, experiencing how drained the other two were; then she focused only on sending energy to them.

You got some screamin' optics, babe, Tzader's voice whispered in her mind.

And her vision isn't her only asset. Quinn searched through her thoughts like a warm flood of fine whisky.

If she wasn't so concerned over the threat entering as soon as the wall disappeared, she'd have smiled at the flirt.

Don't move until I give the signal. Tzader gave that order with enough heat to let everyone know he was in no mood to joke.

Guess we'll allow him to lead this one, eh? Quinn's sarcasm took the edge off Evalle's anxiety and filled her with a flush of confidence. She glanced over at the rogue and winked, then sent them a message. *I'll wait for the word to attack, but let them unshackle me before you do anything if you want the full force of my power.*

Tzader gave a curt nod of his head.

Quinn lifted a finger in acknowledgment.

The wall cleared. Four warlocks in swirling gray robes with no hoods carried torches into the room, all headed for Evalle. Without her sunglasses on, she squinted to be able to see in what, for her eyes, was brilliant light.

Serpent tattoos wrapped their thick necks, then swept around each bald head. The pointed tip of the viper's head stopped at the bridge above each warlock's wide nose. The vipers' eyes glowed yellow-orange and had narrow black diamond centers. When one warlock stood in front of each of Evalle's arms, they chanted in unison, releasing the shackles.

She dropped to the floor.

One of the other two warlocks extended his hand, not touching her. His fingers kinetically circled her throat and lifted her off the dirt floor.

She fought to breathe. *Tzader? What are you waiting on?*

"She is secure, Priestess," the warlock choking Evalle called out in a loud voice.

Kizira appeared at the entrance, her face stoic.

16

Quinn shot his thoughts to Evalle. *Tzader was waiting on Kizira to enter. I'll deal with her.*

Kizira closed her eyes and held her hands in front of her with the palms turned up. Her eyes glowed yellow. She began murmuring foreign words that sounded ancient and deadly.

Now, Evalle, Tzader roared in her mind.

Evalle willed herself into battle form, a minimal physical change all Beladors were approved to use when engaging with an enemy. She tightened her fingers into fists. Spiked cartilage rose along the lengths of her arms. Power surged throughout her, expanding muscle tissue and driving her adrenaline to a volcanic level.

She gripped both hands around the invisible arm holding her and bared her teeth. "You're dying first, just to kick this party off on a high note."

The blunt-nosed warlock smiled and squeezed tighter, drawing tears to her eyes.

Using her kinetic ability, she knocked the torches into the dirt, killing the flames. The warlocks howled in anger.

Ready?

Tzader and Quinn broke free of their shackles, drawing the other three warlocks around to face them.

Battle screams ricocheted off the walls, gathering force like the wail of a banshee.

Pulling in opposite directions with each hand, Evalle snapped the force holding her throat. The warlock screamed in agony, his arm falling uselessly to his side. Released from his power, Evalle again dropped to the dirt floor. He snarled with pain and dove at her. She shoved her hands up, palms out, blocking him with a shield of power. He bounced back, falling to the ground.

Kizira swayed, caught in a deep trance.

Evalle stomped each foot and silver spikes with razor-sharp tips shot out from around the boot soles. She took a step toward Tzader, who fought two warlocks.

Quinn snapped the neck of the Medb he battled, tossing the body aside quicker than yesterday's trash, then snatching one of Tzader's opponents away.

The warlock Evalle had knocked out gained his feet. He charged her, his mouth opening wide to release demonic curses on a stream of black breath.

She spun, whipping her boot high, the lethal tips slicing his neck like a buzzsaw. Purple liquid bubbled from the mortal wound, filling the air with a soured-orange stench. Evalle whipped her boot up again in a crosskick. The warlock's head flew off sideways, hitting Kizira in the chest. That jolted the priestess out of her trance. Her glazed eyes started clearing.

Oops.

Evalle swung back to the fight, but she couldn't jump in kicking and risk killing the Beladors, who now fought the only two warlocks still alive. Of the two dead, one lay facedown on his chest with his head spun around to stare at the ceiling.

Tzader battled a warlock armed with a three-pronged sword he hadn't possessed a moment ago.

Quinn blasted the fourth warlock backward with a shot of energy, then produced three Celtic Triquetra with jagged blades and threw them with deadly accuracy. The blades struck the warlock in his throat, heart and eyes, killing him instantly.

"Not my brother! No!" Kizira screamed. She looked at Quinn, her agonized face a mix of shock and betrayal. When the priestess lifted her hands at Quinn, Evalle dove at her.

"No, Evalle!" Quinn shouted.

She slid to a stop at the side of Kizira, who froze in mid-motion with arms extended, eyes stuck open, full of fury.

Quinn appeared next to the priestess. "I've locked her mind, but I can't hold her long without harming her." He cut eyes teeming with sadness at Evalle. "Help Tzader."

She nodded, then felt a blow to her midsection and doubled over. Quinn groaned but held his position with his back to the room. When she turned to Tzader, she found him on the ground, the three-pronged spear staked through his chest.

Tzader looked over at her. His face twisted with pain. *Unlink . . . before I die, and leave me,* he called into her mind. *You can't kill this one.*

Evalle looked at the last warlock, who laughed in triumph until he eyed Kizira immobilized. That's when the eyes on the serpent tattoo on his head came to life. That meant he carried the same blood as the Medb High Priestess.

Evalle looked at Tzader. *Escape or fall, we stand as one.*

Agreed, Quinn confirmed on a gasp. *But I can't help you and hold Kizira immobile.*

Evalle faced the warlock. Intimidation played a role in every battle won. "You don't look so hard to kill."

The warlock whispered a chant, lifting his hands to his lips and blowing across the palms. Both hands tripled in size, extending into claws. He swiped one long talon at the nearest wall, digging a trough through stone as though cutting butter with a cleaver. He crooked the same claw, smiling when he goaded her to attack.

Well, crap. She hadn't really expected to get out of this mess without facing this decision. But she'd only shifted once—partway—and that had been in reaction to terror. Returning to her normal physical state had been a struggle. Could she do it again? Or would she remain a mindless beast?

No time to worry about what *might* happen.

If they stayed, they died. If she shifted . . .

Evalle mentally reached inside herself, deep into the core of her life force. She urged her body to free itself. Power rolled through the center of her, surging into her legs and arms. Bones cracked and popped, skin stretched tight. Her clothes split, shredding into tatters that fell away from her body.

Leather ripped with a squeal when her feet thickened, toes growing the length of a human hand. Her jaw expanded to accommodate a double row of teeth that sharpened into jagged fangs.

Nerves and tendons cried out in pain. She roared an echoing, haunting sound, now able to stare down at the warlock from ten feet off the ground.

He dared to laugh, then threw a ball of energy at her.

She batted it away, blowing a hole in the rock wall.

The warlock cocked his head, still smiling, but with a little surprise. He flew at her, arms drawn back to swing a clawed hand at her neck. Before he could sever her head, she blocked him, using an over-size arm that sizzled with unspent power.

He bounced back, stunned for the two seconds she allowed him to live.

She curled her leathery fingers into a fist and smashed his face, slamming him backward into the wall, where his body clung, shaking. Bolts of energy popped and sparked around him before he dropped to the ground. When she stepped close to the warlock, he gasped, "You're a dead monster—"

She lifted a foot as heavy as two cement blocks and slammed down on his midsection, crushing him into two halves.

His last breath screamed out of him, a sound of agony Evalle never wanted to hear again.

Brilliant orange light blanched the inside of the cave. His body foamed purple, then disintegrated into a puff of brown smoke. A sure sign he was Medb royalty.

Evalle took several breaths, calming the power pulsing through her. She begged her body to pull back into itself now that they were safe. Each breath she drew forced another part to tighten and shrink, but hallelujah, she was reversing the change. Sweat covered her skin. Pain daggered her arms and legs, sickened her stomach. Her head felt as though a stake was being driven through her temples, but she'd end up facing worse if the Tribunal found out she'd shifted.

Feeling the last of her body return to human form, Evalle swung around to Tzader, who lay perfectly still. When she reached him, she yanked the spear free. Blood gushed from the three holes. Mortified by her naked state but unable to repair her shredded clothing, she dropped down on her bare knees and pressed her hands over the gaping wounds to stop the flow of blood. But she had no power to save him from all the internal damage.

"He can't be dead, because we're alive," Quinn said in a wheeze over his shoulder from where he still controlled Kizira.

"You're right." Evalle and Quinn had a chance to survive if they unlinked and escaped, but she couldn't walk away from Tzader. He was not the traitorous Belador. If she unlinked, he'd lose the strength she still gave him. Her abdomen hurt, too, but . . . not as though she'd been stabbed. Why didn't she feel like she was dying?

Could an Alterant linked to a Belador not die?

Tzader's eyes fluttered.

"I'm here," she assured him. "I won't leave you."

He gasped hard for air, chest heaving. His hand shot up to grab her arm with a strength that surprised her.

"He's living . . . I feel him getting stronger."

Evalle glanced over her shoulder at Quinn. "Me, too."

Tzader groaned. "You can move your hand now."

When she looked down, his face was robust with life. She pulled her hands away. The holes in his chest were shrinking. She stared in shock. "What'd you do?"

Tzader sat up and stretched; then his shoulders slumped with the effort. "You saved my life, Evalle."

"No, I didn't." She stood up and backed away from him. "I do *not* have those powers."

Pushing up to his feet, Tzader turned to her, politely avoiding her naked body. "You ought to grab a robe."

She yanked a robe off the ground where it had been left behind when one of the warlocks had disintegrated. She shoved her arms through the sleeves. "Now. What happened to you, Tzader?"

He moved slowly, still recovering. "Best I can tell, the spear tips were made of lava from a volcano I'm not telling either of you about since it's the only thing that can kill me. But the tips have to stay in place while I die a slow death. If you hadn't defeated the last warlock and pulled out the spear, I'd be dead."

Beladors were not immortal, as a rule, as far as she knew. "Why can't you be killed?"

When Tzader didn't reply, Quinn did. "Might as well tell us. Then Evalle can share what it takes to kill her, too. I'm not leaving here without knowing more about both of you."

She gave him an arch stare. "I think you two know all you need to know about me right now."

Tzader shrugged. "Let's just say I'm the descendant of a Belador who had me blessed, or cursed, depending on your point of view, and leave it at that, okay?" He walked over to Quinn. "Can we get outta here?"

"Yes. I pulled the exit route from Kizira's mind."

Evalle stepped up to both of them. "I doubt she's going to let us go without a fight once you unlock her mind."

"I won't kill her," Quinn said with quiet conviction. "I can leave a blank place in her thoughts when I release her that will last maybe a minute after she comes out of this state. That's enough time to reach the surface."

"Do it." Tzader glanced at the still-open wall. He whistled shrilly. Two spinning knives with Celtic designs on the handles flew into the room and circled him, landing at each hip. The tips of the blades snarled and hissed.

Evalle missed her boots more than her clothes, but she had bigger worries. She knew better than to believe these two would protect her secret unless they gave her their word. But what Belador would risk his existence *and* his family for an Alterant?

"We have to go now." Quinn stepped away from Kizira, who stood motionless, like an eerie statue. He led the way, racing through a maze of dark corridors that climbed upward to the surface.

Tzader followed Evalle, who kept pace with Quinn.

"We're all good with keeping a few secrets, right?" Evalle was dying to know why neither of the men had commented on her shifting. She'd do anything to protect her tribe, but she would not go willingly into a cage again.

Not after spending her childhood locked away as a freak.

Tzader's steps pounded close behind. "Let's get outta here first, then talk."

Fear went through her. He was going to throw her to the higher-ups. She knew it. He just wasn't man enough to tell her until he was safe. "You can talk *and* run. Admit what you saw. I changed right back into my normal state. I'm not out of control. I chose when to shift and when to come back."

"It's complicated, Evalle." Quinn led them with confidence, choosing turns without hesitation and running all-out.

Until he reached a pile of rocks that blocked their path.

Everyone skidded to a stop.

Neither man made a move to clear the rocks, and their minute of a head start was close to ending. Evalle looked at them. "Let's get kinetic, shall we?"

Quinn shook his head. "We can't move these rocks that way. I pulled several chants from Kizira I believe are connected to this route, but—"

"But what?" Anger mixed with fear inside her. "Start the freaking chant before your crazy priestess wakes up from her little nap."

"I might *kill* us if I use the wrong chant. And she's *not* crazy." Quinn's tone told her his patience was strained.

An unearthly shriek right out of a B horror movie rocked the underground tunnel.

"Sounds like Sleeping Beauty's awake," Evalle sighed.

"I liked you better when you didn't talk," Quinn snapped, losing all hold on his composure.

"I don't like either one of you right now." Tzader glared at them. "Open the damn exit or I'm gonna have to kill one seriously pissed-off priestess."

Kizira's shrieks grew in volume.

Quinn faced the rocks and spewed out a rapid sequence of mumbo jumbo Evalle couldn't begin to translate or remember.

Boulders started falling away to each side, parting to make an opening. She took one quick look behind them for Kizira. Quinn might not want to hurt his evil-eyed honey, but Evalle did. If not for the Medb she wouldn't be facing imprisonment—or worse—for shifting.

"Let's go." Tzader grabbed her arm and dragged her through the opening. *"Seal that mother, Quinn!"*

Quinn's chant was lost in the sound of rocks piling in behind them.

When Evalle caught her footing she was above ground.

In daylight. No shelter within a mile.

An August sun blistered the desert landscape, and it blistered her.

"No!" She curled inside the robe, pulling the thin protection around her. Skin on the back of her exposed hand started turning a nasty green color.

23

Tzader and Quinn shouted something, but her screams drowned them out. Heat scorched through the blood vessels in her arm and into her body, carrying the poison into her system.

She wouldn't face imprisonment after all.

The sun would kill her first.

CURRENT DAY
ATLANTA, GEORGIA

ONE

Evalle kept a city block between her and the Cresyl demon skulking along Peters Street through one of the riskier sections of downtown Atlanta after dark.

Three-in-the-morning dark. Graveyard quiet for a Sunday morning. Where were all the people leaving the bars? There should be more on the street than this.

But more importantly, who had sent a Cresyl demon into this territory—again—and why? Second time in ten days, and she wouldn't have identified this one so quickly if not for having studied up on them after the last one showed up and ruined her day.

So many nonhumans to learn about, so little time. Especially while hunting them. But the last Cresyl sighted in Atlanta had disappeared before causing any trouble.

This time, they weren't so lucky. A human had died, and in a suspicious manner for a demon attack. A death that meant trouble for Evalle in the worst way with VIPER.

The body of a young female had been mauled with only the heart missing. Worse had been the stink of sulfur, which told her exactly how nonhuman the attack had been. But that didn't make sense. A demon had to ingest the entire human to take a soul, so why only one organ? Why maul the body?

It didn't smack of demon. It smacked of the way Alterants had decimated bodies in the past.

Was someone intentionally trying to make the killing appear as though an Alterant had attacked the woman?

Or am I just being paranoid?

27

She wished Tzader and Quinn hadn't both been called out of town. They could sort reality from paranoia. She hadn't been really good at doing that for herself since surviving their escape from the Medb two years ago.

Had the Medb sent this demon?

Were they still trying to get her?

But that didn't make sense either. Cresyls were South African and not Celtic, therefore they weren't the kind of demon the Medb would use.

Stop with the crazy thoughts and catch that friggin' thing sneaking around the city. If she handed proof of what had killed the human to VIPER *before* they opened an investigation, she wouldn't face even suspension. If not, the first finger would point at her the minute they found out about a ripped-up human.

Always worked that way.

Guilty beyond doubt. Burden of proof on me, no matter how much I prove myself.

Bastards.

She'd never harmed a human, but she was an Alterant after all, profiled in the purest sense of the word as a predatory threat for nothing more than breathing their air.

Even temporary suspension would be unbearable, because it meant having her powers stripped to a minimal level. That would leave her practically defenseless in a city where preternatural beings moved silent and deadly.

With purpose.

Like the being that crept along steadily ahead of her.

If *she* ran around Atlanta without her powers, it'd be open season on her and she'd end up on a slab in the morgue next to that poor woman missing a heart.

Much as the idea of losing her powers gave her the shakes, her greater worry would be that the sudden stripping of powers might trigger an involuntary shift into her beast form out of a natural instinct to protect herself.

That would end any question of her guilt as far as VIPER was concerned, and she'd be doomed.

She'd face a room full of demons to avoid that scenario. Besides,

VIPER needed her out here working. She had the best informants in the city when it came to supernatural intelligence.

That's how she'd found this demon in so little time.

The Cresyl stumbled, caught his balance, then stopped as though stuck in place. Dividing her attention between him and her path, she barely sidestepped a pile of putrid-smelling ick on the sidewalk that he'd left in his wake.

Great . . . like walking behind a horse. Jeez. Didn't they have any sense of cleanliness?

He—the demon's gender as determined by the size of his horns—glimmered in and out of shape, appearing more as shadow and mist than anything lifelike to unsuspecting humans at three in the morning. Even through her dark sunglasses, Evalle's natural night vision picked up his bony spine, slinking tail and leathery skin as clear as a high-resolution image.

Why was he moving at such a sluggish pace? Cresyls were generally quick and dangerous . . . and traveled in pairs.

Where was this one's mate?

Which one had ripped into a human tonight . . .

Or had they?

Something had, and they were the most likely candidates. The remains of the young woman had shown up in the Atlanta city morgue a few hours ago. The morgue where Evalle worked part-time as a maintenance tech from ten at night until five in the morning. All agents at VIPER were expected to integrate into the community, preferably somewhere that allowed them intel on supernatural activity.

The morgue was a perfect place to be. Not just for VIPER but for her own personal reasons as well.

The dead were not a threat.

Most of the time.

And what better place to hear about unusual killings or strange DNA evidence? Being on call for early Sunday morning usually meant processing run-of-the mill Saturday night violence, not a demon mauling. The graveyard shift supervisor who'd received the woman's body had filed a request that animal control come inspect the ravaged body and gouged chest.

That visit wouldn't happen until Monday during business hours. But Evalle couldn't gamble on the possibility of VIPER finding out about the mutilation before Monday, since they had other spies with morgue access besides her.

Even if a wild animal from the zoo *could* have ripped the heart out of the body so cleanly, any investigator would question why an earthly predator would leave the rest of the body uneaten.

Animals tended to be sloppy killers. Demons not so much.

Everything about this death was off, didn't fit anything she'd ever seen or heard about with regard to Cresyl demons—or any other kind, for that matter. Her Spidey sense was tingling off the charts, and she couldn't shake the feeling this was bad for her. *Real* bad. Having been alone right before work, she had no alibi for the time of death.

Not paranoia. I'm being set up. I have to be. Nothing else made sense.

Quinn and Tzader would help with a minute's notice, but they were in Charlotte, and she refused to call them like some helpless female. *I came into this world alone and I can handle anything it throws at me.*

And by the gods, she could handle the Cresyls.

If she didn't make a mistake.

Or run out of time. With daylight coming in less than two hours, she'd be forced off the streets to hide from the August sun. That was why she'd faked a case of nausea at the morgue and clocked out early to go home. It wasn't a total lie. She really was feeling sick to her stomach that someone wanted her butt in a sling.

Or more to the point, a cage.

Evalle flinched as unwanted memories tore through her with sharp talons at that thought. Nothing set off her panic attacks worse than imprisonment.

Well, there was one other matter, but she wouldn't think about that either.

Focus. But it was hard. No matter how much she tried to keep the past buried, things like this threat unearthed her worst fears and made the old wounds burn anew.

Which was why she'd much rather battle the demons without. Once she killed them, they stayed dead. Too bad the ones inside her weren't so cooperative. Even when she did manage to kill one, a dozen more cropped up to attack her.

As Quinn would say, bloody inconsiderate wankers.

But that was neither here nor there. She'd made the ten-minute ride to her secure apartment beneath a downtown parking deck only to pick up a weapon—the special dagger she carried, which had a bone handle carved with Celtic designs. The blade shimmered with a death spell. Badass to the extreme, it could be used to kill most demons if she stuck the blade into the creature's forehead between where horns grew above each eye. The dagger had been a gift from Tzader after he and Quinn had saved her life in Utah.

Just one of several treasured gifts from Tzader and Quinn, with friendship and trust being the most cherished of all.

But she was on her own right now.

The demon paused in the middle of the next block at the newspaper-wrapped feet of a sleeping vagrant, a poor wadded-up piece of humanity not bothering anybody.

Was it sizing up the guy as a meal?

Evalle paused, perfectly still. Sweat trickled beneath her top to streak down the naked skin on her back and soak the top of her jeans. The back of her vintage BDU shirt stuck to her back. She wore the cotton military shirt for comfort, but nothing felt good in this heat. Her steel-toe boots were hot, but much handier and safer than sandals if someone or some *thing* wanted a throw down. She fingered the dagger in the sheath at her hip and wrinkled her nose at the sulfuric odor trailing off the demon. The odor was too faint for a demon who had eaten a human heart.

Although one of them might have discovered the magic of deodorant or perfume.

Then again, perfumed crap still stank no matter what you did.

Maybe this thing hadn't attacked the human. She didn't like the idea of hurting anything on purpose, but that young woman had died a hideous death, and the quickest way to find this thing's mate would be to make him call for help.

Besides, as a VIPER agent, she was expected to do whatever it took to protect the humans from predators.

And she would.

A car turned onto the street half a mile down and headed toward her, the burned-out muffler rumbling loud in the still night. She kept her eye on the demon. The last thing she wanted to do was attack one in front of a civilian who would see the demon clearly if it solidified to do battle, but she wouldn't let him kill the vagrant.

The demon shook his head and mumbled under his breath, then continued on as though reluctant to pass up the human.

She let out a breath of relief, but why had he passed up this chance?

When the approaching car's headlights flashed on the demon, the creature sprinted ahead then disappeared to the left down a side street.

Evalle sucked into a recessed doorway until the car passed her then rushed forward, holding her breath as she leaped over the vagrant, who reeked of body odor and urine. Man, that stench gave the demon a run for his money in the stink department. Maybe the demon had paused to wonder if the guy was kinfolk.

At the corner, the side street turned left and shot through a dark shadow cast by buildings on each side.

The street stopped at a railway embankment.

Empty. No demon.

Damn. She couldn't have lost him.

Evalle moved ahead carefully, sniffing for any wisp of sulfur in the air. Luckily, she caught the scent by the time she reached a weed-infested concrete pad twenty feet square at the end of the street.

The demon, now in solid form and hunched over, sat on a stack of tires, patting his scaly head above the horns. He mumbled incoherently. The scent of rotten eggs stank up the air, but the smell would be even more overwhelming at this distance if *he'd* fed on a human recently.

"What're you doing here?" She spoke with authority even though she doubted he'd just blurt out the truth. Had to open the conversation with the Cresyl somehow.

He slowly lifted his head. Drool slid off one side of his wide mouth. His dull yellow eyes were unfocused. He started muttering again, a low guttural sound. "You."

Huh? What was wrong with him? She took another step but kept a ten-foot separation. "You working with anyone?"

"You."

For a Cresyl, this one didn't act dangerous. He acted demented . . . or drugged.

Or maybe sad. Could he be sad about something? And why had she sensed it? She'd have thought her emerging empathic side was more discerning. "Who killed the human?"

His eyes moved around in strange circles, then focused on her. "You."

"Guess I should make it multiple choice. Got any more words, or do I have to buy a vowel?"

Where are you, Evalle? Tzader called to her telepathically.

Off Peters on the south side of Atlanta. Not far from where we busted that Midnight Moon Fae ring last year. Why? Where are you?

In Atlanta. What are you doing?

Thank the goddess Macha that Tzader was back. Evalle wouldn't turn down his help. *I've cornered a—*

The demon snarled and jumped to his feet, shoulders hunched in an aggressive stance. His eyes glowed white hot. "You killed her."

"Killed who?" She pulled out the dagger and spun it once, preparing for him to attack.

"You killed her." He started howling, and his body shook as if reacting to a drug, but drugs didn't work on demons, did they?

He took a step and stumbled.

Had someone cast a spell over this thing to accuse Evalle of killing the woman? "Who's your master? Who sent you here?"

Evalle?

Get back to you in a minute, Tzader. Busy right now.

"She died. You. Die." The demon launched himself at her.

He had to be talking about someone else. A Cresyl would never avenge a human.

She dodged to the right and swung around when he missed her. "*Who* killed the woman?"

"You." He stumbled around and snarled.

"Could we fast-forward to a new answer?" She needed a question he couldn't answer with "you." "Where's your mate?"

That had been the wrong question.

He lifted the stack of tires and threw them at her, but she was too quick and spun away.

Or he was too slow for a demon. When she stopped spinning, she faced him. He curled over his chest, moaning so pitifully she almost felt sympathy for him.

Why wasn't his mate coming to him?

If he stopped making that horrid sound long enough to talk, she might get some answers out of him. She'd planned on his fighting her so she could catch his tail. Cresyls were like opossums. If you could wrap one's tail around your forearm, he was under your control.

Something had screwed up his mind.

Maybe he had some kind of weird sickness. Did demons get sick? Like demon Parvo or something?

She couldn't hurt something that wouldn't fight her.

Evalle softened her voice and eased toward his tail as she spoke. "Look, buddy. Just tell me who sent you here and I'll find someone to help you feel better. Or tell me where your mate is and I'll go get her for you."

The demon howled a screeching sound so high-pitched no human could hear it. His tail lengthened, whipping around to slap her legs out from under her. She slammed backward, her skull bouncing on the concrete.

Dazed, she blinked and touched her sunglasses, which were cock-eyed on her face. No one had told her Cresyls could do that with their tails.

He dropped down over her, landing his knees on each side of her legs, arms arched above his head with claws extended to attack and a mouth full of teeth open to rip a chunk off her body.

Survival instincts shoved her mind past the pain in her head. Someone called her name from far away . . . or had it been Tzader in her mind?

The demon swung downward in slow motion.

She kept her eyes locked on the crazed look in his gaze. Blood rushed through her ears. Her heart pounded like war drums in her chest the closer his sharp fangs came to her face.

At the last minute, she whipped the dagger up in both hands and stabbed him in the forehead.

Putrid yellow dust swirled, then disintegrated, confirmation he hadn't killed a human. If he had, she'd have been able to capture his essence in her fist before it disappeared.

Crud. No evidence. She had to get the other demon.

"Couldn't you wait until I got here?" an angry male voice yelled from the alley.

She rolled over and pushed up to her knees to find Tzader running toward her. He had on a T-shirt, jeans and boots that were all so dark she'd never have seen him with normal vision.

Dusting off her jeans, she stood. "No, I couldn't wait."

"What's the point of saving your butt in Utah if you're going to put it at risk every time we turn our backs?"

"Can we *not* have this argument again?" She would forever be appreciative to Tzader and Quinn for saving her life and guarding her secret, but they were like two overprotective brothers at times.

Most of the time.

"This was just a Cresyl, and a whacked one at that."

One of Tzader's eyebrows rose in question. He crossed his arms. "So you fell down on the ground to even the odds?"

Rather than admit she'd made a tactical error no trained warrior should by underestimating her opponent, she shrugged. "Seemed like a good idea at the time."

"What was the rush?"

She told him about the body at the morgue. "I didn't find out who sent the demon and I can't prove that *any* Alterant—including me—is innocent of killing that human until I get that second Cresyl."

Another Alterant surfacing wouldn't draw the attention away from her either. In fact, it created more problems. Things had been quiet for a long time, but two months ago a new Alterant had shifted and attacked humans. Evalle had been brought into VIPER once again and questioned extensively about her ability to prevent involuntary shifting. In reality, Sen—the top dog at VIPER—had been trying to catch her in a lie so that he could put her in protective custody.

Protective? Yeah, right.

Tzader sent his gaze up at the sky that was lightening by the minute. "You're running out of time."

"I realize that. Now that you're back, we can split up and search." She started walking toward Peters.

He fell into step beside her. "I can't go hunting yet. I came back to meet someone who has a lead on the Belador traitor." They had yet to identify the bastard who'd betrayed them.

Two years . . . Two friggin' years and they weren't a bit closer than they'd been while shackled in the cave. Meanwhile a traitor was moving undetected in their ranks, and who knew who else he'd killed and betrayed.

"That's great." She'd wondered many a night if they'd ever find out who'd betrayed them in Utah. Whoever it was, they were resourceful and smart.

"It *would* be great if I didn't have to worry about you out here on your own chasing demons. Give me an hour to make this meeting and we'll go together."

Was he nuts? She looked up at the pale night sky again. "Don't have an hour. Clock's ticking and I can handle a Cresyl demon. If VIPER gets word of this first, you know what they'll do to me. Sen has zero tolerance for anything with my name on it." She stopped at the corner, her hand automatically at rest on the dagger handle.

"I doubt he'll hear about the killing before Monday. We'll find the other demon first."

"What if we don't, Z? What if he does find out before Monday?"

Tzader looked away, bitter worry clouding his gaze. "Then I'll make sure Brina knows. She'll be there for you."

Yeah, right. She'd sooner trust a cottonmouth not to bite her in the woods.

Evalle didn't consider Brina as supportive and benevolent as Tzader did, not when it came to Alterants. Brina was the counterpart to Sen, since they were both in liaison positions, but with one difference. Whereas Brina was an advocate when acting as liaison between

Beladors and their goddess Macha, Sen was strictly a conduit between VIPER agents and the Tribunal.

Sen enforced Tribunal decisions. No advocacy.

Especially not where Evalle was concerned.

Macha and her Beladors had to abide by Tribunal decree. To go against it would turn all Beladors into enemies of the VIPER coalition. They would all be marked as outlaws and ordered for execution. If that happened, Evalle's tribe would battle on all fronts, not just with predatory nonhumans and other powerful beings.

She shuddered at that thought. "Brina would *never* speak up for me."

"Have a little faith in her. She *will* intervene if I tell her you didn't shift and kill a human."

And Evalle was supposed to trust in that? She could feel the prison door already closing on her.

She clenched the handle of her dagger. "I might show faith in Brina if she'd ever shown some in *me* without you asking for it first. Regardless, she can't stop the suspension. If I don't find proof of what really did the killing, I am screwed. You know what VIPER will do if I don't find the flaming demon to prove otherwise." She held up her hand when Tzader's eyes thinned to his look of lecture mode. "Neither of us has time for this argument, and I'm not walking into VIPER without something in hand to prove my innocence. Call me after your meeting and we'll team up."

"I can hunt after daylight, so don't take any chances. Do you even know where the other Cresyl is?"

"Not yet, but I will soon even if I have to rattle every Nightstalker in the city." But hopefully it wouldn't come to that. She'd try Grady first.

Even though he was a pain in the butt and made her work for every piece of intel she squeezed out of the old ghoul, he was one of the best informants when it came to anything supernatural.

Tzader looked around the street, taking stock of everything seen and unseen. "Your bike in the area?"

"Parked on the next block." Her cell phone buzzed with a text message. She reached to pull the phone from the back pocket of her jeans.

He checked his watch. "I gotta go or I'll be late. I'll call you soon as I'm free, but worst case I'll swing by your place after daylight."

"Okay." She lifted the phone into view as Tzader's swiftly moving form disappeared in seconds. The text was from Kellman, one of two teenage male witches who lived on the streets because they had no family and no coven.

The message was simple: SOS . . . demon.

She took off running and punched up the GPS program Quinn had installed in her phone that would trace back a cell call to a location.

Please, please let the demon threat be the Cresyl's mate. For once in her life, let her be lucky . . .

With fewer than ten demons seen in this region in a year, that was a good bet.

At the next intersection, she hung a left and pulled out her remote key, pressing it when she got within fifty feet of her motorcycle, a metallic gold Suzuki GSX-R. She adored her gixxer, which bolted down the highway like a bullet. The headlight flashed once, scaring away the vagrants huddled around the bike. She kinetically freed her full-face helmet from where it was hooked over the mirror on the handlebar and strapped it on as she straddled the bike, then fired up the engine.

Pulling away from the curb, she rolled on the throttle sharply. The front tire lifted off the ground for fifty feet.

In twelve minutes, she was cruising along Metropolitan Parkway. She turned onto the cross street indicated on her cell phone, drove a quarter mile and stopped in front of a brick building for a trucking firm that was closed on Sundays according to the schedule on the door. She listened for the boys above the low buzz of her engine.

Nothing.

But that being said, the air reeked of a distinct sulfur stench.

Strong. Vibrant. Deadly.

The smell of well-fed demons.

And inside were two scared kids. . .

TWO

Now that Evalle knew where the demon was hiding, she quickly parked. This wasn't the best place to leave a GSX-R after dark, but no one could steal the bike. Someone from Quinn's extensive network of contacts had warded the bike to prevent the engine from firing unless Evalle was sitting on the seat. It really paid to have friends with mad psychic skills.

The bike had to be within her energy field for the wheels to even turn. Go team.

She traded her helmet for the dark sunglasses and left on foot to hunt, picking her way toward the building. Silence followed in the wake of her soft steps, as if no threat lurked nearby.

She knew better.

The air stank of evil.

Her demon was here, and the dead quiet meant the Cresyl knew Evalle was here, too. *Come get some . . .* Shadows whispered, stirring the hairs on her arms as she sensed a presence she couldn't find.

She stomped her boots, and blades shot out around the soles.

No underestimating her opponent this time.

The nasty sulfur stench grew stronger the closer she edged. A solid sign that she was on the right trail, but she hadn't heard a sound from the boys.

Please don't be demon Kibbles 'n Bits . . .

Surely she'd gotten here in time. She couldn't stand the thought of something happening to the twins. The boys annoyed her at times, but they were like family to her.

No wonder they annoy me . . .

She paused at an electric gate, which ran between the brick building and a long warehouse and closed off a wide driveway to the rear loading dock area.

She sized up the ambush potential.

Definitely a trap.

But who or what was the demon trying to catch? Kardos and Kellman were homeless teens no one cared about. No one but her and the Nightstalker Grady, who helped her keep tabs on the pair.

Using her telekinetics, she unlocked and lifted the gate so she could enter. She simultaneously sent out pulses that would interfere with any and all electronic surveillance or alarms the company had. As the gate moved, metal gears squeaked in protest, making her cringe, as it not only alerted the demons about her presence but also telegraphed her location.

Damn, why couldn't her telekinesis come with WD-40?

She froze for a second, waiting for them to pounce. After a few mad heartbeats, she started forward again.

When she reached the back lot, one security light above her head shed enough light for a human to easily navigate the enclosed area. Thirty-foot-long metal shipping containers were stacked along the far side.

Everything was too quiet.

Tzader's warning dug into her thoughts, reminding her not to fight demons alone. *You're not immortal or impervious* . . . One mental call for help would bring the closest Belador running to give her support.

She considered that idea for all of a nanosecond.

Beladors *would* come—grudgingly—if she called. Screw that, and she wasn't bothering Tzader. His meeting was too important.

I can't put this off with those two boys at the mercy of a Cresyl demon.

She drew a shallow breath and walked further into the parking lot. The closer she got to the demon the more foul the air turned. Would the female Cresyl be in her demon form, or could the thing have fed on another human and now be masquerading in that poor soul's body?

Where were the twins? Her panic for their safety was rising high.

A scraping sound above her drew her gaze over her shoulder, up to where two identical blond males clung to a galvanized pole mounted thirty feet off the ground that supported the halogen security light. One of the boys kicked his boot against the brick wall and struggled to keep a grasp, but neither uttered a sound.

Thank the goddess they were safe.

The demon had muted them—something *she'd* wanted to do to the back-talking Kardos on occasion—but this wasn't funny.

Evalle needed something to break their fall. She spied a Dumpster and lifted her hand to telekinetically move it into place.

All of a sudden a blast of energy knocked her backward. She hit the brick wall four feet off the ground and slid down, scraping her arms on the rough edges but landing on her feet.

Ready to fight.

Her hand went to the dagger in her sheath and paused.

The demon that leaped into view from between steel containers on the far side of the parking lot was not a Cresyl or a female.

Scrolled ink designs ran along one side of his face, moving like a tangle of angry snakes. He was pushing eight feet tall, and she had a bad feeling this one could grow larger. She based gender this time on the very human fit of his jeans that were tight enough to leave no doubt about his endowment or sex.

Ah, crap, he was shifting from human to demon form.

What kind of demon was this thing, and what was he doing here? Who had opened the hellmouth downtown?

More to the point, how did she close it again? Preferably with the demons on the right side of it. 'Cause no offense, she was getting tired of the cleanup.

He locked his hands—that now had claw tips—together in front of his chest. A supersized black hoodie covered thick shoulders, but he was still shifting. Horns had already started growing from his thick forehead just above each eye. His nose widened and lengthened to a curved tip. Ew! Boar demons were ugly. A thin red tongue lashed out from between pointed teeth.

And what the heck had happened to his ears? They were cauliflowered like a battered boxer's instead of pointed.

The back of his pants ripped open, and two tails grew six feet long with spikes at the end.

41

Now she knew what he was.

A Birrn demon, far more dangerous than a Cresyl.

Oh, yay! Just what her suckass night needed.

If the stories she'd heard were true, he should smell like tar or burned rubber, not sulfur . . . unless . . .

He'd eaten the Cresyl.

Great. Just great. Even better. He'd eaten her evidence. Did everything have to conspire against her tonight?

But a Birrn wasn't a free agent. He answered to a master, so he wouldn't be here unless he'd been sent. VIPER would definitely go after whoever sent a predator here. If Evalle could show up with this thing smelling of Cresyl, even Sen would hesitate to point a finger at her for the dead human.

She hoped.

The demon bellowed as both horns curled and thickened at full extension.

"Hello, Mr. Ugly. Care to explain why you ran my friends up a flagpole?" And here she'd thought only bully humans were that cruel.

"I want your power," the demon whispered, a deep and menacing sound.

Was he hunting any and all powerful beings or . . . just her?

"Um yeah . . . no offense. Think I'll hang on to it for a bit." Evalle crossed her arms and glanced over her shoulder. "What about those two?" Had he sucked them dry?

"Bait."

Okay . . . how did he know anyone would come to help the twins, much less someone with my level of powers? She'd chalk it up to a good guess, but his kind really weren't that smart. "Let them go and we'll chat."

He shook his head in an easy motion. "Bait always dies."

"Bad news for you then."

The demon pulled back. Dull confusion fogged his glowing red eyes. "Why?"

"Cuz you're not bright enough to come after me yourself, which makes *you* somebody else's bait."

Worry skipped through his gaze for a split second, just long enough for Evalle to take advantage of his lack of attention. She whipped both arms away from her body, throwing an arc of hot energy at him that knocked him backward. He slammed into the steel shipping containers, which crashed down on him, the sound shattering the predawn quiet.

Using her telekinesis, she directed a Dumpster to cross the parking lot and park below the boys. "Jump!"

A sick thought hit her at the same moment.

What if the Dumpster was empty?

Or worse, had something in it deadly for them? Surely they wouldn't be that stupid.

Well . . . Kell wasn't that stupid.

But when the boys dropped, it sounded as though they'd landed on a cushion of garbage. Thank Macha.

"Get out of here," Evalle ordered the twins when they scrambled over the top and jumped down in front of her. "And get a bath. You smell like rat piss."

"We wouldn't've if you'd caught us instead of dropping us in a shithole." Kardos brushed off his hands, then paused to take her in from head to midriff. "Hellooo, hoochie mama."

His brother Kellman shoved at him. "Excuse my mentally defective brother, Evalle. Real glad to see you again. Thanks for the assist."

"You're welcome. Gotta fight demon now. Go."

Kardos eyed her greedily before he did his idea of a bad boy pose. "Baby, we're not abandoning you. Wouldn't want to see anything happen to all that . . . *software* I've got a hard drive for."

"Gah, I think I just threw up in my mouth. Yeah, I definitely taste bile." She had to find a coven in the city that would take them before they ended up in the metro Red Guard gang.

Evalle stepped close to Kardos, who stood at eye level with her. Both the twins did, but Kardos tried to sound another four inches taller. "First, your powers only work on small animals, not demons. Second, you'll get in my way. And third, you really need to grow some more, especially in maturity. Now stop acting like a warlock and get moving or get eaten."

Kardos grimaced at the male witch slur she generally reserved for a Medb.

Steel banged against steel. The demon was pushing his way out of the pile.

Kellman grabbed his brother's arm and dragged him toward the street. "We're just going to get her hurt if we stay."

Kardos groused two steps, then picked up his pace, calling out arrogantly, "We'll harrumph harrumph later."

In your dreams. She opened the gate for them, then shut it again and swung to face the demon, who was pushing up to his feet.

She winced. She should have been attacking him while he was down instead of letting the twins distract her.

He'd grown larger in size, thick body ripping out of his hoodie. Black scales covered the top of his arms, the middle of his face and his chest.

Crud. That meant he was gaining strength. She should feel flattered that he considered her that much of a threat. But really, she'd rather put him down quick.

"You know, I've been looking for you." She hoped to stave off his attack until she got some answers.

He stopped growling. "Why?"

"You ate a female Cresyl, right?"

The belch he released blew across the expanse to smack her in the face with sulfuric halitosis. Added to his twisted grin, that sufficed as a yes in her book. "What about the male? He know you ate his mate?"

Another grotesque demon grin. "You kill him?"

"Yes."

"Thought so."

What did that mean?

He flicked a hand at her.

She jumped sideways, barely missing the blast of energy that struck the ground at her feet.

The Birrn howled with laughter.

She *tsk*ed at him. "Didn't your mama tell you it's rude to play with your food?" This Birrn eating the other demon was no coincidence, not in her line of work. "What are you and the Cresyls doing here?" Besides eating the tourists and making her life hell.

The demon spread his arms wide, hands open in a show of indifference. "I hunt. They died. You might not . . . yet."

She'd have liked to feel encouraged by that, but demons could do things that made death look appealing. "You'll understand if I don't make the same offer in return."

He lunged, his body going airborne, diving at her like a demon torpedo.

She went to the right, rolling and coming up on her feet, now facing the wall where the boys had hung. The demon hit and flipped, landing sure-footed and ready for her. She spun her hands around each other as though winding invisible knitting yarn at hyper-speed, then threw a ball of energy at him.

That should plow his fat head through the brick building.

Her roll of power hit him square in the chest, but he just made an *umph* grunt, then laughed, a deep, sinister cackle. He was enjoying himself.

She doubted he'd play with her for long or that he'd let her get past him again.

The Birrn dropped his head down and growled, pawing the ground with the focus of a bull after a trespasser in his pasture.

She threw up a force field of energy to stop him when he barreled forward.

Didn't work.

He struck so hard that he knocked the force field *and* her backward, up in the air onto the loading dock, slamming her into one of the wide loading doors. The corrugated metal folded in around her and slid across the concrete floor—with her on top—plowing through shipping boxes.

Now that just hurt. She wouldn't be able to move tomorrow. But she better move tonight or she wouldn't have to worry about anything ever again. And her favorite doctor would be weighing *her* organs on Monday.

When she came to a stop, her back and legs screamed in pain. She sat up, shoving boxes off her, and rubbed her head.

No alarm sounded. Good, her powers were holding and still interfering. The last thing she needed was the police. If they came, it'd only make her job that much harder.

She really wanted to kill this demon, but that wouldn't help her one bit with VIPER. All she had to do was contain him, then call Sen, who would teleport the demon to headquarters, where they could extract answers. She didn't know how Sen interrogated, but Tzader and Quinn said the word was Sen could get answers out of hell.

All she had to do was hand him the Birrn. To do that, she'd have to blind the thing.

The demon roared and pounded the last few steps across the parking lot, then jumped up to the loading dock. Now up to full size, his head just cleared the fifteen-foot-high opening left by the wrecked loading door.

The inked designs continued down one half of his body, but now she could see the shapes better. The scrolled lines were a Celtic weave . . .

What the . . . ?

Birrns were Nigerian in origin. There shouldn't be anything Celtic on him.

On the other hand, there were millions of demons from all over the world. Sometimes things weren't listed, and as she'd learned the hard way, many research websites sucked.

Not wanting to think about that, she had to stop him from getting too close so she could set up for her attack. Birrn demons were dangerous, but stupid.

Best of all, they hated to be mocked.

"You don't even know why you were sent here, do you? Poor little bait demon." She laughed sarcastically, slowly moving up to sit, then sliding forward until she was on her knees. He'd think she was acting submissive.

Must have worked.

He stopped to answer, probably because he couldn't walk and think at the same time. "Do, too."

"Yeah, right." She rolled her eyes. "If you knew, you'd say. But you don't. Forget I even asked. I didn't mean to insult your lack of intelligence."

"I do too know." The demon sounded as though he was going to pout, which would be funny if not for the jagged teeth and claws curving out of thick fingers.

"Awww, don't feel bad, little demon." She softened her voice to one she'd use with a three-year-old. "Nobody expects a Birrn to know why they do anything. You're only a gofer demon for someone else." She smiled good-naturedly, keeping his attention on her face and not the subtle movement of her hand to her dagger.

Blind a Birrn and he was at your mercy.

His horns dropped low over his eyes when he frowned. "I *do* know. Looking for the Alterant."

Those words jolted her. Who was after her?

More to the point, *why* were they after her?

"Who sent you?"

When he shook his head, she raced through what had happened and how she'd ended up here. "Did you . . . *know* that I'd find the other Cresyl?"

Smiling seemed to be his yes, so she took his smirk as an affirmative. "Did you put a spell on the Cresyls?"

"No."

"Your master did."

He puffed up with pride and nodded.

Feeding his ego was working, so she stroked it again. "Okay, that's impressive, but the female Cresyl didn't eat the human. She made the death look like a beast attack, but I doubt your master's spell could have made her do that. Killing the human that way was clever. Had to be the Cresyl's idea, right?"

"No. My master's."

That's what she needed. If he'd tell *her* that, then Sen should be able to squeeze the same confession out of him. Plus the Birrn had said he was here looking for the Alterant, which confirmed someone was targeting her. Definitely not paranoid. "How'd you know to grab the two male witches to get me to come here?"

The demon's mouth opened, then he shook his head. "No more talking."

"But we're getting to know each other. Who's your boss?" She rocked back on her heels like a runner at the start line. Except she was preparing to go for his eyes instead of sprinting and hoped she hadn't underestimated his power or overestimated hers.

He bent his head back and bellowed an unearthly howl that slammed from wall to wall, echoing through the building. Birrn demons also liked to posture. When he faced her again, his eyes glowed, red embers with yellow centers. He raised his hands and murmured words she could barely hear.

Time was up. She hoped that what she'd read about blinding a Birrn was more than some urban legend. She took three steps and leaped into the air.

Something invisible grabbed her body in midair and held her ten feet off the ground.

No one had told her a Birrn could do *this*.

She better not find out Tzader and Quinn knew.

Getting caught in the demon's power wasn't ideal, but she didn't think he'd eat her if he was supposed to deliver her alive to someone else. If that happened, she'd meet his master . . . who wanted an Alterant for what?

She hoped Parcheesi, but since she couldn't play . . .

The demon flipped her back and forth like he was shaking a toy. Then her body started floating toward him.

Oh, come on. . .

She tried to use her telekinesis to drop a chunk of the ceiling on his head.

For once nothing happened.

She called to Tzader telepathically.

No response.

He had her powers blocked . . . This was bad. Very bad. The scent of burned rubber filled her nostrils. Could there not be one single demon who didn't stink?

The demon's power was filling the warehouse, closing in on her.

Not looking good for the home team.

Her only hope was to distract him. "Oh, I see. You just don't know *who* your master is. He won't tell you, huh? Sucks to be you. And I hope you just made up the part about looking for an Alterant. Because I'm not one."

Her body stopped floating toward him.

"Yes, you are."

"Nope. You got the wrong person. I'm just a witch. What's your master going to say when you show up with a witch instead of an Alterant?"

She'd stumped him to the point of being mute. Go back to the important detail of who was hunting her. "No one *important* is looking for an Alterant or word would be all over the city." She tried to shrug, but she couldn't move her shoulders. "You're good at what you do. You should find a master you deserve, one with a higher rank on the food chain."

The demon had a puzzled look, as though trying to decide if telling her would win this game. "He's powerful."

"So *you* say. But I'm betting he's so insignificant I've never even heard of your master."

She might have pushed him too far with that. The pressure around her chest tightened until she could hardly breathe. Even if he didn't mean to eat her he could crush her.

Flames licked at the corner of the Birrn's mouth, and his eyes flared solid red. "My master *is* powerful," he said so low that she almost couldn't hear him. "He is called—"

Bright light erupted behind the demon on a loud blast.

A bolt of power shot a hole through his middle, barely missing Evalle's feet. The invisible binding that had held her body captive fell away and she could feel the demon's power withdrawing.

She hit the ground and stumbled backward, but kept her footing. The demon remained upright for the ten seconds it took his body to suck into itself and disintegrate into a pile of smoldering black chips that reminded her of manure . . . right down to the stench.

She cursed at the bad timing. She'd been a slip of a second from finding out who was directing the demon, and now she had *nothing* to give VIPER.

All her evidence gone into one steaming pile of demon sludge.

And she wanted blood for it.

As the smoke cleared, Evalle looked up to find a brute of a man standing where the door had been before she went through it. He held a black-and-silver weapon that looked like an oversize six-shooter with a cylinder big enough to hold six hand grenades.

He started toward her with purpose, weapon aimed straight at her chest.

Crap. It was Dr. Doom, and she was now the patient.

THREE

"**W**ho are you?" Evalle widened her stance, ready to fight and bash in his head, since he'd destroyed her Birrn and ruined her chances for an easy alibi.

But the two most important questions bubbling through her worries were: What was that weapon he'd used to take down the demon and was he going to use it on her?

She didn't have time for more company. Daylight would break in less than an hour, and while she had a suit in her bike that would protect her in an emergency, it wasn't comfortable to be in anything black that covered her from head to toe during Georgia's dog days of summer, when the temperature usually hit ninety-four degrees by 8:00 a.m.

The man walked forward with an arrogant stride. The closer he came, the more she could see of his Mack truck body, wide and bulked up beneath a black outfit that resembled an ACU—Army Combat Uniform—with Kevlar plates. His sleeves were rolled up over bulging biceps. Obviously he wasn't afraid of demonic acid spit.

He wore a night-vision monocular, which allowed him to see her just as easily as she saw him in this cavernous building with no light. All in all, he was a handsome man in a lunatic, over-the-top, *I play way too much Call of Duty and Resident Evil* kind of way.

"You okay?" His lips barely moved, then returned to a tense line. The short black hair fit his abrupt personality.

Didn't sound like he was a threat, but he definitely looked like one. And he hadn't lowered his weapon.

"Fine. You are?"

"Isak." He gestured with the tip of his weapon toward her sunglasses. "You blind?"

She got that a lot because of her tendency to keep them on even at night. Her sunglasses had been custom-made by a friend of Tzader's, who'd used a lens that would allow her eyes to be seen in low light but shield their freakish color. Let's hear it for special variable tinted lenses—if she could only get something like that for her skin with SPF 5000. "No. I see fine in low light, right down to your Batman belt buckle."

His eyebrows moved slightly at the dig, as if questioning how sensitive anyone's eyes could be in this pitch-black warehouse. But obviously she'd seen enough to out his strange taste in belts. "What're you doing here?" he asked.

Like she was going to tell him that . . . "What are *you* doing here?"

"Hunting demons."

Dang, that was brutally honest. Most people who hunted demons didn't blurt that out to strangers for fear of an all-expenses-paid visit to the local psycho ward.

Was this guy an unfamiliar VIPER agent? Agents, she didn't mind, unless they got in her way.

Or killed a Birrn she needed to capture.

But if he was an agent, she didn't sense power coming off him.

No. Definitely human.

Weird and gorgeous, but human.

"Who do you work for?" she asked.

"Myself."

Her stomach clenched. He could be a merc, anybody . . . especially with that superblaster. Just what her already-screwed-up night needed.

Isak kept visually sweeping the area around them, then paused to look her over again. He finally shifted his weapon to hold it across his chest. "What'd that demon want with *you*?"

Yeah, this was an odd conversation to have with an unknown civilian.

"Dinner and a movie. How'd you know he was here?"

"Smelled 'im a mile away."

Too bad the twins hadn't.

She searched again with her powers but still felt no unusual field of energy from this guy. Nothing to mark him as anything other than a human with a demon-killing fetish.

And where had he gotten that wicked weapon?

She glanced over at the pile of stinking demon dung. She couldn't use her powers to clear that out of here with Isak present. Nor could she call VIPER for a cleanup team until she had a plan that would keep her head off their chopping block.

And there was no way in hell she was touching *that* with her hands. She'd managed to walk away fairly clean from the Cresyl, but this would be harder to clean off her skin than skunk odor. Not that she had any interest in getting frisky with a man, but stink like that would ensure her peace and solitude for months on end.

More important—VIPER would smell Birrn demon on her.

"Did you *have* to kill him?" she asked.

He arched a brow suspiciously. "What? You *friends* or something?"

She returned her gaze to his face, then looked up to eyes so impervious to emotion a shiver of warning ran up her spine. Isak didn't seem surprised she knew about demons.

What was his story?

And what had the demons done to him? The average human didn't track and kill demons.

What could she possibly say that wouldn't end up with her dead or exposing VIPER . . . which still might mean her dead? This guy walked, talked and shot like a vigilante. She knew the type. If you didn't uphold their hatred, you needed killing, too.

She gave him an insincere smile. "I was kind of hoping to ask him a few questions. Thanks for killing that opportunity. Literally."

Interfering moron.

"A demon?" His one uncovered eye widened, then creased with a suggestion of humor that didn't fit the serious GI Joe face. "You wanted to interrogate something with the IQ of lettuce, that sees humans as a major food source? Good call. Are you drunk or mental? Or are you one of those freaks who thinks nonhumans just need love and understanding while they munch our brain matter?"

Her internal defense alarms went into high gear at the way he said *"nonhumans."* As if the word alone was repulsive. What would Isak do if he knew she wasn't exactly an everyday citizen? "So you just arbitrarily kill any nonhuman even if they're not harming someone?"

He curled his lip. "Kill 'em all and let their various gods sort them out. In case you haven't noticed, hon, it's open season on us. Either you kill the demon or the demon eats you. Way I see it, you should be thanking me. I just kept you from being digested."

She let out a curt breath of aggravation. "I can take care of myself, Terminator, and as for thanks . . . yeah. You just screwed up something I needed to find out. So thanks a lot."

His amusement vanished. "Ah, God. Don't tell me you're with that paranormal tree-hugging group that's trying to convince everyone malevolent poltergeists and demons are just misunderstood friends who need hugs."

Of all people, that wasn't her. But *he* didn't need to know her stance on demon slaying.

Her organization wasn't any of Rambo's business. "Want to tell me what group you're with?"

He shook his head slowly from side to side.

"Then I'd say we're done here. I've lost enough ability to smell for one night." She debated calling Tzader, who must still be in his meeting, otherwise he'd have called her. She had to get this mess cleaned up.

When she made a move to step past Isak, he closed his fingers around her arm.

She froze in anger at that touch and glared at his huge paw of a hand as old memories surged. She wasn't a terrified helpless teen, and no man would ever lay hands on her again without her explicit invitation. "You got three seconds to remove that or your new name's going to be Lefty."

He held his hand up in surrender. "You got a ride nearby?"

"Yes."

"I'll follow and—"

"No. I've had enough favors for one night, and now I have to clean this crap up before anyone finds it."

"My people'll deal with it."

"Really?" She deserved one lucky break tonight. But honestly . . . did he really know a group who would come in here, clean up smelly demon goo and not report or arrest her? "Do you work with law enforcement?" Working for the morgue, she'd met a lot of the local LEOs—law enforcement officers—but never Rambo. He tended to stand out.

Isak smirked. "Not even."

Believe it or not, that was good news in her world. VIPER employed a long list of different people that included a large number of Beladors, many of whom worked with local police, the FBI and other agencies. But if his people didn't work with any of hers . . .

She might stand a chance after all.

Even though she had no idea who this guy was, she'd bet Tzader would know or could find out.

Continuing toward the smoldering hole the Birrn had left in the warehouse, she reached the loading dock, where the hot air was muggy but fresh. She jumped down to the parking lot and started walking.

Heavy boot steps followed right behind her. "Look, I don't think you realize what you're up against. Hotlanta is steaming tonight because someone has unleashed major mojo on the city. And they're not here to play with us, little girl. They're here to feast on entrails."

Little girl? Mr. Macho had no idea who he was dealing with, and right now, he was lucky he wasn't limping. "I'll take my chances."

"What's your name?"

"It definitely isn't Little Girl. Honey. Or Babe, Baby Cakes. Now run along, little boy. Us girls need to be alone." Because she couldn't clean up the demon crap with him standing watch over her.

Unless she used her hands.

Nah. I'd rather VIPER burns me. 'Cause that's just g-r-o-s-s.

Evalle had barely reached the middle of the parking lot when sirens rang out, coming closer.

Ah, crap . . . police were headed this way and would most likely enter the same way she had.

Please don't let there be some stray kid with a cell phone. That's all she'd need tonight. Her face on the local news, fighting a demon. Her luck, it'd be picked up by the AP and on YouTube and she'd be more famous in twenty-four hours than Paris Hilton on a bender.

Look on the bright side. It might make Sen choke on his fury so hard that he'd stroke and die before he could cage her.

C'mon, think, Evalle, think. She needed every minute she had left until daylight to figure out who'd sent the Birrn. Why it'd had Celtic branding and what the demon's master wanted with an Alterant.

Her . . .

Oh, and come up with an explanation for the slashed body in the morgue that didn't involve her being accused of eating the woman's heart.

Some nights it didn't pay to leave the house . . .

With the blue light specials flashing outside the gate, her most immediate problem was the lack of time to deal with the flaming pile of demon churras on the floor. Could she sell the cops on the idea that she was a disgruntled employee trying to plant prairie pastries on her old boss's desk?

Not with my luck tonight.

What were the chances she could trust Isak's people to clean up this mess?

She turned around as Isak jumped down from the loading dock and jogged in her direction. She gestured toward the cops. "Nice present. Thank you so much for the arrest record, Mr. Shoot-to-kill. Appreciate it. Know any good bail companies?" 'Cause with his hair trigger, he should be getting a volume discount from someone.

He stopped in front of her, his weapon slung across his back. "I don't need no stinking bail company. I've got something better."

This she couldn't wait to hear. "A rocket launcher and a tank?"

"No. Exit strategy. You coming?"

She didn't think so. "Thanks, but I'll find my own way out."

"By now the cops are crawling the building like ants on a cake and *you* are about to become the ice cream cherry."

He was right and she hated him for it. "All right, First Blood. Lead me to freedom."

Police racket clamored near the front gate.

Isak paused at the wall on the side of the building, where she could now see a thin aircraft cable running vertically from the top. Sneaky little booger . . . how clever. A metal clasp with a heavy D ring dangled at shoulder height. From inside his shirt he pulled a short length of thicker cable that was probably hooked to a harness and clipped the karabiner on the end to the clasp.

But if he thought she was going up the side of *that* wall, he was crazy.

Ten or fifteen feet off the ground, no problem.

Any higher . . .

Big problem.

Evalle didn't do heights. Ever.

The sound of the huge electric gate at the street opening was followed by the sounds of the cops coming closer. Flashlight beams danced ahead of them.

Stealth was not the forte of Atlanta's finest. Lucky for her.

She looked around, quickly assessing a potential alternative route. "Tell you what, Isak. I'm—"

An arm hooked around her waist and yanked her backward against a body so hard, it was like slamming into the brick wall. Panic at being touched got shoved aside by a greater fear when her feet came off the ground and they shot up the wire at a speed that left her sick.

No, no, no!

She hissed in outrage. "Put me down!"

"Hon, at this height, you definitely don't want me to do that."

Stupid her, she looked down before she could stop herself. The world below was shrinking at a rapid pace. Her stomach threatened to show her a replay of the slaw dog she'd eaten for dinner. Snapping her eyes closed, she clenched her teeth and fought down her panic.

He wasn't going to drop her. He wasn't.

Still, the fear was there, and it was debilitating as her past slammed into her with a reality she despised. Her shoulders trembled. She forced her muscles to lock tight.

Never, ever show a weakness. Not to anyone.

Too late for that.

She ground her teeth at the conflicting voice in her head that she hated. *Stay calm, Evalle, you can do it. You've survived a lot worse than this.*

Why, why wasn't flight one of my powers?

But as they neared the top, she realized she wasn't going to fall . . . and Isak wasn't trying to grope her.

He wasn't attacking her. This wasn't her past and she wasn't a defenseless child anymore.

Both of his arms hugged her against his chest. An act of protection, *not* violation.

She smelled his human scent, warm and a little sweaty from his exertions. Raw, natural male. He pulled her closer, as if he'd keep her safe from anything.

No one had ever held her this way.

Like she was precious to them.

Didn't matter. End of the day, she couldn't stand the sensation of hands confining her. Of someone pressing her against his body.

Let me go, let me go, let me go . . .

He whispered against her ear, trying to calm her. "We're almost there. I'll release you in a sec."

You're not a helpless teenager. He's not the bastard. Why couldn't she banish those memories? Why did they sting most when she could least afford them?

You ruined my past, you worthless dog. You will not destroy my future . . .

She bit the inside of her mouth to keep from screaming and giving away their location to the police.

The vertical movement slowed.

She was trembling, couldn't open her eyes and look. *Coward.*

What kind of demonslayer was scared of heights *and* human contact? She could face down Satan in hell, but let one geeky guy lay a casual hand on her shoulder and she was petrified.

Think about the cops, Sen . . . anything.

Excited shouts came from below where the police must have found the demon drop treats. She shook her head in frustration over having left them behind.

Maybe they'll write off the fried remains as toasted rubber and ignore them. 'Cause God help her if they took a closer look and discovered the chips were actually scales.

Maybe they'd write that off as a visit from Puff the Magic Dragon . . .

Unfortunately, she wasn't that lucky. And she cringed at the thought of what Sen would do once he found out about this *and* the body in the morgue.

Maybe she could join the French Foreign Legion . . .

Did they still have one? It might be worth investigating.

Focus, Evalle. 'Cause she had no intention of Sen or anyone else other than Tzader learning about this.

"Don't panic," Isak said quietly as they stopped moving upward. "I'm going to turn you around so you can climb into a window." What was it about that gentle tone that could almost make her forget he was a loon?

When she felt her body spin, she opened her eyes to find an old-fashioned sash window with the bottom half opened enough for her to squeeze inside. *Don't look down at the parking lot. Just get into that room.*

Isak slid one arm beneath her legs and lifted her so that she could stick her feet through the window opening and slide in to safety. The minute her toes touched the floor, she jumped away.

He entered right behind her, disconnected the rigging and looked out the window before turning back to her. "Typical. They didn't see a thing. Good thing about cops and demons . . . they seldom look up."

She gave him a nod, the best she could do until she caught her breath and stopped shaking so badly.

Oddly enough, his weapon no longer bothered her. His size and hands on her body did.

But Isak hadn't made any threatening moves at all. He'd been nothing but kind and respectful to her . . . at least while they'd escaped.

In fact, she owed him for getting her away, even if he *had* been part of the problem. To prove to him, and to herself, that she *could* touch a human and not freak out, she offered her hand to him. "Thanks."

He closed his fingers around hers in a friendly, gentle hold. She had large hands for a woman, but his swallowed hers. In that moment she saw him more as a protective grizzly than a demonslaying tank.

He stepped forward.

She held her position, refusing to let a man intimidate her. Especially a mere human. One male had gotten away with that in the past, but he'd paid for it.

I'm not sixteen and locked in a basement. I have powers. No human can harm me ever again.

Not without a serious maiming.

When she looked up—had to because Isak was another six inches taller than her five foot ten—she realized he no longer wore his monocular. She couldn't tell his eye color, but based on the light shade, she'd bet on blue. A soft color for such a hard man.

"Is 'thanks' and a handshake all I get for risking life, limb and imprisonment?" His gaze burned into hers, daring her to back down from his challenge. His finger rubbed across the back of her hand.

She shook her head at him. He'd been sucking in too many demon fumes if he thought she was *that* easy. "Sorry, slick. Not that kind of girl. I require at least a couple of nice dinners and some flowers first."

Isak smiled. "You're going way off track mentally. Not that I wouldn't be happy to go there with *you,* but all I want is your name."

Oh. Idiot. But then she'd always been socially awkward around people, especially men—it was the whole raised-by-herself-in-a-basement thing that tended to put a crimp on her people skills. She'd rather battle a demon any day than banter with a man. And don't get her started on trying to navigate catty women. "Name's Evalle."

His eyes twinkled in the dim light, teasing her in a way only Quinn had ever done and never with such effect on her stomach. He actually made it flutter for a second . . . or was that the gag reflex still working from her height fright?

"*Evil?* Interesting name. You sound like my kind of woman."

She rolled her eyes. "E-vahl. Not evil . . . unless the situation calls for it."

He laughed a warm, rich sound that resonated from deep inside his body. "Nice meeting you, E-valle." His tone deepened, as if he savored the cadence of her name on his tongue. "Guess you *can* take care of yourself." He lifted her fingers before she could stop him and kissed her scraped knuckles. "I always say beauty is best when it comes mixed with danger."

This time there was no mistaking her attraction to him. *Oh, yeah, I'm definitely high on demon fumes.* She pulled her hand away. "On that note, General Bison, I really need to go before I turn into a pumpkin."

He inclined his head to her. "Head out. I'm right behind you."

She wanted desperately to argue with him about following her down through the building. He had a team out there, and for all she knew, one of them might tail her back. And that she couldn't have. She needed to find Tzader or Grady before daylight, someone who could help her figure out what was going on.

She glanced over her shoulder to find Isak had his monocular back in place. He'd have no problem following her down this dark hole.

On the ground floor, she paused at the door and cautiously cracked it open to make sure no one was there. The reception area was on her right, two long strides away. Bright blue lights flashed through windows that faced the street, letting her know that even more police had been called.

What? Had they found drugs in the building? Surely her little demon pile hadn't caused all that.

Evalle turned to Isak, who was touching his ear where a wire curled from his earbud and down the back of his shirt.

He lifted his hand and pressed the tiny throat mic. "Everyone clear?"

So he hadn't been kidding about his team. Just what had she walked into? And how much of her interaction with Isak had they been privy to?

She didn't like being spied upon.

Isak held up a finger, silently asking her to sit tight as he rattled off his location to whoever was on the other side of that system. "Report on all perimeters." He paused again, nodding. "Affirmative. Need a diversion on the west side. Target located and neutralized, but doesn't matter. We know the source. DHQ located. Mission accomplished."

Evalle scowled. DHQ? What the devil was that? Demon headquarters?

Was it possible that Isak might actually know where the Birrn had come from and what it was doing in Atlanta?

More to the point, did he know anything about Alterants and why the Birrn had been seeking her?

He turned to her. "You set?"

She gestured to his mic. "Can they hear us?"

"No. The mic sensor only picks up my vocal cord vibrations." A slow smile curved his lips. "What you got in mind?"

She didn't trust him one bit, but he was the closest thing to a lead she had since he'd turned her demon into roadkill. "You have a card or a number?"

Interest glowed in his gaze. "Not one I can share, sugar. *You* got a phone number?"

Yeah, right . . . "Don't normally give my digits out to demon-blasting strangers who call me 'sugar.'"

He laughed. "Tell you what. I've got to pick up something, then I'm free for a bit. Want to meet somewhere in a half hour?"

She had maybe an hour before daylight, and then her activity would be severely limited. She could ride in daylight, but it had to be fast and furious in full gear that would boil her in this heat. Which meant meeting close to her home. "You familiar with downtown?"

He gave her a droll stare. "No, the demons only hunt in the burbs."

She ignored his sarcasm. "Meet me at the Varsity. I'll be in the drive-in on my bike." Yeah, it would be open to daylight, but she didn't plan to stay long enough to get caught. The Varsity was two minutes from her apartment, and she'd stay on her bike. And it was a public place.

If he tried anything, she could be outta there in an instant.

"See you there . . ." He gave her an evil grin. "Sugar."

Evalle let it go as she prepared to head out.

She was sure she'd catch grief from Tzader for not calling him in to meet this guy, but she didn't know how Isak would react to someone showing up unannounced. And there was no way she could miss this chance. Besides, she hadn't heard a word from Tzader. Which probably meant he was having trouble with his informant, and bugging him in the middle of that was not the smartest thing to do.

While he loved her like a sister, she didn't want to test the limits of his adoration by making him strangle her.

Not to mention she wouldn't mind seeing Isak again. It was, after all, only natural for her to be curious about a new player in town. She had a duty as a VIPER agent to find out who Isak and his people were.

Nothing more.

She cast a look back at his massive form that filled out the black ops garb nicely. Better than nicely. Her heart quickened.

Seeing him again was only work-related . . .

Evalle drew a long, easy breath and worked to accept that along with the inevitable. Isak considered nonhumans the enemy, and she didn't encourage male attention.

Ever.

Don't start now.

True to his alpha DNA, Isak took charge. "Here's the plan. In sixty secs, my people will draw the police's attention. I wave you out, you go right. Once you're clear, I go."

She normally bristled under any authority, but she'd let him have his way since she had to make the most of every minute between now and daylight. "Works for me."

He started past her, then paused and swung around. His fingers wrapped around her upper arm in a firm, but nonthreatening, way.

Her muscles clenched with the need to lash out, but hitting someone who was trying to help her wasn't a normal response. She might even hurt him if she didn't keep her power in check.

His fingers slid off her arm, erasing her irrational sense of threat. "Thirty minutes. The Varsity . . . or *else.*"

Or else what?

She would've asked, but time was ticking and she needed to get out of here.

Turning away, he went to the door and held an electronic device up to the security panel. He waited for the lights to turn off before he opened the door an inch and peered out.

She stared at his back, glued to the spot. Her skin still felt embossed where he'd touched her. No man had *ever* left her breathless before. Not even the ripped warrior gods at VIPER who were as daunting as a fully loaded tank . . .

And Isak was *only* human.

Then again . . . She swept a look down his shapely backside.

Most women would call *that* a god.

And in all honesty, he did make her wish she could break through the scars of her past and feel normal—like any other woman around an attractive man.

But that had been cruelly ripped from her, and she didn't know if she'd ever be able to overcome it.

Sometimes dead wasn't dead enough . . .

Isak gave her the high sign. It was time. She took a deep breath and moved forward.

Racing past him, she gave a quick glance at the cops on her left who'd gathered around the electric gate with their backs to her. She took off fast in the opposite direction.

She didn't stop until she was out of sight. Stepping into a dark alcove, she peered over her shoulder in time to see Isak walk across the street with a deceptively nonchalant pace and dissolve into the shadows like he owned them.

Who was that guy?

She shook her head. Now was not the time to contemplate him, his hotness or his bizarre quirks.

She took a convoluted trek back to her bike since Atlanta's finest stood between her and the most direct route. The detour cost her ten of her thirty minutes.

That was all right though.

The Varsity was an easy eleven-minute ride. She could have made it in eight, provided a state trooper wasn't running radar.

But why take the chance for only three minutes?

Just as she reached for her helmet, her cell phone vibrated with a text message. She fished her phone out of her jacket pocket and read the message:

Red-V-2.

That was code for "your butt needs to be at VIPER HQ in two hours, not one minute late."

The only excuse Sen would accept for running late was death. And even then he'd want blood.

He'd probably write her up for it, too. After all, death was no excuse for dereliction of duty.

But there was one slight problem with his order. VIPER's HQ was two hours north of Atlanta. *If* she left immediately, she'd barely make it in time.

Of course . . . she'd also be riding in full daylight.

Isak would be at the Varsity to talk about his Birrn hunting, and he didn't strike her as the kind of guy who'd handle being stood up real well.

So that left only one question. Which one of them could she least afford to severely piss off?

FOUR

Where's the Alterant?

Tzader didn't care for the way Sen always referred to Evalle as "the Alterant," as if she was a tumor on his ass and not one of their most valuable assets. He gave the man his best eat-shit-and-die glare.

It didn't faze VIPER's head ballbuster one bit.

So Tzader tried a little more tact to soothe Sen's trauma. "She'll be here."

"By 0700? The others are already in the war room. We don't have time to wait on a mongrel."

Tzader had to ride herd on his tongue, which really wanted to put Sen in his place. Tzader didn't like him on his best day.

And this definitely wasn't one of those.

It seriously griped him that Sen couldn't give Evalle her due. She was twice the agent of many of them, yet Sen continued to pick at her like some inept newbie fresh on their force.

However, punching the arrogant prick in his face wouldn't accomplish much, so Tzader changed the topic away from Evalle. "Why are we here, anyway?" If VIPER had caught wind of the Cresyl attack, Tzader was sure he'd have been contacted by Brina herself. And Sen would have teleported Evalle up here immediately. If for no other reason than Sen knew she hated teleporting.

Worthless pig.

Sen gave him a snide once-over. "If you want to hear about the mission this morning, stay. Otherwise have Trey brief you and Quinn later. I refuse to waste breath going over details twice." He checked his watch. "The Alterant has sixteen minutes to arrive."

"You sure old Mickey there isn't fast?" Tzader shouldn't have bothered. Sarcasm was usually lost on imbeciles.

With one last parting sneer, Sen teleported to the war room, leaving Tzader alone in the sterile hallway. Sighing, he stared at the dull stone corridor that went on for what appeared to be forever. Hallways like this one formed an intricate spiderweb through their isolated haven set beneath the North Georgia Mountains. This was a safe zone for all preternatural beings, since *almost* no one could use majik or powers here.

No one except Sen, who, as a rule, was as surly as a hungover Hells Angel left naked in the desert. Sen didn't hide the fact that he considered his position with VIPER on par with mucking out pigsties. Something that made Tzader wonder why the first Tribunal had chosen Sen to mediate between them and their VIPER agents.

Or better yet, who Sen had pissed off to rate this assignment. Whoever it'd been, they had to be extremely powerful to stick Sen with this gig against his will.

And there wasn't much mediating involved when it came to Sen; just hard-nosed enforcement.

He ran VIPER according to only one set of rules . . .

His.

Of all the wizards, shape-shifters, Beladors, empaths, witches, centaurs and a list of other beings that made up the VIPER international coalition, no one but the gods and goddesses knew what Sen was or where he came from.

Tzader's bet was the lowest bowels of hell, but that was just his opinion.

That lack of knowledge kept agents on edge around Sen. You couldn't even look at him and tell his genetic origins. He was like an amalgam of all races. Almond-shaped blue eyes, mahogany brown hair and possibly Nordic bone structure.

As the Belador Maistir, Tzader commanded the North American contingency, answering only to Brina and Macha. He considered Sen a peer at best, regardless of Sen's position in VIPER. He didn't care why Sen was stuck in this role or how much he hated it as long as Sen didn't treat any Belador—including Evalle—unfairly.

Which meant Tzader had his work cut out for him most days.

Working his way through the tunnels, Tzader reached the checkpoint at the entrance to the cave where Jake, their resident troll, stood guard. At five feet tall, the repulsive troll might look unimpressive, but he was a dangerous beast. A ragged, unkempt beard covered the entire lower half of his face.

Tzader paused upwind from him—something everyone with a brain did. "Anyone call for clearance recently?"

Jake held one side of his headphones against his ear as he shook his square head, disturbing the shaggy gray-brown hair that'd been shaped into an unattractive bowl cut. "Got one call a minute ago, but it didn't come through . . . broke up."

A bad feeling went through Tzader. The troll was always screwing with Evalle. Jake used a façade of incompetence to cover a mean streak so wide the other trolls swam in it. But Tzader wasn't fooled.

Jake was out to get Evalle as much as Sen was. "Thought you had the comm unit fixed."

Jake wiped at his nose. "I did, I thought. I mean, it worked fine when everyone else came in this morning, but something isn't syncing now. The new hydraulic door got stuck a few minutes ago, so I closed it. I can't do anything about the audio breaking up until I get the door to function properly. Sucks really." Jake lifted a slim voice recorder to his lips and made a couple of notes, then fumbled with the digital settings and the keypad on a black electronic box supported by his enormous gut. "Wouldn't have this problem if Sen would trust me to use my powers. What's he afraid of? I'll fart and take out his office?"

Uh, yeah, that *was* the concern. "Didn't you once use your powers to conjure a pen and instead took out the entire northeast corridor?"

Jake bared his teeth, looking more like a hairy hog posing for a family picture than a dangerous troll from his native Jotunheim. "I can control them, I—" He stopped and angled his head to listen, then frowned.

If he was screwing with Evalle again, Tzader was going to eat troll balls for breakfast. "Put it on speaker."

"Calm down." Jake hit a button on his little box.

A female voice came through the static intermittently. "VIPER 66—" The next part skipped, then Tzader heard, "—caid."

"Call sign not clear," Jake responded in a voice washed with boredom. "Repeat—"

There was no mistaking who it was anymore when Evalle's fury-ridden voice yelled, "*Open the wall . . . now!*"

Tzader saw red. "Cut the shit, Jake. That's Evalle and you know it." And she was in mortal danger. The longer she was out there, baking in the sun, the closer to death she came. "Open the door, Jake."

Jake's eyes turned completely black. "It's jammed again. I can't."

Tzader felt his knives rattling against his thighs as his fury mounted. The bastard could have kept the door open long enough for Evalle to get inside out of the sun. "Open the damn door!"

"I. Can't!" Jake roared. "Why don't you use *your* powers and open it?"

For the same reason Jake couldn't.

No one was allowed to use powers here . . . except Sen.

"Get down here, Sen!" Tzader shouted, sending his voice straight into the bastard's head. "Kincaid is coming in hot and the door's jammed tight. If we don't get it open, we're going to be scraping her off your new door." Or worse, scraping her boiled ooze off the pavement.

Sen appeared at Tzader's side and lifted his hand, flexing his fingers at the entrance forty feet away.

Rock disintegrated.

The whine of a high-powered engine screamed ahead of the motorcycle that pierced the dense fog hanging in place of the rocks.

Evalle came in like the Ghost Rider hell-bent for his contract holder. The front tire squealed when she engaged the brakes, laying a strip of rubber across the hard rock floor. The rear tire lifted off the ground, rising chest high, while the bike skidded the last fifteen feet, then stopped eight feet in front of Tzader. It swung around and slammed down on the rear tire in a one-eighty Enduro finish, complete with the side stand down.

Evalle ripped off her full-face helmet and pitched it at Tzader like a sideways pass. He caught it without hesitation. She shoved a pair of dark sunglasses on her face, hiding her scary luminescent green eyes. But the glasses did nothing to conceal her fury, which pulsed through the room in sonic waves.

She snarled in Jake and Sen's direction. "Which one of you bastards was trying to kill me?"

Jake went rigid. "Let's not get into questioning each other's parentage, shall we? After all, you're the one with a faulty bloodline."

Tzader cringed at what had to be the most blatant act of suicide he'd seen in awhile. Even a troll should know the limits of his stupidity.

But obviously Jake had flunked Survival 101.

Wet strands of black hair clung to Evalle's neck and face where the Georgia heat had boiled her inside that insulated black suit she was forced to wear to keep the sun from searing her skin.

"Alterant," Sen warned softly when she slammed a boot to the ground and stepped off the bike.

She pinned him with an acid-lined glare and a curled lip. "Don't 'Alterant' me." Tzader could swear he heard a "you prick" in that tone. "What took so long to open the wall?" She stormed across the twenty-foot space between her and Sen.

"Alterant," Sen cautioned again.

Jake swallowed hard. "We're evaluating a new door system and it's got a flaw . . . or two."

"Of course it does. One conveniently programmed to only act up when I'm coming in during daylight hours." Evalle stopped inches from Jake. Standing almost six feet tall in her riding boots, she stared down the guard, whose snarly attitude waned.

He shrank under her blistering glare and flinched when she lifted her hand.

She pointed her index finger at him. "You ever hesitate to open the wall for me again when I'm treading daylight and I'll rip off your balls and wear them for earrings." She turned away, taking wide steps on those toned legs.

It was all Tzader could do not to smile. But he couldn't fault her for her anger. They'd come close to ending her days, and if anyone had a right to be pissed, it was definitely her.

"Like this was my idea," Jake mumbled.

She strode to her bike. "What lazy moron thought hydraulic doors were a good idea when there's enough psychic juice in here at any given time to move an entire mountain?"

Sen cleared his throat and narrowed a deadly look at her. "*I* would be the moron who came up with that idea since I'm the one stuck opening it most of the time. Not like I have better things to do than play butler to VIPER." His nostrils flared. "Good thing for you I was here so promptly, but don't rush to thank me."

She lifted a shoulder with indifference. "You the same person I should thank for hauling my ass in here during daylight?"

The look he gave her said it all. *I don't answer to you and you better remember that . . . bitch.* "Get to the war room." Sen vanished.

Evalle curled her lip at his departure, then smoothed out her expression as she looked at Tzader. "Thanks for getting the door open, Z."

He inclined his head to her. "Don't thank me too soon. I just didn't have time to waste picking out caskets today. And speaking of your blatant death wish . . . could you stop antagonizing Sen?"

"Why would I ever want to do that? I've had no sleep in two days and he calls a red alert, knowing I'll cook all the way here." While Evalle kept protective motorcycle gear on her bike, it was black to help her blend in with the night, which was when she was out and about. Not the coolest color to wear in full sun. And she couldn't ventilate it, because any bit of daylight on her skin bubbled it.

Unzipping her black jacket, she discarded the suffocating outer layer, leaving on her soaked BDU shirt and damp jeans. "So what crawled up Sen's ass and died?"

"I don't know. I saw Trey and Lucien here, but I haven't been to the war room yet."

Digging a towel out of her tank bag, she wished she could trust talking to Tzader in this place—even telepathically—but he wouldn't want to risk Sen overhearing anything they discussed.

She whispered low to Tzader. "We need to talk . . ."

"Find some*thing*?" Tzader leaned heavily on the last syllable. He meant the second Cresyl she'd been hunting.

71

"Sort of." She looked over at Jake, who acted as though he wasn't tuning in to every word, but she knew better. One of his jobs was to spy for Sen. "Not here."

Tzader nodded. "I'll swing by your place tonight, but I've got to leave right now."

She scowled at that. The last thing she wanted was to be stuck in a meeting without him. "What about Sen's powwow?"

"I already told him that I'm tracking a lead on Noirre. I could stay, but I've got a window of time for finding someone." He put emphasis on "someone," clueing her in that Tzader meant his informant.

Ah, that made sense.

Far more lethal than black majik, Noirre majik was the most ancient of all and thought to be practiced only by a few covens. The Medb being one of them.

She put her towel down. "I got you. Is Quinn privy to this mission today?"

Tzader stepped close and lowered his voice. "Yes, which reminds me of something. Keep your head down in this meeting. And you better get going. You're about to be late."

"Don't worry. I'd hate to cause Sen to stroke. Then again . . ." Wrinkling her nose at him, Evalle grabbed a bottle of water from the nylon MotoFizz bag strapped to the back of her seat. "So why should I keep my head down? What are you worried about?"

"You. Sen said Trey would fill me in later, as if he thought I wouldn't hear about it from you. That makes me nervous."

Yeah, her too. She didn't like the sound of that at all, but she dismissed it. "I'm sure Sen was just pointing out that Trey is available any time, not just at night. Like everyone else, he finds me lacking. Thinks I'm only good for intel and grunt work, nothing more."

"Not everyone thinks of you that way."

"I know you and Quinn don't." The rest of them . . .

She might as well be called Fido.

"Brina considers you a valuable member of our tribe."

Yeah, right. Evalle groaned silently. Replying to that honestly would only open a debate neither of them would win. Holding Tzader and Quinn's respect mattered more than being shunned by

Brina. Evalle pulled her shoulders back and tried to sound at ease over Tzader leaving when she couldn't entirely dismiss his concern.

He was intuitive when it came to others.

"Don't worry, Z, I'll be fine."

"If not, have Trey get word to me."

She hated that, but she wouldn't be able to reach Tzader herself once he left. No one could break through this fortress telepathically. That always left her with a sense of unease whenever she had to come up here.

Inside mountains no one could hear you scream . . .

Cue the scary music.

"You're down to two minutes. Don't be late." Tzader stepped away from her and raised his voice. "I'm ready to leave, Sen. Don't forget my truck."

By the time Evalle chugged the last of her water, Tzader had vanished. Teleported by Sen. The only thing worse than riding through the sun in full gear was teleporting. Sen had done it to her once and she'd thrown up on him when she'd arrived.

Might be one reason he didn't like her. But it'd been a great day for her. Not often she got the last word where Sen was concerned.

She kicked off her boots and slipped on a pair of sandals before heading to the war room. The temperature this deep within the mountain was even cooler than back at the entrance. The upside of being in damp clothes was the quick chill that slid over her skin.

Reaching the war room with a minute to spare, she scoped the team assembled so far. Three men lounged around the room, all positioned to face the door with their backs to a wall. The only other Belador present was Trey McCree. He'd stretched out on a leather sofa the color of sand. Since he lived in the Atlanta area like her, he couldn't be much happier about the run up here than she was.

On the other side of the room, in a wood-and-black-leather antigravity chair, a cowboy sprawled with a nonchalance she was sure he didn't feel. Reece "Casper" Jordan. He'd been with VIPER for over six years and hailed from Texas—thus the bone-white Stetson hat covering his face and the snakeskin boots he always wore. His personal bane was sharing his body with a thirteenth-century ghost.

Little was known about the third guy in the room, a dark Castilian who leaned one shoulder against the rock wall. Lucien Solis. His name might mean "light," but he was as dark as sin. No matter where he was, he studied everyone like they were test specimens he'd like to pin to a board and dissect.

"Mornin' sunshine." Casper grinned at her, shoving his hat up on his head as he moved the chair upright. "How *do* you see with those things on?" He indicated the almost opaque sunglasses she wore all the time. "Hell, I walk into stuff all the time and I *can* see."

"Sunshine?" Evalle smiled at his dig at her nocturnal life. "Think I heard there were thunderstorms in the forecast for today."

Casper grimaced. "Not funny." After being struck by lightning during a visit to Scotland ten years ago, Casper sometimes morphed into the reincarnation of a Highland warrior who'd lived in 1260.

He'd hated storms ever since.

But honestly, she liked him a lot. Unlike most of the operatives, Casper held no allegiance to any deity or clan—only to VIPER.

Having finished off the first bottle of water, Evalle lifted a new one from an aluminum tub against the wall that was perpetually filled with bottled water, iced tea and cold drinks for them.

She settled on a second leather sofa near the entrance.

"Anybody know what this is about?" Trey scratched his head, rumpling his light brown hair, which suffered from perpetual bedhead. He sat up, dropped his feet to the stone floor and propped his elbows on his knees, holding his head in his hands. The heather gray T-shirt and jeans he wore covered a body that would give most nightclub bouncers pause before tackling.

"I don't have a clue." Evalle set her water down and watched the entrance.

Trey yawned, eyes red with lack of sleep. "I could do with a little more notice next time."

Married life must be keeping him up late. He'd taken a wife two years ago. Childhood sweetheart. A nice young witch who, along with her sister, upheld the laws of their coven and practiced a spiritual life within the bright light of peace and compassion. Beladors were rarely allowed to mate outside the tribe, but Brina had approved the marriage. Tzader had told her their union removed the emptiness inside Trey, and he was right.

Trey did seem happier these days, at peace.

Lucky bastard.

Evalle felt a twinge of something akin to envy, a stupid emotion she shoved way back in her mind. She didn't want what he had, not if it meant the risk of being vulnerable again.

Never.

She envied the peace he felt, that was all.

Besides, she couldn't get involved with anyone. Not until she figured out where Alterants came from and understood her place in the world. Something that was her number one priority at night whenever she had a chance to breathe.

Of course, that came after her obligations to VIPER. Then there was her job at the morgue and taking college classes online.

Yeah, she really had no life.

But this wasn't the time or place to think about that. Right now, they had a meeting to attend.

She stifled a yawn herself. "This better be important."

"Sen cutting into your beauty sleep, precious?" Casper winked at her.

"Like he gives a flip when any of us sleep, since he doesn't ever seem to." She should probably get up and walk around to keep from nodding off in this cool air.

The loud thump of boot heels approached, banging the slate floor in the long hallway. All VIPER doors were ten feet tall and four feet wide to accommodate the majority of body shapes.

"We're waiting on two more," Sen said as he entered. No salutations, his SOP. What agent was he allowing to arrive late? That didn't sound like their unforgiving Sen.

And if Lucien was a mystery, Sen was a dark secret. Speculation on Sen ranged from god to demigod to the devil himself.

She'd made the Lucifer suggestion.

At six feet in height, he stood with his arms crossed over his chest. His black jeans rode snug against his hips. She'd seen him taller and thicker. Sen's body seemed to be a fluid thing, never in one state for very long.

75

Gone was the dark chestnut ponytail he'd had at the last VIPER meeting, replaced by short, thick hair.

Trey made a sound of irritation. "What's going on?"

"There's a serious problem in the southeast." Sen didn't elaborate.

Evalle snorted. "We have problems everywhere . . ." When no one else spoke up, she went on. "So how big a problem are we talking and where *exactly* is it?"

Utter contempt radiated from Sen's glare.

Tzader's warning went through her head, reminding her she would gain nothing by pushing Sen.

Nothing but torture.

Still . . .

Who or what was he waiting on?

Sen allowed no one to delay his meetings. Something was a beat off with all of this.

She picked up the approach of someone different. Energy and a swirl of anxiety rushed into the room and scuffed her arms. Her senses had hinted at an empathic gift for a couple years, but this was the strongest assault she'd had to date.

In that same instant the other three agents became alert.

All eyes went to the doorway as a woman entered.

Chin-length blonde hair framed a perfect face. The stunning hazel eyes and smooth, unblemished skin would be enough to hate her for, but she sealed the deal with average height and a figure models tortured themselves to maintain.

Then she smiled.

In that instant, Evalle's empathic sense went wild. As expected, she sensed lust from the men . . .

But what caught her off guard was a lash of hatred from one of the men so severe that when it whipped through the room she felt the sting on her skin.

What the hell was that? And who had it come from?

FIVE

"This is Adrianna Lafontaine," Sen said as the blonde female took several steps into the war room and paused as though allowing everyone to enjoy her beauty. Her fire red jacket and short skirt ordered all eyes to start at the top and continue to the sparkling red shoes.

Evalle wished she could reach Tzader right now to find out if he knew anything about Adrianna. Everything about this woman raised Evalle's alarms.

"And this is Storm." Sen's second introduction yanked Evalle's gaze to the man who'd walked in behind Adrianna.

His presence spoke louder than any introduction. Black hair fell to his shoulders—an obsidian color that was matched by his dark eyes. Sun-drenched skin and high, proud cheekbones spoke of ancestors who'd lived in North America long before invaders had shown up. Pebble-sized mixed stones interspersed with inch-long carved claws were strung on a length of rawhide tied around his neck. He wore a lightweight leather jacket over a white T-shirt tucked inside worn jeans . . . jeans he filled out nicely.

His alpha presence doused the wave of male lust that had flashed through the room when Adrianna had entered.

"Have a seat," Sen instructed the new members.

Adrianna took a spot on the couch next to Trey, using the motion to show off her shapely legs.

May Macha bless Trey because he ignored Adrianna. That was a happily married man.

Evalle expected Storm to stand only because his mysterious

appearance reminded her of Lucien, who rarely sat, but Storm sauntered across the room and settled next to her, stretching out his long legs. She didn't think he was much over six feet tall, but he packed a lot of man into that space.

And why was she noticing that about him if he was a new agent? *I think the sun boiled my brain.*

Swinging her attention to Sen, Evalle started to lean back when she felt the stuffed leather behind her head move with Storm's arm sliding across. She considered sitting upright and stopped herself before reacting. Never wise to show any reaction that could be misconstrued as apprehension around another nonhuman. *Let no one see your weakness*—it was the one code she'd never break. Storm didn't touch her, but that presence she'd felt when he'd walked in barged into her space.

What exactly was he?

And what were his powers? . . .

Sen cleared his throat. "Now that everyone is present, pay attention so that I don't have to repeat myself. We have a problem here in Georgia."

"Again? Can't the demons find a new place to play? I hear New Orleans is dying for some action. And New York's nice this time of year," Trey muttered.

For some reason, Evalle couldn't resist taunting him. "What's the matter? Married life making you soft?"

Trey cut an annoyed glance at her, then cocked a cynical smile. "If that was the case, we'd all chip in to find *something* to marry you."

"Enough." Sen's no-nonsense stare struck Trey, then drifted to her.

A short, deep laugh rumbled out of Storm.

Evalle's eyes widened at his audacity. Somebody should give him the Sen Survival 101 talk.

"The Ngak Stone—"

"'Nack' like 'knick-knack'?" Casper interrupted him.

Sen cut a vicious glare at him. "The Nah-yak"—he enunciated slowly, then spelled it so that they'd understand the term—"Stone was lost in Atlanta during an unsanctioned battle two years ago." Sen paused, his condemning gaze now firmly affixed on Trey, who sighed and covered his eyes with his hand, as if knowing what was coming next. "The stone will choose a new master soon. It has boundless power and moves through history with a certain autonomy. It's believed this stone caused the Yellow River to flood China four thousand years ago when a high-level adviser inside the Yao Dynasty stole the stone from a Tibetan monk with intentions of using it to multiply their crops and build an empire that could not be defeated. The Yellow River flooded the next day, killing the thief and washing the rock away. But the stone must have been extremely angry over its theft because the Yellow River still floods to this day. And don't get me started on what it did to Vesuvius. *That* is the kind of power we're talking, people."

Sen paused while a grim murmur buzzed through the room.

So that's why we're here? Evalle schooled her face to be concerned and not show her relief that she hadn't been exposed. Thank the gods, Sen hadn't found out about the demons or their quest for an Alterant . . .

Yet.

But that relief was only minor given the severity of what was happening. The Ngak Stone showing up again created all sorts of deadly possibilities, especially for the Beladors, since the last person to hold it had been a Kujoo warrior.

I think I'm getting a migraine.

Because the last thing she needed thrown into this mix was a bunch of angry Kujoo running around town with an all-powerful weapon, trying to settle an ancient score with the Beladors.

But at least this meant a common enemy that for once wasn't *her*.

Sen glared the room into silence. "The Hindu god, Shiva, contacted our Tribunal a few hours ago to let us know that the Ngak Stone will soon reveal itself in the same area where it was lost. He has no idea when or exactly where. But the time is drawing near, and once the stone is ready to be located it will call a new master."

Trey let out a sound of aggravation. "Shiva didn't say if choosing a new master would involve a Kujoo, did he?"

"No, but he didn't say it wouldn't."

Casper slid a glance to Trey. "Wanna lay odds with me? Cause my luck and money says if a Kujoo don't find it, my favorite song ain't 'I Love My Truck.'"

Trey shook his head.

Ignoring them, Storm frowned at Sen. "I'm unfamiliar with the Kujoo. But if Shiva's involved, I take it they're Indian in nature?"

Sen inclined his head to him. "The Kujoo were once a race of Hindu humans until eight hundred years ago, when a band of rogue Beladors, drunk on bloodlust, plundered their village and killed their families. Before Macha could punish them for it, Shiva answered the Kujoo's call for vengeance and granted them supernatural powers so that they could fight back."

Adrianna scowled at him. "Why are the Beladors still enemies then after all this time?"

Sen sighed. "The Kujoo weren't content to kill the handful who'd wronged them. They declared open warfare on any and all Beladors. It was bloody and brutal. And the Kujoo quickly lost sight of why they'd originally fought. It became a matter of killing off anyone with a trace of Belador blood in them."

When he said "a *trace* of Belador blood," Sen sent a derogatory glance at Evalle before continuing. "Finally, when there were only a few of each left, Macha and Shiva came to an agreement. She would corral and sanction the remaining Beladors, and Shiva would lock his now insane Kujoo beneath Mount Meru—where they continue to live, train and plot the Belador communal deaths. Two years ago, one such plot resulted in a Kujoo warrior escaping Mt. Meru with the Ngak Stone. During the ensuing fight against some of our operatives, he lost the stone in Piedmont Park."

Casper sat forward. "Wait . . . you're saying that we *knew* where this potential Belador kryptonite has been sitting the whole time but didn't send a retrieval team to find it and put it in our vault?"

Sen gave him a duh stare. "Yes, Casper. We purposefully left it there. It made such a great resting place for the pigeons and tourists that we couldn't bring ourselves to move it."

Trey spoke up. "It's only the size of a goose egg, not a damn boulder. There was one good thing that came from the battle. Macha fixed our eyes. Our powers are no longer linked to our vision."

"Speak for yourself," Evalle muttered. Many of the Beladors, like Trey, had been subject to weakening of powers if their eyes were compromised. After the battle with the Kujoo two years back, Brina had lobbied Macha to fix that, which the goddess had. Be nice if Brina had lobbied Macha on Evalle's behalf to allow her to walk in sunshine. "*I* still have sensitive eyes."

"But it doesn't affect your powers the way it did ours," Trey pointed out.

Sen broke in. "Think you two can save the drivel for your own time?" He addressed the whole room. "The stone becomes invisible until it wants to be found, sometimes for centuries. We could have excavated the entire park and never found that rock. It chooses when and where to be seen or found."

Trey let out an elongated breath. "I suppose it's too much to hope that we have some idea who or what the stone has chosen for a new master."

"In the past, it's always chosen someone with significant powers. Someone with an unknown history. The only clue Shiva could give us is that he believes it'll select a woman this time."

"Well, there goes the neighborhood." Casper winked at Evalle.

Evalle rolled her eyes. That cowboy was asking for trouble and some female would oblige him one day, but not her. He didn't interest her at all, not like Isak, whose touch had been . . .

No, don't go there.

Because she had no interest in a relationship with anything other than Häagen-Dazs. Especially not with a man whose favorite extracurricular activity was hunting nonhumans.

There was no telling what he'd do to her if he ever learned who and what she really was.

Sen crossed his arms over his chest, the action bringing her thoughts back to the matter at hand as he continued. "Shiva has agreed to let us put the Ngak Stone in our vault *if* the stone allows its owner to hand it to us *voluntarily*. Shiva warned he will not interfere with the stone's destiny. He can't. So we must find that woman and get that rock."

"What if the rock is destined to remain with the woman it

chooses?" Adrianna's voice was filmy as smoke, soft and tainted with hidden undercurrents. "Why are we assuming this woman shouldn't wield its power?"

If not for hearing an ulterior motive beneath Adrianna's words, Evalle might have seen her point.

Amazingly, Sen showed no sign of annoyance at being questioned by the blonde. "Shiva had a vision. He saw two paths for the stone once it passed into the woman's hands. The first showed it resting in a guarded space—the outcome we prefer. The other ended with it being used for cataclysmic destruction. If this stone lands in the wrong hands, it could change the landscape of the world as we know it. Every time it shows up, it changes human history, and never for the better."

"Where's Indiana Jones when we need him?" Casper wondered aloud.

Sen's jaw twitched, but he continued the briefing. "In the past, our people were lucky and managed to prevent total destruction of our planet. This time? It's up to us. Things are going to get ugly if we don't get our hands on the Ngak Stone."

"How do you plan to take the rock from its new owner if we find her?" Lucien's question surprised the room when he spoke.

Evalle imagined that deep voice and melodic Latin accent played well with the females. Oozing testosterone and looking like sex on two legs probably didn't hurt either.

Sen sighed. "We can't take the Ngak Stone from her. She has to willingly hand it over."

"Not exactly true." Lucien paused, his voice softening with a lethal quality when he added, "There is one other way to take possession."

Evalle arched an inquisitive look at the Castilian, grasping what he insinuated. The new master could die.

Remind me to stay on his good side.

Sen glared at him. "You will *not* kill her to take that rock."

Lucien smiled, an expression his stony gaze failed to support. "*I* don't intend to. However, accidents happen and other creatures besides us are hunting for it. Who knows? She could easily slip and fall on someone's knife. A few dozen times."

Sen sighed. "As you said, we can't stop that, but anyone who tries to take the stone by force would have to be out of their mind. The stone might accept a new master, or it might turn on the person who attacked the chosen one. The gods help them then, because it won't be pretty."

Casper gestured to the agents in the room. "Are we it? Please tell me given the nature of this beast that we're going to have more folks looking for it."

Sen hesitated before he spoke. "This is a highly delicate situation. The fewer people who know the stone is up for grabs, the better off we'll be. So do not share information with anyone outside this team, not even other VIPER members, and especially not that we're searching for the Ngak Stone. I can't risk sending in a large contingent that would alert our enemies. If word of the stone's reappearance surfaced, any and every *thing* with supernatural power would show up to get their hands on it."

Lucien scoffed. "Word *will* get out."

Wasn't he Mr. Encouraging? Evalle didn't think Lucien would live long around Sen if he kept that up, but she welcomed anyone drawing Sen's attention away from her.

"Then we have to find that stone *and* the woman quickly." Sen's terse words sent in Lucien's direction made it clear he wasn't up for any negative attitude or slackers.

Trey shook his head. "Atlanta's spread out. Do we know where to look for this woman?"

"No, but we know where the stone should reappear since it can't physically move itself. The stone *can* create environmental changes that cause it to be moved, but it still has to wait to be picked up."

Trey let out an angry sound of frustration. "Damn, this sucks." He leveled a serious stare at Sen. "You do realize that I now have to choose between the end of the world as we know it and my balls, right?"

Sen's eyes widened in surprise. "Pardon?"

"My wife's in her last weeks of pregnancy, and if I'm not there when she goes into labor, she will annihilate my testicles. *Both* of them. Without anesthesia. I'd rather the earth end in a bloody ball of flames than I lose the boys. I think every male in this room agrees . . ." He glanced over to where Lucien leaned against the wall. "Well, maybe not Lucien. The jury's still out on his sexual preference, but I don't want to be a soprano."

Lucien's eyes held a wicked threat when he chuckled. "You keep that up, *cabrón,* and you won't have to wait on your wife to remove them. I assure you, it can be arranged here and now."

The tic started again in Sen's jaw. "Go to your respective corners, both of you." He looked at Trey. "As for your personal matter, I suggest then that you locate the stone quickly before your jewels are handed to you. And trust me, once her labor pains kick in, even if you're there, you'll be lucky to walk away with them intact anyway."

Sen turned his attention to the rest of them. "Now if we can focus on something other than Trey's testicles, we still have Armageddon to deal with. Tzader's spearheading this mission, and Trey will handle communications with headquarters. Quinn will work with Casper. Storm will become part of the southeastern team. Evalle will show Storm around."

Evalle stiffened. When had she become a tour guide? She started to complain that she couldn't be saddled with a new guy when she had to be inside during the daylight, but Sen would love nothing more than to have her admit she was lacking.

Again.

But with that came a sense of dread. The last thing she wanted was to deal with Storm tonight. Not that he hadn't seemed like a decent guy at first glance. Still, she didn't want to be alone with him for several reasons.

One, she didn't trust *any* man when they were alone.

Second, she didn't know what kind of powers Storm had or how he felt about being stuck with a woman. Then there was the small matter of her being an Alterant. Her experience with Beladors was that they tended to freak whenever they found out about her heritage. He'd put her at the bottom of the food chain, right under Birrn demons and pond scum.

With any luck, Tzader would take Storm off her hands to train.

Lucien jerked his chin toward Adrianna. "What about her?"

84

Sen glanced at Adrianna, then back at Lucien before he answered. "She'll be working on her own, but you're to assist her."

Lucien's eyes darkened with an emotion Evalle would call loathing that matched his tone. "Ah, I would say *gracias,* but that would sound as though you did me a favor. Perhaps now you'd care to tell everyone *what* she is?"

Evalle had found the source of the hatred she'd felt when Adrianna had walked into the mission room.

And Adrianna didn't appear any happier with Lucien than he was with her.

When all eyes focused on Sen, he explained, "She's a Sterling witch, working with us on this one mission. We needed a consultant who was there the last time a witch opened a portal for the Kujoo."

Evalle shook her head. "Are you out of your mind? You want us to trust a witch from the *Sterling* family? A black-majik-practicing dynasty?"

Sen's eyes narrowed to slits. "A Tribunal has approved her. This is not *your* decision."

Evalle had to force herself not to argue her point. Tribunals weren't infallible by any stretch of the imagination. But Sen wasn't about to listen to her, even though all of them knew better than to trust a Sterling.

What was the Tribunal thinking?

Sen's threatening gaze shifted to Lucien, whose only reaction was a muscle twitching in his jaw. "Another thing. I had a report that a Birrn demon was executed in a warehouse off Metropolitan Parkway in Atlanta this morning. I want to know who or what took him down and what the demon was doing there. I know it couldn't have been one of our agents, since no one called for cleanup." His face tightened. "At least it better not be one of our people. The gods help them if it is and I expect answers by sunset, or it won't go well for any of you."

With a snap of Sen's fingers, a low wooden table appeared in the middle of the room, along with a stack of file folders. "This is what we have from Fulton County law enforcement on the slaying."

Holding her breath in fear, Evalle lifted a file and tried to look normal. She went immediately to the pictures of the scene, hoping there was nothing from the county investigation that would betray her.

Grace be to Macha, nothing in these pages looked damning.

For the moment, she was safe.

But the question was, did Sen have a sniffer in this region who could use the chips to catch a trail and follow it the way a blood-hound tracked scent? That was one of the few powers she envied.

And while she was at it, she needed to locate the twins and tell them not to mention the incident with the Birrn to anyone, especially a Nightstalker.

Her thoughts turned to Isak, and her stomach sank. How was she going to find a man who no doubt was unfindable *and* convince him not to tell anyone about seeing her with the demon?

I should have been late for this meeting.

Apparently she'd flunked basic survival, too.

Sen wouldn't need any help getting rid of her if she kept putting her own head in the noose. Her heartbeat jumped into high gear.

Her time for locating the Birrn's master was running out. Sen would suspend her, strip all of her powers, then lock her away in hell.

She'd absolutely lose her mind if that happened. There was no way she could take that again. Not to mention the small matter that she was their target. Without her powers, there was no telling what the demon master would do to her.

But she couldn't do a thing until dark without risking her life. Her breath came in shorter and shorter gasps as she fought down her panic through clenched teeth.

Trained agents would be looking into the Birrn slaying.

I'm so dead. I'm so dead. I'm so dead. She couldn't breathe or focus. Her panic continued to swell. She had to keep it hidden from the rest of the agents. *Get a grip!*

Suddenly, a gentle wave of energy floated over her, soothing her distress and wrapping her in a cocoon of comfort. Her breathing steadied.

Someone in this room had done that.

Evalle slowly looked around, but no one seemed to be paying her attention. Who had reached out to her?

Who knew she'd been closing in on panic?

Was it Lucien or Casper? She didn't think Trey had that kind of power, and Sen definitely wouldn't have done squat to help her.

Her gaze skipped around the room until she looked into the dark eyes of the man sitting next to her.

Storm.

Her breath got tangled in her throat.

His expression had been void of emotion when he'd entered the room, but interest burned through his gaze now. A purely male gleam. He stretched back, looking even more relaxed and utterly confident in a room full of alpha males.

Confidence like that was incredibly sexy.

And he knew it. The corner of his mouth lifted a tiny bit, letting her know he'd seen her purely female reaction.

Her pulse thumped wildly in response. The room was hot and crowded all of a sudden. She wanted everyone to leave.

Maybe not Storm.

The smile peeking from his eyes picked up heat.

Crap, what was wrong with her? Had her hormones blown a gasket?

Or was Storm using majik to heighten her attraction?

It took all of Evalle's control to break away from that gimlet stare and calmly shift her attention to Sen, whose briefing she was missing.

". . . the Ngak Stone chooses its master in the next twenty-four to forty-eight hours. It will use its powers to call her out and to seduce her into accepting her destiny while she carries the rock. The morning after the next full moon, when the sun touches the spot where she found the rock, the stone will bond permanently to her. At that point she'll be a force to be reckoned with. We have to separate her from the stone without killing her before that happens. Once bound, the woman will have full use of the stone's power, but it will also have control over her."

Casper sat forward. "The next full moon is Tuesday night. So you're telling us that we have three days to find this rock and the woman. *Three days* to save the world?"

The room groaned.

Sen nodded. "Get moving, people. In the hands of a preternatural predator, that rock is invincible."

"We'll all be dining in hell," Trey said under his breath.

Casper turned a thoughtful look toward Evalle. "You think the stone's looking for Evalle? She has power and an unknown history. Seems like a good fit to me."

Every set of eyes turned to her. *Thanks, cowboy. Just toss my hide out for the skinning.*

Sen curled his lip derisively. "I seriously doubt it would pick an *Alterant* when it has the entire universe to choose from."

Evalle went from terrified to humiliated with one sentence. Anger scorched the back of her throat, but she knew better than to let it show. So what if he felt that way? She didn't care about him either.

Still, it stung, and the fact that it did just made her all the angrier at herself for giving him that kind of power over her emotions.

By the time she stood up, everyone else had left the room except Storm and Sen.

The sun would be out in all its glory by now, and she'd have to ride back home with the heat climbing to a hundred. Gotta love baking in Georgia's summer heat. Not.

Evalle couldn't squelch the irritation she'd kept bottled until now. "Did we have to come all the way up here to hear this? Couldn't Trey have briefed us from home?"

The pleasure that burst into Sen's gaze took her breath, and not in a good way. "Trey could have briefed the others, but I wanted *you* here for another reason. Storm's SUV has been warded to shield the interior from the sun. And there's a motorcycle trailer hitched to it for your bike. He'll be driving you back so that you won't damage yourself." Could he be any more snide?

Tzader would have been proud of her for not saying a word. But in all honesty she'd gone blank. Ride two hours with a man who had . . .

What had Storm done to her? She still didn't know what kind of powers he possessed.

"Looking forward to the company on the drive down." Storm's tone was professional, yet his gaze was anything but.

She'd be the first to admit she found him sexy . . . if admired from a distance. However, the last thing she wanted was to be trapped inside a vehicle with an unknown male for two hours.

Especially one her senses were yelling at her to avoid.

Sen's expression was creepily pleasant, like that of a lion licking its chops while eyeballing its prey. "I want you to review the Birrn death with Storm. Tell him everything you know about paranormal activity in the city and the recent proliferation of demon visits."

"Okay."

Sen's gaze sharpened, like he'd just cornered her. "By the way, I didn't tell you why I brought Storm in."

"He knows something about Birrns?"

Sen shook his head. "He's a Navajo shaman who can track unnatural beings. But he has one special talent I think you'll find fascinating. It's one that will be of great benefit to VIPER. Storm has the ability to know if someone is lying or not." An evil, smug smile curved his lips. "And he's going to be *your* new partner, which should expedite your efforts in finding out why the demons are here, as well as ensuring the Ngak Stone doesn't end up in your hands."

Bile rose in her throat. "Thought you said the stone would never pick an Alterant."

"The gods occasionally have a sick sense of humor. And I can't take the chance that it will seduce you."

Oh, I'd like for it to choose me. 'Cause you'd be the first one I'd go for, you arrogant bastard. That alone would make it worth her soul.

And now she understood what had caused Sen's happiness.

He wanted her out of VIPER, since he didn't like an anomaly on his team. The little pig thought Storm would catch her in a lie that would land her in suspension . . . or a Tribunal hearing.

Sen was wrong.

Storm could catch her in a whole string of lies, and any one of them could doom her.

SIX

"**M**y lord, my lord," Ekkbar called out. "I have news."

Batuk flicked his hand, tossing an arc of power at the magician to prevent him from rushing forward.

Ekkbar's skinny legs continued to run where he stood, but they didn't carry him forward.

Batuk growled at the half-wit he'd warned not to show his face again in the great hall. At least not for a thousand years if he wanted to continue breathing. After all, it was Ekkbar's fault their Kujoo people had been cursed to live beneath Mount Meru for the past eight hundred years.

Snakes carved as arms on his throne began to undulate beneath Batuk's tense muscles.

Ekkbar's high voice pleaded, "Please, my lord, you must listen. I have found a new portal, I have."

"Lies!" Batuk roared. They'd all been searching for a new portal. It was inconceivable that this lowly piece of excrement would be able to succeed where the rest of them had failed.

Rock walls glowed, shifting as if molten lava. Flames spit out between cracks in the stone.

By the gods, he would kill that scab if not for one problem.

Every member of his Kujoo tribe was immortal.

Because the gods hate us. Better we should have been slaughtered in battle than subjected to this horror of eternal, never-relenting hell. He curled his fingers, muscles tight with the need to kill Ekkbar.

His fingernails sharpened into metal claws.

The elite guard drew their swords and moved forward. His men couldn't kill Ekkbar, but with a little encouragement they would make the magician scream for mercy, which might alleviate a few minutes of his boredom.

Batuk's fury stoked the temperatures high until the *nihar* billowing around his throne turned from fog to hot steam.

Ekkbar bowed his head in reverence—a lying act, like all his other actions. "But, my lord, I bring you good news. You said not to return *unless* I could free you of this place. I would not defy you, my lord. Not defy you."

Batuk held his hand up to stay his guard. What if this pathetic maggot had actually found a way for more than one of them to escape?

Could his army ever be free again? Batuk's silent question echoed back at him from the weary eyes of his men.

He glared at the magician. "For my tribe, I will hear you. But heed me now when I warn you to take care. If you use lies to sow false hopes, I will have your skin peeled off daily."

Ekkbar swallowed hard, then bounced his head up and down. "Yes, yes. Free my legs, my lord, and I will tell you great truths."

Grunting with disbelief, Batuk lifted his chin in the magician's direction to release his legs.

The magician hurried forward until he stood in front of the throne. His silvery silk pants rustled against his scrawny limbs. His body shriveled along with his manhood, Ekkbar weighed no more than one of Batuk's legs.

"Speak fast or I'll unleash the guard on you."

Ekkbar swallowed hard. "I have spoken to a witch in my dreams—"

Batuk cut his words short with a vicious hiss. "Not another witch. I've had my fill of them for a thousand lifetimes." Which at present he'd be living here as he fulfilled them.

Ekkbar opened his arms in a gesture that questioned why his master lacked simple knowledge of how majik worked. "I know of no other save a witch who can open a path for us, my lord. But this one is different, far more powerful than the last one."

"The *last* witch fell into league with the Beladors and betrayed us. How do we trust that this one will not as well?"

"When you've heard all I have to share, you will know the answer to that question, *O Revered Highness*." Ekkbar shifted from foot to foot, an impatient dance he performed whenever he was anxious.

Batuk wasn't so easily sold. "You're treading dangerous landscape, worm."

The dance stopped immediately. Ekkbar fell to his knees, stirring the *nihar* that smoked around his chest. "Never, my lord."

"What does this witch claim she can do?"

"To release you and eight more warriors from our realm—"

"Nine? Only *nine* of us? I want all of my men freed!"

Ekkbar bounced his head up and down again. "I understand, my lord. I do. I do. But she says once you pass through the portal you will be able to free all those loyal to you. She says ten will be enough men to—"

"Ten?"

"Vyan is still alive from when he escaped. I have spoken to him in his dreams, too. He tires of waiting and stands ready to free his warlord."

Batuk grunted, pleased at the unswerving loyalty from his first in command, who had gone through a portal two years ago. Vyan had tried to capture the witch who'd opened that first pathway to force her to help his people. He'd battled her Belador lover and lost only because more Belador warriors had entered the battle, outnumbering him. "Does Vyan know this new witch?"

"No, my lord. I would not share this news with anyone until I spoke with you." The humble curve of Ekkbar's shoulders sat poorly on a man who bowed only when forced to do so.

"How am I to free the others once we leave here?"

"The witch says all you have to do is gain control of the Ngak Stone—"

"It is gone. Forever."

"No, no, my lord. The stone hides until it chooses to be found. I did not even know the Ngak Stone had lived with me beneath Mount Meru all these years until the stone revealed itself in my chest two years ago. Did not know until Vyan stole my treasure," he accused, muttering to himself.

"*Your* treasure?"

Ekkbar's yellow eyes turned almost white with fear over his slip. Batuk knew without a doubt that Vyan had taken the stone to find a way to save the tribe, whereas Ekkbar would have saved his hide only.

The magician's shoulders trembled. He clutched his hands together, twisting them as an old woman begging for mercy. "I meant only that I treasured the stone, yes, only that. All treasures are yours, my lord. All yours." He bowed his head again.

Batuk had to fight the urge to kick him. But he didn't want to sully his foot. "You never did tell me how the Ngak Stone came to be in your possession to begin with, Ekkbar, did you?"

A shadow fell across Ekkbar's face, guilt peeking through before he brightened. "You did not ask, and I could not say while banished from your sight. I found the rock glowing in a creek near where you battled the Belador heathens back before we were cursed. Wicked heathens. I had just placed the stone in my chest upon returning to camp—but only to keep it safe for you, my lord—when Shiva sent us to live here. Most unkind of our god. Most unkind."

Don't remind me. "Where is the stone now?"

"I know not for sure—"

Batuk pounded his fists on the arms of his chair. The carved snakes came to life, striking out at Ekkbar, who slid backward on his knees as if gliding upon a majik carpet. "I warned you not to sow false hopes."

Steel clanged throughout the great hall when each warrior struck his sword against the rock walls in anger, hungry for Batuk to toss Ekkbar to them.

Ekkbar remained on his knees, shoulders now quaking with fear. "My lord . . . please. You are an honorable warrior. Hear me out before you decide if I have deceived you."

Lifting his hand to silence the noise, Batuk released a sigh that built from deep in his gut. "Speak."

Ekkbar floated forward again, his folded legs a hand's width above the floor when he stopped just out of striking distance. He warily eyed the snakes, which had returned to carved serpents, and continued, "What I meant to say was that I do not know the precise location, but I have had a vision of the Ngak Stone. It still resides in the creek where the stone was lost during Vyan's battle with the Beladors. The Ngak Stone will cause a giant shovel to dig this creek up soon, bringing the rock to rest upon the bank. The stone will reveal itself to a new master before the full moon three nights from now."

"Will the Ngak Stone choose Vyan again?"

The squirt of noise from Ekkbar's lips conveyed his disgust for Vyan, no doubt because the warrior had outwitted the magician the last time a portal had opened. "I believe the stone chose Vyan *only* for his two hands that carried the stone out of here, not to be a master, or the stone would have remained within his grasp. The stone has always chosen a powerful being, but this time it waits for a woman."

"The witch?" Batuk ground his fists against the arms of his chair. Snake eyes glowed with life.

"No, no, my lord. The witch does not want to touch the stone. She claims it carries majik that will fight hers. And she warns that if you or any of your men touch the stone when you arrive in Atlanta, the Beladors will know that you are in their world before you have the chance to use the rock. She tells me she has seen this in a scrying bowl."

"If neither I nor my men can touch the stone, how will it serve me to be at the mercy of Beladors, who will outnumber our ten?"

"The witch has a plan, yes, she has a plan." Ekkbar's kneeling body floated up with his excitement. "Once she brings you and your men out, she will tell you how to find a being who can gain the Ngak Stone for you."

"What is this being who will help us?"

"An Alterant."

Batuk scowled at the unfamiliar term. "A what?"

"Someone who is born part Belador . . ." Ekkbar lifted his hands palms out as he waited on Batuk's snarling to quiet. "And part unknown. Yes, this being has the blood of your enemy but is shunned by the Beladors."

"I trust *no* Beladors!"

"This is not a true Belador but one who is considered a lowly mongrel, a castoff their tribe holds in low respect. Alterants change into dangerous beasts and have killed Beladors."

Batuk sat back in his throne, scratching his beard. "A Belador beast that kills its own tribe? I have not heard of this."

If a shriveled-up male could preen, the foolish magician did just such. "I am most pleased to bring you good news. Most pleased."

"What does this witch want in return?" Batuk began to believe this hairless blight on his existence might actually have found a way out of Shiva's curse.

"After you have gained what you most desire, the witch says you may take the Ngak Stone and do as you please if you give her the Alterant to do with as she pleases."

That was it? He could keep the most powerful stone in creation and all the witch wanted was this Alterant?

Batuk hesitated. *When something seems too easy, it always is.* No one would give up the stone for something so petty. Not without good reason.

But that being said, they could deal with the witch and the Alterant once they escaped and had the stone. Then the world would bow and tremble before them. Their wrath would be legendary.

"Tell the witch she has a bargain."

SEVEN

Storm slowed his 1979 FJ-40 Land Cruiser to a crawl. Not by choice. He doubted anyone else caught in this gnarled I-75 traffic slowed down by choice either.

At least he had sweet-smelling scenery inside *his* cab.

He shifted his gaze sideways to where Evalle Kincaid leaned her head and shoulder against the passenger door.

As soon as they'd left the war room, she'd told him how tired she was. He didn't doubt her exhaustion—she had the bags under her eyes to prove it. That's why he'd allowed her to bail on him after she'd executed an exaggerated yawn on the way to his truck and asked if he minded her taking a quick nap.

Avoidance would only work for so long, but he'd agreed.

Evalle had hugged her body as tight as she'd been able against the passenger door, acting as if she rested. But the muscles in her folded arms had been tense and her shoulders had curved inward defensively.

Nobody that tight would have been able to sleep no matter their exhaustion.

He was a hunter, a patient man who could wait out skittish prey, so he'd murmured a few words asking the spirits to ease her soul and allow her to rest.

Within minutes of their leaving VIPER's HQ, Evalle had relaxed into a boneless heap. He'd slipped off her sunglasses, since the interior was so dark with Sen's protective warding that the dash lights were on even though it was midafternoon outside. Sen hadn't warded the truck from the sun or stuck the motorcycle trailer on the back with her crotch rocket as any favor to Evalle. He'd wanted to force her into an uncomfortable situation for two hours.

Sen hadn't said he was gunning for Evalle, but even the blind could see he had a private agenda when it came to her.

Storm understood private agendas. He had one as well and would fulfill his agreement with Sen, but on his own terms.

Which was why he'd helped Evalle sleep almost the entire drive. She shifted, her black Gore-Tex riding clothes shushing against his vinyl seats. The movement stirred her scent around the cab. She had an earthy smell, something that piqued his interest in a way Adrianna-the-sex-toy-witch hadn't. With all the lacy trimmings on the outside, Adrianna blew cold as an arctic winter on the inside.

Took more than window dressing to make a woman desirable.

He liked his women with fire under the surface. Evalle might project a chilly façade, but she had a core of heat he'd bet would burst into an inferno with a little encouragement.

But he couldn't afford the distraction right now or get close to someone he was tasked with keeping an eye on.

No hardship there.

Her unzipped jacket had fallen open while she slept.

She wore a loose T-shirt underneath, but from the way she slumped it was pulled tight over her hard stomach, showing her body off to perfection. A wisp of thick lashes hid her finely shaped eyes above soft cheeks. He'd seen the shape of her eyes through her sunglasses, but not the color.

Didn't matter. They could be purple or blaze orange and she'd still be beautiful. Her hair had dried during the ride, sweeping loosely over her shoulders. One long tendril lay quietly along her neck.

Only his iron will stopped him from reaching over to stroke his fingers through all that plush hair, black as a sinful thought.

He hadn't enjoyed a female since . . .

He'd lost his soul.

Just another reason not to touch this one.

Traffic started moving again in his peripheral vision, pulling him back to the task of reaching downtown by three. He wanted time to snoop around after dropping her off at her home.

He caught a tiny movement within the cab. A human without heightened powers of perception would not have noticed, but it drew his attention to Evalle.

She studied him surreptitiously from beneath eyelashes hovering low over her pink cheeks.

He could let her sleep, but he wanted her company. "Feel better?"

She hesitated for a second, but to her credit she opened her eyes—exotic green eyes the color of a baby salamander—and sat up right away, stretching. "Much. Where are we?"

"Just inside the perimeter."

She stopped moving as she realized her eyes were uncovered. "Where are my sunglasses?"

"Above the visor over your head."

Once she had them on again she sat back and rested her arm along the edge of the window, tapping her fingers. "What's got traffic bogged down in the middle of the afternoon? This sucks, even for Atlanta."

"Wreck two miles ahead, but it'll be cleared soon."

Her eyes took in the radio he hadn't turned on since leaving VIPER. "And you would know this how?"

He laughed at the obvious leap she'd made. "You think I'm psychic?"

"In our line of work, that wouldn't surprise me. I don't know what shamans can do."

Storm suppressed the wry chuckle stirring in his chest. Sen had called him a Navajo shaman because Sen believed what he'd been told by an agent in the northeastern division where Storm had spent the last eight months. A fair assumption, based on what Storm had led everyone there to believe. Tracing a person's background in the world of humans was much easier than determining the origins of those with supernatural powers.

He was not entirely Navajo nor exactly a shaman.

Storm grinned at her. "You think shamans can't read electronic message boards with traffic warnings . . . like the one a couple miles back?"

"Oh, crud. Forgot about those." She smiled at herself, unable to stop a flush of embarrassment.

Seeing her face light with a casual happiness pulled at him, rousing a warm feeling he hadn't experienced in a long while. A human feeling. He considered telling her the truth—that he *had* seen the car collision ahead in his mind. At one time he would have shared something so simple.

That had been before a woman he'd cared about had used things he'd told her, simple details, to steal first his soul then his father's.

Right before she'd killed his father.

The bitch had sent his father's spirit to wander for eternity, then turned Storm into her personal weapon.

After what seemed an eternity in hell, he'd finally figured out how to break free of her.

She'd disappeared, but he would find her. No matter what—even if he had to hunt her through multi-dimensions. And when he did, he'd free his father first and get his own soul back next.

"So *are* you or are you *not* psychic?" Evalle looked anywhere but at him.

"Sometimes." That was all she was going to get out of him.

He'd been born with a few gifts—thanks to his South American Ashaninka grandfather—such as the ability to affect emotional response around him and to strip the truth from a liar.

"Hmm." If she moved any closer to the passenger door, she'd meld with it.

He opened his senses to Evalle's emotions. She was as calm as a summer sky ahead of a brewing storm, waiting for him to pounce on her. Might as well get to the heart of what had her agitated. "Tell me about Alterants."

"Like Sen hasn't filled you in?"

Storm ignored the swirl of anger Evalle generated and pressed again. "Is it true the last one killed nine Beladors before it was destroyed?"

Her anger whipped through her as she tensed. "He."

That anger confused him. "He what?"

"You called the Alterant 'it.' We're not things. We're people, just as much as you or anyone else born of human parents. Yes, *he* shifted and killed Beladors."

During the time Storm had been with VIPER, little had been said about Alterants until that incident. VIPER had a no-tolerance policy when it came to talking about agency business.

They silenced those who spoke too freely. Permanently.

But word traveled fast when one beast killed nine powerful beings. Impressive for any creature. He doubted mentioning that would encourage more dialogue at this point. "What else can you tell me about Alterants?"

"Like I know anything?" Evalle scoffed softly. "I'm the only Alterant walking around free I know. Never met any of the ones they caught even." The anger smoldering beneath her earlier bout of apprehension flamed up. "Want to cut to the chase? Even if I could tell you something about Alterants, you don't really care if they live or die, do you? Especially since the *only* reason you're here is to report everything I say and do back to Sen."

"If that's what you want to believe—"

"That's what I know. But I'm willing to consider testimony to the contrary if you think you can convince me."

Storm switched lanes. "Just be a waste of time from what I'm hearing." He had a choice for the next fifteen minutes they'd be in the truck. Try to settle her back down by talking about the city and how her division of VIPER operated, or stir her up a bit.

He'd never been one for the easy way, and he knew her current hot button. "If you don't want to talk about Alterants, then tell me about your local demon problem. Counting the Birrn killed this morning, that makes two, right?"

He paused for her to answer. Not a word. "Going to be hard to work together if we don't share information."

"What do you want to know?"

Time to find out if she lied as much as Sen indicated or if Sen really was singling her out unfairly, as she believed. "What do you know about the demon killed in Atlanta this morning?"

Silence is usually the first sign of a lie, and her lips were buttoned tight.

EIGHT

Evalle cursed herself for letting her mouth walk her from an annoying conversation into a dangerous one.

She shouldn't have gotten her dander up when Storm asked about Alterants and played the conversation for a bit. Now she had to talk about the demons, a topic where she might not be able to answer every question truthfully. With his ability to tell a lie from the truth, running blind across an interstate in Atlanta at rush hour was safer than any discussion with him.

"Your demon problem?" Storm pressed.

As if there was only one?

The blasted clock and traffic were conspiring against her. She needed a diversion. "Got any water in here?"

Storm didn't respond or acknowledge her comment.

Not verbally anyhow.

He drove his olive-green Land Cruiser—not one of the hot new models but a classic from the '70s—with one hand on the steering wheel, eyes staring at nothing, yet taking in everything. Including her, but the only change in his face that indicated he'd heard her speak was the dubious tilt of his mouth. She wouldn't call it a full commitment to smile, just enough to let her know he'd only allow her to evade him for so long. "Water's behind your seat. Grab me one, too."

She wrenched around and lifted the lid on a scarred-up six-pack-size cooler and dragged two plastic bottles out of the ice. After handing one to him, she slumped back against her seat, wishing she could use her power to lift cars out of the way.

It would take maybe another fifteen minutes to reach her exit. Sen had never liked her much, but bringing in Storm to hang her surprised even Evalle.

That she'd actually fallen asleep in front of him surprised her even more.

Storm cleared his throat. That would be warning number two that he was not going to wait much longer.

She zipped her jacket, appreciating the cool air circulating through the truck even if it did push his attractive scent past her defenses to make her notice. "What do you want to know about our demons?"

"I'm most interested in the Birrn."

Of course he was, 'cause she was just that lucky. "What about him?"

"Did you kill him?"

That was direct as all get-out, but she had an honest answer. "No."

"Do you have any idea who killed him?"

Think, Evalle . . . If she gave up Isak, it would implicate her in the worst sort of way. So she settled on another truth that would keep Polygraph off her back. "Yes, but I'm not ready to say until I have solid evidence. VIPER's rules," she added, reminding him that agents couldn't make claims of any wrongdoing without proof. Isak hadn't killed the demon.

His friggin' awesome gun had.

More to the point, the Birrn's master had killed him by sending the demon into the line of fire.

Storm flipped on the truck's turn signal and slipped into a space in the bumper-to-bumper traffic that magically opened up. She eyed him closely, trying to discern if he'd used any power to do that. He drove with a fluid grace, confidence in every move.

This guy could probably do ten things at once, so why had he stopped rattling off questions?

She would normally welcome silence right now if she didn't feel as though she was waiting on the hangman to build his gallows.

"Sen said you had other demon problems?" He asked that in a smooth and disarming voice, but she lived every day watching over her shoulder for a threat, with Sen and Tribunals leading the pack.

Nothing Storm could say in any tone could disarm her.

"As far as I know we have no current demon problem, especially since the Birrn was killed." Truth. Technically. The Cresyl demons were also dead so, poof, no demon problem at this very minute.

However, the mauled body in the morgue?

Still a problem.

But she was getting the hang of maneuvering around his questions. She allowed her shoulders to relax.

"Is there any other problem connected to the demon death I should know about?"

"No." That was the absolute truth. The less *he* knew, the better for her. She cheered silently when Storm turned onto Centennial Boulevard. A couple minutes and she'd be out of this truck. "Take the next left, then cross over Peachtree Street. I'll show you where to park."

He gave her a quiet nod.

Something warned her quiet was not necessarily an encouraging sign with him. He couldn't have run out of questions, and she'd sparred nicely so far, if she did say so herself.

Bring it on.

When he reached a parking lot at the rear of a closed restaurant off Peachtree Street near North Avenue, she directed him to pull in and park. He should appreciate that the lot was empty, which allowed him plenty of open space for jockeying the motorcycle trailer.

As he parked the truck, his mouth quirked with that hint of a smile again, one that lacked any humor. "You want me to believe you live in this abandoned restaurant?"

"No. I don't live here." Evalle zipped her jacket up the last few inches to her chin and pulled her leather gloves on. She reached around to lift her helmet from the backseat. Every inch of her skin would be covered before she stepped outside. "Thanks for the ride."

"Thank Sen. He's the one who warded the truck so the sun wouldn't affect you."

Yeah, so the bastard could spy on her. She lowered the helmet to the top of her thighs. "I'll be sure to do that." She let her sarcasm flag fly high.

Other than the lifting of one eyebrow, Storm didn't ask why she and Sen were like a cobra and a mongoose around each other. "First watch is scouting Piedmont for any sign of the Ngak Stone or anything out of the norm during the daylight hours. You and I are to take over for that team at dark. Give me your address and I'll pick you up at eight."

Did he really think that would work? That she'd tell him her address when she hadn't let him drive her home? She had to find Isak, deal with a mauled body in the morgue, find the twins and talk to Grady first. "I've got a few things to do before I get to the park. I'll meet you at the Piedmont Road entrance at midnight."

No smile this time. Storm didn't take the brush-off well. "Sen *expects* you to work with me."

"Sen doesn't own me, and VIPER doesn't feed me or pay my bills." She'd spoken softly, but he shouldn't have missed the warning in her words.

"He *is* your superior."

"Only in *his* mind. I answer to him because, as a Belador assigned to VIPER, I have an obligation to the team and I always honor my commitments." She should just go along to get along, but she'd learned a few things after working around so many alpha males. The worst mistake she could make was allowing one to think he gave her orders. Storm was no higher in rank than her, even if Sen treated everyone else—even a Sterling witch no one in their right mind would trust—with more regard than Evalle.

For me, Sen brought in a two-legged truth serum who could track preternaturals.

But the bitch-witch had carte blanche.

Yeah, Sen was an idiot who let hatred blind him and make decisions he would one day come to regret.

Her thoughts went back to Storm and what he'd done to settle her panic during the meeting. Had he been giving her a sample of his powers, proving he could influence her at will? She hated being at anyone's mercy and would not tolerate him using his powers or majik to get his way.

No one controlled her. Ever. She was free and she intended to stay that way. No matter who or what she had to sacrifice.

Storm turned to her, a picture of calm if you didn't notice the anger kindling in his brown eyes. "You have a duty to VIPER, which means following orders even if you don't like Sen. You don't want to answer questions. You don't want to meet at a reasonable time to get started. You don't want to work together, period. Sen said no one else would work with you besides your buddies Tzader and Quinn. I'm starting to see why."

Oh, that set her off. The others wouldn't work with her over a birth defect she couldn't help, and all of them were quick to rub her nose in it. As for Sen . . .

"Let's get something clear, Storm. My *duty* requires that I follow the agency rules—just like every other agent—but *no one* dictates what personal information I share, like where I live or what hours I work." Because if they knew, they could come for her, spy on her, or worse, find evidence to lock her up for eternity. "Not unless Sen wants to make that a new rule for *all* the agents to declare their addresses on a community database."

"Look, I didn't mean—"

She didn't take a breath. "I also have a job at the city morgue, a position that allows me access to vital information we need, especially for containment to protect the civilians. If I don't check in with my supervisor there tonight, I will lose my job, and you don't ever want to know how hard it is to find a night job with flexible hours that pays over minimum wage. And in case you were born on the sun and haven't noticed, it's summer and the night hours are short."

"I understand—"

"No, you don't." He had the option of living a normal life in a normal world. People didn't judge him based on genetics he couldn't help, and no one had ever locked him away like an animal because of it.

She curled her fingers against the helmet so she didn't throw it out of frustration as her emotions swelled. She was so tired of all the crap. So tired of always having to be on the defensive. Having to weigh and measure every word ten times over to keep from condemning herself by a simple slip. "My *day* starts at sunset and ends at daylight, which gives me extremely limited time to accomplish anything in the summer, so I can't afford to waste even a nanosecond. Everyone knows I'm nocturnal, especially Sen."

"Your point?"

"He got his kicks once today by making me drive two hours in the heat in full gear while my skin boiled. So I don't give a flying effing fig what he wants right now. I'll do my job. I always do, because I am not the animal that bastard thinks I am." She lifted the helmet halfway and paused, shooting a glance loaded with warning at Storm. "And one more thing. About that little show of power at headquarters this morning? Don't ever screw with my emotions again or I'll make you regret it."

She pulled on her helmet and stepped out of the truck before he could answer. The driver door slammed at the same time hers shut. When she reached the trailer, Storm was already there. She'd order him to get his hands off her bike if not for her helmet, which would muffle her words.

He cranked open the wheel chock that prevented the front tire from moving, then leaned the bike against his hip. Someone walking along the street wouldn't notice the harsh flex of his shoulders as he moved.

She'd hit a nerve, but taking the words back or smoothing things over would destroy any ground she'd just gained with him.

When he had the wheel free to move, he toed the gearshift up one click to neutral, then rolled her bike off the trailer with the same graceful ease with which he seemed to do everything else.

The bike would roll for him as long as he didn't straddle it and the motorcycle was within her energy range.

The minute he put the side stand down and backed away, she walked over and slung a leg over the seat.

Storm stepped in front of her and stood alongside her front tire, waiting.

Ignoring him wouldn't budge that determined angle of his chin. When she did look up, she was glad for the black shield on her helmet that prevented her from having to meet his eyes.

Or so she'd thought.

He put a hand on her handlebar and leaned forward, eyes staring as though he saw right through the mirror shield. "Are you finished issuing orders?"

The quiet words would have sounded like a gentle caress if not for the low vibration of anger thrumming in his voice. She didn't say a word, just gave a slight move of her head to indicate she was listening.

"Good. I have a job to do, too, and it's not all about you. It's about saving the world and all those humans who know nothing about what might hit this world in three days. I'll be at Piedmont Park at midnight. Come prepared to work together, which means answering questions. Truthfully. Not playing a word game two-step. And as for the comfort spell I sent you at HQ, I didn't do it to screw with your emotions or show off my powers. I did it because I didn't like seeing you feel threatened and figured you didn't want to give Sen the pleasure of knowing he'd rattled you."

Her heart thumped an extra beat. Storm had been trying to do something nice for her when he'd used his power to calm her? That floored her. Kindness from strangers was not something she was used to, and she was sorry she'd misjudged him.

While he'd been handsome to her before, this set him up a few notches in her book.

Storm clenched his teeth before he spoke again. "I'm heading over to where the Birrn was killed to pick up a trail. I should know something tonight."

No, no, no. She had to clamp down on her panic before he sensed it.

Going to the killing site would have been enough to raise her blood pressure without the way he swept a gaze over her that thawed out the frigid shield she used to keep all men at bay. His gaze scorched her. "You don't like me using my powers on you . . . that's fine. I'm much better with my hands anyway."

NINE

The crisp smell of fresh-cut grass reminded Laurette Barrett of life as a child during a more hopeful time when mistakes hadn't had such dire consequences. Long before she'd become a twenty-four-year-old woman who lived at the crossroads of adversity and fear.

Her granddad would shake his head at her and say, "You'll survive this, Laurie girl."

If he were still alive, she might. But he was gone, and her life was ruined.

Daylight was abandoning her by the minute, which made walking through the park that much more difficult, but she had Brutus by her side. When she'd been looking for a small dog with spirit, a nice lady at the Humane Society had jokingly told her she had a twenty-pound dog that was a cross between a terrier and a hedgehog.

Laurette had fallen in love at first sight with the patchwork mutt and named him Brutus to build up his self-esteem.

How was she going to take care of him if things got worse?

How was she going to pay any bills if she couldn't make a living? Negative thinking had never solved a problem—she knew that. She'd survived on her own for seven years by not letting anything defeat her.

Surely she could figure her way out of disaster once more. But she was tired of getting so much practice at it.

Being played by a con man happened to everyone, even bright women. She wasn't stupid, just too ready to believe the best in people.

Didn't see that one coming, did you?

She laughed at her unintentional joke about her failing eyesight to keep from giving in to the panic that clung to the walls of her chest. Seeing much of anything was getting more difficult by the day. All she'd been able to see in the mirror this morning had been the flaming red hair she'd gotten from her granddad and vague dots of blue where her eyes were supposed to be. Putting on makeup had gone by the wayside.

But she couldn't blame lack of vision for allowing Chuck to swindle her. That man had the ability to sell ketchup Popsicles to women in white gloves.

Especially because they were women.

If using her hadn't been humiliating enough, Chuck had accessed her meager bank accounts and depleted every dime she'd had.

When they first met, she thought Chuck would be the perfect salesman for her large outdoor pottery urns. Her grandfather had told her that as long as she had her pottery with her signature design painted on the side, she would be secure in this world. He'd also said she'd meet a man she could believe in, a stranger who would show her an unexpected kindness in her darkest hour.

Stupid her to have believed for even a minute that would be Chuck. But it'd seemed so perfect and fit her grandfather's prophecy. A man like Chuck showing up right as her sight was starting to fail.

Wish you were here, Granddaddy. He'd never steered her wrong while he was alive, but he was gone and she had to figure this one out on her own. And without turning to another man. The one thing this had taught her was that no one could be trusted.

She was alone in the world and no one cared.

If only she could save her sight, she could continue to sell her art. She could still shape the large outdoor urns with her hands, but painting the intricate patterns and whimsical letters on each one—her signature patterns—wouldn't be as possible. If she did figure out how to clear that hurdle, she still needed to find clients and deliver the pots. She had no one to help her.

She'd tried to train herself these last months by painting the designs blindfolded. She doubted someone looking for abstract art would spend lunch money on her last disaster. Without her eyesight, her career would be the first casualty and her independence the second. She didn't know how to do anything else.

Best's disease. That was the name of the thief that had caused her blindness. She'd never even heard of it until her diagnosis. Now she knew everything about the macular degeneration that had no cure.

In the last couple of months, she'd gone from seeing well enough to drive with thick glasses to a blurry world that no lens could bring into focus.

At the rate things were changing, she'd be completely blind in only a few more weeks.

With no savings and no way to keep working, she'd end up on the streets, where she'd be at the mercy of men who made Chuck look like Galahad.

Her heartbeat sped up, thumping louder and louder in her ears. She felt light-headed and sick.

An urgent whining broke through her panic attack. Brutus tugged on his leash, pulling her forward and out of her downward spiral.

Laurette blinked to clear her mind and wished she could sharpen her sight as easily. Because of the foggy shadows, it took her a few moments to realize she was standing off the jogging path, in the grass. Brutus jumped up against her legs, his whole body moving when he wagged his stubby tail.

She took a breath to calm her nerves and dropped down to hug him. "You're right. I said let's take a walk and not think about *it* for awhile."

He must have taken that as a sign to take off and drag her over the footbridge at the south end of the park. She squinted through her glasses to see, but all she could make out was the creek running beneath the bridge. She saw undulated globs that were probably piles of plants and mud.

Brutus pulled her down the foot of the bridge and across the grass to where he sniffed clumps of rock and mud along the bank. She could tell he practically went on point at one spot when he yanked his head down.

"No, Brutus. We can't take anything from the park for our garden." That was all she needed at this point . . . an arrest record and a fine she couldn't pay.

110

When he refused to leave, she knelt next to him to see if she could discern what had gotten his attention.

One rock seemed to shine as though catching the last bit of light before the sun set. *Wait a minute . . .* She stared at the goose-egg-shaped stone for the longest time, mesmerized until Brutus barked—well, more of a yap—breaking her attention.

She could *see* that rock.

Clearly.

No, she couldn't see one rock when everything else was a rush of colors and shapes. She was imagining things.

"Right. Time to go." Before she had any more hallucinations that ended up with her in a straightjacket.

Laurette stood up and turned away. But she couldn't leave. She felt the strong urge to glance back at the rock.

The stone was now very clear. And sort of brightlooking.

Laurette rubbed the heel of her hand over her eyes. Was she losing her eyesight *and* her mind?

That rock had *not* glowed. *Am I really seeing that or not?*

She stared at the stone again. The shape seemed like that of a soft lump of red-orange lava with purple and yellow ribbons. All the colors shifted, moving as though molten.

Brutus dropped down in front of the rock with paws outstretched as if told the "down" command.

Yeah, right. Like that would happen in her lifetime.

Pick up the stone and prove to yourself it isn't molten and that you're not nuts. While she couldn't take it home, there was no law against holding a rock for a few seconds to convince herself she wasn't going bonkers.

She squatted down and touched the rock with one finger, quickly, in case it was hot. Not injurious hot, but a comforting warmth. That made no sense. She closed her eyes and let her fingers curl around the smooth shape, lifting it into her palm to identify the rock with a sculptor's touch.

She could swear the stone moved as though it was a living thing.

When she opened her eyes, the colors in her hand glowed.

She glanced around the park, but something was odd about how everything looked blurrier than before through her glasses. She used her free hand to slip her thick glasses off, and her breath backed up in her throat at what she *could* see.

Everything.

A young man threw a Frisbee for his dog halfway across the field. The Border collie leaped high to snatch the toy from the air. A young couple sitting on a blanket fifty feet away played with their baby, who had a new front tooth.

This couldn't be happening.

Laurette pushed her gaze to Tenth Street, which separated the park from a residential area. She wouldn't normally be able to see that street from here. Car headlights burned crisply against the twilight darkening the city.

She'd never had vision this good, even with glasses. Even before her diagnosis.

The rock sat in her hand, pulsing with a vibrant energy.

Her head wanted to argue that this couldn't be happening, that rocks did not restore eyesight, but her heart didn't care.

She could see.

Testing her theory, she opened her fingers away from the rock, then scanned the busy park activities again. She couldn't see as clearly as before but still better than she had with the best glasses she'd ever worn.

"What am I going to do, Brutus?"

He gave her a yap and danced around, happy.

Laurette closed her fingers once more around the rock and the world came back into sharp focus. She hooked her eyeglasses through the scooped neck of her sleeveless top.

Was this really happening? Or was she losing her mind?

If insanity *was* taking over, she'd use that as a basis for her defense if she got arrested for taking a piece of city property, because she held a miracle.

And she wasn't telling anyone about this rock. Or ever giving it back.

TEN

"You've got one minute, then I'm leaving. *With* your surprise." Evalle muttered the warning on her second hike past the back side of Grady Hospital in downtown Atlanta, where heat hovered in the eighties at close to nine at night. What she wouldn't give to use her power and stir a breath of wind, something to blow away the stench of urine oozing through the humid air in this spot.

Where was that ornery Nightstalker?

The temperature dropped ten degrees to a comfortable chill.

"What happens in one minute, E-*valle*? Not like you gonna leave 'till we talk." Grady's deep Southern voice brushed past her ear like charred wood scraped against rough concrete.

Evalle stopped on the sidewalk running along Pratt Street. She didn't turn around. A waste of time, since no one stood behind her. "I'm in a hurry, Grady."

The translucent form of a thin male took shape, wavering in front of her. The coffee-colored skin on his jaw was covered with gray whiskers that stopped just below a slash of cheekbone. His creased nose had failed to dodge a fist or two that had left their marks. Bony elbows interrupted the long arms sticking out from his red-and-black plaid short-sleeved shirt.

The air continued to cool, a welcome change.

From what Grady had told her, he looked the same way now he had the day he'd died homeless on the streets at age sixty-eight, a decade and a half ago.

When his head came into focus, sharp eyes with two chips of coal for pupils glowered at her before his gaze dropped to the denim shoulder bag hanging against her hip. "*What* surprise?"

"Not until we have a deal and shake." Negotiating with Grady was like dealing with Charon on the River Styx. If you didn't set the price before you got on the boat and refuse to pay until he ferried you safely to the other side, he'd dump you in the river and leave you to drown.

Grady lifted his stubborn chin. He was a wily old bastard who gave up nothing for free. He, like all Nightstalkers, was the metaphysical remains of the less fortunate who'd died on the street. They would do anything for a craving. Sometimes it was drugs or food, but usually it was alcohol, and in Grady's case, there was only one thing he wanted.

Mad Dog 20/20.

All a Nightstalker needed was one quick handshake with any powerful being—and they could take human form for ten minutes.

"Whatya got?" He eyed her bag.

"Clock's ticking."

"I'm listenin'."

"I need information on two Cresyls and a Birrn demon that were running around town this weekend. Got anything on them?"

"Maybe."

"I can't play this game right now, Grady. My butt's in a sling."

"With who?"

"Everybody if I don't find out who sent the demons."

"Who'd you piss off this time?"

"*I* didn't do anything." *Other than being born an Alterant.* "But a demon mauled a human. The body's in the morgue and word is going to be out by tomorrow morning, if it takes even that long. If I don't come up with evidence to prove the demon mauled that human, everyone's first default will be that an Alterant did it. Not a good thing for me. You got anything on the attack or not?"

"Why would a Cresyl attack a human and not eat the body?"

She wanted to choke him and his game of twenty questions. But then, she hadn't mentioned that it was the Cresyl who'd killed the human. Grady definitely had information. "That's what I'm trying to find out. It's tied to the Birrn, I think."

"That don't make sense." Wrinkles on Grady's face piled together in a frown. "Cresyls belong to a German practicing dark arts and the

Birrn to Nigerian black majik. What makes you think they're connected?"

He probably knew why and was testing to see how much information she had. "I'll share if you do. Got information or not?"

"Maybe."

He could be the most obstinate of ghouls, but he was one of the better preternatural informants *because* of that annoying trait. Hoping to nudge him along, she bluffed, "If you can't help me, just say so."

"Didn't say that, but I still don't see why you're in a jam, 'less you got mouthy with somebody. *That* I'd understand."

I will not let you bait me. But Grady had that look, the one that said he wouldn't budge until he got *his* questions satisfied. "Things have gotten a little more difficult for me than normal over the past eight weeks since those nine Beladors were killed in North Carolina."

"By that Alterant?" Grady floated off the sidewalk.

"Yes. Get back over here," she hissed at him.

"Oh. Didn't realize I drifted." His flickering form moved back as though blown gently, but there wasn't a breeze to be had. His gaze puckered with concern. "That ain't right to come after you every time another one shifts into a beast."

"True, but we're in the minority with that opinion." What was it going to take to move this along?

"How much you know about that Birrn killed this morning?" he asked.

She flexed her jaw muscles. *Patience.* "Give me a break tonight, Grady. I got a lot to do and not much time."

"You wouldn't be so wound up if you did something other than work at night. Maybe found you a nice young man to give you a—"

"Grady!"

"—back rub." He pulled off a look of mock despair a Catholic mother would be proud of. "Not much chance of that happening when you can't even get a date."

"I'm not wound up." Yet. "And I *can* get a date, old man."

"Better an old man than an old maid. Who dates a woman that lives underground like a mole and has weirdos for friends?" His lips stretched into a dog-happy grin. No sense of urgency at all—a luxury of the not-entirely-dead, which Evalle couldn't afford.

"You have a twisted sense of humor, Grady, but I wouldn't call you a weirdo."

"Was talkin' 'bout Tazer and Quill, those two goons you hang out with."

"His name's Tzader. *Z!* The T's silent and it's Quinn, not Quill. He and Quinn are *not* weirdos or goons." She tapped her foot. "Can we move this along?"

"And that thing you call a pet—"

"Grady!" She no longer felt guilty about her surprise for him. "Back to my *demon* problem. Please, for the love of Macha."

"Which you still haven't explained," he interjected. "I'm surprised those two goons aren't here helping you." The irritating rascal didn't take a breath. "But you don't need them or anyone else. Some hard tail come at you, he'd end up with his ass booted into next week."

She was glad one person, even if he was dead, had faith in her ability to defend herself.

Grady scratched at his beard. "But that's another reason you can't get a date. Men want a sweet woman, not some Amazon what's gonna kick their butts."

How did he always manage to run so far off track? "We are *not* discussing my love life—"

"That's for sure. Nothin' to discuss." Grady's bushy eyebrows lifted in an all-knowing way as he nodded.

"If you don't stick to the topic, I'm going to someone else." Evalle wiped a bead of sweat from her brow with the back of her hand, prepared to dicker. "I'm *out* of time. You ready to shake?"

"No free nothings."

"Like that ever changes? Here's my deal. We'll shake *if* you agree to share everything you know about the Cresyls and Birrn who were here in the Atlanta area over the past forty-eight hours," she said, spelling out the specifics.

He acted like he considered it, but they both knew he wouldn't walk away. "You got it."

She pulled her thumb free from her jeans pocket and extended her hand. Due to fear that too much power shared would alter the normal state of a Nightstalker, VIPER rules forbade an agent from shaking for more than ten seconds without special dispensation. A rare exemption she'd seen allowed only once when national security had been at stake.

But with her level of power, she could give a Nightstalker human form for ten minutes with a five-second shake.

"Ready?" she asked, glancing around to make sure they were still alone. The only living thing anywhere close to this dark stretch was some poor old vagrant across the street covered in newspapers and sleeping shoved up against the hospital's back wall.

Grady's hand trembled when he started reaching for hers. He licked his lips, anticipation blooming in his sagging gaze until he paused and pulled back. "What'd you bring me?"

She shook her head, refusing to tell him what was in her shoulder bag. "Not until we shake."

"Should have made that part of the deal," he grumbled and stuck out rough fingers that had fought to survive. "Do it."

When her hand touched his, heat spread across her palm with the energy flowing from her.

The exultation on his face always plucked at her heartstrings. His life had come down to ten-minute visits to this world. She could go to other Nightstalkers, who would agree in a snap to anything she asked, but Grady was far more intelligent than the rest when it came to information, and the grouch behaved like a grandfather who gave unsolicited advice.

Her fantasy of a grandfather, since she'd never had one she knew of.

Within seconds, Grady's body turned completely opaque, his dark flesh hung loose with age, but the old coot's body emitted a quiet strength.

She withdrew her hand. "Start talking."

"What's my surprise?"

Evalle sighed and dug into her shoulder bag for the McDonald's sack filled with a hamburger, French fries and a bottle of water she lifted into view.

"You're kidding, right?" The look he gave her questioned her ability to chew gum and walk.

She ignored the hiss of irritation that slipped from his lips and pointed out, "Last time you said how much you miss the taste of hamburgers."

He rolled his eyes to the heavens as if someone up there would explain demented women to him, then swung around, searching the other side of the quiet street. Grady limped over to the homeless guy asleep.

Evalle would have zapped him with a lick of power if not for her aversion to hurting Grady in any way. Especially during his ten minutes of Nightstalker nirvana. "You forget you owe me information and that I'm on a tight schedule?"

He slipped a half-drunk bottle of wine from the bony fingers of the comatose bum and limped back. "I agreed to talk after we shook, but not how *soon* after." He downed a swig of wine and jerked the bottle away. "Lord Almighty, that sucks."

"What? Is your palate spoiled by Mad Dog 20/20?" She grabbed the bottle away from him. "I need answers."

He sighed as he stared longingly at the bottle. "The Cresyls were on a leash, part of a spell. What were you doing with the Birrn?"

Figures that Grady would know about her fighting the Birrn. "Where'd you hear about that?"

"Those two junkyard heathens."

She rubbed her hand over her forehead. "I've got to find those twins and shut them up."

"They'll sure as hell spill their guts if someone grabs 'em and plays hard."

She didn't have a nurturing bone in her body, but if someone hurt either of those two teenagers, she'd make that person beg for death.

Grady reached for the wine. "What have you got on the demons?"

She pulled it away again. "One of the Cresyls killed the human, then the Birrn ate the Cresyl. The Cresyls set me up, but I don't know if it was to bait *me* into a trap or any Alterant who happened to be here."

"You're the only one I've ever heard of that ain't caught yet."

That was the unfortunate part. But she could hope there were more, couldn't she? Just one more would shed doubt on the death being related to her powers. "Oh, and here's the kicker—the Birrn had Celtic markings."

Grady shook his head. "That don't make sense with the Birrn bein' Nigerian."

"Yeah, I know. So where does a Celtic connection come in? Every way I look at this, I still come up with someone out to set me up by making the mauled human appear to be an Alterant attack."

"Here's what I got." Grady finally turned serious. "The Cresyls were on a spell leash connected to the Birrn. That would mean the Birrn's master was controlling all three demons."

She handed him back the bottle. "I've never heard of that, but we could fill a library with what I don't know about demons. What about the Celtic link?"

Grady turned the bottle up, swallowing a long gulp. "The majik holding the Cresyls was Noirre."

That sent a shiver through her. Tzader's lead for the traitorous Belador had something to do with Noirre majik. But Tzader was too involved in something to break free or she'd have heard from him telepathically by now.

"Any idea who conjured the majik?" Evalle glanced up when Grady didn't speak, and she caught him considering his answer. Oh, she knew that look, and it was trouble. "Don't even *think* to negotiate a new deal."

He covered his heart with the bottle in his hand. "I'm hurt that you'd question my integrity that way."

Nightstalkers had no integrity or loyalty as a rule, willing to sell the same information over and over as soon as they could shake again. But Grady had been different, an exception to the rule, and he'd protected intel in the past.

However, that show of insult on his face right now was nothing more than an act.

He belted down another quick slug and wiped his mouth on the sleeve of his flannel shirt. "Most likely, it's a witch conjuring Noirre, but that doesn't rule out another being, since we ain't got a Who's Who directory of black majik folk around here. There ain't been a Noirre in the south for the past fifteen years I been hangin' loose. Only ones I ever heard of worked alone."

Evalle smiled at how he described his years of being a Nightstalker as "hanging loose." More than once she'd wondered if Grady was the derelict vagrant he presented to the world with his ragged speech or if his core personality was the highly educated man who peeked out from beneath the charade at times.

But that didn't matter right now. If he was right about a lone witch being behind the Noirre majik, she jumped to the only conclusion she could.

Adrianna.

The witch who came from a long line of corrupt witches. After all, most witches were good people who harmed no one. That was their code: Do no harm. Whatever you send out into the universe will return to you threefold. That kept almost all witches in line. However, there were those who did dabble with the darkness, and Evalle couldn't rule out the possibility of the Medb being here either.

But still she couldn't let the thought of Adrianna go.

Those like Adrianna and her family who danced on the dark side didn't adhere to those happy pony rules. They were the deadliest of all because they had no conscience, and all that mattered was what they wanted.

If Adrianna really was here to work in VIPER's favor and not turn on them, her first test would be finding the witch behind the Birrn.

Would that help or hinder Evalle's position if Adrianna found out the Birrn had been looking for an Alterant?

Then again, she couldn't see Adrianna doing anything to benefit her.

The heavens grumbled, threatening to turn this into a full sauna evening.

"I've got to make the most of tonight. That all you got on the demons?" Evalle gave her watch a quick glance. Grady would start to fade soon, then he'd be hard to find for an hour or two.

VIPER didn't want her mentioning the Ngak Stone even though Grady would know about it being lost in Atlanta two years ago. But he might have something new to share if she positioned the question creatively. "Or anything else? Any unexpected energy floating around? Maybe a female with unusual powers who's new on the scene?"

He took another swig. "Not part of the original deal."

She should take his bag of French fries back, but the whining would be worse than pulling a sack of trick-or-treat candy away from a four-year-old. Not a pretty sight on a ghoul his age. She tried a sly approach. "I need intel *now* on anything unusual and quick. Something to show VIPER I'm on the ball."

Grady shrugged. "And I'm running out of my anytime minutes. Want to shake again?"

"You know I can't shake for another hour."

"Then give me an hour of prime time Wednesday night."

She grunted a disparaging noise at the ridiculous request. Even from Grady. "Want the Brooklyn Bridge while I'm at it?"

He growled and stomped around, putting on a show to let her know she'd ticked him off. Then he stopped suddenly, concentrating on something. His eyes stared off into the black skies.

She kept silent, since that was how he looked when he listened to some invisible spirit.

His lips moved without saying a word, then he flinched at something he heard before his gaze shot to her. "That's all I got on the demons, but Kardos has more."

She frowned at that. "What does he know?"

"Not sure, but I heard he and his brother were outside the Iron Casket when the Birrn caught him."

"I'd believe Kardos was stupid enough to hang out in the parking lot of Deek's nightclub, but not Kell. What makes you think Kardos knows more?"

"Because he's at the Iron Casket right now."

"Inside?"

"Yep."

She didn't like the suspicion raised in her mind at hearing all that. Had she made a mistake with Kardos and Kellman? Had they set her up with a demon? She just couldn't believe that but would give Kardos a chance to explain. That meant her next stop was the IC.

Someone shoot me. She absolutely did not want to deal with the owner of that nightclub tonight. Or any other night, for that matter. "Can't that boy stay out of trouble for five minutes?"

"He don't seem worried about making his next birthday, that's for sure."

Yeah, and the first thing Kardos was going to explain when she found him was how he'd gotten past Deek's tight security that didn't allow teens into the club. "Okay, bud. Back to—"

Grady started fading. "I don't have nothing for sure yet, but there's a synergy moving through the city. I might have more later if you want to trade something like . . . more time."

She'd lose him for a couple hours now, because unlike the other Nightstalkers, who tried to stay in one spot so they could be found easily, he tended to reappear anywhere in a ten-block area. "You be here when I come back *with* information on that synergy."

His form flickered as he took a deep drink before answering. "You *know* I ain't got no control over where I go next."

"You would if you'd just concentrate when you start fading."

"Like I need to be stressed out over anything at this point in my life? I am *dead,* dammit."

"Yeah, and if you don't get me the info I need, you'll be even deader."

He laughed. "Like you'd ever do me that way." He guzzled the last of the booze before he faded out and the bottle tumbled to the ground.

Evalle felt a tingle run down her spine. Something in the air wasn't right, but she didn't know what it was.

The stone has been found.

She had no idea whose voice that was. Yet it'd been crystal. She shook her head to clear it. Was that a witch messing with her?

Or a warning sent by Grady?

She didn't know, but it didn't matter. She had to do what she had to do. Turning around, she headed back to her bike so that she could go to the last place she wanted to.

May Macha have mercy on her, because Deek would not.

ELEVEN

Evalle rode fast to the Iron Casket in a quick downpour that knocked a couple degrees off the hideous temperature but did nothing to beat down her concern over Kardos and the possible danger he might be in.

Over and over, she saw him being bludgeoned or worse if one of the staff had discovered him in the club. There were so many hideous things that could be done by ancient beings to a young person, especially an untrained male witch.

Just thinking about it made her blood run cold.

She parked her bike in a half-filled parking lot and turned off the engine. She couldn't believe she was about to head into Deek D'Alimonte's territory alone. An immortal centaur who could morph into a human, Deek owned the Iron Casket and was without a doubt one of the nastiest creatures who'd ever lived. No one knew why really. He just hated the entire universe.

I am courting death here.

There was serious bad history between the Beladors and Deek. He had no patience for any of their kind, and if he saw her inside, there would be a brawl.

Just don't let me get arrested.

All she had to do was retrieve one pain-in-the-ass male witch before Deek saw her. *Dame Fortune, don't be on vacation tonight.* 'Cause she was about to need her badly.

Evalle quickly scanned the area, looking for threats. Whoever was seeking her probably had even more demons gunning for her. Every shadow could hide an assassin or demon whose only mission was to take her unawares.

Rule Number One: Stay Vigilant.

She put on her sunglasses and checked the back pocket of her jeans for cash.

Kardos was so going to pay her back for the cover charge. Little snot. She headed for the entrance. The rain was fading. Droplets clung to her vintage BDU shirt. Not as stylish as most of Deek's clientele. But that was all right. She wasn't here with the same intent as the rest of the patrons, looking for a victim or a lay. She was here to beat sense into one severely testosterone-poisoned idiot.

Deek's warehouse had multifaceted panels of slanted black and silver covering the entire outside. Panels that gleamed in the rain. In full sun, she'd bet this place flashed like a polished black diamond.

Deek had turned the inside into a showcase of black marble and glitter intended to lure a Fae to the sparkle like a werewolf to fresh meat. Then the ever surly Deek had forbidden any Fae to tread here. If any were dumb enough to do so, it invited a major ass-whipping.

Next on his kicking list—a male witch not yet twenty-one.

The real question was, how had Kardos gotten past the two bouncers who looked like Goth gargoyles standing outside the door? She hoped the teenager hadn't used majik to gain access, because Deek would kill anyone who used majik in his place.

Anyone.

Even more frightening, she couldn't see any way Kardos would have gotten past those two guards *without* majik.

As she neared the front door, the dull staccato of throbbing music vibrated through her. She smiled at the first of the two black-swathed mountains she reached. "Any chance I could go in for five minutes without paying? Just got to find somebody, then I'll be right back out?"

He lifted an eyebrow in amusement. "Any chance we can spend a night at your house?"

"When the devil sits on icicles." She handed him the ten dollars and let him stamp the inside of her wrist.

When he opened the door, the music charged forward, slapping her body and ears. Not a packed house, but enough gyrating bodies and clusters of groups moving through the three levels that she'd have to poke around to find her target.

Unless Kardos had left.

Rushing through the crowd, Evalle covered the downstairs in a matter of minutes and was just taking the first step to go up to the second level when the music ended. She glanced across the room just in time to catch a bright flash of familiar blond hair moving through the room.

Kardos snaked his way off the dance floor and into the hovering crowd that swallowed him.

Or had he seen her and taken off?

She spun around and plowed through warm bodies smelling of silky cologne and sweat to reach the other side of the room just as Kardos zipped through the rear exit. How had he gotten past the bouncer at the back door, who was carrying on a conversation with a patron?

Deek killed unobservant bouncers. Crap. Kardos was definitely using majik.

Flaming moron.

"Hey!" The bouncer stopped *her*. Now he decided to be alert? "No one leaves through the back door and that means you, baby. The bathroom's upstairs. The front door is on the opposite end."

Oh, to be able to blast the arrogant snot until he bled. But that would no doubt tip off Deek that a Belador was here.

Grinding her teeth in frustration, she all but left a vapor trail as she rushed through the club, trying to get outside to catch Kardos.

She ran to her bike and shoved her helmet on.

By the time she circled around the street along the back of the club, Kardos was hauling ass, but still in sight.

That was the good news.

The bad news was that he had a young woman with him.

The really bad news?

That girl was Bettina D'Alimonte, Deek's nineteen-year-old sister he treated like a goddess.

As in an *untouchable* virginal goddess. And Deek demanded that any man who came within a mile of her must sacrifice his penis or his life.

Damn, that boy was working hard to die young.

Deek wouldn't care that Kardos was a year younger than Bettina, only that Kardos was a witch who came with a full set of male running gear.

Evalle raced forward and sped twenty feet past the teenage pair strolling along as if Kardos's death wasn't imminent. She slammed onto the sidewalk, cutting them off. She flipped up her face shield, which should have made anyone walking toward her on a semi-lit street take notice, since her eyes glowed in the darkness.

A sick lump clenched her stomach when they kept coming as if they didn't see her.

How could one person be so stupid? All she wanted was a five-minute conversation with him. Not a new migraine. She had to separate those two and return Bettina to the nightclub before the girl was reported missing and Deek started a manhunt. Or more to the point, a testicle hunt.

Evalle glared at Kardos. "What do you think you're doing?"

Bettina answered in a lifeless voice that said someone else had control of her. "Walk out the back door to the first street. Turn left."

Oh crap.

Who had them locked in a trance? More to the point, *what* had them in a trance?

When the teens reached Evalle, she held up her hand. "Stop."

They walked right past her, still heading down the street that extended into a dark void where the streetlights didn't reach.

After kicking down the side stand, she ran forward to grab them. A wave of power blew past the teens, stirring their hair. They stopped walking.

That energy came at Evalle.

She put up a shield an instant before it blasted her. Her shield allowed the energy to flow over her without effect.

But it gave her a blast of something she could use. The majik smelled old, centuries old, and dry as a desert.

Kardos and Bettina stood still, facing the dark end of the street.

Evalle lifted her hands and shoved back at the majik, pushing it toward the source.

Sparks exploded around the teens.

Okay, that hadn't worked.

She was lucky it hadn't hurt one of them. "You can't have these two." She moved around to position herself in front of the teens. Wary of what was coming for them, Evalle braced herself.

The air stirred like a sinister cloud, announcing that something badass wasn't happy.

Out of the darkness came a man with the slow, casual lope of a predator heading for his prey. His leather duster fanned out behind him. Since there was no air current to move it, it was a sign of his power radiating around him. Black hair fell past his shoulders, with two thin braids hanging along each side of his face. His eyes radiated bright yellow in the darkness, their double pupils making a spot in each one that was obvious even from this distance. Gorgeous and masculine all the way, he didn't stop until he reached the streetlight.

The hairs on the back of her neck rose as fury sped through her veins.

Vyan.

The Kujoo who'd pulled the Beladors into an unsanctioned battle two years ago and almost unleashed an army that would have destroyed everyone and everything. Never had the Beladors confronted an enemy so strong, but it was because Vyan had possessed the Ngak Stone then.

A sick feeling of dread permeated her bones. If he was here now, it was so that he could reclaim the stone and finish what he'd started.

His gaze radiated his hatred and repugnance for her.

That was okay. She didn't like him much either.

"You interfere with me once again, half-breed," Vyan said as if Evalle merely stood in his path and wasn't a true threat.

She *tsk*ed at him and returned the disdain full force. "Poor Vyan, ever posturing. Trey kicked your ass once, and I can do it this time." That threat had a nice ring to it even if she was bluffing her boots off. Had it not been for her linking with Tzader, Quinn and Trey, Vyan could have annihilated her along with everyone else while he'd held the Ngak Stone.

Hopefully, he'd forgotten that part.

She looked over to Kardos and Bettina, who were still in his thrall. "I have to say that you are brave to risk your freedom for *them*." Shiva had allowed him his freedom on one condition—he had to behave in the human world.

He laughed evilly. "The terms were that I not attack the Beladors." He glanced over to the teenagers. "Lucky me, neither of them are in your ranks."

True, but she was admitting to nothing, and he wasn't touching these two kids. Cocking her head at the pair, Evalle asked, "What do you want with them?"

"I merely played Cupid. The boy said he wanted the girl. Voila. Isn't love grand?"

Evalle sucked her breath in sharply. "You in a diaper . . . just can't see it." She sharpened her gaze on him. "You with an arrow aimed at someone's heart . . . that I believe. And I know you're lying. Kardos would never trust a stranger with something so personal. He's a street survivor, not an idiot." Well, actually not true, since he'd have to be mentally deranged to have a crush on Deek's sister. "Release them, Vyan. I have no patience tonight, and I will cut your throat rather than deal with you."

A strange glint darkened his eyes, like he was silently laughing or mocking her. "I have no quarrel with the Beladors. Guess I better set them free. When they wake up, you might want to tell them the tale of Hansel and Gretel." He turned and disappeared into the black abyss he'd emerged from so fast that it took her several heartbeats to realize he was gone.

What was that action?

She stood there, completely stunned. That had been way too easy, and nothing with Vyan ever was.

She thought about his parting words. Had he just told her to warn the teens about a witch who lured children into a trap to eat them? Was he giving her a warning that a witch was behind this? It seemed inconceivable, and yet . . .

"Evalle?" Kardos's tone held a note of fear in it. "What are you doing here?"

Turning around, she focused on Bettina's shocked expression, which changed to confusion when the girl looked at her hand clasped in Kardos's.

He realized they were holding hands at the same time. His cheeks flaming bright red, he quickly let go and stepped away.

Evalle let out a relieved breath that he did in fact have a modicum of survival instinct. "We have to get Bettina back quick, before—"

The sound of running feet rushed toward them.

Or was that the sound of hooves?

She felt ill at the doom that was headed their way.

"What are you doing with my sister?" a male voice bellowed.

Ah, crap. But at least Deek hadn't changed into a centaur, which was the ultimate harbinger of his lethal intent. However, he and his brigade would reach them any second.

Bettina's olive skin turned pasty white. "What am I doing here?"

Kardos's cheeks turned even redder. "You asked me to take a walk with you."

"I did not."

I am so glad I don't have kids. Evalle wanted to shake them both.

Instead, she turned around and braced herself to defend them from the death squad that was about to demand the heart out of the one person she needed desperately to interrogate.

TWELVE

Evalle held up her hand and hoped Deek didn't take that as a sign of war. Hard to tell with a centaur, and too late she remembered the sign of an open palm was an insult to Greeks.

Was Deek an Italian or a Greek centaur? The name suggested Italian, but most were Greek.

Oy! She closed her palm.

Centaurs didn't have a sense of humor.

Deek stopped in front of her, his seven men spread out to the side and behind him. He was beautiful, but like a cobra, deadly with one bite. "What's my sister doing out here?"

"It's not my fault," Bettina called out from where she and Kardos stood behind Evalle.

"Shut. Up." Evalle ignored Bettina's gasp. The girl was spoiled beyond heiress level and had probably never heard those words in her life. But right now, Evalle had much more important things facing her than some brat's feelings. Like a centaur ready to rearrange her body parts.

She forced a smile for Deek. "It's not what you think—"

Deek cut her off. "Bullshit. I ran the security cameras to find Bettina." He jerked his chin toward Kardos. "That underage punk walked right into my club without paying or getting stamped. Which means he entered by majik. My territory. My rules. He's going with me. Now."

Kardos had moved forward and stood on Evalle's left. Bettina had done the same, ending up on Evalle's right, which was telling. Did she believe she was safer with Evalle, or was she staying on this side as a show of support for Kardos in some way?

Or was she just being an obstinate teen?

Evalle figured now might be a good time to redirect Deek's anger. "You got bigger problems than a teenage witch whose powers are too immature to be a danger."

Kardos ground out a sound meant to counter her insult.

She gave him a quelling look and returned her attention to Deek. "Someone else lured him into your club and used majik to get them past your guards."

Deek scoffed. "Who would dare such?"

She'd known he was going to ask that, but she couldn't tell Deek about Vyan while VIPER was trying to quietly flush out the location of the Ngak Stone. It would serve Vyan right to turn Deek loose on the Kujoo. She bet Deek could find him, but having an enraged centaur in the middle of things could hamper covert operations—kind of like tossing a live grenade into a group of paranoid schizophrenics.

And no one wanted that rock to end up in Deek's possession.

She turned her hands palms up. "I'm trying to figure out who he is myself."

"What'd he look like?" Deek directed that question at Bettina, who took a step back.

Bettina shook her head. "I don't know. I was in the club one minute, then Kardos asked me to take a walk—"

"I knew it!" Veins popped up like cords beneath the skin on Deek's thick neck.

Kardos took a step back. "I didn't mean to ask her out."

When Bettina hissed at him, clearly not happy with the way he'd said that, Kardos looked over at her. "Oh, baby, I didn't mean it that way, just meant I had no idea that guy was screwing with me. Of course, I *want* to ask you out. I just had more sense to—"

"I'm going to kill him." Deek bolted for Kardos.

Evalle cut him off and forced him back. Stopping a freight train would have been easier. She wouldn't be surprised if her shoulder was bruised from it.

"Look, Deek, I can appreciate the feeling, since I've wanted to strangle him myself a few times, but he isn't the danger here. Someone else is. Someone with a lot of juice that neither of us wants to confront without prep. And right now, I'm on the hunt for him. Until we find this guy, let us pass in peace. You take Bettina back with you, but make sure you keep an eye on her in case our mutual friend infiltrates her mind again and has her leaving with someone a lot more dangerous than a teen witch who can barely use his powers."

Deek immediately postured, puffing out his chest and crossing his arms. "She's always well guarded."

Things were going Evalle's way until Kardos snorted at that comment.

Deek went for his throat and she again had to ram her body into the mountain of steel—an action that left her winded.

Kardos, you idiot. If you want to die, there are much less painful ways to go about it. As well as ways that wouldn't leave her bruised.

If Kardos kept this up, she'd reconsider handing him over to the centaur.

She forced Deek back a step, sure he was refraining from using majik only because a human might see them. But if this had been in the basement of the Iron Casket, there would have been no discussion. "Look, Deek, I'll be in touch if I have anything new to share with you on the guy who breached your security."

Deek let his gaze swipe across the three of them and finally gave a nod of assent. "Time to go, Bettina."

The girl released a stream of air so quickly that she must have been holding her breath. She lifted her chin like an offended queen and headed toward the Iron Casket. Guards opened a path for her, then surrounded her, moving en masse with Deek at the rear.

Impressive.

Scary, but impressive.

"Sheez, that was close," Kardos said in a spurt of relief.

Evalle rounded on him. "No shit, Sherlock. What did you think you were doing messing with the centaur's sister? Since the moment she came on the scene a month ago, he's let it be known to all creatures that to even look at her is suicide."

"Well, I didn't think he meant *forever*. Besides, that old guy doesn't scare me."

She rolled her eyes at his youthful arrogance. "When a being as powerful as Deek says, 'Death to anyone who touches my sister,' you can take it to the bank and make a deposit on it. Two-thousand-year-old centaurs aren't known as bluffers. He's forgotten more painful ways to kill someone like you than you and I will ever know."

"Bluffers? What kind of word is that?"

Evalle ground her teeth as rage shot through her. Was that really the only part of her caveat that the imbecile had heard?

No wonder I don't want kids.

"Did you miss the part where I said he was not kidding and you are the next bonehead on his menu?"

That seemed to permeate his stubborness. "Then maybe we should get out of here."

No duh.

At least he was now making sense but unfortunately it wasn't that easy. "First, I need you to explain a couple of things." She took a look around, making sure they were alone. "I heard you met the Birrn demon here at the club. Is that true?"

"Yeah, it was crazy. Me and Kell were looking for some silver . . ." His face clouded with guilt. "I mean hunting for new revenue stream when a Nightstalker told us there was a guy at the IC who was willing to pay runners to pawn his goods."

Evalle frowned at him. How could he have contacted a Nightstalker for information? Grady had talked to them once when they'd irritated him by almost getting killed trying to steal a hubcap on a moving vehicle, but the others ignored the boys. "You aren't powerful enough to shake hands with a Nightstalker."

"I didn't. Kell was playing chess in Woodruff Park when I saw one shimmering, so I went over to talk to him 'cause it was just freaky weird. Never saw this one before."

It still didn't make any sense. "Are you sure it was a Nightstalker you saw?" She'd never known one to give up anything without a handshake, and it wasn't like them to just hang out and shimmer. Fireflies they weren't.

"I thought it was off, but he seemed sincere and then disappeared as soon as he told me about the deal at the IC."

133

Yeah, it smacked of a setup. What the hell had he been thinking? "I'm surprised Kell got involved." He usually knew better.

"He thought it sounded suspicious, so he went as backup." Kardos got serious. "I told him to hide and not let anyone know he was with me, but when the Birrn grabbed me, Kell tried to help. Idiot."

Relief blanketed her at the confirmation that the boys had been set up and had not pulled her into a trap. "Did the Birrn tell you anything?"

"Not really." Kardos locked gazes with her. "Just that he had to find you."

What was this? Open season on Alterants?

Or just open season on her?

She was the only one walking around free that she knew about. "You're sure he wanted me specifically?"

"Yeah. He said he knew we were friends of yours. Kell still wasn't going to call, but the Birrn threatened to eat me if he didn't." He shifted his feet. "Even then, Kell hesitated for a minute. Kind of sucks for the twin brother, right? Anyway, then Kell thought between the three of us we could get away even if he did call you. That was before the demon tossed us up to the light pole, where you found us. Sorry about walking you into a trap."

Evalle shrugged. "It's what I live for. And I'd rather you do that than the two of you get eaten by a demon." She didn't want Kardos to hesitate to call her again. "Now I've got to get going." She walked over to her bike.

"You going to let me ride bitch?"

That stopped her as quickly as getting backhanded. Her anger reignited so fast and furiously that she was surprised she hadn't already blasted him. In fact, she would spare Deek the trouble of killing Kardos.

Evalle turned slowly, expecting to find a smug look of arrogance on his face. "What. Did. You. Call. Me?"

His mouth was open but no words came out. Shock, or fear, sucked the color from his face. He was doing a great imitation of a fish suffocating from lack of oxygen until he finally squeaked, "*What?* You thought . . . I would never . . . no, I didn't call you that." He pointed to the bike. "The seat, Evalle. I was asking if I could ride on the back."

"Oh." She'd heard it with a comma before the word *bitch*. He'd meant the slang term for riding two up with the one on the back *riding bitch*.

Yeah.

"Okay, I'll let you live. This time only."

His cheeks flushed heavily with color.

Good. Maybe he'd lose some of the cockiness around her. She'd let Kell slide for most any infraction, but this brother would be right back in trouble in an hour if she gave him any leeway. "Your mouth is going to be the death of you. You know?"

"God, I hope not. I want to go out in my sleep next to some hot babe after a great harrumph harrumph." Kardos stared at the ground and shuffled his feet. "How'd you end up here anyhow?"

She shouldn't let him change the subject just to distract her from reaming him, but the truth was even if she spent all night chewing on Kardos she'd only end up with a sore jaw. With him, it went in one ear and out the other. "I was looking for you and Kell. Grady told me you were here. I need you and Kell to do something for me."

"You got it. Whatever you want."

She sighed at how fast he'd agreed. Yes, they were friends, but there were many of the preternatural kind who would bind him into slavery with that.

"I don't want you or Kell talking to *anyone* about being with that Birrn last night or about seeing me there either. Especially about seeing me with the Birrn. You got it?"

His gaze slid away, but not before worry jumped into his eyes.

She was too late. "Crap! Who'd you talk to?"

"Not me." Kardos held up his hands in surrender. "Kell talked to someone he was playing chess with at the park."

Everyone from office workers to street people hung out in Woodruff Park. A favorite loafing spot for elderly men. And chess games cropped up like weeds beneath the shade of sprawling oak trees on the south side. Kellman picked up games with the old guys because, unlike Kardos, he didn't go around seeking activities that would shorten his life. He liked the challenge.

Evalle had only seen the chess games in passing during the rare times she'd come above ground during the daylight and never long enough to remember anyone. "Do you have a name or any way to identify the old guy Kell told about the demon?" "Old guy" wasn't much of a hint, since to the twins it could have been anyone over twenty-five.

"Wasn't an old guy, not one of the regulars. I walked up while they were talking and asked Kell what was he thinking talking to a human about the Birrn. Kell said the guy wasn't human and it was weird when he started talking, like everything around them slowed down and Kell felt compelled to tell him, like it was a relief." Kardos squinted, thinking. "The dude was thirty maybe. Beefed up. Long black hair. He was Native American I think."

Her stomach clamped down tight enough to make a diamond. Double crap.

Storm had tracked the boys from where she'd killed the Birrn. She lifted her watch into view. A little more than ninety minutes until she had to meet Storm at Piedmont.

Had he found out about the body in the morgue yet?

If he had, there was about to be another body in the morgue.

The only question was would it be his?

Or hers?

THIRTEEN

Since Kardos couldn't ride without a helmet and there was no way with her luck they wouldn't be stopped and ticketed, Evalle sent him to the closest MARTA subway station and gave him money so that he could ride back downtown and meet up with his brother. He complained about public transportation, but in the end he went.

As soon as she was sure he was safely on the train, she took off for the morgue, hoping to circumvent yet another disaster.

It didn't take long to reach it, and she swung into a parking spot near the front door of the two-story building, which looked out onto Fulton County Stadium, where the Braves played baseball. She yanked her white coat out of her seat bag and rushed to the door. In one well-practiced move, she pulled the lab coat over her shirt.

Inside the glass doors, she walked straight ahead down the hallway until she reached the examination area, where Medical Examiner Beaulah Layton was dissecting a cadaver on the other side of the glass window. Beaulah's eyebrows moved up and down in rhythm with her humming some music from the '70s that Evalle couldn't really place. Beaulah moved like a silent movie screen star, short black hair perfectly styled, as if she'd had dinner plans instead of slicing up bodies until five in the morning.

When Evalle wasn't tracking demons, she performed simple maintenance on equipment and some cleaning, but she preferred to stay as far away from cadavers as possible. Unfortunately this morning she'd been face-to-face with a mauled body.

She tapped on the glass.

Beaulah turned just far enough to make sure whoever disturbed her peace got the full brunt of her glare. She put down the bone saw she'd been using and sidled over to the door Evalle had opened.

Evalle did her best to ignore the scent of stale death that invaded her nostrils. "Sorry I had to bail this morning. Must have been something I ate. It came and went though."

"Good. I don't want no H1N1 running through here, and especially not through me."

Evalle smiled. "I hear ya on that. Just wanted to check in, see how things are going. Any problems with the equipment?"

"The equipment's fine, but things were crazy here this afternoon."

Evalle frowned. "I haven't been listening to the news. Did we have a tornado or something? Somebody bomb the airport?"

"Uh, no. It wasn't bodies coming in, but one that left."

Evalle's gut tightened in apprehension. *That didn't sound good at all.* "What do you mean?"

"The chewed-up Jane Doe disappeared."

For a moment, Evalle thought she might actually be sick. This could not be good for her. "What? How?"

Beaulah shrugged. "No idea. She was here when I went off shift at noon. I came in at six tonight to meet with the animal control investigator, who wanted to see the body, and I pulled out an empty drawer. No one knows what happened, and she sure as the devil didn't walk out on her own. Cops dusted for prints, but the only sets were mine and the intern's who helped me load the tray."

Evalle cringed with every word that brought her just that much closer to disaster. "What do you think happened?"

"No idea. Security ran through the tapes of everyone who came in after I left. Nothing unusual. No one who wasn't supposed to be here."

That was understandable, since all the security staff Evalle had met were human and wouldn't know that some nonhuman beings could enter and remove a body undetected.

The question was, who had been here and what had they wanted with the dead woman's body?

To use as evidence against me? Her paranoia revved into high gear. And who could blame her?

Think, E, think.

138

Would Storm have taken the body? She had no idea what the extent of his powers was or what exactly Sen expected him to do while partnered with her, but she wouldn't rule out his stealing a body to use as evidence against her, then returning it to the morgue.

Evalle fought the need to take deep breaths until she got outside, where the air wouldn't taste like formaldehyde. "I don't want to hold you up any longer. I'll see you on Tuesday."

"You take care." Beaulah headed back to her cadaver.

Evalle made haste to get out of the building as soon as possible. The minute she stepped outside, she sucked air into her lungs and hurried to her bike. She'd just packed the white lab coat in her seat bag when a male voice startled her.

"Did you think I was joking when I said 'or else'?"

She'd forgotten about Isak.

Evalle rearranged her panicked expression into a look of pleasant surprise before she turned toward him.

He didn't appear quite so menacing tonight in a collared blue shirt that was tucked inside jeans, but she'd seen him in demon-killing mode and gear. Judging his relaxed pose as casual would be a mistake. All a person had to do was look into his steely gaze to see the danger lurking there.

Danger could be sexy as all get-out to a woman in her line of work. *Like you care.*

Funny thing was, she almost did.

She tucked her hands into her pockets. "How'd you find me here?"

"I have friends in low places."

Just how low was the question. She glanced to the gate, where she'd swiped her card earlier. "How'd you get inside the security gate if you're not law enforcement?"

She'd always considered this a safe place to park, but she started wondering now.

"Creative conversation. What happened to you this morning?"

"Sorry about that, but something unexpected came up and I didn't have a number to call you to let you know. See what happens when you don't share?"

No reply. No reaction. No sale.

139

She added, "It had to do with my job and my boss."

"This job?"

Oops. She'd forgotten how sharp Rambo was. "No, uh, my other job. I do some courier work and had to make a run up to Chattanooga on short notice." Good thing Storm wasn't here or his lie detector needle would be buried far in the red.

"Must have been pretty damned important for you to get a call that early on a Sunday morning."

You have no idea. "More like an offer I couldn't refuse."

He didn't appear convinced, but neither did he call her on the lie. "Doesn't change the fact that you were a no-show."

"Sue me."

"That wasn't what I had in mind."

Just the way he said that ruffled her skin and made her nervous. She swallowed before she could stop the telling motion.

His lips curved up on one side, not quite smiling, but enough that she didn't think he was angry. His eyes were blue, a deeper blue than she'd expected.

She still needed to find out what he knew about the Birrn, if he'd share. "We were just meeting for coffee. How about we reschedule for a meal and I pick up the tab? Your choice."

He took his time making up his mind on how to answer. "Okay. How about lunch tomorrow?"

Lunch? She couldn't do that, nor did she want to explain why she really didn't want to come out in the daylight to a man who had no compassion for something unnatural. "I'm on a different body clock schedule because of working nights here."

"In that case, what about tonight?"

She had less than thirty minutes to make Piedmont by midnight and to find that rock. If they didn't get their hands on the Ngak Stone, her problems would become moot in comparison to the coming Armageddon. Even more important, she couldn't bail on Storm without drawing additional suspicion.

Isak didn't crack a smile, but his voice was full of humor. "Is there a decision coming out of all that heavy processing I see going on?"

"Tonight's a little busy. I was just trying to find a break in my schedule. But I can definitely meet you at four thirty in the morning."

He looked a little doubtful that she'd make it again. "Where? Since you have a busy schedule, you pick the place." He heavily emphasized "busy schedule," questioning the validity of her words.

"There's an all-night diner on Peachtree just south of the Fox Theater." Since they seemed to be back on good terms and she had the patience of a gnat, she went for a quick bit of intel. "Find out anything about what brought that Birrn to the city?"

"Few things."

She waited, hoping he'd expound, but no. Instead, he took a step forward and wrapped two fingers around her wrist, gently, and lifted her hand, turning her wrist into view.

The casket-shaped IC stamp glowed in the narrow dark space between them.

She should be pulling her arm out of his grasp and giving him reason to keep his hands off her if he'd like to continue using them. That would show more self-preservation than standing here drinking in how delicious he smelled.

"Girls' night out?" His question had come partnered with a smile that warmed his appeal even more.

She shrugged. "I don't have girlfriends." On second thought, she did have one female she considered a friend, but Nicole was a witch and Evalle had never done a girls' night out with anyone. No point in recanting that now.

"Boyfriends?"

"No." She'd answered too quickly and realized too late how that sounded. No girlfriends. No boyfriends. No human friends. "I mean I have friends that are male but not like a *boy*friend."

That answer pleased him, which left her feeling the need to explain her lack of social life. "I work a lot."

"At night."

"Yes. Never been much for the daytime."

"Why's that?"

The more she said right now the easier it would be to hang her later. She lifted her watch into view just for show. "I'd love to finish this conversation, but I've got somewhere I have to be in the next twenty minutes."

He studied her face and hair, his gaze pausing on a detail, then roaming again, intimately, like a visual caress that made her shiver even in this heat.

Being the center of that intensity bumped up her heartbeat in a funny way. Part suspicion and part attraction.

Neither made her comfortable.

She took a step to the side, then busied herself with checking that everything was ready to go when her bike was *always* ready to go. "See you at the diner, okay?"

"I'll be there."

She could feel him thinking. If he was Tzader or Quinn, she'd just demand he tell her what was bothering him, but she hesitated with Isak. He was an unknown entity.

He had a gleam in his eye that made her wonder if he picked up on her thoughts. "There's one thing I haven't figured out about you."

She'd pulled on her helmet, but the face shield was up as she straddled the bike. She laughed derisively. "Just *one* thing you haven't figured out? I can't wait to hear what."

"I'm curious about your aura. Yours is . . . different."

He can see auras? Crap. She'd anticipated a lot of questions, but not that one.

"Different?" she asked, hoping he missed the slight quiver in her tone. "How so?"

"It's not human."

FOURTEEN

Piedmont Park covered over sixteen city blocks of open green space that linked thick stands of trees, a small lake and recreational areas most people found relaxing.

Evalle knew what could lurk in all those dark corners at night, and none of it was relaxing or fun—at least not for the victims. She left her bike parked two blocks away and hiked to the park, reaching the Piedmont entrance a minute after midnight.

No Storm.

While she paced outside the gate, she sent a telepathic call out. *Tzader or Quinn. Are you in Atlanta? Helloooo?*

Nothing stirred along the sidewalks, human or otherwise.

I'm here, Evalle, Tzader's voice brushed through her mind. *Quinn'll be back in the city in another hour or two. Where are you?*

At Piedmont Park, meeting the new guy. You hear about Storm?

Trey filled me in on the Ngak Stone and Storm, but he didn't have much on this guy.

She sighed out loud. *All I have is what Sen told me when he stuck us together. Storm's a shaman who can track supernatural activity and tell if someone is lying or not.* She hesitated to mention how Storm had influenced her emotions, since Tzader only needed pertinent details at this point. *I think Sen brought Storm in intentionally to find proof that I pose a threat to the rest of you so he can lock me up for eternity.*

Eve . . . I know he stays on your ass, but I wouldn't say he's trying to get rid of you. VIPER needs your power and skills. You don't help the situation when you go out of your way to bust on him.

Don't tell me you're justifying Sen's actions?

143

Not even, but I have to keep peace between him, VIPER and the Beladors for the safety of our tribe. I won't let Sen get away with abusing his position when it comes to you, but antagonizing him only makes it easier for Sen to justify his actions.

The fact that she breathed antagonized Sen. But she understood what Tzader was saying. *I hear ya. Where are you now?*

In Decatur. Still trying to find my source on the Noirre. He disappeared, running from something. I'm hoping no one got to him.

She felt Storm's presence an instant before he stepped into her path. "Thought you weren't going to make it tonight."

"I've *been* here," she told Storm, then silently informed Tzader, *New guy's here. I need to have all my attention available to deal with him. Meet you at my place by daylight.*

We'll be there.

Good. Quinn would be there, too. For some reason, she needed to feel less alone tonight. Though she prided herself on being independent, there were times when even the strongest needed reinforcements.

Storm made no move toward the park as he eyed her with an intentness that unsettled her. "Finish all your errands?"

"For now." She'd have to come up with a believable reason for taking off to meet Isak by four thirty, which was only a few hours away.

And before that she needed to come up with a reason why her aura wasn't human. Luckily Isak's phone had buzzed less than a heartbeat after his declaration that her aura didn't appear human. She had no idea what it'd been about, but it'd caused him to excuse himself and take off immediately.

She had a couple hours to come up with some way to explain her nonhuman aura.

In the meantime, the safest conversation around her foremost problem—Storm—would be for *her* to ask *him* questions. "You find anything on the stone yet?"

"Just got here myself."

"Where've you been?" She inwardly cringed the moment the words were out of her mouth. *Why didn't life have an Undo button?* He'd been tracking the Birrn and looking for her ties to it. Which was *the* last thing she wanted to remind him of and talk about.

His expression gave nothing away. "Running down rabbit trails trying to confirm some leads."

When he didn't share anything more like playing chess with Kellman, she decided a change in topic was the safest course of action. "Let's start walking the park."

"After you."

Double cringing at the thought of having him at her back, she angled toward the darker parts of the park, where her vision thrived.

But honestly, her thoughts were not on the stone. They were on her goose getting fricasseed.

How would she know if Storm had found something damning? The quickest way would be to ask, but that was also the fastest way to walk herself into verbal quicksand if he turned the conversation around to what she knew about the demon appearance—especially with his powers. Better to stay with safe subjects. "Anybody have new intel on the stone?" She still couldn't shake that feeling she'd had about it being found.

Or forget the voice in her head that had warned her.

Had it been real or imagined?

Friend or foe?

Until she knew for sure, she wasn't putting any stock in the unidentified voice. It could just as easily have been an enemy trying to throw them off the scent and get them out of the vicinity before one of them unearthed it.

Storm cleared his throat as he kept pace with her. "No one's found anything yet, but the creek running through the park had an unusual overnight eco-change with hyacinths growing like . . ." He paused, clearly at a loss for an analogy.

"Like Audrey II in *Little Shop of Horrors*?" she supplied.

"I guess so."

Evalle paused and took in the confusion in his face. Where had Storm been in recent years not to know what she was talking about?

He stepped up beside her. "The city had to send in a crew to clean out the creek before a storm flooded the area. Since the stone has the power to affect its immediate environment, like using fast-growing hyacinths to lift it out of the creek and place it in sight of its next owner, Lucien thinks that's a good sign it'll be found in that area."

Evalle scowled. "But Lucien and Adrianna didn't see it?"

"They found plenty of rocks that looked like rocks. Nothing that matched the one Lucien saw the night Trey fought the Kujoo."

"Has Trey taken a look?"

"Yep. He came straight here from the VIPER meeting and arrived as workers were unloading the backhoe. He watched the entire time they dumped rocks and mud on the bank, then stayed until Lucien and Adrianna showed up. Those two spent their shift walking the park, but . . . nada."

"I feel for them. It really sucks when you have to look for something. The least the inconsiderate bastard could have done was have a miniature billboard with an arrow pointing down that said Ngak Stone Here." She couldn't help the sarcasm, but did everyone think the rock was going to jump into their hands?

Storm laughed, which surprised her. He had a nice laugh, one that warmed the air and brushed across her skin. Under different circumstances she might actually like working with him.

He added, "Lucien had Adrianna walk along the bank by herself hoping the stone would reveal itself to her, but no luck. Apparently she's not the powerful female it wants."

Evalle stopped and turned to search his face to see if he considered that as bad an idea as she did.

He lifted his hand in a gesture of dismissal. "I don't know if *I'd* have done that, but I wasn't assigned to work with her."

Did she hear relief in his voice on that last part? She should leave well enough alone, but the need to know where she stood with everyone, even Storm, gnawed at her. "Can't be any worse than working with an Alterant, can it?"

"I have no issue with witches. I've known some I now call friends and trust to watch my back in any situation, but not a Sterling witch. I told Sen up front that I had limitations when it came to working with any of his agents. I normally work alone."

He hadn't really answered her question about being partnered with an Alterant in particular. "So why did you agree to partner with me? Or is the truth that you're not really here to be a partner?"

No answer.

And that made her sweat. She plodded along beside him, waiting for a response, but Storm still hadn't said a word by the time she stepped on the paved road that ran across the upper end of the park. Within three long strides she passed through the streetlights along the drive and returned to the black abyss surrounding the rest of the park.

"Did you hear me, Storm?"

"Yes."

"And?" She stopped walking.

He paused, then turned around slowly, taking a step toward her until they were only inches apart. Close enough to feel his soft breath ripple across her hair and forehead.

He raised his hand and extended a finger to touch her face.

She didn't want to retreat and give up any ground to him, but neither did she want to allow a second man to eat up so much of her personal space tonight.

Indecision destroyed any chance to react.

His finger touched her hair, then traced around the curve of her ear. "Do you know you smell like mint and flowers?"

Her pulse ticked harder. Did he like the way she smelled?

She could understand the flowers, since she grew a few in her underground home, but she had no idea about the mint. "Not really. What's the way I smell got to do with answering why you agreed to work with me?"

"I had no idea I'd ever agree to partner with you until I walked into the war room. Trust me, it shocked the hell out of me, too. The mint hit me first, but it was the floral smell that threw me. There you were, all decked out like a tough biker, yet you smelled like a delicate flower. When I sat down by you, those two scents hit me at once and I knew instantly what they meant."

"What?" That whispered question had slipped past her lips without waiting for permission from her brain.

"Mint is refreshingly different and so strong that it's overwhelming to many. Flowers may look fragile, and yet some, like the lotus that only thrives in mud, withstand the most brutal of environments to beautify a world that has tried its best to destroy them. They both suit you, and I knew that I could go against my grain and work with someone like you."

His words seduced her with an ease she found frightening and unsettling. It felt as though he'd peered straight into her soul and laid bare her scars.

Storm thought she was different, fragile and determined.

He was wrong about fragile.

But he'd exposed something she refused to analyze about herself, and the last thing she wanted was for him to think he'd figured her out or had reached her in any way. Not this man who worked as Sen's eyes and ears.

She stared at him blankly. "Wow, you're one of those men who can read a bubble gum wrapper and see the decoding of the entire universe." She leaned in closer, like she was imparting the world's greatest secret. "But sometimes, it's just a wrapper. I chew a lot of mint gum and must have brushed up against a flowering bush at some point. Simple explanations that have nothing to do with my personality or humanity . . . or lack thereof."

His eyes crinkled, seeing everything she tried to hide. "No, this isn't something that clings to you. It's a scent born from who you are."

She'd forgotten that his finger still rested against her neck until it circled around to toy with a thick lock of her hair. If she pulled away, he'd know how much that tiny connection between them affected her. Be damned if she'd give him even that much.

Her heart thrummed with a feather of excitement that slid along a blade's edge of fear, but she wouldn't show a weakness. Not to him or to anyone.

Ever.

His touch left a path of skin sizzling in its wake. "I agreed to partner with you because you're not like the others."

Not like the others.

A freak.

Which brought her back to reality and the real reason Storm had been teamed up with her—to catch her in a lie.

Allowing this attraction to blind her to the danger he presented would be a fatal mistake. He was playing with her, toying with her emotions. He'd already proven he could influence her with his powers.

Was he doing that right now? Was any part of her current emotions real, or were they sent to her by him?

If she didn't get her guard up, he would help Sen destroy her.

She stepped back, breaking the connection. "Don't play games with me or think for a minute that I'll fall victim to your charms."

If not for her night-vision ability, she wouldn't have seen his brow tighten into a frown. He gave a harsh laugh, then shook his head at some inner thought. "I don't think you've ever played games in your life, have you, Evalle?"

Games were for children who didn't know about monsters.

And some of the worst monsters out there were actually human.

Admitting she'd never been a normal child who'd played with other children just made her look more like a freak. Keeping silent was the safest course of action.

He let out a long breath. "I only used my powers one time, and it was *not* to harm you in any way. Have I given you any other reason not to trust me?"

Let me think . . . besides working with Sen?

Wasn't that enough?

And he still hadn't confirmed or denied her charge that he was here to help Sen. He might not have used his powers to harm her, but he'd used them to influence her. In another situation she might have appreciated his intervention that had shut down her silent panic during the meeting. However, Storm had no reason to do something just to be nice.

She didn't trust nice. She knew better. Altruism was a lie people used to disarm the weak. She didn't trust that he liked how she smelled. Didn't trust that *she* liked how *he* smelled.

Rather than admit any of that, she shrugged. "You haven't *given* me a reason to trust you, and talking isn't going to find the stone. We need to get moving."

He stayed where he was, blocking the path. "What are you always so torqued about?"

"We don't have enough time to go through the list." She folded her arms, striking her I'm-done-with-this pose.

"Let me narrow it down. What have *I* done to piss you off? And don't give me your baseless conspiracy theory about how I'm working against you."

"Baseless? Maybe I'm not PO'd so much as that whole 'we can be friends' routine doesn't work on me any more than your flirting." *Wonder if that lit up his lie meter?*

He wanted her to trust him?

Right.

Not without a test, and the one she had in mind was a simple pass or fail.

"If you want to prove yourself trustworthy, how about telling me what you found out about the Birrn killing?"

"You want to keep this all business? Fine." He closed the distance between them until she could see the black pupils in his eyes drilling her. "I picked up a couple scents. One was mint."

In spite of the heat simmering the air around them, her skin chilled at that and felt clammy. He *could* link her to the Birrn demon.

Had he told Sen yet?

Before she could utter a word, light sparked on her left. Evalle backed away from Storm and the flash of light.

Sen's face and body appeared as bright as a match struck in the dark. "I've come for you, Alterant."

"Why?" But her brain filled in the blanks.

She looked at Storm. The bastard had betrayed her. She knew it. "You dog."

"I'll drive her up," Storm offered.

Sen's eyes closed to slits. Both Evalle and Sen shouted, "No!"

Taking a step back, Evalle looked toward the street. If she could get away from Sen, she could contact Tzader and let him know what was happening without Sen or Storm overhearing her. "My bike's two blocks from the park."

"Leave it," Sen ordered. "*They* are waiting for you."

"They? They who?"

But Sen didn't answer, and the only "they" she could think of was the Tribunal.

She tried again. "Don't I get a suspension hearing?" She swung around to argue with Sen and froze when she saw his hand outstretched toward her. "No, no, no . . . don't—"

The world spun into a gray cloud. She heard Storm call out something, but it was lost in the sickening vertigo building in her head from the gut-wrenching turmoil of being teleported.

The world sucked out of sight and she was gone—heading straight for her worst nightmare.

FIFTEEN

S he hated the smell of the past.

Almost as much as she hated Sen.

Peeking through her sunglasses, Evalle snuck a look at the Nether Realm where Tribunals convened, a neutral zone for all entities who supported the VIPER coalition.

A Tribunal was composed of three entities whose pantheons had no direct or indirect relationship to the situation surrounding the supernatural being in question.

Decisions could be made here without danger of retribution. Decisions about whether she remained free or not.

She kept her head down and held her body perfectly still as though she hadn't regained her equilibrium yet, but with her insides shaking, that required supreme effort. The last time Sen had teleported her to a Tribunal meeting she'd come to and retched all over his boots. Must be why he'd left her kneeling on a pad of dense grass this time and stood several feet away, glowering at her.

He was no longer her major concern. Not here.

Power sang through the air from the two gods and one goddess standing on the raised platform of white marble streaked with veins of gold. The dais was set in the center of a circular tract of land the size of a city block where the world fell away at the edges and a star-lit black sky overhead crossed from side to side.

Sort of like kneeling inside an unshaken snow globe at night.

Imposing on the time of powerful beings was never wise. However, her life, for some unknown reason, was in question, and she needed to quickly gather her wits.

She mustered humility. "Might I have a moment to recover my balance?"

"You may have *a* moment." The Polynesian goddess Pele was incredibly beautiful and obviously the only one who was gracious. Surprising, since Pele was known for her temper as much as her exotic beauty. Black hair swept around her bare shoulders in stark contrast to the vibrant flowers woven into the material of her strapless gown.

Standing on Pele's right was Ares, the Greek god of war, who might sympathize with Evalle's struggle to retain her freedom, since he'd been held captive by two giants for thirteen months once. *Might,* if he wasn't one gigantic, aggressive mass waiting to attack someone or something. He crossed arms that bulged with muscle on top of muscle. His legs were positioned in a wide war stance, his body battle-ready, with a bronze cuirass and greaves. Wavy blond hair fell to his shoulders and matched the well-trimmed beard around his terse mouth.

Loki rounded out Evalle's supreme court of justice. The Norse god was a trickster at heart. Narrow horns as long as Evalle's arm snaked out from his forehead and curved up until the tips pointed forward. He had demonic tendencies running through his veins, but she'd bet he wouldn't go quietly into a cell either. His gaze traveled everywhere and back in seconds while he flipped a furry glowing orb back and forth from hand to hand.

Any other time, Evalle would consider Loki's presence a plus, since he might see the trouble Alterants had caused as no different than things he'd done in the past. But putting him in the same space as Ares could turn lethal. Fast.

Probably why the two gods had been positioned on each side of Pele.

This whole deal was wrong.

Sen couldn't take Evalle straight from suspicion to a Tribunal, not without irrefutable evidence that proved beyond a doubt that she was a threat to humanity.

"Alterant." Sen growled deeper than an agitated lion.

She ignored him when she lifted her chin to let everyone know she was ready to proceed. "I come before you both humble and confused, as I don't know of any infraction I am guilty of."

Sen addressed the Tribunal. "It would appear that the *Alterant* has recovered from being teleported."

Evalle held her composure, but one day she'd pay Sen back for every slight and indignity.

It was a day that couldn't come soon enough.

Pele spoke first. "Do you call upon one to witness for you?"

Evalle had only faced the Tribunal once before, which was one time more than any other agent she'd ever heard of. The last time she'd been given this option she'd requested Tzader's participation. Sen had treated her as though she was an imbecile for not realizing she could only ask for Brina or Macha to be called forth.

The Tribunal's version of phone-a-friend. She'd passed on asking for Brina last time rather than be humiliated when the warrior queen failed to show for an Alterant.

But last time, Tzader had told Evalle she was being called in as part of an inquisition. This time Tzader had no idea she was here, and everything about this meeting felt threatening. She'd risk embarrassment and more to stay out of captivity.

Evalle kept her voice steady. "I wish to ask Brina of the Isle of Treoir to be present." Not really, but she sure as the devil wasn't going to bother Macha. Tzader kept telling her Brina would help any of the tribe who asked.

This would be a good time to test that theory.

Pele nodded at Evalle's request and announced for all to hear, "As you wish. Brina of the Isle of Treoir, Warrior Queen of the Beladors, beholden to the goddess Macha, your presence has been requested. We will not proceed with this forum until you appear or send word that you refuse. Sen, you may leave until we call you back."

"Yes, O Goddess." Then Sen just vanished.

Evalle would love the ability to make him do that.

As the seconds ticked by on soggy feet, worry banded her chest so tightly that she could hardly breathe.

What was taking so long?

Would Brina deny her request?

Time passed at a different speed in this dimension. When the delay stretched into what felt like thirty minutes, Evalle struggled not to cross her arms and tap her fingers. Showing any sign of impatience wouldn't be wise. Not with three entities watching her.

Plus Brina might take that action as a bad reflection on the Beladors.

Loki stopped juggling the orb. It immediately sprouted wings, then floated above his shoulder and stayed there. He glanced around as though just noticing the proceedings. "I see no reason to wait any longer."

Pele arched a brow. "As if your time is more valuable than ours?"

Evalle had come and gone quickly the last time she'd faced a trio of entities.

Was Brina making them wait so they'd be angry enough to ship Evalle off forever?

Loki returned her arrogant stare with one of his own. "I know only that *my* time is valuable. And I can make a decision where others may not."

"You will hold your tongue unless you wish to lose it for the insult you wield." Ares took a bold step around Pele to face Loki, who grinned like a wicked brat.

Evalle was ready to recant her request for Brina when a spinning blur of autumn colors appeared between her and the Tribunal. Hair the color of a brilliant red sunset fell to Brina's waist. She wore a gown of ocean green that challenged her matching eyes for dominance. But this wasn't the real-life Brina, only a hologram of their warrior queen, who could not physically leave her mystical island in the Irish Sea.

"Please forgive me for delaying the proceedings." Brina's voice was soft with deference but lined with steel. "I was attending to a matter for my goddess."

Why did Evalle not believe her? Anything could be construed as a *matter for her goddess,* like talking to Tzader first to see if Brina should waste her time helping an Alterant.

"Your delay is acceptable." Loki spoke before Ares or Pele could voice an opinion.

Pele eyed him with quiet malice, then slid her attention to Brina. "We have the unfortunate task of informing you another Alterant has shifted and killed."

Evalle's mouth slipped open. *Now* she understood why she hadn't been given a suspension hearing. This wasn't about the Birrn demon.

They'd found out about the human.

Macha help me.

Brina dropped her head, a sign of shame in front of the Tribunal.

Evalle would not drop hers. Not while she was innocent and being wrongfully accused.

"May I speak?" Brina requested.

Ares jumped in first this time. "Granted."

Brina swept her gaze around the gods. "We have kept a close watch on Evalle, and she has shown no signs of being a threat to humanity. I would ask that she continue in her current position with VIPER and under our supervision."

Not that she didn't appreciate Brina's support, but Evalle hated being spoken about as if she was a feral animal, incapable of living among humans like everyone else unless someone kept a choke collar on her.

Pele's eyes turned to acid. "Evalle has been allowed to remain free all this time based on your recommendations in the past. But this situation is different."

"How so, Goddess?" Brina's voice flowed as easy as an undisturbed stream.

But then it wasn't her neck at risk here. Evalle held her hands in front of her to keep from fidgeting or running.

Pele glanced at Loki and Ares with a look of *are-you-through-posturing?*

When neither god spoke up, she answered Brina's question on how this attack was different. "The Alterant that changed into a beast this time was a female. She killed three innocent people and had to be destroyed, but not before VIPER agents learned that she was pregnant. That child died with her. Until now, Evalle was allowed her freedom based on her unique position. Now that a female Alterant has proven capable of shifting *and* being impregnated, we see two potential problems with her continuing to live among humans."

On the one hand, she was grateful they still didn't know about the mutilated body.

On the other, this was worse. She wasn't being accused of something they thought *she'd* done. She was being condemned for the actions of someone she'd never even met.

The injustice of that burned deep inside her and made her seethe. How dare they judge her?

She released her hands to grip the front of her thighs, fighting against the pressure that closed in around her.

They were going to lock her away. Now.

Had she known what this was about, she'd have fought Sen with everything she had.

Sweat ran down the insides of her arms. "Brina, please."

"Silence!" Brina didn't even look her way.

Evalle sent a telepathic plea. *Tzader, I need help.*

Silence! Brina's shout was even louder in Evalle's head.

"I understand your joint concerns." Brina addressed the Tribunal in a much calmer voice. "As Evalle has proven to be an exemplary follower of our beliefs and valued VIPER agent, I would ask the Tribunal to provide her the opportunity to produce evidence that she is not a risk to the humans, that she is different from all the other Alterants."

The three entities exchanged glances, then turned their backs to Evalle and Brina as they conferred quietly among themselves.

Evalle couldn't believe Brina had actually stepped up and spoken for her, just as Tzader had said she would. He was right about showing trust in return.

Brina was doing her best to buy her time. *Goddess be praised.*

Evalle rubbed her damp palms on her jeans, cheered at the possibility of putting all suspicion about her to rest. Even with Tzader and Quinn's help, she expected that rounding up the evidence needed to cement her case would take a while.

But surely Brina would petition VIPER to allow her a leave of absence so that she could focus on this. Would Brina finally share information on the caged Alterants?

Evalle would be willing to give the Tribunal updates every few weeks. Whatever they needed to make this work.

"We have come to a decision," the goddess said as she and the other two faced them again. "Your request is acceptable to us—"

Hallelujah! Evalle almost staggered in relief.

Until Pele spoke again. "—with the caveat that Evalle remains loyal to VIPER and does not associate with another Alterant while collecting her evidence."

I haven't even seen one in eight years, and if I had, it would probably have killed me. Evalle pulled a calming breath into her chest, preparing to thank the Tribunal for this chance.

Brina nodded. "Agreed."

Ares cleared his throat. "She may have until the first hour of Thursday to prove there is no danger in her remaining among humans. If her status changes at any moment between now and then, she'll be teleported to a secure location immediately."

Evalle's stomach hit the floor. Three days?

Three flippin' days.

Were they out of their divine minds?

Surely these weren't the same three days she had to spend hunting the Ngak Stone or she'd appear disloyal to VIPER?

Oh dear goddess . . .

No matter what she did, she was screwed. If she proved her innocence, she was disloyal, and if she was loyal, she'd never be able to prove her innocence.

Finally Sen would have his wish and she would be caged.

In only three days.

SIXTEEN

Vyan stared at his warlord, who was about to march all of them straight to their deaths. He wanted to call the man a lunatic, but his intelligence and desire to live kept that word out of his vocabulary. Instead he used a moderate tone that flew in the face of his true nature. "I would warn you one last time, my lord, to rethink this plan with so few men."

After passing through the portal that'd been opened by the witch, Batuk had been driving the men relentlessly to invade the city.

"Ten is all we need," Batuk finally said. "We have waited long enough. I have a duty to my men, to *our* men." With one cut, he sliced his sword through a tree the size of Vyan's arm. "Every hour we waste my people spend another day in immortal misery beneath Mount Meru. Can you not understand that?"

"*Me* not understand? I stepped through the portal two years ago for the chance to free our people." Vyan slashed a path through thick undergrowth of this jungle called Amazon, so different from the streets of Atlanta, where he'd been living.

"Has your time in this new realm softened your hatred of the Beladors?" Batuk asked without looking back at him.

"How can you say that? The Beladors killed my wife. I only question how much we risk by facing a monster with less than a legion of warriors."

"We have something the beast will want. This beast will be our

159

shield against the Beladors. How fitting that one of their own will aid us." Batuk chuckled to himself.

Vyan saved his breath. Monkeys raced across branches above his head, screeching to one another. He eyed a fat one that would make a fine meal if he were allowed to stop long enough to hunt. His warlord had less patience than a dog on the heels of a bitch in heat.

"Batuk!" one of the men called out, and raced forward. When Vyan and the warlord turned, Nhivoli plowed through the jungle, past the men marching in line, and stopped, breathless. "I have your peace offering."

Batuk's face split with a satisfied smile. "Excellent. Keep it at the back of the line until I call you." He dismissed Nhivoli, who trotted away and disappeared behind the string of men hidden by vegetation.

Batuk planned to sacrifice an animal to the monster.

That reminded Vyan of the witch's serum he carried to feed the animal. "Are you not curious what animal Nhivoli captured?"

"No. I have no doubt he followed my precise orders, as *every* soldier should." Batuk scratched his grizzly black beard. "I expect my first in command to show the same commitment and loyalty."

Vyan wished for the millionth time that as a young man he'd sought another way to acquire the land he and his wife had intended to farm. Taking up a sword to follow Batuk upon the promise of his own tract of land had made sense at one time. A foolish decision observed clearly in hindsight. Just another way he'd failed his wife. Time had stolen her face from him, but not the sense of failure to protect her.

Vyan blinked away the hot sting in his eyes and swallowed to wet his dry throat. His saliva tasted bitter with salt and remorse.

A sizzle of energy washed across his skin in a cloak of warning.

"Stop." Vyan raised his hand to enforce his order. Hair pricked along his arms. He sniffed the air for a hint of danger. The breath he inhaled burned his throat, indicating the threat was near and powerful. They'd entered the monster's invisible cage. Vyan's hearing sharpened with the possibility of facing a creature in battle. Thin twigs snapped beneath his feet, loud as a tree being axed.

He and his men moved to circle their warlord.

Batuk shook his head and lifted a single finger to indicate all of his men should remain behind him except his first in command. An arrogant move when facing an unknown enemy.

Resigned to his fate, Vyan fell into step with his warlord, who pushed into a clearing.

The entire jungle stilled. Nothing scuttled across the ground or swooped through the air between the webbed branches overhead. A foul odor assaulted Vyan's nose and throat.

He caught a sound, a deep, rasping noise coming from a large animal. He gained Batuk's attention before pointing across the opening to where a palm frond shot fifteen feet above the ground and trembled in sync with each ragged breath from whatever hid there.

Batuk took another step into the opening.

A strong vibration tripped through the air, followed by a low, keening howl filled with menace, as if the animal warned them they had trespassed in his domain and there was no way out.

Vyan's blood pumped hard in his body. He touched his sword, which hung in the leather sheath at his hip, but had to take care. The witch who'd freed their small number had warned that any use of majik in the monster's spellbound cage would backfire against them.

A snarl bellowed in the dense forest in front of them. Trees swayed and the ground trembled.

The animal raised its head.

Vyan had never seen anything so repulsive. How could something alive smell of swamp rot? Most of the body was covered in sores and scabs. The small parts that weren't were a hideous patchwork of filthy hair and scales. Batuk believed they sought some form of a man, but this thing stood ten feet tall and could be nothing other than a monster.

Vyan drew his weapon, heartened at the shirring sound of eight more swords drawn behind him.

"No!" Batuk ordered. "Sheathe your weapons. Now!"

So we die like slaughtered lambs? Vyan held his frustration in a firm grasp. He did as ordered and stood beside the warlord he'd sworn fealty to many centuries ago.

The animal drew its cracked lips into a snarl, fully exposing uneven saber teeth. He tipped his head back and bellowed, the sound

161

neither human nor animal but clearly a message that they had wasted the head start the beast had given them. In its haste to get to them, it uprooted trees as thick around as Vyan's waist and bounded forward in heavy steps, shaking the ground.

When the beast entered the clearing, it *was* half human. At least, the barrel chest, two long legs and two dangling arms were humanlike in structure. It wore threadbare jeans but no shirt over the hair on its chest, which was matted with blood. Scales wrapped its abdomen and ran across its hunched shoulders. Each three-toed foot was twice the length of Vyan's.

Black eyes peered from beneath a jutting forehead.

"By all the saints, what is that?" Vyan whispered, but he never got an answer.

The animal raised its bulging forearms with four thick fingers dangling from each hand. It pointed jagged fingernails at Batuk.

"I am here to offer you a deal," Batuk said, raising his hand in a silent order for the animal to stop.

Instead, the beast took another step and clenched its stubby fingers into fists that cut his palms. A warning, but the monster was curious, or it would have slain them all by now.

The men mumbled in harsh whispers, clearly questioning the sanity behind this march. Even Vyan wondered if his warlord had lost his mind while traveling through the portal.

The animal sniffed the air, grunted, then peered past Vyan and Batuk. On its next sniff, it growled, as if preparing to attack.

Batuk called out over his shoulder. "Bring the woman."

Woman? Vyan went cold at that one word. He caught the scent of innocence before Nhivoli and another soldier marched forward with a young female bound and gagged, hanging by her hands and feet from a narrow tree limb supported across their shoulders. She appeared to be unconscious at first, but the animal's growl roused her. The poor girl took in the scene with wide eyes, then jerked back and forth, bleeding where the ropes cut into her soft skin.

Fury screamed through Vyan's brain and threatened to explode. He stopped the men from entering the clearing and spoke to Batuk. "You cannot do this."

162

"Do not argue with me." Batuk's hand moved to his sword. His face gnarled with rage. "This is the only way to free our people. Without the beast's help, we have no chance against the Beladors once they learn of our escape from Mount Meru. Do you not care for your people? Have you forgotten all you have lost to them?"

Drawing a sword on Vyan would have been less of an insult.

The animal snarled and growled, pawing the ground.

"Wait, I have an offering." Batuk waved the men into the clearing.

The reminder of all Vyan had lost in a bloody war with the invading Beladors crashed through him. Pain forged an alliance with his anger to tear a fresh gash through the heart that had withered in his chest over time. He'd spent centuries dreaming of revenge, willing to do practically anything to make the Beladors pay, but using this woman stirred something inside Vyan he'd been sure had died along with his wife eight hundred years ago.

His conscience.

First the men slid the ropes holding the woman's hands and feet from the pole then they backed away quickly.

"All wars require sacrifice," Batuk whispered to Vyan. "Besides, you have no power inside this cage, so do not kill my men with misplaced honor."

Vyan struggled to find a solution to the impossible situation he'd marched into. Since they had no way to retaliate, this animal would definitely kill all of them. In truth, Vyan would welcome the end to his private hell, but not at the cost of another innocent life.

Keeping an eye on Batuk and his men, the animal dropped down on one knee next to the squirming girl, whose skin glistened with fear. Muted noises gurgled beneath the gag on her mouth. The beast studied her, as if not sure what to do, then flicked a sharp fingernail across the ropes holding her feet, slicing cleanly through. She froze, staring with horror-filled, bloodshot eyes at the monster. It cut the ropes binding her wrists. Her body shook, her small shoulders rocking with tremors. The simple blue sack she wore as a dress clung to womanly curves that belied the girl's youth.

The beast gently slipped a talon between the gag and her face, slicing the rag with little effort.

She screamed, eyes bulging in terror.

Vyan began to wonder what the beast would actually do. He swung his gaze to Batuk, whose black eyebrows drew tight over his hard expression.

This clearly confused his warlord.

The young woman began crying hysterically and spewing garbled words in a language Vyan did not speak. He understood the meaning behind them, though. She pleaded for her life.

The self-hatred he lived with each day for failing his wife would be nothing compared to what he'd feel if he found no way to stop this travesty. What was left of his soul would be a true wasteland.

When the girl moved to crawl away, the creature roared and slapped the ground with its open palm. Vines exploded from the earth, pushing her onto her back, then tethering her arms and legs. It bared its teeth. A thin tongue slinked out, stretching all the way down to touch her face.

She cringed, turning away and crying harder.

Vyan closed his eyes, damning himself along with the others. This was wrong!

Her scream snapped his eyes open and shook loose what was left of his humanity. He could not let Batuk do this. They'd all sworn revenge on the Beladors, but offering this poor woman to a monster was not his idea of war.

"Wait!" Vyan fully expected to pay for this interference with his life.

The beast's glare was only outdone by Batuk's murderous gaze, which should have backed Vyan away, but didn't.

"The girl has not taken the serum the witch gave us," Vyan quickly explained.

The warlord's face blazed red with anger, embarrassment, or both. "Nhivoli, why did you not give it to her?"

"My lord, I do not have the serum, Vyan does."

Batuk's fingernails lengthened into sharp metal claws, a sign he wanted to kill someone. With his glowing yellow eyes locked on Vyan, it wasn't hard to figure out who. "She is nothing more than a meal if she does not drink it. Give her the serum!"

Her wailing filled the jungle. The air trembled with her despair.

"The witch said it was not necessary to drink all of the brew," Vyan hedged. "In fact, she warned us about using too much." The witch had actually said to give the serum to an animal, then stake the offering for the beast to feast upon, because she believed the potion would work slower and hold longer if not taken directly, but she did not know for sure. Vyan really didn't care what it did to the monster, but he would not allow this girl to be a sacrificial lamb.

"Feed her the brew now!" Batuk bellowed.

Vyan struggled to think quickly under the threat of his impending death. "What if she drinks the serum then her stomach tosses it back? We can't risk wasting any of the liquid. The beast's body is much stronger than hers. Give the beast some and see if it works. If not, then give the rest to the girl, but do not let him kill her first." He had no idea how he would get the woman away from this monster and Batuk, but he'd bought himself a few minutes with which to plan.

Ignoring them, the monster raised a hand above her, fingers curved to attack. She screamed, then fainted.

Vyan took a step toward the beast, his hand going to his sword. The creature's head spun to the side. He stared at Vyan with raw hatred.

"Sir." Batuk extended his arms, palms open in offering. "I have brought something better than the girl. I have a serum that will give you what you most desire."

The beast's rumbling breaths came quicker. Its black eyes crept from the girl to Batuk, then returned to its prey. It seemed to struggle with indecision until it slowly moved its hand back and forth above her. The silent order caused the vines tethering her to slide away from her body and into the jungle as frightened asps. Moving its hand again, the beast levitated her limp body to lie across one extended arm before it stood and, to Vyan's disappointment, turned toward the dense woods.

What now?

Vyan was Batuk's best strategist, but he'd come up with no idea of how to deter this beast from the girl. If all else failed, he would use his sword. To do so would decidedly result in his own death at Batuk's hands, but Vyan had enough nightmares without draping this woman's death across his shoulders, too.

He called out to the beast. "So you do not want the serum that will cure you of being a beast? Too bad. We shall leave then."

At his challenge, the beast turned a gaze on him so soulless that there appeared to be no eyes in the black sockets.

Vyan took a deep breath he hoped would not be his last. "Lay the girl down and I will give you the serum."

"It is *my* gift to you," Batuk quickly interjected with enough emphasis to let everyone know he was in charge. He steepled his hands in front of his chest, then bowed to the monster, but his eyes seethed with ire when he glanced at his first in command.

Vyan only hoped if they survived this that he could convince his warlord later he'd been trying to save all of them. He withdrew the metal flask and stepped forward.

The beast swung around. The woman dangled from his arm.

"Put the girl down," Vyan repeated, his tone one of counsel rather than an order.

When the beast still hesitated, Vyan opened the flask and angled it as though to pour the contents out on the ground. Hearing Batuk's harsh intake of air, Vyan prepared for death in the next minute.

The beast flung the girl to the side, where she landed on several bushes, then slid to the ground. Vyan winced, but so far she was unharmed. Bruised and probably mentally scarred. But physically she'd recover.

He placed the flask on a bare patch of dirt and backed away.

The beast lifted its hand over the metal container, which rose in the air to eye level. It stared at the flask, clearly questioning the contents as it breathed in and out in a low rumble from deep in its chest.

"I need you to help us, so why would I poison you?" Batuk asked in an encouraging tone.

The beast stomped its foot.

Vines lashed from the trees down upon Vyan and the others before he could draw his sword. He fought to free himself, but he might as well have been tied with braided metal.

The men called out for Batuk to free them.

His warlord stood tall in his binding and stared at the beast. "Kill me if you choose, but free my men. The only mistake they made was in trusting me. My only mistake was believing you, too, wanted revenge on the Beladors, to make their leader Brina pay for what she has turned you into."

The beast stopped snarling and studied the warlord.

In that moment, Vyan witnessed a flash of longing in the empty eyes. The beast wanted to believe Batuk.

Silence bound everyone for several seconds.

Then the beast raised its hand and pointed a finger at the flask that floated chin high, but he did not touch it. The metal tin moved to the beast's mouth and tilted as it dropped its head back to allow the brown liquid to flow down its throat.

"He still may not help us," Vyan warned under his breath.

Batuk was unbelievably calm given their situation. "We have never known the outcome of any battle before the first strike of swords." He turned his head and staked Vyan with a menacing glare. "You have never doubted my ability to lead my men before. Do you now?"

"No. My loyalty does not waver." Vyan made sure his voice was solid with conviction to hide the lie. Though honestly, his faith should have wavered sooner.

Much sooner.

The flask hit the ground hard. The beast clutched its middle, moaning. Fire glowed red in its eyes when it raised its head. The beast clawed at its chest as if trying to let something out, then twisted into an impossible shape.

A cry of agony tore loose from its cracked lips.

Vyan could not believe what he witnessed. He prayed they lived long enough to make the witch pay for what she'd given this beast, which would rip them into pieces as soon as it could physically do so.

Red dust appeared from nowhere, swirling in bands around them, faster and faster until the beast was engulfed in a cloud that roared like a loud horn. Sand, loose branches and stones lifted from the ground in the spinning cloud, pelting Vyan's skin, cutting his face and shoulders. The men's cries were lost in the noise until the wind died all at once.

Peace ensued so abruptly that the soldiers quieted, until Vyan heard only the thumping of his heart and each panting breath he drew. He tasted dust and blood on his lips.

When the haze settled, the beast was no longer a beast. Still wearing ragged jeans and no shirt, he now stood only a few inches over six feet tall. His golden hair and pale eyes were as out of place in this jungle as the straight white teeth and perfect features.

Those unnaturally bright green eyes were not human.

They were the unique shade of an Alterant's.

"What do you want, warlord?" the man asked, the glint in his gaze as hard as the cut of muscle wrapping his upper body. He folded his forearms over a smooth chest.

Batuk remained calm. "I was told you are Tristan. And that you are an Alterant, not a pure Belador, even though you were born under their star. It is rumored you have the blood of a dark spirit, but your fair hair and pale eyes surprise me."

Tristan snorted. "Surely you didn't go through all of this to talk about my looks?"

"As I said earlier, I came to make a deal with you. I need one with your powers to help us."

"Why should I care what you want?"

"Because if you agree to my offer, you can remain the way you are now . . . forever. You will no longer be known as a beast."

Tristan's eyebrows flickered in surprise, then he shook his head and shoved a testy glare at Batuk. "Who are you to think you can offer me the impossible?"

But curiosity had slipped through the bravado in his words.

"I am Batuk, the Kujoo warlord. My men and I are willing to lay down our lives to make the Beladors pay for murdering our families and raiding our lands. We will not stop until every one of them lies dead."

Vyan felt encouraged at the slight catch of interest in Tristan's eyes when Batuk mentioned warring with the Beladors.

"You have yet to answer my question, warlord." Tristan shifted, his bored stance reinforcing a lack of patience.

"Release us so we may talk as men. I have proven I am not your enemy by the form you have right now."

Tristan tossed his head to one side, as if silently ordering someone to leave. The vines unwrapped from Vyan's body and snaked away to nearby trees. The witch had warned that this part of the jungle was entirely under Tristan's rule and power, but it was also his prison. The two-kilometer-square area had been shrouded in a spell that prevented him from leaving.

Once the men were freed, Batuk stepped closer to him. "I have sworn revenge on the Beladors for murdering our people and causing us to lose favor with our god Shiva. My men escaped through a portal we've opened between the two worlds. I am willing to help you obtain what you want if you will in turn help me obtain what I need."

"What exactly do you need?"

Batuk hesitated just long enough for Vyan not to trust his warlord's answer. "To free my people from imprisonment beneath Mount Meru, but I feel certain we will encounter the Beladors before this is accomplished. If so, we will need your help to defeat them, as our god forbids us from warring with the Beladors. You can fight them. We cannot."

Tristan chuckled, a derisive sound meant to mock. "You do realize the Beladors who live *today* are a bunch self-righteous pansies, right? That bitch Macha protects them as long as they uphold an oath of honor."

Batuk curled his lip. "I care not about their oath, and neither should you." His righteousness swelled with each boom of his deep voice. "I was told how Brina denied you your birthright. That she caged you here, refusing to let you leave without her permission. Do you not yearn for revenge for being cast away as unworthy?"

"You know nothing about me, only rumors and stories traded by Nightstalkers and black witches," Tristan shot back. "I have no reason to believe you. Leave now while I'm feeling relaxed. Or I might choose one of you to take back to my cave and show you how I've entertained others who ventured into my space." His eyebrows lifted with the grin that appeared on his too-pretty face.

Vyan touched the handle of his sword.

Tristan's gaze slashed at him with eyes that blazed hot as the setting sun and could have cooked the monkey Vyan had wanted for dinner. A bolt of fiery light shot from his gaze to the ground at Vyan's feet, close enough to smoke the toes of his boots.

In return, Vyan quirked an unimpressed look at Tristan that said, *Is that all you got,* an amusing phrase he'd heard from the street kids in Atlanta. Tightening his fingers on the hilt of his sword, he considered using his majik to answer the insult, but he would not risk injuring the other soldiers.

He didn't miss the fact that Batuk failed to address the insult.

"I know this." Batuk drew Tristan's attention back to him. "No man would continue to live as a beast when he could walk this land freely in the body you own at this minute. If you agree to my offer, I have a key that will unlock this cursed existence forever."

Tristan made a noise in his throat that dismissed Batuk's offer. "Listen closely, warlord. A local witch doctor came here out of curiosity. I held him captive for a month and gave him every opportunity to work his voodoo to cure me. Didn't happen. In fact, he tried to kill me for my blood. His skull now decorates the entrance to my cave. I'll give you one minute to convince me why I shouldn't use your head to make a matched set."

Batuk smiled confidently. "The serum I gifted you with was brewed by our witch who knows much about Alterants. My men and I all bled into the mixture to share our powers with you, but the witch warns this will not last long. She says you will be able to escape this prison while you are in human form this time, but it will only last for three days. Before then, if you join my army, we will locate the Ngak Stone, which has the power to break your curse forever."

Now Vyan understood the rush.

Three days to find the stone *and* gain control? They were destined to die in this time. Legend held that the stone had always chosen a powerful being in the past. What were the chances they could find the stone's new master or that Tristan as Batuk's envoy could take possession of the stone in so little time? How could they trust Tristan to keep his word if he did agree?

Would have been nice to have known everything before Vyan traveled here and risked his life for nothing.

Tristan narrowed his gaze on Batuk. "What are you *not* telling me?"

"That we cannot battle the Beladors without drawing the attention of the gods. We do not have our Shiva's support, so I need you to . . ."

There was that hesitation again, making Vyan wonder what game Batuk played.

". . . agree to stand with us should we face the Beladors before leaving this world. Second, the Ngak Stone has chosen a new master. Shiva would know immediately if one of us gained control of the Ngak Stone, or I would have gone after it myself by now. I need someone with your power and lack of ties to any entity to take possession and wield the stone for us. The Beladors infest the earth now and will no doubt *also* learn the stone has taken a master."

Tristan shook his head. "So basically, you need to keep a low profile until you can get out of town, so to speak?"

Batuk tilted his head in confirmation. "Once you convince the new master to willingly give you the stone, you will hold the power in your hand to break the curse of being an animal. In return, I want you to use the stone's power to send all of my tribe back eight hundred years to our home—not Mount Meru but when we lived as men with families. And, as I said, *possibly* battle the Beladors if a conflict arises."

Tristan's eyes twitched, narrowing on Batuk before his gaze evened out with a look of silent understanding that Vyan trusted even less than Batuk's words. Something had just transpired between the two. If only he could determine what.

The Alterant's entire body relaxed. "Why would the stone's master help me?"

"Because the master will be a woman. With the face and body you now possess, can you not sway one female to do your bidding?"

Tristan actually smiled. "There are many ways to make a woman bend to my will. Some are more enjoyable than others. Looks like we have a deal."

171

Batuk might have a deal, but Vyan had no intention of bending to Tristan or trusting the bastard to help his people.

Vyan no longer trusted his leader either.

That left him with only one person he could rely on.

Himself. And only one choice of action. He'd have to find this woman who possessed the stone before Tristan did *and* convince her to help free his people before Batuk's real agenda killed them all.

Vyan clenched his teeth as the task ahead daunted his conviction. Damn, his conscience had picked a terrible time to return.

SEVENTEEN

The sense of spinning ended abruptly with Evalle standing upright. She shoved her hands out for balance. Her palms hit a surface that flexed, but it was the lungful of raw sewage she breathed in that told her exactly where she was.

Sen had teleported her to a port-a-potty.

In the middle of the summer in Atlanta. Gross.

That bastard's sense of humor came from the same place his head was shoved up most of the time.

She fumbled with the door handle and stumbled out onto a dark sidewalk on shaky legs, gulping fresh air. The sidewalk pitched with her vertigo.

Nausea threatened to finish off her perfectly crappy day.

At least it wasn't dawn yet. That would be more like Sen to stick her in a port-a-potty in the middle of a hundred-degree day without sufficient clothing to leave.

A hand latched onto her shoulder. "Hey—"

She came around swinging out of reflex, her mind a rush of red fury. No one would ever hurt her again.

He blocked her right cross. She shoved her knee up. He used another hand to deflect her slam to his groin. That gave her an opening to throw an uppercut with her left fist, clipping the edge of his chin.

"Ow, dammit. Stop!"

He spun her like a top on a string.

Vertigo won at that point. And she figured out who she fought.

"You stop or I'll throw up on you," she warned, sure that would be enough to make Storm shove her away.

"You don't transport well, huh?"

Was he laughing? She *could* break his hold even though he had her back pinned to his chest, but her legs were so weak she'd probably land facedown on the sidewalk. She hated to ever feel weak, but the shaking wouldn't stop. "We call it teleporting in VIPER. You make me sound like fresh fruit that gets damaged in shipment."

He did laugh this time, a warm, throaty sound. His grip changed from one of containment to one of comfort.

She tried to make herself push away from him, from being held, but her body refused to help. His fingers wrapped her abdomen and moved slightly, cupping her waist. He breathed deeply, a motion that gave her an up close and personal idea of just how wide his chest was.

The air changed from one of joking to awareness.

Not the fight-or-flight mode she usually experienced this close to a man.

She was torn between wanting to stay in this moment a few seconds more and shoving away from someone who was helping Sen.

"You better now?" Storm's voice was next to her ear and sounded as though he didn't want to hear yes, but that was the answer she gave him. "Okay. If I let you go, will you promise not to hit me *or* throw up on me?"

"For now."

When his arms fell away she experienced a quiver of disappointment. And surprise at not feeling the bone-deep fear of being held and hurt in his grasp.

Would she ever want a man to touch her . . . to *really* touch her?

She stepped away, recognizing the street and buildings as she turned and located her bike in the same spot she'd left it. Satisfied nothing had happened to her baby, she faced Storm. "What time is it?"

"Right around five. Be daylight in a half hour."

Crud. She'd lost almost five hours even though the Tribunal meeting had seemed to pass in less than an hour. Isak had to be ticked off about her blowing a second meeting. One problem at a time. She cut her eyes at Storm. "What are you doing here?"

"Waiting for you to show up. Again." He canted his head in the direction of the bike. "I found your gixxer after you left. Figured I'd hang around and keep an eye on it."

"Why?"

Storm had a way of looking at her that made her think she'd missed something in the conversation, as though she shouldn't need to ask that question. "Bad enough to get yanked off your feet by Sen, but it would be worse to come back and find your ride gone."

It was nice of him to look after it, since he had no idea no one could take her bike. His kindness touched her a lot more than she wanted it to. "What about looking for the Ngak Stone?"

"Sen came back not long after you left. I told him I'd just finished my shift in the park and if he expected me to work with you, then you had to be here for that to happen."

Why would Storm purposefully bait Sen? Especially about her? Was he telling her the truth or trying to manipulate her into thinking they were on the same side? She kept her curiosity hidden. "We've got to find that stone."

"VIPER agents have been in the park and the surrounding areas all night, so it's not like the mission was entirely abandoned. Besides, I can't see any of us finding that rock until it chooses its woman."

He made it sound like some horny teenager. "What agents have been here since I left?"

"Casper came by for a while, then Tzader was here. Another guy joined him—"

"Quinn?"

"Yeah, he showed up. They both left a little while ago."

But Storm had stayed. She wished she knew how to feel about that, but she'd only slept a handful of hours in three days and was too tired to think at this point. "I'm going home. Thanks for keeping an eye on my bike."

"No problem. What time do you want to team up again?"

Wow, he'd finally figured out that demanding she meet him at a specific time wouldn't work.

But what to tell Storm? She'd stood up Isak—again—and still had no way to find him. Isak might know why the Birrn demon had been looking for an Alterant, information that could be useful with the Tribunal, but she doubted he'd share a thing with her after this.

Heck, she'd be lucky if he didn't turn that big cannon he toted on her.

Storm waited patiently for her answer, his eyes full of quiet under-standing she really wished she could trust.

"I'll see you at the same gate at nine tonight." She considered the conversation over and headed to her bike before she did something foolish such as offer to grab coffee with him.

"That'll work. I've got to catch some sleep then follow up on a couple leads."

Evalle was halfway to her bike when his words stopped her. "What leads?"

"On the Birrn killing." Storm walked over and stood in front of her. "You could help by answering some questions."

That's right. He'd picked up a mint scent.

Hers.

"Why would you think that?"

"One of the two male witches I found said you'd been there and helped them escape the Birrn. Want to elaborate?"

Not really.

Had he asked her that before the Tribunal meeting, she'd have had to fight a rush of panic. Now she had much more to worry about than Sen's agenda. She was sick to her stomach from being dizzy and had no energy left to verbally fence with Storm. "Yes, I was there. Yes, I helped the twins get away from the Birrn. And, yes, I could have told you that this morning and saved you from working so hard today to give Sen the information he needs to put me on suspension. Sorry I didn't want to help you put a collar on me."

Trying to outmaneuver Storm was like playing dodgeball with an octopus. She could only do it so long without losing.

"I know all that, *and* that you fought the Birrn *and* that you were present when the Birrn was destroyed."

She had her arms crossed and her hands fisted, ready to tell him just what she thought of anyone who was Sen's go-to man for infor-mation, but Storm didn't let her.

"Get some sleep and cool off some. My questions will keep." Storm used the back of his finger to wipe a layer of sweat off her brow, the motion wiping away her anger just as easily. "Regardless of what you think, I didn't agree to transfer to Atlanta for the sole purpose of handing you to Sen on a platter. You want me to be straight? Fine. He does think you're hiding something from him, and when he told me he specifically wanted to know if someone was putting the VIPER coalition at risk, I knew he was talking about you. That doesn't mean *I* think you're a risk. When Sen asked about the Birrn earlier, I told him I was tracking the person who killed it, which I am. But you didn't kill it, did you?"

She didn't dare tell Storm about Isak for fear of his running to Sen with the information—which would definitely not work in her best interest. Also, she still had to find out what Isak knew about the Birrn.

That is, if he'd ever speak to her again after she'd left him double hanging.

"No. I didn't kill it."

"Then you better run along." His tone was fierce.

"Why?"

"Because you'll turn into a toasty Alterant if you don't," he teased.

She allowed a smile. "Why didn't you tell Sen about me being at the site where the Birrn was killed?"

Storm could turn a minute into the longest stretch of time with one look into his searing eyes. "Because I'm not Sen's hit man. I decide for myself who the good guys are." He turned his hand over to brush his palm through her hair, letting his fingers rest at her shoulder for a brief moment before he stepped back. His eyes were darker than before. Whatever he was thinking disappeared in his shuttered gaze. "Now head out before something even more evil than a Birrn comes along tonight and decides to eat you."

She would have questioned him more, but every instinct she possessed told her to get out of here as quickly as possible. Because if she didn't, something wicked just might devour her. Not that it would really matter. At the rate she was going, she'd be dead in three days anyway.

Or would she be able to find the miracle that could keep her free and save the world from those who wanted to destroy it?

EIGHTEEN

Monday predawn traffic poured into the parking lots Evalle rode past. She slowed to scan the area around each one.

No trolls working the pay booths. No demons lurking in the shadows.

She kept an eye on three parking garages in downtown Atlanta for Quinn, who probably owned more real estate than some small countries did. If he wanted to consider a nightly ride to keep an eye on his businesses a part-time job, who was she to argue? Especially since Quinn gave her a reduced rent in trade for surveillance.

All missions completed for the evening.

She turned her gixxer toward home.

When are you going home, Evalle? Quinn asked in her mind.

How did he know she wasn't there yet? Was the man psychic on top of his other gifts?

She glanced up at the sky threatening to unleash sunshine in another ten minutes. *I'm a mile from my elevator.*

Z and I'll meet you there.

Not much for chatting, that Quinn.

She cut down Marietta Boulevard and turned on a side road that deposited her below Atlanta's traffic level. The rutted street her narrow tires bounced over ran along the railroad tracks that once fed into the original Underground Atlanta, where civies came in groups for safety. Today's Underground Atlanta was a thriving tourist attraction safe enough for the kiddos.

She preferred the spooky early morning darkness down here in Atlanta's underbelly, where dock workers sweated out an honest living, to the pristine world full of suits . . . a world full of doctors who . . . *Don't go there.*

Parking in front of the overhead door to her personal elevator, which could carry a full-sized vehicle, she pressed the remote opener clipped to her tankbag and climbed off.

Footsteps approached, crunching gravel layered over the pavement. She pushed her bike into the dark elevator stall, turning it to where she could face her guests. "How's tricks, boys?"

"Must you always cut it so close to daylight?" Quinn asked.

She grinned at him. "Gotta make hay when the sun don't shine and all that. Besides, Sen ran me late."

"What'd he want now?" Tzader entered last, sounding whipped. Had he rested at all since yesterday?

"He snatched me in for a Tribunal meet—," she started explaining.

"Without contacting *me* first?" Anger boiled off Tzader.

Evalle supported the bike against her hip and lifted a hand, hesitating to say much out here. "It wasn't a suspension hearing that would have required due process."

No happier than Z, Quinn picked up on her reluctance to expound. "Let's get inside her apartment where no one can hear us."

She keyed the remote, shutting the door, and turned her attention to where a panel of six toggle switches was mounted behind bulletproof glass.

Getting inside the elevator would be simple for an intruder.

Breaking the bulletproof glass over the switches would set off alarms in her living quarters down below. But even if someone made it this far, they'd have to know the correct sequence for flipping the toggles. That changed daily, and only the three people inside this elevator car knew those codes.

Tzader and Quinn could flip the toggles kinetically, which one of the two did before she could, because the elevator started moving.

"You got any food down here?" Tzader got downright surly when he was hungry on top of being tired.

She thought about it. "Sure, I got a new recipe for—"

Tzader and Quinn both said, "No."

"That's cold. You haven't tried anything I've cooked since that first time." When the elevator stopped twenty feet belowground, she mentally flipped the toggles in reverse and pushed her bike into the twenty-by-thirty-foot garage area of her private world. She rolled the gixxer onto the hydraulic motorcycle lift she used to service her baby and tightened the wheel chock to lock the bike in place. White upper and lower cabinets lined one side of the room, but she was the only one who could see all that right now.

A string of fluorescent lights overhead flickered on.

Quinn's doing, since he had no patience for being in the dark.

"I got the door," Tzader said and the elevator closed behind them.

With one quick glance to ensure everything was as she'd left it, Evalle led the way through a series of unlit tunnels toward her apartment.

The tension in her shoulders eased the closer she got to her home. Quinn would have let her live here rent-free.

No way. She'd sleep in a public bathroom—and had—before she'd owe anyone for something as basic as a place to live. He'd set a fair price, and she earned her way between working at the morgue and receiving pay from the Beladors' fund as an agent to the coalition.

VIPER negotiated payment arrangements with all their agents except Beladors, who chose not to accept money from the coalition. She guessed Brina and Macha didn't want to be dependent on VIPER any more than Evalle wanted to be dependent on anyone.

Quinn was on the board of Belador financial barons, who invested funds accumulated over generations. They took care of their own.

"What happened to the lights in *this* hallway?" Quinn groused.

"Saving on your power bill." As she approached the steel door that had no handles or locks evident, she channeled energy to open it.

Quinn growled something low. "I'm not a bloody slumlord. All my properties are green efficient and you know it. Not like your eyes can't take a little lighting."

"You got better places to spend money."

He could be overbearing some days, especially when it came to what he considered her well-being, but he respected her need for independence.

She stepped into her abode, where wall sconces and tiny overhead puck lights strung along a wire brightened the simple room. Quinn maintained she needed enough light for *guests* to move around safely.

She didn't have guests as a rule, but even a blind person could navigate around the few pieces of furniture she'd accumulated.

This was home and hers. She came and went at will. Her one indulgence was plants, especially flowering ones that she had to trick into blooming with artificial lighting.

Tzader dropped down on her lumpy sofa, let out a groan born of deep exhaustion then kicked off his boots. He leaned back, stretching out his jean-covered legs and crossing his arms over the sleeveless black T-shirt, so completely different from Quinn's pewter gray collared shirt with a golf logo on the chest and creased slacks.

"I see you've decorated since I was last here." Quinn sent a reproachful frown at the oversize orange beanbag in the middle of the room. "Having a time deciding on the most advantageous location for *that*?"

"Too bad there's no snob police, Quinn. They'd make a fortune writing you up."

He sighed with strained patience.

She loved tweaking his aristocratic nose.

A noise from the back of the apartment snapped her into action. She hurried over to stand by the offensive beanbag.

Growling rumbled from down the hallway that led to her bedroom.

Footsteps slapped the hard concrete floor, heading toward the living room, picking up speed, running full bore until the pounding echoed like bomb blasts.

"Evalle?" Tzader issued the sharp warning and came to his feet. The knives hanging at his hips snapped and hissed. He took a step toward her.

"Oh, good Goddess," Quinn muttered.

She ordered both of them, "Stand back. I got this." Keeping her attention on the hallway, she prepared for the attack that flew out of the darkness at her.

The two-foot-tall gargoyle went airborne, wings flapping, like a cannonball with mouth open to expose sharp teeth. All that heading for her chest.

"Dammit, Evalle!" Tzader reached for her arm and missed when she jumped aside at the last second.

The gargoyle landed on the beanbag, his momentum sliding him with the bag all the way across the room until he smacked the solid wall.

She laughed out loud, enjoying the best sound that had traveled up her throat all day. "Nice one, Feenix. Come here, baby."

Feenix made a noise that sounded part growl and part snort when he was happy. His mouth spread wide, showing off sharp incisors that were as deadly as they looked. He clutched his little potbelly and tucked his batlike wings close when he rolled off the bag, still chortling over his NASCAR-worthy slide. They were both fans of American car racing.

"That thing doesn't know his strength," Tzader growled, but his knives had settled down. A sign he was at ease. "He's going to hurt you one day."

"No, he won't." She squatted down as Feenix waddled to her, wings flapping happily. His huge eyes were two orange orbs that glowed bright as a Halloween pumpkin against his dark-green-and-brown scale-covered body.

"I could have acquired you a dog—something adequately trained that wouldn't kill you." Quinn stepped aside, moving his expensive pants out of snag range from the sharp points on Feenix's wings.

"A dog or a cat would want to go outside in the daylight and need more care than I could give it. Feenix likes the dark and he's self-sufficient and he loves me. He's perfect." She opened her arms and he walked into her embrace, tucking his wings so she could hug him. It was like holding a soft alligator that was as cold as a dark cave and smelled like freshly tanned leather. The skin covering his wings was the smoothest part of him. "I finally settled on the perfect name. Feenix."

"Because Lucifer was taken?"

"Careful, Quinn," she said with mock threat. "Or I'll tell Feenix you want a hug."

Tzader chuckled and shook his head.

Quinn shuddered on his way to the recliner she'd picked up last week from a late-night going-out-of-business sale.

Hard to hit yard sales when most of them ended by nightfall.

"He's no bird rising from the ashes of destruction," Quinn muttered.

She argued, "Yes, he is, but his name is different." She spelled it for him. "I picked *Feenix* because this little critter survived that demented sorcerer and crawled out of a burning building when all the other *things* the sorcerer had created died even though they were bigger and stronger."

She released Feenix, who waddled across the room making grunting noises. He picked up a stuffed alligator and tucked the soft toy into the crease of his bent arm, holding it like a baby doll. "And *phoenix,* the bird name, means 'the most beautiful one of its kind.' Just like my Feenix."

Quinn cleared his throat. "Evalle, darling, you may need prescription glasses after all. That creature is *not* attractive."

"He is to me," she whispered, then smiled at Quinn, who groused about most of her choices in life. He hated that she wouldn't let him hire people to finish the interior of this place or buy any furnishings. She did allow him and Tzader to give her plants, which was why it looked more like a jungle than a home.

"Food, Evalle?" Tzader reminded her.

She swung around, grinning. "I've got frozen pizzas."

Neither of the men made a sign of interest. She added, "And, I stocked my bar. I'll throw in a Boodles and water for Quinn and a Guinness—on draft, no less—for you, Z."

"Now you're talking." Tzader stretched out again, propping his feet on the arm at one end.

"With enough Boodles, I can eat anything." Quinn waved at her dismissively.

"Wouldn't want to ruin your taste buds for caviar," Tzader muttered.

"Or yours for Vienna sausage." Reclined and with eyes at half-mast, Quinn stretched his hands along the chair arms, as if he enjoyed the pedestrian furniture more than he wanted her to know.

"What happened with Sen?" Tzader asked before she left.

"It'll hold until I get food cooking and your drinks."

Tzader made a noise of acceptance.

Evalle headed for the kitchen and paused when she remembered the treat in her pocket. "Feenix?"

The gargoyle looked up, eyes round with anticipation.

How could someone not love him?

She dug out the lug nut she'd found and pitched it in the air.

His tongue shot out, swiping the nugget out of midair and into his mouth. He made an "mm," sound and his cheek fattened as if he was sucking on a caramel.

"Was that a *steel* lug nut?" Quinn missed nothing.

"Yes. He loves anything silver."

"Oh, good Goddess . . ." Quinn mumbled something else she laughed at, and she went to the kitchen.

Her heart warmed at the strange feeling flooding through her. Happiness. What a time to finally be happy when she might be dead or caged in three days.

She got busy heating the oven. She had Quinn to thank for the stainless steel chef's kitchen, since it was already here when she moved in. He and Tzader had only stopped by twice since she'd moved in four months ago, never staying long.

Could it have been fear of being invited to eat again after what she'd cooked the first time? Who knew duck smelled that bad when it burned?

She pulled a mug out of the cabinet and started the slow process of pouring a Guinness draft between pushing pizzas into the oven and mixing Quinn's drink.

Having company tonight after the harrowing Tribunal meeting was . . . nice.

Quinn and Tzader could visit her sanctuary whenever they wanted, but no others. Even after two years, she didn't know much about their backgrounds, but she did know the one thing that mattered—that she could trust these two without question.

When Tzader had a chance to transfer her to the southeastern division, she'd accepted immediately, moving across country at night over three days. That had been five months ago. After arriving in Atlanta, she'd found a gym where she could work out and shower at night. Then, during the day, she'd slept in a climate-controlled storage space nearby, where she'd had a bedroll and a bag of clothes.

Same thing she'd been doing since she'd started living on her own at eighteen.

When she'd put them off about coming by where she'd been staying, they'd tracked her down to the storage locker.

Quinn had at first been appalled, then angry, then he'd just sighed and told her, "Prepare to move in twenty-four hours."

Tzader had refused to even discuss another option.

She'd finally agreed under the one condition that she paid for the apartment. No charity deals and no owing anyone. She'd live in a storage room or worse the rest of her life before she'd ever be at anyone's mercy.

No one would ever own her life again.

She'd never shared the ugly details about her childhood that drove her to remain independent.

Not even with these two men.

Quinn had assured her he had a location that was within her budget, and he'd even swap out some of the rent if she'd keep an eye on several of his parking garages.

That's how she'd ended up in a place with all the charm of a fall-out shelter, which was paradise compared to the claustrophobic hole she'd spent twenty-four hours a day in for eighteen years. She had over two thousand square feet here she could do with as she pleased. On her limited budget, that meant very little.

Eventually, she'd turn this into a true sanctuary.

If the Tribunal didn't decide to lock her away.

If so, Brina would put her somewhere no one could find her. Not even Tzader.

Evalle squeezed the dish towel in her hand. If that happened . . .

Something tapped her on the leg, breaking her out of the desperation cartwheeling through her chest.

Feenix stood there with his alligator baby tucked under one arm. His eyes drooped, a sign he was unhappy or worried.

"What's the matter, baby?"

He leaned his head against her leg and patted her foot, something he'd done the last time she'd come home shaken up after the Tribunal had yanked her in for a meeting.

Did he sense that she was under threat?

She wouldn't go down without a battle, but she would make sure Feenix was taken care of if the unimaginable happened and she lost.

"Everything's fine." She smiled to give the words a ring of truth. Reaching over to the counter, she pulled open a drawer in her cabinet and took out a foot-long stainless steel cooking spoon she'd found in a garbage can and sterilized. "Here ya go, sweetie."

When she pushed the spoon under his nose he bit it, flipping the handle out of her hand. "Go back and keep the boys company. I'll be in there in a minute. Okay?"

Feenix tottered away, licking the spoon he now held in one hand and dragging his stuffed animal clutched in his other four fingers.

She carried a small plastic tray with a bottle of Powerade, Z's mug of beer and Quinn's mixed drink into her living room. One day she'd have a television and stereo system in here, but her laptop in the bedroom and boom box in the kitchen would suffice for now.

"Get the table, Feenix." Evalle carried the drink tray to where he pushed a cardboard box into position to act as a coffee table Tzader and Quinn could reach. "Thanks, baby."

Feenix clapped his hands and went back to playing with his alligator.

She cracked the plastic cap on the Powerade bottle and took a swig. "Ready to catch up while the pizzas are cooking?"

Tzader sat up, rubbing his eyes, then lifted the mug and looked at the top of the beer. "Impressive. Where'd you learn how to draw the four-leaf clover in the foam?"

"Internet. There's a YouTube video on everything." She didn't have to ask if Quinn's drink was okay. He had a look of euphoria after taking a sip. "Why don't you two tell me what you found out in North Carolina, and I'll fill you in on the Tribunal and what Trey didn't know about the demons, since I figure you caught up with him by now."

Tzader's eyes simmered with building fury, but he nodded.

"We did speak with him." Quinn sat back. "I'll give you what I know, then Tzader can tell you about the informant. The Alterant that was caught in North Carolina two months ago was thought to be in his late teens or early twenties, according to Nightstalkers there. He was a thief, breaking into businesses, stole a couple cars, robbed a convenience store, but nothing major."

Evalle tapped her fingers on her knee, thinking. "Was he ever arrested?"

"No. He had an unnatural speed, like Trey's ability, which we suspect he may have inherited as a Belador trait. The police just thought he was a professional criminal. No fingerprints, and they never caught his face on a security video. It took me a while to come up with a common denominator in the crimes until I started thinking about your aversion to the sun."

"Was he a freak living like a vampire, too?" Evalle joked. She walked over and kicked the beanbag closer to the cardboard coffee table, then sat down on a poof of air.

"You know how I hate it when you call yourself a freak," Quinn admonished. "But, no, he wasn't nocturnal. The police set up a trap, thinking an unlocked car with a camera bag in the back would be an easy heist if left alone during three days of rain. The male Alterant stole the car on day four in bright sunshine. We discovered that all of his crimes were committed only when it was daylight and not raining. A Belador on the police force who started following this case realized the perpetrator might be a preternatural being, so he asked to work the stakeout. When the Alterant stole the car, the Belador cop followed, sure he'd located something nonhuman, so he called in support."

Evalle nodded. "That's how nine male Beladors cornered him, right?"

"Yes. During the six hours they pursued him, the weather began changing from partly cloudy to an approaching weather front. Four of them cornered him at the back of a school on a Sunday, and the other five Beladors came when called telepathically. Before the thief realized they weren't human cops he could outrun, he jumped out of his car to flee just as it started raining. The Beladors had linked by now. The thief was like any other panicked criminal until he got wet, then he screamed as if hit with acid. He shifted at that point, turning into a beast that ripped the head off one Belador before they realized what he was and had a chance to unlink."

She chewed on her bottom lip, sick at the loss of life. The families whose father, husband, brother or son hadn't come home. "How'd you find out all that when VIPER couldn't get anything the first two weeks?"

"Another Belador in the area heard their call for help when the Alterant started shifting and showed up after the killings, but before any law enforcement got there. He had the good sense to pull the video out of the police cars and call for Brina, who brought in Sen to clean up the mess and teleport the Alterant to a secure location. Brina told the local Belador to hold onto the video until Tzader and I showed up, since this was more a Belador issue in her mind than a VIPER issue."

Evalle cocked an eyebrow at that. "Brina just wants to keep the dirty laundry under wraps."

Tzader uttered a gritty noise. "Don't get started, Eve. Brina's first responsibility is to our tribe, which includes you."

"Even a mutt gets a bone once in a while." But Brina *had* spoken up for her today.

Quinn stood up and glanced down at Tzader. "Why don't you pick up from here, and I'll refresh our drinks."

Tzader handed off his mug. "While we were investigating in Charlotte, we caught someone stealing from the Alterant's booty stash. Someone with the ability to change his physical appearance."

"A troll?"

"You got it. When Quinn figured out about the weather, we mapped an area where the thefts took place and drew lines until we figured out a general area where they intersected. Once we had that, we started shaking down Nightstalkers and found the Alterant's hideout in a derelict auto repair building. Before going in, we spent a week watching the hideout to see if someone was connected to him in any way. What we found was a troll who showed up on the sunny days while the Alterant was out and took a couple things like jewelry or motorcycle chrome. Never enough to make a huge dent in the pile we found, but consistent."

"What was the Alterant doing with the stolen goods?"

"Looked like he was pawning most of it and stashing the cash in a wall air conditioner in his hideout. He had a newspaper folded to a section on custom vans, as if he was trying to get enough money to buy one."

Evalle understood immediately why someone who couldn't take rain the way she couldn't handle sunlight would want a low-profile vehicle he could live in when need be. She'd have loved to own a van like that instead of traveling in late-night buses on the trip she'd taken across the country. "What happened with the troll?"

Tzader accepted his beer from Quinn, then eyed the smooth foam. "No clover?"

Quinn released a put-upon sigh and opened a supersized Mr. Goodbar she'd splurged for, because that was his favorite confectionary indulgence. He told Tzader, "No little paper umbrellas either. You were telling her about the troll."

Swallowing a drink of beer first, Tzader continued. "We caught the troll and threatened to alert VIPER that he had not declared his residence in Charlotte. He swore he was leaving that day."

Evalle snorted at that. "To go home and take care of the elderly sick mother he didn't have, right?"

"Close enough to the lies he spewed," Tzader agreed. "We told him he wasn't going anywhere unless he could bring us information on the thief he was stealing from within twenty-four hours. If he did and the intel was confirmed as usable, he could leave. He came back nine hours later with two pieces of intel. The troll said someone was looking for the Alterant."

Feenix padded over and climbed onto Evalle's lap, gurgling noises on each breath. He was a heavy little guy. Once she had him settled, she clarified, "So the troll *knew* the thief was an Alterant?"

Quinn cut in. "Not until after he'd spoken to others in his underground community and put it together. The troll was pretty shaken up to realize he'd been stealing from an Alterant, especially after word circulated about the thief killing nine Beladors."

Trolls fearing Alterants. Now that cheered her up, except for the downside of Sen figuring a way to use that against her. "You said two pieces of intel. Who'd the troll say was looking for the Alterant?"

"A Rak had feelers out for the Alterant."

Just add that to the list of today's demons, Sen and the Tribunal. She felt like the baby in a Mardi Gras king cake.

Eventually something with teeth would get her.

"What's a Rak?" Now that she had a computer, any waking minute when she wasn't working at the morgue or running down VIPER leads Evalle spent studying websites Z and Quinn had given her. Still, her working knowledge of preternatural beings, supernatural abilities, entities and anything related was pretty limited compared to Quinn and Tzader's expertise.

"*Rak* is a slang term for a Rakshasas, a malevolent being or demon who can shift into any form, not just human," Quinn explained.

"Another *demon*?" Was it a slow news week? She could hear the six o'clock anchor now. *Alterant becomes dinner at demon convention. Film at eleven.* Three demons in ten days and two of them had been hunting for an Alterant. "What happened to the Rak?"

"He fled to Atlanta," Quinn told her. "The second thing the troll told us was that the Rak had left a cryptic message for a Belador. The Rak is the informant Tzader came back to Atlanta to meet with."

Yet another demon in Atlanta. Three in one day had to be a record. And this one had been looking for an Alterant, too.

Coincidences were for people with a normal life, not her.

The walls of her world started closing in, and for the first time in two years she had serious doubts over how much Tzader and Quinn could do to help her if someone was targeting Alterants . . . and knew where to find them. Them? Her.

But this many demons popping up in the southeast was not coincidental.

With the Tribunal breathing down her neck, Evalle needed anything this Rak demon could provide, like who knew how to find the Alterants. And maybe the origin of Alterants. Brina didn't know how to find or identify them in human form or she'd have captured the one in Charlotte before it had a chance to shift and kill Beladors.

Evalle's skin pebbled with excitement. This could be the key to providing the Tribunal with answers.

If anyone could pull information from a snitch, it was Tzader. Her gaze slid over to Tzader, who still hadn't said what had happened to the Rak.

She squeezed a hand full of beanbag, using it like a stress-relief chair. "Tell me you found this Rak guy, Z, and got the information you were after."

"Yes and no."

Not the answer she was hoping for.

NINETEEN

"What do you mean yes *and* no? Where is this Rak-demon-thing?" Evalle kept a lid on her frustration since it wasn't aimed at Tzader or Quinn, but what the hell!

When had she turned into the pinup girl for demons?

Tzader let out a sigh pumped full of frustration. "Here's the whole rundown. None of the trolls or Nightstalkers over in Charlotte had heard of an Alterant until the Rak mentioned it, because Brina has kept the handful of attacks in the past out of mainstream intelligence. The trolls also had no idea who had sent the Rak to Charlotte. The Rak offered a lot of flash that brought trolls out of every hole, but nothing surfaced on the Alterant until word got out about the Beladors killed."

Evalle ground her teeth. "The trolls *knew* he was looking for an Alterant? They could have told VIPER before we lost nine Beladors."

Quinn made a sound of disdainful humor. "That would require a conscience."

Tzader made a sound of disgust, then continued explaining. "Soon as the Rak heard about the Alterant killing Beladors then disappearing he knew he'd lost his prey and that his master would kill him for the failed mission. So the Rak left a coded message in Gaelic with the trolls, assuring them a Belador would pay well for it, then fled to Atlanta."

"You can understand Gaelic?" Evalle knew very little about Z and Quinn's history. When Tzader nodded, she tucked that new piece of knowledge away. She currently studied languages in her online classes, Gaelic being one.

She'd send her next email in Gaelic and surprise him. "What did the message say, Z?"

"The Rak wanted a deal to trade information on a Belador traitor for safe passage to a destination of his choosing. And the note explained how to find him in Atlanta. Quinn stayed in Charlotte to guard the troll until I found the Rak and made sure we hadn't been tricked."

Her nerves tightened at Tzader's heavy pause. "And?"

"I found the Rak, but he wouldn't tell me everything until I got an agreement from Sen to put him into VIPER's protective custody first."

"He had to be scared spitless to want to go into a VIPER holding cell," she muttered.

"He was." Tzader rubbed the back of his neck. His dark eyes showed long days of wear and tear. "All I had to do was tell Sen this guy had intel on Noirre majik, which the Rak said he could prove was being used in this area. Sen agreed to pull him in and protect him until we determined if he was lying or not. That's why I couldn't stay for the meeting yesterday."

She understood but would have liked to have had Tzader in the meeting to get his feedback on Storm, Adrianna . . . oh, and Isak, who Evalle had to find sooner than soon for any hope of figuring out who had sent the Birrn.

At this rate, if another demon showed up, she'd need a whiteboard to keep track of the players.

And what about the missing body in the morgue? Argh.

Tzader's voice flattened more with each sentence. "When I got back to the meet point for the Rak he wasn't there. I chased leads all yesterday, but he was running like a rat from one hole in Atlanta to another because someone else was after him. I figured his master had come for him, which would have worked for me if we'd caught him—or her—too. Quinn got in around eight last night. We teamed up and finally found the Rak just after nine."

"Where was he?" She looked from Tzader to Quinn, who took over explaining.

"In five pieces, stacked neatly inside a suitcase placed in the middle of an empty hotel room with a note that read 'Our company has a zero tolerance policy on traitors.'"

"So not funny." Evalle thought on it a minute. "What *did* he share with you when you first talked to him, Z?"

"This is where it gets screwy. The Rak said he had information on a Belador working with the Medb and knew why his employer was searching for the Alterant, but he wouldn't say until he was safe."

"Crud!" Evalle slapped the beanbag.

Feenix jumped up, wings flaring and pointed ears laid back in attack mode. Smoke whistled from his lips, which could shoot fire next.

Oo-kay. Note to self to up the Zen factor when living with gargoyles. She cooed to him. "Sorry, baby. I didn't mean to startle you."

Quinn laughed. "You think you frightened something that could blow a hole in the wall behind me?" He pitched a chunk of his Mr. Goodbar at Feenix. "Catch, boy."

Feenix snapped the chocolate bite out of the air.

"Don't feed him *that!*" She was going to strangle Quinn.

"You feed him *lug nuts* and you're worried about a little chocolate in his diet?" A laugh sputtered from Quinn's lips.

"Chocolate makes him fart, then I have to spend two hours in the shop working on my bike while the air clears, dammit."

"Yeth, dammit." Feenix nodded.

Tzader and Quinn both looked up. "He talks?"

"I'm teaching him a few things." She kissed his scaly head.

Feenix tucked his wings, then climbed out of her lap to waddle around the room saying, "Hello, one, two, three, fork, five, thix, dammit." After that he continued mumbling things that made no sense.

Evalle stabbed Quinn with a look of accusation. "But I hadn't wanted to add *that* word to his vocabulary."

Quinn lifted his hands in surrender. "I didn't tell you to curse in front of him. If he farts from chocolate, I can only image the piles of rusty poop he leaves from lug nuts."

"He absorbs the steel into his system. We blew a hole in the back of a closet that gives him a cave to hole up in when he needs his space. He's very tidy."

"Yeth, dammit." Feenix flapped his wings, then settled in the corner and started counting his toes. He had eight, but he only knew how to count to six so far, so he had to start over when he reached the extra two.

Tzader shook his head at her. "You take him outside again and he'll pick up an even more colorful four-letter word than *damn* to say for the number 'fork.'"

"I'll get earmuffs for the next time I take him over to Nicole's. She loves to see him, and Feenix likes riding the bike." Evalle wouldn't take Feenix around just anyone, but Nicole was a witch in Rowan and Sasha's coven, where some feared her because she had unusual gifts and a strangely lethal air about her. But her coven did not permit any black majik practice, and Nicole would never practice dark arts.

She was one of the most honorable and kind people Evalle had ever met. Maybe she'd always felt a kinship with Nicole *because* she was different even from other witches.

That Nicole treated Feenix like a prince made her even more special in Evalle's book.

"I don't want to know anything about you taking Feenix out in public at all or riding him around on a motorcycle." Tzader shook his head. "Let's get back to real problems. The Rak did confirm that someone from the Medb coven was working Noirre majik in the southeast and it had something to do with the Alterants."

"Alterants walking around free as in plural?" Evalle tapped her fingers against the beanbag. Was there any positive news to be had?

"Possibly." Tzader allowed another long pause, then looked her square in the eyes. "We'll have to inform Brina and VIPER about this."

She knew that look and tone but glanced at Quinn to confirm her guess. The unguarded worry in his angular face was answer enough that they were telling her not to share something with them that they would be forced to pass along.

Quinn cleared his throat. "We told you two years ago we'd always have a plan if it became necessary to get you somewhere safe, and this may be the time."

She started shaking her head. "You said I could never come back or be around either of you again. I can't do that."

"Evalle, darling, we don't want you to go away either," Quinn told her. "But we'll do whatever it takes to keep you safe *and* uphold our vows to the tribe."

Give up what little life she'd finally gained after twenty-three years of struggling? She'd fight first. But that meant not putting these two in a position of having to choose between her and the tribe. She wouldn't do that to any Belador, and these two meant more than all the other Beladors put together.

She *would* find a way out of this mess without putting Quinn or Tzader at risk. Or she'd suffer the consequences on her own. "I understand what you're saying, and you know how much it means to me that you would do this to keep me safe, but I have to try to find the answers. And I have to help find the Ngak Stone. If I can show my value to VIPER, maybe the Tribunal will give me some more time."

"What's going on with them?" Tzader's body tightened when he leaned forward, propping his forearms on his knees.

"Yes, what's this about *more* time?" Quinn shoved the recliner footrest down and sat up.

Evalle took a deep breath and let it out. "That's the part you two don't know yet. The window for me to leave has passed. Let me tell you about what's happened since I ran into Tzader yesterday." Since Quinn didn't have all the details, she explained about the mangled body in the morgue that was now missing, the Cresyl demons and the Birrn. She'd just finished telling them how she'd escaped before the police found her with the smoked Birrn demon, but stopped before she said anything about missing the meetings with Isak, when she noticed Tzader. He'd covered his face with his hands. "What, Z?"

"You said the shooter's name was Isak? Big guy with a super-weapon?"

"Yes. You know him?"

Tzader's jaw flexed. "Know *of* him. Isak Nyght. Runs a team of mercs called the Nyght Raiders. Former military from different branches, all special division Black Ops types. Isak has a source for the weapons, and some think he actually designs them. In the past, he and his men have been sent to investigate and deal with *unusual* situations, but on other continents."

Quinn frowned. "Unusual . . . like nonhuman?"

"Exactly."

Evalle kept her tone casual. "Is *Isak* human?"

"Yes, but he has an uncanny ability to find information and locate nonhumans." Tzader scratched his chin thoughtfully. "Based on the report from our people on the ground in Tehran, we're pretty sure the Nyght Raiders killed an Alterant that shifted into beast state."

The hairs along Evalle's neck danced with anxiety. Isak had killed an Alterant? "Does Brina know there's an Alterant Terminator running around?"

Bigger question . . . would it matter if Isak terminated Evalle?

Tzader lifted his chin in confirmation. "Brina knows about the Alterant Isak eliminated, but she stayed out of it because she isn't responsible for anyone outside her tribe. Isak is dangerous in a lot of ways, Evalle, but mainly because he's not on board with VIPER. We discussed it a few years back with a Tribunal and the consensus was that Isak wouldn't play well with any*thing* or any*one*. Steer clear of him."

That'd be a lot easier if she didn't need answers from Isak, but she couldn't tell Tzader and Quinn that without putting them in conflict with Brina and the tribe. Isak and his team had been familiar with the Birrn, maybe knew where it had originated or who had sent it.

The question was how much Isak had figured out about her if he was familiar with Alterants.

Evalle moved ahead and covered the VIPER meeting, which included the new members of the team, concluding, "Adrianna worries me, but Lucien should be able to keep an eye on her. I'm more concerned about Storm."

Quinn studied the ice melting in his glass. "I'll check into Storm and Adrianna. Wish I knew how Sen ended up in his position. He needs to be replaced."

She should be so lucky. "Like that's going to happen when none of us voted him *on* the island to begin with?"

"Sen's not going anywhere." Tzader made that statement in a dismissive tone. "Now, what the hell happened with the Tribunal? When we found Storm at the park tonight he said Sen had taken you to headquarters, but I figured it couldn't be anything serious, since he didn't contact me."

Storm hadn't told them about her going to the Tribunal?

She recalled the conversation right before Sen had teleported her. Sen hadn't said anything about the Tribunal in front of Storm, so Storm really hadn't known where she'd been going.

And Storm had let Tzader and Quinn know she'd been taken.

Why did that stir up a warm feeling in her middle?

Her conscience prattled at her to believe in Storm's good intentions, but Evalle had once paid a heavy price for believing in another man who had convinced her he was trustworthy. Sen had brought the shaman in for one reason—her. She had to keep that in mind.

Tzader glanced at Quinn, then at Evalle. "Well? Is the problem with the Tribunal worse than last time, Eve?"

She gave him a grim smile. "A Tribunal was called because another Alterant changed yesterday and killed a human."

"That's getting old," Tzader grumbled.

Tell her about it.

"Where?" Quinn put his drink down and crossed his arms.

"In Birmingham." Sen had told her that little bit just to let her know the attack had been only two hours west of Atlanta, in Alabama. "You know the standard procedure. They pull in the likely suspects. Oh, wait. That's right, there's only one. Me. Then they threatened to lock me away. Nothing new there."

"They can't do that without bringing in Brina. You *did* ask for her, right?" Tzader's smooth eyebrows dropped low over his intense gaze.

"Yes, I did. And, yes, she appeared. Eventually." Evalle took a breath, considering her words so as to prevent putting these men at odds with Brina. "Brina convinced the Tribunal to give me time to prove I'm not a threat to humanity."

Quinn shook his head. "You've been through this with them over and again. Why do they persist in dragging you in?"

"Because the Alterant that shifted this time was a female Alterant . . . and pregnant." She let that sink in for a second. "Now the Tribunal feels there's a precedent for not just a female shifting and killing, but the fear that other Alterants might seek me out to breed or that I might do that with something else, because, you know, you can't trust an Alterant."

If anyone knew that a doctor had raped her at fifteen, they'd realize the chances of her getting pregnant were close to zero if it meant allowing a man to do that again. But that was no one's business except hers, and that of the doctor she'd sent running in terror when she'd shifted partway into a beast.

He wouldn't have told anyone about what had happened with her even if he hadn't lost control of his car and died in a fiery crash that day.

She looked from man to man. "That's why your escape plan will only hang you with me, because VIPER will hunt me to the ends of the earth if I run. I have to beat this."

"We're going to help you." Tzader spoke the words, but Quinn's agreement was written all over his face.

"I think Isak may have some information on the Birrn." She broached the topic just to see what Tzader would say.

"Don't go near him. Farther you stay from him the better."

Shouldn't be much threat of running into him socially after standing the man up twice in twenty-four hours. But she needed to know what Isak had on that Birrn and hated to go hunting him without telling Z or Quinn, so she tried again.

"What if Isak has information on these demons? I could just talk to him—"

"No, you of all people shouldn't talk to him." Tzader's jaw muscles worked for a second as he thought. "Remember that Alterant Isak was suspected of killing in Tehran? The beast ripped his best friend in half. Isak *hates* Alterants. The number one mission for his Nyght Raiders is to track down every Alterant they can find and destroy them."

That gave her pause.

Did all Alterants have the same aura as hers? How was she supposed to protect herself when she'd never met another Alterant and had no idea where they'd originated? Had Isak seen the other Alterant's aura? Had it looked like hers?

The Rak demon had alluded to more Alterants. Was Isak only

playing along with her thinking she'd lead him to the others, then he'd kill her once he knew where they were?

She swallowed against the bile trying to run up her throat. If Tzader and Quinn thought Isak was a threat to her, they wouldn't leave her side while she helped search for the Ngak Stone. Isak would probably not come near her with Tzader and Quinn around. Or with Storm around.

But Isak was the only one with any possible lead on the demons and maybe even the Alterants.

Between Isak and Storm, it was a toss-up as to which one might be the more dangerous to her existence.

TWENTY

"The men are tired, Batuk." Sleep pulled at Vyan as he changed to clean jeans and a faded blue shirt with buttons, preparing for the first night of hunting for the Ngak Stone in Atlanta. The sun had vanished minutes ago. "The men need rest after the march through the jungle and the trip back here."

Batuk did not look up from where he sharpened his sword. "The men can sleep when we return home. We have less than two days until the full moon and no idea what woman the stone has chosen. We cannot rest until we find her and take the stone."

Thumping music shook the walls behind Vyan when a car rolled by outside. A common sound in the area known as West End, where he'd found this crumbling building that smelled worse than fresh camel droppings. Cobwebs wide as a blanket spread across the corners.

"I hate that noise," Batuk muttered. "Two more days in this world will be torture. We must find that stone. Our scouts should return soon with Nightstalkers."

Vyan held his tongue for a moment. He'd caught Batuk and Tristan talking secretly once during the trip, which removed any doubt Vyan had about how far he had fallen as the first in command in Batuk's eyes.

Had the Alterant monster and his warlord struck a new deal?

Vyan saw no point in talking in circles. Not with so little time left. "What is the plan when we have the Ngak Stone? Do we leave quickly or fight the Beladors?"

Batuk's face had not been shaped well for smiling. No humor

gathered in his eyes. "We shall leave as soon as Tristan has fulfilled his agreement."

"I thought sending us home *was* the agreement."

"As your leader, I have ensured we will never be at the Beladors' mercy again. When we return home, our ten will be powerful enough to slay any enemy. Then we will have none."

His warlord spoke the truth, but he hid something among his words. Vyan wrapped that away in his mind to look at later and see if he could unwind the lie hidden inside. He kept his voice soft to address his more important concern. "I'm not convinced Tristan can collect the stone without harming the woman."

"Tristan knows the stone could choose to destroy him if he killed the woman." Batuk's tone wavered some, giving reason to believe he was not so confident.

If not for endangering the woman, Vyan would enjoy watching Tristan pay the price for his arrogance. "He may be unable to control his actions or his power. The serum is not holding. Maybe it is because he is an Alterant. You saw what happened on the way back here when—"

"—you provoked him," Batuk finished. "I have little worry as long as you do not anger him *again*. Tristan will control himself." He walked away to where the men had begun stockpiling supplies they'd scavenged.

Vyan hid a knife in his boot in addition to the sword strapped to his side. He had a knee-length black raincoat for concealing it.

The access door to the building opened and Tristan strolled through. The cocky bastard was now dressed in a shirt the color of dark clouds tucked inside sleek sand-brown pants similar to clothes worn by the businessmen who scurried around this city during the day. White teeth glowed in the dim lighting when he smiled at Vyan.

A smile that said he knew something Vyan did not and the knowledge amused him.

Vyan noted Tristan's blond hair was both shorter and damp. "Where have you been?"

"Showering and locating decent clothes, since I have no intention of dressing . . . like you." A folded pair of dark sunglasses hung from where they were hooked at the neck of his shirt. Fancy eye covering that the Alterant had probably taken from an expensive shop, whereas Vyan wore a discarded pair of dark glasses he'd found.

But his were to hide his double pupil eyes from the public. Tristan wore eye covering as a king would don a crown.

"In my time, clothes were merely protection from the elements." Vyan had bathed in a lake and changed to the comfortable clothes he would miss when he returned to his time. Maybe he would pack a bag to take back. The strange clothing would bring good coin if the cloth survived traveling back through time.

"Dressing like a sheep herder is probably why I heard you had no woman with you when you were sent below Mount Meru, but then I guess it's a matter of so many sheep, so little time."

Vyan's heart thumped at the reminder of losing his wife, but he'd never let Tristan know he'd struck his mark. Instead, he answered the insult. "Yes, I was alone when I arrived beneath the mountain, which meant I had all the consorts I wanted while there, because they wanted only virile men. What I should have explained about clothes was that in *my* time, a *warrior* wore clothes only for protection, not to preen as a bird would. The *pretty* men who spent hours worrying over their face and clothes turned more heads of young men than women." Vyan smiled to punctuate his taunt.

Tristan stopped short, eyes glowing a hot green. His lips rippled with an unspoken snarl. He twitched, his head jerking to one side. His forehead jutted out with a loud snap, and his jaw extended down from the sharp teeth, which lengthened.

"Tristan, stop it!" Batuk ordered, rushing over to where they stood.

Tristan growled and clenched his fists. He twisted his neck, straining as his face cracked and distorted into jagged planes of skin over misshapen bones.

Batuk swung around to Vyan. "What did you say?"

"Me? Nothing. I merely complimented him on how nice he looked." Vyan crossed his arms and turned to face Batuk. "I told you when this happened the last time he could not be trusted alone. *Now* do you believe me?"

"I believe you are causing him to change." Batuk opened his mouth to say more, but Tristan spoke.

"Don't worry, I'm okay. Just a little tired."

Vyan turned to find Tristan once again perfect.

"That is understandable considering the past few days, but we will all rest tonight." Batuk swung his black gaze to Vyan. "Do not provoke him again."

Vyan started to argue further when the air cooled unnaturally without warning. His arms pebbled from the chill.

Batuk and Tristan straightened, alert and glancing around.

Two soldiers walked in. One said, "These are the only Nightstalkers we found so far that would leave their area."

A smoky figure, thin and shaky, appeared. The hollow eyes stared straight ahead as three more transparent figures floated into the room from different directions. Vyan's next breath slipped out in white puffs against the frigid air. None of the Nightstalkers acknowledged the existence of one another.

"Do you know what we want?" Batuk asked the translucent bodies floating in front of him.

"Yes. You want the woman with the Ngak Stone," one Nightstalker answered in a hollow voice that swirled around them. The others echoed his words.

"How will you recognize her?" Vyan asked them.

"She'll be glowing bright pink like the boots of a streetwalker," one ghoul answered. The other three nodded, which meant they were aware of each other.

"The first one to find her will shake with me for a full fifteen minutes," Batuk declared, offering an enticing trade. "But the one whose lead ends with us finding the Ngak Stone *and* taking possession will be rewarded with a twenty-minute handshake with both me and Tristan."

All four images quivered, blinking in and out with undisguised excitement over the exorbitant offer. Vyan disagreed with this, too, as he'd heard it was dangerous to shake longer than ten minutes or with two powerful beings.

What if Batuk and Tristan created monsters that turned on the Kujoo?

"Two of you go with me." After giving that order, Tristan headed for the door.

All the ghouls rushed after him in a blur and collided with each other in a mob of confused shadows until Tristan swung around and snarled. "Cease!" When the cloudy forms separated, he pointed as he spoke. "You and you, come with me."

Two ghouls whisked to hover above each side of Tristan when he walked out.

Vyan snatched his coat from where it hung on a nail, then stepped forward. "You other two come with me."

"I will remain here to meet with more Nightstalkers as they arrive," Batuk announced. "When the woman has been located, I will send someone to let you know."

Vyan paused at the door but did not turn around when he replied. "Have you no faith in *my* ability to find this woman?"

"On the contrary. I have no doubt you will find her. My concern is if you will bring her back."

That struck at his honor.

Vyan did not want to see the woman hurt, but gaining that rock was the only chance of saving his people and returning to a life he had once known and was quickly forgetting. This time he wanted a new life of spilling sweat as he tilled the land instead of watching other men's blood run.

"I have always given my best for you and my people," Vyan told Batuk. "I will give no less now." With that, he pushed through the door. Once outside, fumes belched from the metal cars, assaulting his nose. By all saints, he missed fresh air. He searched the streets until he saw Tristan striding along the opposite side.

Tristan paused at the corner to glance back with a look so full of challenge that he might as well have produced a gauntlet and tossed it at Vyan's feet, before vanishing around the side of the brick building with his two ghouls in tow.

So be it.

Tristan might have been born of this world originally, but Vyan had spent his last ten months learning Atlanta well. He would start his search in Piedmont Park, where he'd once held the stone during a battle with the Beladors before losing it in a small stream there.

Now he wondered if he had actually lost the powerful rock or if it had been choosing its path even then.

Neither Tristan nor Batuk had considered what kind of being the stone would call to it or how powerful the woman would be if she resisted giving up the magical treasure.

Vyan's powers were mighty, but he would lose a battle against Tristan if the Alterant shifted into a beast.

The woman would lose as well if that happened.

One of his ghouls became agitated. "The stone is revealed."

Vyan's blood pumped fast. "In the park?"

The ghoul shook with excitement. "Yes."

TWENTY-ONE

Evalle came ready to deal. But it had to be fast.

"What kind of trouble are you in to show up with *that* and to come out this early?" Grady's pale form hovered at eye level.

"Plenty." She sat six feet off the ground on the top of the concrete wall that backed up to the interstate embankment behind Grady Hospital.

Grady's gaze was stuck on the bottle of Mad Dog 20/20 clutched in her hand. She held a McDonald's bag in the other. She hated to give him alcohol when she'd rather just feed him, but it was hard to deny the old guy one small moment of happiness.

Rain drizzled off the bill of her Braves baseball cap. The storm that had rolled in at twilight to completely blacken the skies had given her a faster head start tonight, but she only had forty-five minutes until nine o'clock, when she had to meet Storm at the park.

"I'm waiting." Grady's eyebrows crawled up his forehead.

She tapped her little finger against the bottle. Monday night rush hour squealed, honked and banged a hundred yards behind her while it sounded as though the god of thunder, Taranis, played a solo backup overhead. "Okay, here's my offer, and I'll warn you right now I want quick answers."

"Then make a quick deal."

"I am not breaking down specifics. If you want a handshake *and* this bottle, I want any question I ask answered." She didn't demand, just laid out her cards face up.

Grady lifted his chin in his way of thinking and floated sideways into the embankment, then flickered back in front of her. "Things must be really bad."

Evalle didn't reply. The less she said, the better her chances were of getting a carte blanche deal, since Grady was one big mass of curiosity.

"All right," he said. "But only this one time."

Not a problem, because if she didn't figure out what to do soon, she wouldn't have a reason to make future deals. "Understood."

Evalle jumped down from the wall and landed on the sidewalk as Grady floated down to face her. After giving the area a fast once-over to ensure no one was paying attention to a woman in rain gear and soaked jeans standing in the dark, she extended her hand and connected with his.

"Damn, I hate the rain," Grady said as soon as he was a solid form. Water shed off him like it did off her GORE-TEX riding gear. "Hand it over."

"Have you found out who was controlling the Cresyl and Birrn demons?" She gave him the bottle and he twisted the top off and guzzled a three-finger slug of the cheap wine.

Lowering the bottle, satisfaction softened his face. "Not exactly, but I think it's someone who's in the city now."

"Why do you think that?"

"Because there was another demon here, a Hindu one."

Evalle nodded. "A Rakshasas. I heard."

"I think the same person is controlling all the demons."

"What or who could be doing that when all the demons should be originating from different power sources? I've never heard of such a thing before."

"Might not be specifically one power behind all of them but a partnership of some sort between two dark powers," Grady suggested.

She tilted her head to one side. "What would have caused two groups to join forces?"

Grady barked out a sarcastic laugh. "Oh, I don't know, maybe the bad guys decided to do their own recruiting when VIPER opened an ark for every weirdo with an extrasensory ability."

"Guess you've got a point." She hooked her thumbs into the corners of her rain slicker pockets. "We had someone tracking the Rak and his master, but the master got away and the Rak ended up repackaged in a suitcase. What do you think the chances are of finding his master?"

"Not good. Not if he's sending in demons to do his dirty work, and I'm betting those demons aren't the original forms but some kind of copies. Especially with that Birrn having Celtic markings. You need to find the source of the power for the demons to determine who the master is, but that's going to be hard to do when you've had a Nigerian demon with Celtic markings, a Cresyl demon that is German and now a Hindu Rak. No common denominator. If I *am* right and they're all being controlled by the same power, then they're being sent out with a glamour disguise to hide their true origin."

"A Fae glamour?"

"No. Some kind of witch spell that disguises the demon."

Witch, as in Noirre majik? She was back to her conspiracy-against-Evalle theories. "Crud. Can this get any more difficult?"

"In a word, yes."

That got her attention, because Grady hadn't been kidding. "Why? What else have you got?"

"An ancient synergy has entered the city."

She immediately thought of Vyan, the Kujoo she'd seen last night near the Iron Casket, which she'd forgotten to tell Tzader and Quinn about. Crap! That wouldn't have happened if Tzader hadn't gotten an urgent cell call from headquarters and taken Quinn with him when he'd left—and if she hadn't needed to catch up on two days of lost sleep so she could work tonight.

She'd have to start issuing hourly bulletins at this rate to keep the boys in the loop.

Evalle pushed her soaked ponytail off her neck. "You know the origin of this synergy?"

"Got an idea who." He paused for another libation break then said, "Remember that time a couple years back when you and those other two Belador hoodlums had a smackdown in Piedmont Park with a Kujoo?"

"Yes." She didn't even bust him for calling Tzader and Quinn hoodlums. Grady was confirming her worst fears.

"Same synergy this time, but much stronger."

The only reason the synergy would be stronger was if Vyan had found a way to bring more of his kinsmen forward in time. "I think you're right. Probably the Kujoo and they've come for a reason."

"I doubt VIPER'll be happy with the Beladors or the Kujoo if they have a showdown in the city again for no reason."

She wanted to tell Grady about the Ngak Stone, but there was a limit to how much she could share even if he had held her confidences in the past. She hedged, "I don't think the Kujoo are looking for the Beladors since that didn't go well with Shiva last time. But they're here for something. If you find out what, I need to know."

That was as close as she could get to telling Grady about the stone.

"I'm giving you something important about this synergy," Grady said in a quiet voice underpinned with need. "Maybe something worth more like an hour of solid time?"

She growled under her breath. "What has gotten into you? You know I can't give you an hour."

"Just one time, that's all."

"Why?"

Grady snapped his lips into a firm line.

She wasn't the only one with trust issues. "If you've got word on anything else going on, you *have* to give it up. We've got a deal."

"Let's see." He twisted his face into an exaggerated look of seriousness. "There's a Chattahoochee Faerie lifting trinkets from street vendors, the twin heathens are trying to make pigeons steal tip money off outdoor café tables, heard a troll and a ghost were squabbling over a stretch of dirt up under Spaghetti Junction . . ."

"Never. Mind." She didn't have time for squabbles about living under Atlanta's notorious interstate interchange. "I gotta go."

When she stepped away, Grady pressed, "I want that hour on Wednesday evening, Evalle."

That made her take another look at him. Getting one hour of human form was important to Grady, so she didn't blow him off with a wisecrack.

"If I could do it, you know I would, Grady. I'm the last person who can do something like that right now. And even if I could, I have no idea what it would do to you." She couldn't look in his sad eyes without her heart aching for him, but neither could she give him what he wanted without putting him at risk with VIPER. Or turning him into some kind of monster.

If she did try and Sen found out, his reaction was unpredictable at best.

She put her hand on Grady's forearm to stall him from lifting the bottle again. "I won't do something I think might harm you further and I won't pull you into my mess, which is what would happen if I got caught giving you an hour. I'll help you figure out whatever it is you're trying to do once this is over, okay?"

He stared at her for the longest time, then patted her hand in an understanding way. "That's okay. It'll wait."

She released his arm reluctantly and walked away.

Grady had just lied to her.

Whatever reason he had to want human form for an hour would not wait. But she'd help him the minute she got herself out of trouble, which wouldn't happen unless she found Isak. First she had to do her rounds with Storm in Piedmont Park.

Waste of time. Did VIPER really think the Ngak Stone was just going to be sitting there waiting on them?

And what would Grady give up for an hour of time in human form?

TWENTY-TWO

Storm leaned back against the stacked stone gate to Piedmont Park. He gazed through the misty air for a hellion on a motorcycle who had three minutes to show by nine o'clock if she intended to arrive on time.

A line of headlights cut a swath of light through the nighttime blanketing Atlanta's busy midtown streets. Tires shoved leftover rainwater up on curbs, but the thunderstorms had beaten August's heat into temporary submission.

Getting wet didn't bother him in the least, but he'd taken advantage of the rain to wear a poncho.

Nice cover for a weapon.

"Rainy night in Georgia, huh?" Evalle appeared on his right, walking up to him from the park instead of the street side, where he'd expected her. Figured.

He hadn't heard her approach, but he should have smelled her at least with his senses so sharp this time of night. Not as acute as when he took jaguar form, but sharper than a human's. "Plan to put in more than a half hour tonight, or you hanging out with Sen again?"

"That's a tough one. Teleport with the Grim Reaper or spend an evening playing truth or dare with you?"

Storm's lips twitched. "I haven't caused you to toss your cookies."

"There is that. Sad to admit I'd have rather worked the park with you last night." With her gunmetal gray riding jacket unzipped, her unusual silver navel ring flashed when the streetlight hit it.

"I knew you'd eventually see the bright side of partnering with me," he quipped.

212

"Yeah, right." She wiped water off her slender neck and shoved loose hairs under the ball cap. Every move was intended to reinforce her tough attitude and the ability to take care of herself, just as the midnight black sunglasses were meant to keep the world at a distance.

He didn't like the way she pushed him away.

What was it about a man that made him notice a woman who was prickly as a wet cat? Notice every little move she made, like the fact that she tried to hide her case of nerves around him. Call it raw instinct, but he had a strong inkling that it wasn't his powers *or* his association with Sen so much as his just being a man that was making her fidget with her zipper pull and avoid his eyes right now.

That made her even more intriguing.

He had some kind of contrary nature to want her, but want her he did.

She caught him looking at her and glanced around as if seeing the park in the pitch of night was interesting. "What've you heard from the team?"

"Lucien and Adrianna were here when I arrived. The only word I got out of him was short and crude." Storm paused while a couple walked out the gate huddled beneath an umbrella, hanging onto a taut leash being pulled by a bulldog. "Adrianna says there's Noirre majik in the city."

"I knew that."

Instead of asking Evalle why she hadn't shared her knowledge of the Noirre activity, he just raised an eyebrow at her defiant posture and tone before continuing. "She also said the Birrn demon was controlled by Noirre—" He held up his hand when Evalle looked ready to claim knowing that, too. "And that the Noirre is Celtic in origin."

Evalle's eyes widened.

Got you there. Storm added, "You didn't get a chance to see last night, but the creek under the walking bridge at the south end of the park was dug up. The landscape crews finished clearing the creek today and most of the work is completed. We think the stone has already been found."

"Crud. It might not even be in the city anymore."

"Sen talked to Shiva, who only confirmed the Ngak Stone was still here *and* close to the park."

"*If* we can believe Shiva," she said softly.

"Even though the gods and goddesses are capable of lying with impunity, Sen indicated that Shiva seemed worried about something to do with this stone, though he offered little else."

"What'd Shiva say that gave Sen the impression the god was concerned?"

"He said the stone might not have ended up in the intended hands."

"Why can't he just say who has it? Is there a penalty clause for gods giving a straight answer?" Evalle slapped the side of her hip, which was covered by a pair of jeans molded to her shapely lower half.

He wished she hadn't pulled his attention down there. Forcing his eyes back to her face, he said, "I have no idea. Until we're told differently, we're still hunting a powerful female, so you ready to roll?"

"You going to be able to see in the dark areas without a monocular?" She turned to stride ahead, always wanting to take the lead.

He let her this time. "I can see." Actually, he could see the sway of her hips exceptionally well and could navigate the dark areas of the park just fine, but his sight, like his sense of smell, would be sharper in jaguar form. Animal energy prickled beneath his skin, wanting to break out and change shape so he could slip through this park as a practically invisible predator. He didn't feel pressure to change because of the upcoming full moon. He was part Ashaninka Spiritwalker and part Navajo Skinwalker, not a lycanthrope.

No, the urge came at dark, period. He fought the pressure to change the minute the sun set every day, but he had control over that urge even if his body wanted to argue just now.

He hadn't encountered any real difficulty for the past seven months or he wouldn't have left the backcountry of Chile to come around civilization.

The urge to shift was eating at him and he'd bet it was that vixen striding ahead of him. Not just any female, but that one. Something as simple as a woman's scent would get under a man's skin to make him want one particular female, and nothing Storm did would stop his body from reacting anytime this one was near.

The animal inside of him wanted her or wanted out.

He couldn't allow his control to slip. Not even for a woman that fine. She'd only get in the way of his mission to find his father and get both their souls back.

"What'd you find out on the Birrn?" Evalle asked, tossing a look his way over her shoulder as she made her way around the north end of the park.

"You mean besides that you were there and a Cresyl was involved?"

She paused and stared into the darkness for one second, two, three. "Sen doesn't know."

Not a question, just a confirmation.

He could withhold the information, but he wouldn't make her work for this. "No. I didn't tell him."

She continued on, weaving her way around the base of old oak trees that hovered over the park protectively. After another gap in the conversation, she asked, "You wouldn't know anything about a female body missing from the morgue, would you?"

"The female victim who had been mauled was gone when I got there. Anything you want to tell me about that particular body?"

"I don't think so." She picked her way as carefully as she chose her words. Pushed hair behind her ear. Nervous move. "You track the Birrn to anything or anyone . . . else?"

"I found where the Cresyls were killed. The fear and pain lingers. A third demon entered the city. Not sure what it was other than Hindu in origin. When I found that demon, he'd been tortured and cut up into pieces."

She stopped about fifty yards from the footbridge at the south end of the park and turned to him. "I heard about a Rak demon that was cut up and left in a suitcase."

"I'm not familiar with Raks, but that sounds like the one I found."

"Did you pick up anything on the Rak's killer?"

"I tracked him for all of a half mile, and the trail disappeared in a MARTA subway station. He must have teleported at that point for me to lose him."

Crossing her arms, she stopped again and stared off into infinity. Debate played through her eyes. She glanced up at his face and he saw her dilemma.

Share information, or not?

He waited for her to come to a decision.

Her fingers tapped against the rain slicker. She gazed off into the distance. "Okay, this is what I have. I talked to a Nightstalker tonight who thinks the demons are all controlled by one source or by two that are working together."

Storm kept his surprise hidden that Evalle had actually shared anything. "Unfortunately, that doesn't narrow the field much."

"Except when you add in the Noirre majik." The bill of her cap swung around toward him, bringing her dark glasses almost eye level with him. He liked a woman with substance. Evalle was tall and tough. They matched physically, and noticing that little detail only sharpened the edge on his frustration.

What had they been talking about? Noirre majik. "Isn't that Celtic?"

She shook her head, water flying off her cap. "Not always, but there's one major source of Noirre that is Celtic."

"I don't know much about that history."

"There's Celtic history that is *known,* then there's the history that is only known by Beladors," she began. "I'll tell you what is not necessarily common knowledge but known by more than just the Beladors. There was a witch way back in the thirteenth century known as Medb, though some knew her by other names. She had a daughter called Findabair, who was sent to one man, then offered to a bunch of other men. Supposedly seven hundred men lost their lives when a war broke out over her virginity lost in the wrong bed, and Findabair died of shame just after that."

"Another war fought over a woman, huh?"

"Not the first time men used the little brain to make a big decision. You want this history lesson or not, Storm?"

"Since you make learning a real joy, continue."

Her finely cut lips pulled taut. "Back to the how, there are two versions of history. Another story circulated about Findabair says that while she was dying of shame, a druid named Cathbad found her and asked if she wanted to live. But Cathbad was a sly one. He'd actually been sent by Findabair's mother, Medb the witch, to get a child from her that she could raise in secret."

"I thought the Medb was a coven of witches."

"Are you listening? Did you have to go through remedial shaman classes?"

Storm couldn't help himself. Annoying Evalle brought out the color in her cheeks.

"There was a powerful witch named Medb from which the Medb coven developed." Evalle composed herself in her next breath. "Got it now?"

"Got it. But the druid broke the deal by letting Findabair die."

"No, Findabair didn't ask how *long* she would live. Just like witches and any other being, druids are not all good or all evil. He brought the baby to Medb, who wanted to create a Medb coven of witches and warlocks for the sole purpose of destroying all Beladors."

"Why?"

"Long story, but the Medb coven believes the island where our warrior queen Brina lives is rightfully theirs."

"Where's that?"

"I can't tell you exactly."

Storm wanted to keep her talking. "Based on just the Beladors I've met, it doesn't seem like the Medb coven has fulfilled their duty of wiping out the Beladors."

"They came very close when Brina's family was destroyed. She's supposed to be the last descendant of the Treoir family, which has always been the keeper of the Belador power on earth. Beladors draw their power from the Isle of Treoir, which is hidden somewhere in the mist over the Irish Sea, but only as long as a Treoir family member lives on the island. That's why Brina can't leave and only shows her face in a hologram-type form. If the Medb coven ever figure a way to take that island, or to kill Brina before she has a child, they will hold our power by the short hairs."

"So you think the Noirre majik in Atlanta is tied to the Medb?"

"Maybe. That's the only form of Noirre that I've ever heard of that's Celt in origin, but I'm not as well schooled as other Beladors."

He considered the last demon he had found dead. "You think the Rak killer was connected to the Medb?"

"I don't know. Whoever killed the Rak demon can teleport, but I didn't think the Medb could disappear without leaving a power trail."

He couldn't figure this woman out. She'd held onto her thoughts tighter than a banker to his wallet . . . until now. "Why are you finally telling me any of this?"

"Isn't it obvious after Sen zapped me out of here last night?"

Was that a trick question? "No."

"You say you aren't here just to help Sen put me away. I'm thinking either you are and you already know some of this, or you aren't working with him, in which case I need you to know enough to be able to help . . . "

"To help what?"

She wouldn't look at him when she whispered, "Me."

Even after a couple years spent in isolation from much of the world, Storm knew when he was being given an olive branch of trust. This woman wouldn't extend faith easily or often, so when she offered anything, a man should pay attention.

The problem was that *he* couldn't afford to be responsible for that trust, and neither could he tell her why.

Letting her think she could gamble on him was a mistake. The best thing he could do was help her and the VIPER team find that damn rock, then rework his deal with Sen, which would piss off Sen.

Piss off Sen or Evalle?

Sen would smoke him.

But Evalle would lose her war with Sen.

Storm couldn't find the person he had come here to hunt down if he gave Sen reason to pull him off the southeastern team. Neither could he do anything for Evalle if that happened. Getting any closer to her than a teammate wouldn't do her any favors with Sen either.

Keeping his tone brisk, Storm asked, "Why do *you* need help?"

She turned those dark glasses on him, and even with that separation he could feel the power of her focus. The strength that lay behind that plastic shield. Her scent steamed off her when she generated any power like she was doing right now, while she tried to decide just what she could say without showing any more vulnerability than she had already.

The urge to reach out with his power and comfort her rose up inside him, but she'd bow up if he did that again. Too much pride to allow anyone to protect her. If she didn't back off the power that was spinning around her he'd have to do something soon. Like put his arms around her. That'd get his clock cleaned. "Look, Evalle, I can't help you if I don't know what I'm looking for."

She dipped her head and the power fell away.

Thank the spirit gods. Storm drew a breath, unaware he'd been holding his.

"Sen wants me off the team."

"Then leave."

She gave a wry laugh. "Not that easy. My existence depends on remaining with VIPER. Didn't he fill you in on Alterants?"

"I heard about the ones that have shifted and killed. I know he thinks you're hiding something from him." Storm wanted to smile when her lips parted in surprise. She had a damn nice mouth. "I know he thinks you're lying to him sometimes, which we established last night was credible."

That flattened her lips across clenched teeth. What would it be like to see her eyes fire up with passion for once?

"What else do I need to know, Evalle?" He had to get moving, away from her preferably, or he wouldn't keep his hands to himself with her putting out anxiety waves like a cornered animal. He had no choice but to push her a little more. "You're the one who asked for help. What's the deal with being an Alterant? What makes you special?"

That shoved the last bit of her rancor over the edge. "Just freakin' forget I said anything." She started past him.

He caught her by the arm.

She swung around and ripped her glasses off with her free arm. Her eyes glowed a brilliant green. Not anything like what he'd seen in the truck when they'd ridden to Atlanta from VIPER headquarters. "Take a good look. This is just a *little* pissed off. The really nasty side comes out if I shift, which Sen thinks I'm already doing anyhow

219

and just keeping it hidden. The minute he has proof I'm a threat to humans, a Tribunal will lock me in a cage where no one will ever find me. That's what he brought you in for. Take your hand off me before you lose it."

Her body shook beneath his fingers.

He understood anger that raw and painful. It came from deep within when everything in your world was beyond your control. Storm's jaguar wanted to come out and kill whatever threatened her, wanted to roar at the anguish buried inside each of her sharp breaths and force the world to stop hurting her.

When he ran out of choices, he kissed her.

TWENTY-THREE

Evalle had prepared herself for any reaction from Storm when she yelled at him and showed her glowing green beast eyes, but his kissing her had not been one of them. A rush of shock stole her ability to think or react. Then she only thought about how his lips were soft for someone with hard corded muscle beneath the skin where she clutched his arm.

He hadn't touched her anywhere except her lips.

She, on the other hand, had her fingers wrapped around his arms. Holding on was sending the wrong message.

Allowing him to continue kissing her was sending a way wrong message. She let go.

He lifted his mouth from hers.

She remembered to breathe again. Noticed the rain still misting. Remembered they were in Piedmont Park, where thankfully few humans visited late on a Monday night. When she met his gaze, she expected a look of apology, but she didn't see an ounce of regret. Before she could stop herself, Evalle licked her lips.

He looked away sharply and released a morose laugh that sounded half sigh. "Don't do that unless you want me to keep kissing you."

His laughing at her dumped cold water on whatever brain lapse had caused her to stand still like an idiot and allow him to kiss her at will. She'd never let anyone get that close to her face since the night the doctor had hurt her.

Why had she let Storm get away with that?

Because he'd surprised her before she'd been able to think to stop him. Because he hadn't put his hands on her. And once his mouth had touched hers, she hadn't wanted him to quit kissing her.

She was treading in dangerous waters with this man.

Hormones might do her in before her remaining lies buried her.

She stepped back, pulling away from the gentle blanket of his heat, which had wound around her senses. "Why'd you kiss me?"

He angled his head thoughtfully. "I could tell you it was because you're pretty, which you are, or because I want you, which I do. But the truth is I don't like seeing you upset."

"I want you"? As in . . . She wasn't even going to touch that part. In fact, she was in so far over her head in this conversation she'd need a floatie if she didn't get out of it. "I was angry, not upset."

The smile that spread across his face called her on the lie.

She huffed at him. "What*ever* you perceived my emotional state to be, that does *not* give you permission to kiss me whenever you want."

He took a step, closing the distance between them to an inch.

She stood her ground in spite of her feet itching to back up—a smarter part of her body than her hands, which itched to touch him. Well, hell, she might need a whole armada of floaties to save her at this point.

Storm shoved his hands into his jeans pockets and dropped his head close to hers. "I won't ever do that again *if* you can tell me you didn't enjoy it *and* make me believe it."

How did she get herself in trouble like this? Telling him the truth—that she'd never been kissed, not in a sweet way like he'd just done—would get her in as much of a jam as trying to convince him she hadn't enjoyed it. "I don't have to tell you anything, and we need to get back to work."

There was that chuckle again, but this time genuine humor spread across his face and reached his gorgeous eyes for several seconds before he turned all business again. "We'll get back to work then. You wanted my help, so tell me about Alterants."

She wished she could read his mind and know what to believe about him. Know if he could be trusted.

When she didn't answer him, he said, "What if I told you we have more in common than not?"

The adrenaline jamming her body from that kiss began to back off so she could think more clearly. Allowed her to breathe again. "I don't see how you and I could have anything in common."

"Let's make this simple and stop beating around the bush. You have your secrets and so do I. I told you I'm not Sen's puppet, but that's all I can tell you about why I'm here. It's up to you to decide if I'm lying or not. If you want my help, ask for it. If I say I'll do something, I will, but that's not a promise I'll say yes to everything you ask, or that our ideas of what it means to help will always coincide. That's the best I can do."

"Did you give Sen the same agreement?"

"Yes, I did."

If he'd taken his time to answer or tried to convince her otherwise, she wouldn't have believed him. Agreeing to share her situation with him didn't mean she trusted Storm completely, but she needed someone who could help other than Tzader and Quinn. She would not put them at risk. "I can work with that."

"Then tell me what the problem is or what you need from me."

She gritted her teeth at the idea of giving him all the evidence Sen would need to hand her over to the Tribunal. Would Storm use what she told him against her, or would he really help her? She was running out of time and there was only one way to find out. "Someone sent three demons into Atlanta looking for an Alterant, and I'm the only one here. I need to find out who is behind the Birrn that attacked me and if it's connected to the Ngak Stone in any way."

"You're sure the demons were after an Alterant?"

"No, I don't have enough real drama. I'm making the demon attacks all about me." She'd gladly give up the spotlight to someone else.

"What makes you think the demons that have shown up in Atlanta are connected to the Ngak Stone surfacing in the park?" Storm asked.

"Too many coincidences add up to a possible connection. For one thing, I ran into a Kujoo the other night, the one called Vyan that Trey was talking about in the VIPER meeting."

"Why don't you tell me about this Vyan while we work our way through the park?" Storm took the lead through the dark.

He moved with the agile grace of a big cat, as if at home in the night. Did he have exceptional vision, too?

Evalle put her sunglasses back over her eyes before he reached one of the paved roads lined with streetlights that dissected the park. She kept an eye out to make sure no one was near them when she continued. "Vyan was trying to grab two teenagers the other night and I intervened."

"How'd you get involved?"

"One of the teens he was after is a street kid, a male witch I don't want to see end up as a demon Snackable. The other one is the sister of a demigod. But here's the odd thing. When I stopped Vyan from taking them, I had the weirdest feeling he was glad I kept the kids out of his hands." That empathic ability she'd been sensing might have given her that insight now that she thought about it.

Striding at a comfortable pace, Storm shook his head. "That makes no sense."

"Tell me about it, *and* Vyan actually told me to read them the fairy tale about Hansel and Gretel. Like he was trying to let me know a witch was planning to use them for a blood sacrifice, which fits with Noirre majik. And here's the other surprise—he didn't at least try to battle me."

"I thought Trey said this Vyan was allowed to walk away free if he didn't battle a Belador."

"Few people consider me a true Belador, so that shouldn't have stopped him. I doubt Shiva would hold him to that agreement when it came to an Alterant."

Storm had reached the steps leading down a ten-foot drop to the south end of the park when he paused and studied her. His eyes logged some thought he didn't share before turning to take the steps two at a time.

She wished she had Trey's exceptional ability to read anyone's thoughts. He was one of the strongest telepaths among the Beladors. Storm would probably catch her snooping around in his mind if she were bold enough to try. She'd love to know just what was going on beneath all that black hair, what gave his coal-black eyes both a contemplative and a hungry look at the same time.

The rain picked up from a bare drizzle to a light shower, running even the most die-hard dog owners from the park. Evalle started to chide Storm over not even bringing a hat to block the rain from his eyes when she caught a movement on her left about fifty feet away.

"What the heck is that?" she mumbled to herself.

Storm turned to follow her line of sight.

The figure of a distorted old man limped through a wide space between two tall pine trees. The man's body flickered in and out of view as though he couldn't hold a shape of any kind.

Evalle took a couple of steps. Her boot scuff must have spooked the thing. He lifted off the ground, floating around with his head and shoulders solid.

His eyes were demon red. Sharp teeth came into view when his lips pulled back in a snaggletoothed snarl.

She spoke softly to Storm. "He looks like a Nightstalker I've done business with." Thankfully, it wasn't Grady.

"Thought they were harmless ghouls."

"They are. Something has happened to that one."

The ghoul flew toward them.

Evalle lifted her open palms shoulder high and shoved outward, tossing a short blast of power that knocked the ghoul backward.

The thing howled, but the sound had no volume. He jerked and shook, looking around with crazed eyes. When his body dropped to the ground still half formed, he turned and ran away faster than she'd expected.

She watched where the ghoul entered the woods. "I have to find out what happened to him. Somebody shook hands with that ghoul too long or put a spell on him when they shook or . . . I have no idea what they did, but he can't run loose. He looks dangerous. I'll check it out."

"No."

"One of us has to catch him before he hurts a human, and we both know Sen doesn't want you to leave me alone with the Ngak Stone."

Storm gave her one of his studied looks. "Would you pick up the stone if you found it?"

"No. I'd call Tzader."

"I believe you. You've seen the stone and I haven't, which means it makes more sense for you to walk the south end of the park and see what you can find out. I'll track down the ghoul. If you find the stone before I get back, we're out of here early." He swept a quick glance around them, then his eyes came back to her. "Close your mouth unless you're trying to catch rainwater."

She was speechless. Was he really leaving her alone to hunt for the rock? She had no quick comeback, which didn't matter since she was staring at his back as he vanished into the thick woods. Swinging around, she headed across the huge expanse of grassed area where people came to hang out and play during daylight.

Not right now, though, on a weekday night with the steady rain churning dense humidity.

She turned toward the creek where the Ngak Stone had been lost two years ago. To the right of the footbridge crossing the creek was another stretch of open space that butted up to Tenth Street. Not a soul in sight, human or otherwise.

A dog barked.

Evalle stopped and searched through the drizzle where the street-lights couldn't reach.

A young woman in a poncho was squatted next to the footbridge, searching the bank of the creek for something. She stood up and gave a little tug on the leash for her mutt, who danced around her feet. "I see you, Brutus, yes, I do."

Human. Not a concern.

Evalle had decided to ignore the young woman when a flush of energy swept the air around her face. She searched the night and found the culprit.

Vyan, the Kujoo, emerged out of the blackness and approached the woman. He asked, "May I speak to you?"

The young woman froze with one hand clenching her dog's tether and the other hand stuffed in the pocket of her parka—holding pepper spray? "No. Please don't come any closer."

Evalle kept her power leashed to prevent Vyan from sensing her presence. She could understand how Vyan saw in this darkness, since he'd have some form of preternatural sight, but how was that human woman getting around without a flashlight?

"I mean you no harm," Vyan said.

"What do you want?" the woman asked.

"I want to warn you. Someone is coming who *is* a danger to you."

Evalle studied the woman closer this time. Nothing radiated from her body that would indicate anything other than human, so this might have nothing to do with the Ngak Stone.

Was Vyan trolling for bodies again like he'd been doing outside the Iron Casket the other night? Was someone forcing him to do that against his will so he tried to warn people in advance?

The possibility loomed in Evalle's thoughts, but she couldn't let him hurt a human, intentionally or otherwise.

And this might be a lead on the Ngak Stone.

"Who are you? I've never met you." The woman pulled her free hand out of her pocket when her dog ran around her legs. She reached down to grab his collar and missed twice.

Was she blind? That would account for no flashlight.

"I am a stranger. My name is Vyan, but I do not want you harmed."

"Then we're on the same page, Skippy." The woman managed to untangle her dog from her legs and straighten up.

"You must leave this park now."

"Are you threatening me?"

Vyan continued in a nonthreatening tone. "No, that's what I'm trying to explain. You have to—"

A whip of bold energy raced across the park, slapping Evalle's exposed skin. She swung toward Tenth Street, easily locating the source. Striding toward the woman and Vyan was a statuesque man with a gorgeous face and light hair. He wore jeans and a button-down shirt.

Who was this guy?

He also wore a pair of sunshades, hiding something about his eyes. The air literally buzzed as he approached.

Considering how her luck had been rolling in the crapper lately, Evalle figured that would be demon-red eyes hiding behind his sunglasses.

Vyan stepped between the woman and the new guy. "Do not come closer, Tristan."

"Get out of my way, Kujoo."

Ah, crud. These two knew each other. Evalle blew out a breath and started toward them from the side. They were not harming a human on her watch.

Tristan whipped a hand at Vyan and a blue strike of power lashed across Vyan's shoulder. He yelled in pain.

The girl shrieked. Her dog barked wildly, then she turned mute. Fear would do that.

Vyan recovered his footing and drew a wicked sword from inside his coat. "You'll have to kill me to get to her."

"As I'm a generous man, I'll grant your wish," the one called Tristan answered, chuckling.

What was this all about? Evalle shoved a wall of power at this Tristan guy and he stumbled sideways.

Then he jerked his head around at Evalle.

Vyan noticed her then, too. "See what you've done?" he told Tristan.

"What's going on, Vyan?" Evalle asked.

"Get out of here, Belador," Vyan said. "I have no quarrel with you."

"Belador?" Tristan said the word as if he'd found something he'd been looking for a long time. Something he wanted to mount the head of.

Evalle opened her channel to the Beladors. *Trey, Tzader, Quinn, get to Piedmont Park. Now.* To Tristan she said, "Stand down or I'll have to hurt you."

The bastard laughed as if he hadn't heard anything that funny in decades. "First I get to kill Vyan then I get play time with you? And here I thought it was going to be a boring night." He ignored her and switched his attention to Vyan. "Move or die. Now."

Vyan turned to the woman, who stood shell-shocked still, and told her, "Run and get rid of that rock."

Rock?

The woman didn't move.

Tristan sent another blast at Vyan that knocked him back into the woman.

Evalle rushed forward and stepped in front of Vyan, blocking

Tristan's next attack with a wall of energy. She turned to see the woman pull a glowing stone from her coat pocket.

The Ngak Stone. Holy crud.

Vyan had fallen at the woman's feet and across her dog's leash, pinning them to the spot. He moaned. Blood ran from his shoulder and his leg.

Tristan roared and slammed Evalle's power field with another shot of hot energy, rocking her backward. If she let her guard down he'd get to Vyan, her and the woman. Had to get that woman and the rock out of here right now.

She could only hope Storm was heading back this way and would intercept the woman if Evalle sent her to him. Evalle told the woman, "Put the rock down and run toward the steps over there."

The woman looked at her with bright eyes that weren't blind. She mumbled, "I just want to go home."

Poof. No woman. No Vyan. No stone.

That just left Evalle with one pissed-off Tristan thing.

TWENTY-FOUR

E valle couldn't believe what had just happened. She was positive
that woman standing in this park a minute ago with the Ngak
Stone was human.

How could that be?

The roar of fury coming at her meant someone else was just as surprised and didn't like surprises.

The man Vyan had called Tristan strode arrogantly across the open
stretch of turf toward her, splashing puddles of water. He flung strikes
of blue hot energy up against the field of power she struggled to hold
in place against his onslaught.

What was this guy? And why did she feel a buzz in the air? If he
was a sorcerer, he'd have dealt with Vyan and pulled the woman to
him, so this Tristan had no majik ability.

Maybe. No absolutes in her world, not when the being was
unidentified.

Evalle stood a better chance in battling this guy one-to-one rather
than just holding up a field of energy. With the rain now coming
down in sheets across the park she might have an advantage with her
speed and agility.

She shoved a wall of power at Tristan that knocked him backward
and gave her a chance to come around into a fighting stance. "Just
what *is* a Tristan?"

"The last thing you'll see alive," he told her in a voice promising
pain as a prequel to death. Then he attacked, rushing at her with
arms raised to slam her.

She kinetically hooked her hands around him and fell backward, using his momentum to toss him over her head, high into the air and crashing down onto the end of the footbridge.

Sen would have to deal with the wrecked bridge.

Tristan rolled to his feet, unfazed. He called out, "Get over here."

"Does that work with other women?" Evalle quipped. "Not so much with me."

"Wasn't talking to you." He lifted his chin, and she realized he was talking to someone else when he said, "Get her."

Evalle swung around just as two hideous half-human-half-ghoul forms flew at her. Things that looked like the demented ghoulish thing Storm had followed.

She slammed her boot heel against the ground, and blades shot out from the sides. Waiting until the ghouls were close enough to catch, she swept her arm wide from side to side. The wave of kinetic energy she dragged across the ghouls knocked one into the other, tumbling them into a pile of writhing arms and legs.

A part of her registered that these had to be old Nightstalkers she'd probably spoken with in the past, so she didn't use her blades to cut their throats. Once she'd dealt with this Tristan character she'd have to call Sen before these two ghouls revived.

Facing Tristan again, she found him sitting casually on the edge of the footbridge railing, one foot propped on a crossbeam, as if waiting on someone to hand him a beer. "What have you been doing to Nightstalkers?"

He didn't say a word.

She took a step toward him and a spike of pain shot into the back of her calf. Evalle fell to her knees. She looked over her shoulder to see one of the ghouls dragging himself toward her with a long fingernail sticking from his finger like a sharpened blade.

Her sympathy for the insanely half-dead flew out the window.

"You shouldn't have done that." She shoved up to her feet, took two steps and cut his head off with a kick of her boots. Turning to the second one, she warned, "Move and I'll quarter you."

The other poor thing quivered and backed up into a ball of fear, huddling against the downpour.

When she wheeled around to Tristan this time, *she* wanted blood. "You're mine."

"I've never been one to disappoint a lady." He jumped down from his perch, gripped his hands as if he had an invisible bat and swung at her.

Her leg throbbed, but she waited until the last minute to dive sideways and roll.

His blast of power disintegrated the remaining ghoul into tiny microscopic pieces the rain dispersed. That had probably been his true target for his first time at bat.

She raced at him from the side before he got to take a second swing.

He spun, using his kinetics to block, but she wasn't a standard-model Belador he could take down with the usual kinetics. At least, not when she was one hundred percent. She'd make him pay for the ghoul cutting her leg.

When she was close to him, she swung around on her good leg and used the bad one to punch through his wall of power.

Didn't happen.

She bounced back as if hitting a wall of stone, landing on her injured leg.

What in the heck *was* this guy? Evalle sucked in a breath and raised her head to get back up.

His body slammed her back into the mud and held her there. He didn't tower over her, but he did have her by four inches and more muscle.

She was on her back, staring up at him. A scream buried deep in her mind came roaring up. She clenched her teeth to keep from letting it out. The memory of being held down and brutalized raced forward with the burgeoning scream, threatening to blind her with panic.

The bastard on top of her was at least winded, chest heaving with a labored breath. "Now we can talk."

"Get. Off. Now." She could only speak in short bursts or the terror would break free.

Never show an enemy a weakness.

Never let a man hurt her again.

Never let one live who did.

This one weighed as much as her couch, but she'd shifted and terrorized the one who had raped her at fifteen and could do worse now.

She shook with the need to shift into a stronger being and protect herself. Blood slammed against the walls of her skin. Her brain tried to warn her to calm down, but the fifteen-year-old who'd screamed in pain burst from the black hole she'd been hiding in all these years.

"Last. Chance," she panted, scrambling for each breath.

"What you going to do?" He shoved his hips against her and she lost all conscious thought.

"This, you bastard!" Cartilage broke free in her arms. Her neck snapped with the first sign of shifting. She let a roar out and kinetically tossed him up and backward fifty feet. He hit the footbridge for the second time tonight, taking down another chunk of it.

Tristan gained his feet and shook his head. His shoulders bunched when he yanked his neck, popping a few muscles of his own. "What the fuck are you?"

That broke through the haze of adrenaline spike and wave of terror to make her look at her hands, where her wrists had split the cuffs of her jacket. Oh, God, oh, God. She had to get her beast under control.

All of a sudden, her sunglasses flew off her face.

Evalle looked up and flicked her hand at him without a second thought, slapping the glasses off his face.

Glowing green eyes swirled like molten stones.

Green eyes unlike anything she'd ever seen before . . . except in her bathroom mirror.

"Alterant?" He said the word with disbelief packed full of deadly suspicion.

TWENTY-FIVE

"A lterant?" Evalle echoed back at the man called Tristan, just as much in shock.

Here was a man with the unusual physical strength and luminous green eyes of an Alterant.

"Where'd you come from?" Tristan asked, stepping away from the damaged footbridge that made Piedmont Park look like a small war zone.

"Why? You putting together an Alterant reunion website?" Evalle wasn't telling someone with his powers anything about herself, but she had to keep him talking. Find out anything she could about the first of her kind she'd ever met.

"Vyan said you were Belador. Why'd he think that?" Tristan took a couple of steps forward.

"Stop right there." Surprisingly, he did. "I *am* a Belador."

"They don't take Alterants into the tribe."

Scarcely a few minutes had passed, but every second of holding his attention became more precarious. Where was Storm? Why couldn't she reach Tzader or anyone else telepathically? Was that strange buzzing she could almost hear a cloaking spell? Had someone placed a spell over the park that prevented her from communicating with anyone?

Did that mean he had majik ability, or was he working with a witch? "I'm proof the Beladors take Alterants into the tribe. I'll ask if they're taking applications."

"Brina took one look at me five years ago and stuck me in a jungle in a spellbound cage."

Five years. Almost as long as she'd been a Belador. "You escaped? When?"

"Yesterday."

"How?"

"Like I'm going to tell you so you can tell the rest of the Beladors?" His eyes brightened with a thought. "Wait a minute. You're Evalle."

Worry scattered along her nerves. How did he know that? For once, shock had stolen her voice. She held quiet rather than confirm or deny.

"I heard about an Alterant called Evalle. A *female* Alterant. I didn't believe it was true."

Few in Atlanta's hidden world of the strange and supernatural did. She'd caught something speculative running along beside his words, a soft sound that harbored dark thoughts.

"This changes everything," he muttered.

She didn't like the sound of that either, since change would probably not be for the good in her case. "What'd you do to those two Nightstalkers?"

"Gave them what they wanted."

She should hammer him into the ground. "If you knew to make deals to shake with them you had to know what would happen when you shook hands for a long time. Those old ghouls never hurt anyone. How could you turn them into something evil and dangerous? Into some hideous halflings?"

"I have my reasons, but I'm not telling a snitch who talks to Beladors."

This worthless dog was not going to insult her. "I *am* a Belador."

"An Alterant? You're living in a dream world. They may let you hang around with them and use you for grunt work, but they don't think you're one of them."

She kept a mask of indifference in place so he couldn't see how deeply his words cut. *She* believed she was Belador even if the majority of the tribe didn't. But this was the first time she'd ever met another Alterant. The first chance to ask some questions and maybe shed some light on where they came from, but she'd have to give Tristan a reason to talk to her. Also, the more she found out about

235

him and how he had gotten here, the better chance she'd have to find the Ngak Stone that had disappeared with the woman and Vyan.

Tristan was clearly after the same thing as Vyan, but maybe not for the same reason.

She gave the let's-work-together-for-the-greater-good tactic a shot. "I'm trying to help Alterants so we won't have to be locked up or destroyed, but I haven't been able to find out any information on them, and I know very little about my own background. Where did you grow up? Who were your parents? Where were you when you were caught?"

Tristan headed toward her again, talking as he moved, but she stood her ground, since he wasn't acting aggressive. "You're free to run around. Why would you care about helping any other Alterants? You don't have any worries."

If only it were that simple. "I don't want to see more Alterants caged."

"You'll never stop Brina from caging them."

That was for sure. She should argue with him, but Evalle couldn't honestly defend Brina when Evalle had her own doubts about the Belador warrior queen. She'd push Tristan and see what he gave up. "I've been working to find out anything I can on Alterants for a long time. I don't want to see them caged. If you don't, then answer my questions."

He crossed his arms, pondering on something. "Finding you has made this an entirely new game. Tell you what I'll do. If you really want to help Alterants and want me to tell you what I know of the others—"

"You know about the other three?" *Now we're talking.*

"Of course. For example, I know where they were caged."

How was it that Tristan had information Brina wouldn't share with her?

He continued, "If you want to help your own kind, then bring me the Ngak Stone before four o'clock Wednesday morning."

Let's think about this. Hand this fool more power? Not. "What are you going to do with the Ngak Stone if you get it?"

"There is no *if* about it. I'll explain when you show up with the stone unless I find it first, at which point I'll move ahead with my plans. But if you bring the stone to me and join me, I'll guarantee your safety for as long as you live and you'll be revered for your powers, not treated as a dog who begs for scraps."

On the surface, that sounded pretty tempting, but she had an oath to uphold. Just not her week for a decent deal. "I don't think you'll be around long enough to be offering protection once Brina finds out you're on the loose. I'm going to be busy finding that young woman with the stone and protecting her."

"You mean to *take* the stone, and put it in the VIPER vault, don't you?"

She was amazed at how much he knew for someone who had been locked away for five years. "I can't discuss VIPER's business."

"If you intend to lock up the stone, then don't pretend you care what happens to me or the other three Alterants." He lifted his shoulders in dismissal. "And you'll never find out the truth about our species, because I'm the only one with the answers to your questions."

"I can find my own answers without putting all the Beladors at risk." Maybe in a couple lifetimes.

Tristan's grin spread at seeing through her bluff. "I doubt you'll figure out what bred with a Belador to make an Alterant. Not without my help. I know my family history and what you, me and the other three Alterants have in common. Are those some of your questions?"

Dead on the mark. Blood thrummed through her at the possibility of actually finding answers. She didn't have a thing to offer Tristan, since he'd been burned once already by Brina—*if* he was telling the truth—and believed the Ngak Stone was his ticket to freedom. But he wasn't the only one after the rock. "What's going on between you and Vyan?"

"I'm going to kill him if he gets in my way again, and I *will* find that woman."

"How did you find Vyan?"

"How do you know he didn't find me?" Tristan quipped and walked past her. "Make plans to come with me, Evalle. I will hold the key to freedom without persecution."

She took a side step to keep him in view, and her leg throbbed at the movement. "If you touch the Ngak Stone it could kill you, or her, and if that doesn't happen the Kujoo might get their hands on the rock and start a war with the Beladors that could turn into a modern-day apocalypse."

He paused from pacing. "Don't confuse me with someone who gives a shit about any of that."

That was the most truthful comment he'd made so far. He really didn't care who lived or died, which only made him more dangerous. Vyan had been much like that when she'd first met him in this very park two years back. He'd lost everything to the Beladors eight hundred years ago, including his will to survive.

Why would Vyan risk drawing the attention of the Beladors?

Grady had told her an ancient synergy had entered the city.

She pieced it together in her mind and made a guess. "You really think the Kujoo warriors are your friends?"

He offered her a smile. "We have Common Enemy Syndrome."

"We." She had to get to Tzader soon and let him know what she'd just figured out. Vyan was no longer the sole Kujoo in the city. "How many Kujoo are here now?"

"Enough."

"You aren't going to have a world to live in once they start a war."

Tristan crossed his arms. "They won't be a problem. The Kujoo aren't hanging around once I get the rock. They want to be sent back eight hundred years immediately. So you don't have to worry about fighting them in Atlanta." His gaze swung from side to side, watching all around him. "Love to stay and chat, but I've got a rock to find and you've got to go suck up to the Beladors."

Just great. An Alterant on the loose hunting a human who had gotten her hands on the Ngak Stone. "If you harm that woman, you'll bring down a lot more trouble on your head than the Beladors. Macha might even get involved."

"Macha won't get involved unless there's a battle between the Kujoo and the Beladors. I'm telling you there's not going to be a conflict in our world."

"Oh, sure, you want me to believe the Kujoo are going to return to their time eight hundred years ago without first coming after the Beladors for revenge?"

"They have a better plan."

She took in his relaxed air and matter-of-fact tone. His body language spoke of confidence. He was telling her the truth. "And you don't want revenge for what Brina did to you?"

"Oh, I'll have my day of reckoning the minute I get that stone. But payback won't come from my hand, and Macha won't act until she has reason. By the time that happens, the Beladors will no longer be a problem for me. A witch is already making plans for moving into Brina's castle the minute she's gone."

"Why would you believe a Medb witch?" Now things started to make sense, but in a way that had her skin crawling. The Medb coven was behind the Noirre majik and must have been the power that had opened a portal to bring the Kujoo forward. Thus, the Medb were orchestrating the Common Enemy Syndrome of joining the Kujoo and Tristan against the Beladors.

"Why shouldn't I believe the Medb witch? She got the Kujoo here and helped them figure out how to free me when Brina locked me away for no reason."

Evalle really hated to stand up for Brina on this, but right was right. "You can't blame Brina for sending you away after your shifting into a beast and killing people."

His eyes thinned with fury. "I never changed into a beast or killed anyone until *after* I was sent away. Even then, I killed only as a matter of survival."

"That can't be right. I heard—"

"Only what Brina wanted you to hear. So before you get all high and mighty on Brina's behalf, get your facts straight, babe. Makes you wonder what else you've been told that were lies, doesn't it?"

If he was speaking the truth, then it did make Evalle wonder.

Tristan's eyes took in her face. He dropped the snarl and said in a calmer voice, "I might be just like you if I'd been the only one free all this time, but I would know the truth when I heard it. Ask Brina if you don't believe me. Her honor will force her to tell you the truth."

239

"I plan to ask her, but you're not helping the Alterants' cause by trying to take the Ngak Stone."

"I'm doing more for Alterants right now by going after that stone than you've done the whole time you've been free. When you get tired of being a lied-to misfit tagging along with the Beladors, come over to my side. I could use someone with your abilities, and you'll be safe from everyone with me." His voice softened when he added, "I'd treat you like the jewel that you are."

She'd be lying to herself if she didn't admit the idea of being safe forever had a certain appeal, but not with this lunatic. She'd given a vow to the Beladors and hadn't taken that lightly. But Tristan was obviously leaving her alive because he believed she might help him gain the stone, and his offer opened the door for her to find out how to reach him. "If I do consider coming to you, how would I find you?"

"Put word out with the Nightstalkers you're looking for me. I'll find you. Otherwise, stay out of my way and don't stand too close to a Belador once I have the stone. I'll find you when they're gone."

"Thought you said you weren't going after vengeance. The Kujoo would take care of that." She didn't hold many kind feelings about Brina, but Evalle would protect her warrior queen just like any other Belador would, and she'd lay down her life for Tzader or Quinn without hesitation. Tristan's confidence in the Kujoo doing his dirty work troubled her.

"I'm not spending any energy on vengeance. The Kujoo will do worse than I could on my own," Tristan said.

"Going to be a little hard to accomplish that if they go home the minute you get the rock, isn't it?"

His smile was full of secrets. "The Kujoo have a plan to destroy the Beladors, and it has nothing to do with them touching the rock or with me battling Beladors, which keeps Shiva and Macha out of the picture. They've created a brilliant strategy with the Medb that will wipe every Belador from the earth, including their ancestors."

Was he jerking her around, trying to convince her he was all-powerful, or was he really telling the truth? She saw a flaw in his proclamation of victory. "You can't let them kill all the Beladors. You carry Belador blood. You'd die, too."

"That's finally the positive side of being half-breeds. The worst that will happen to us is to feel a weakening of our powers for a brief time, but Alterants *will* survive. Once I have the Ngak Stone, I'll share my strength with our new clan of Alterants. *We* will survive and prosper."

Why was he telling her this? He had to know she'd tell the Beladors as soon as she got free. Did he *want* her to tell the Beladors so her tribe would attack the Kujoo?

Did he really think that just because he was an Alterant *she'd* join his side if he was part of the annihilation of everything that mattered to her? "Brina won't sit quietly while you do this."

"By all means, tell her. Tell all the Beladors. The more the merrier. The Medb will be waiting."

That definitely sounded like a trap. "What do you mean?"

"That's all I'm sharing. Be smart and come with me."

"When did you start thinking I was Barbie and you were Ken? What are you offering me to come with you? I'll take a convertible in any color but pink."

"You could save the Beladors."

She didn't believe he would help her do that. "How?"

"Give me what I want and I'll tell you how."

"Oh, sure. Hand you the rock and trust you not to kill everyone with it."

Tristan cocked his head to one side, studying her. "Here's a free-bie to use as you choose. If you tell Brina I've escaped and am working with the Medb, she'll come straight to me and she'll die first, which works for me."

"She only travels as a hologram." That was common knowledge among anyone who knew about Brina.

He shrugged. "The Medb shared a lot of information with me, including Brina and Tzader's history. They *can* kill her if she comes to them this time in any form."

What did he mean about Brina and Tzader's history? He'd said that as if he meant the two of them together. And he knew about Brina in hologram form.

The Medb had been doing a good job of educating Tristan.

He wasn't finished sharing. "If Brina comes to me, so will Tzader

241

and his sidekick, Quinn, who will call in an army of Beladors. They'll play into the Medb and Kujoo's plans, then they'll all die before the Kujoo get to the point of wiping out the Belador race. You decide if you want to tell Brina, because she can find me the minute she learns I've escaped. Up to you to tell them or not."

"If you hurt Tzader or Quinn, you'll wish you were back in that cage," she promised.

"If I was only an Alterant, you might win, but not with the power of the Medb behind me, and I'll be even more powerful once I get the Ngak Stone." Tristan's confidence froze her blood. "You want to keep *your* tribe safe? *Find* that rock and bring it to me *yourself* on Wednesday morning, and I'll tell you how to protect the Beladors."

The pain in her leg interfered with thinking straight. "Let's say I believe you, which I don't. What if I don't find the rock first?"

"If *I* find the rock first I'll give you one other chance to save the Beladors."

Did he think they were playing Let's Make A Deal? "What would you possibly be willing to take in trade for letting the Beladors live?"

"You."

Both offers were unfair, unrealistic and undesirable. Stay with *him*? He was insane on top of being a monster.

Tristan stood quietly for a moment. "I need a female Alterant to populate our species."

Ah, consolation female for the group. He was out of his ever-lovin' mind. "And if I choose to accept either of these incredibly attractive offers, how would I find you if the Nightstalkers don't know?"

He smiled at her sarcasm as if he'd find her entertaining company. "I plan to get my hands on that rock first. When I do, I'll call you to me."

None of this made sense, and he was crazier than bat shit if he thought she'd go for that bunch of hooey. But she'd play along since he was going to let her live. "I'll have to think about it. I don't understand any of this."

Tristan touched his fingers to her chin and she held still only to show him she didn't fear him. She could lie with her body as well as her mouth. "You will eventually, but I've told you enough for now.

Make the right choice when the time comes. I take care of what's mine."

She scoffed. "I am *not* yours."

"Yet." He lifted his fingers and combed them through his thick blond hair. "Don't waste your time trying to follow me. You can't."

Evalle shook with rage over his arrogance to think she'd consider walking away from the Beladors for *him*. Sure, a part of her wanted to be safe and out from under the threat of the Tribunal. But not with this guy, who had been trying to kill her until he'd realized who she was.

What about everything *else* he'd told her?

Could Brina be killed if she appeared only as a hologram? Did the Medb have a way to reach her through that form with the Ngak Stone? What if she didn't believe there was a Medb trap and told the Beladors, then her tribe was lured to their deaths? Doing so could doom Tzader and Quinn. That wasn't a risk she wanted to take. And would they even believe her, given she'd been warned by a rogue Alterant?

Tristan strolled quietly to the street and disappeared. The minute he stepped out of the park, the buzzing in her ears subsided.

Had she been inside a warded area or some sort of spell zone? She didn't think Alterants could do that kind of magic or disappear, but then she didn't know as much as Tristan did about Alterants, Brina or the Beladors, because Brina had kept her in the dark about so much.

And she didn't know how much of Tristan's ability was due to Noirre majik.

She sent a telepathic message. *Tzader, we need to meet. I've got news on the Ngak Stone and it's not good.*

Within a minute, Tzader answered, *Meet at Trey's house. I'll contact the rest of the team. You bring Storm.*

She'd forgotten about Storm and limped around, turning in a circle as she searched the park for him. Using her kinetic ability, she pulled her sunglasses up from the ground and put them on.

Her calf muscle ached like something was trying to chew its way out where the ghoul had stabbed her. It felt as if her skin was burning from the inside out.

The rain had died down to a drizzling mist. There came Storm down the concrete steps in the middle of the park. He jogged up to her, his face lined with worry when he touched her cheek.

She flinched when his fingers brushed her bruised face.

"What happened to you? I can feel sharp needles of pain coming off you."

"Got stabbed in the back of my leg by something like that ghoul thing you chased. You catch him?"

"No. And he's not the only one. I ran into three more in the park. I had to stay and watch over a human couple until the ghouls left." Storm stepped around behind her and squatted down, gently checking her leg.

But the slightest touch sent spasms of pain shooting up her calf and thigh. "Crap!"

"I don't like the color oozing out of this wound."

"What do you mean? I bleed red just like everyone else."

"There's purple running with the blood. You could be infected by some sort of majik. This smells like spoiled oranges."

That would be the color and smell of Medb majik. What would that do to her? "We have to meet the rest of the team at Trey's house."

"You aren't walking far with that." Storm stood up and leaned as though to lift her.

"Don't even *think* about picking me up if you want to draw your next breath," she warned.

"You're so stubborn." He didn't try to hide the irritation in his voice. "Whatever's in your system could cause you to shift involuntarily or kill you if it stays in long enough."

"I'll let you know if I start feeling twitchy." She sounded like a snotty bitch, but she was working real hard not to upchuck.

"That's reassuring," he said in a tight voice. "How far is Trey's house?"

"About a mile."

"We'd get there a lot faster and you wouldn't be in as much pain if you'd let me help you."

"I can handle the pain." Barely. "Let's go." She hobbled along, trying not to think about how sick she felt. What had that ghoul infected her with?

"What's the meeting about?" Storm asked.

"I found the Ngak Stone."

"Where is it?"

"Worst possible place. The stone and the woman who has it are with a Kujoo warrior." And they couldn't have picked a worse person to take control of the stone if Tristan was successful. Had Tristan been telling her the truth about being sent to a cage *before* he'd shifted?

If so, that meant Brina could be lying to her about the other Alterants.

What about Vyan? How did he fit into all this?

She didn't know why Vyan had tried to protect the woman from Tristan, but just the fact that the Kujoo warrior had done so made Evalle wonder if there was some dissent among the Kujoo.

Regardless, Vyan had to relish wiping out all the Beladors as much as the other Kujoo and Tristan did.

Heat crawled up her leg, tugging her awareness back to the most immediate threat. Could Medb majik kill an Alterant?

Just her suck-ass luck to be the test case.

TWENTY-SIX

Laurette waited for the man lying in her living room to get up and kill her.

He could do it. Thanks to her magic rock, she'd had enough vision to see him draw a sword on another guy who'd thrown lightning bolts from his fingers in Piedmont Park.

A sword. Lightning bolts from humans.

All that had been before she'd magically traveled from the park to her little cottage a couple blocks away.

She looked down at the glowing rock in her hand. Magic. She'd never believed in magic, but what other explanation was there for standing in one place one minute then showing up in another the next?

Brutus came running back into the living room, his mouth still dripping water from where he'd gone to his bowl in the kitchen. She'd freed his leash from the inert guy's body the minute she'd gotten here, but his water-soaked body was still sprawled in the middle of her floor. Dripping all over her braided rug that had seen better years.

Grandpa Barrett would hoot over this if he were still alive. He used to tell her how life was full of magic.

That a miracle was just pure magic.

She could understand how a hundred voices raised in prayer to a higher form could result in a miracle.

But a rock?

Brutus sniffed all around the arm of the unconscious man on the floor. Then he sniffed the guy's long wet hair also clinging to her rug.

"Careful, Brutus. He might wake up," she whispered. She wished he would wake up so she could ask him who he was and how he'd known about her rock. And how she'd gotten home.

This guy had told her, "Run and get rid of that rock."

After what she'd seen tonight, there was no way she'd let go of this rock. It had been the only thing to save her at the park. And who was that woman who had shown up and that other guy who'd tried to kill this one?

That tall woman had called this guy Vyan.

She'd *also* told Laurette to get rid of the rock.

The man in Laurette's living room moaned, but the sound barely reached her ears.

Brutus ran over and jumped up on the sofa next to her, where they normally sat to listen to a television show.

Guilt started eating at her even though she'd laid a towel over this Vyan's shoulder. Those lightning bolts had cut his shoulder and stabbed his chest. He was still bleeding.

If she didn't stop the bleeding, he might die.

Then what would she do? How would she explain any of this to the police?

What about the rock? If the rock was full of magic, she could use it to heal him. She lifted the rock and said, "Fix this guy's wounds." Nothing happened. "Make him healthy." Still nothing. "Make him go away?"

His body didn't move an inch.

Dang, dang, dang! She'd have to do something about that bleeding herself or he was going to die.

She got up and eased over a little at a time until she was next to him, then dropped down on her knees with Brutus at her side. "I have no idea what to do with lightning bolt cuts. I need bandages and disinfectant."

A first aid kit appeared on the other side of her. "Now you want to help?" she asked the rock, exasperated.

Inside the kit, she found everything clearly marked. Using a pair of scissors in shaking hands, she carefully cut away his T-shirt until she had the entire thing off his chest. Skin around the shoulder injury and on the side of his chest was red and swollen. She tried to be careful and not hurt him when she dressed the wounds.

By the time she was finished, sweat lined her brow, but her hands had stopped shaking. She cleaned up the mess and deposited everything in the kitchen, then went looking for a blanket to cover him with. Not that her old house was cold in the middle of August, but anyone who went through serious injuries would be chilled from a shock reaction.

Humans would be. Was this guy human?

Her faithful Brutus hung close the entire time, giving her a sense of protection. She kept the rock close, too, but when she reached the living room with the blanket hooked inside one arm she paused before putting the rock in her baggy pants pocket so she could have a clear look at this Vyan from standing above him.

The two braids running along the sides of his angular face gave him a dangerous rogue look. His nut brown skin, shoulder-length black hair and strange accent made her think Mediterranean, but the shape of his eyes and thick lashes hinted at Chinese ancestry somewhere in his background. He sure as heck wasn't your everyday guy.

But that beautiful chest of his could belong to a fireman or a soldier or a guy who just enjoyed working out in the gym.

She'd never been so close to perfection in a male body, or to many men at all.

But this one carried a sword that looked older than time and fought lightning bolts.

Sliding the rock into her pocket, she shook out the blanket and covered him up to his neck. When she reached to pull a pillow off the couch, her gaze stumbled at the sword lying on the floor. She slipped the pillow under his head, then walked around the room, closing the curtains just in case anyone looked in.

The sword rested too close to him even if he was out cold.

She tiptoed over and reached down to see if she could lift the huge thing, and a sizzle of energy ran along the handle as if in warning.

Yanking her hand back, she scooted around his supine body and turned toward her bedroom, planning to blockade herself inside.

A sound from the floor stopped her.

She stood dead still, heart racing, then looked over her shoulder at her patient.

His chest moved with soft breaths, less pained than before she'd bandaged him. She must be tired to think he'd made that sound. He was too wiped out to move. "Come on, Brutus."

Vyan stayed perfectly still until the young woman was out of the room. When a door down the hallway closed, he opened his eyes.

He had kept his eyes shut when he'd awakened at hearing her close by, telling her dog to be careful around him. He'd almost laughed when she'd tried to get the stone to heal him, though he would have appreciated being mended at the time, since the cuts in his body burned.

That was only until this angel had ignored her fear and put her gentle hands on him. He tried to remember the last time a woman had touched him with care. Something deep inside his chest was unleashed, a yearning for what he'd once had many years ago.

Why was that angel caught in this dangerous circle of trouble?

Lifting his head, he looked all around until he saw his sword lying a couple feet away. Close enough to reach.

He would protect his angel, and the best way to do that would be by getting that rock out of her hands.

TWENTY-SEVEN

By the time Trey's house was in view a half block away, sweat gleamed across Evalle's face and upper body, and not just from the heat still rolling through Atlanta at midnight. Her skin pebbled with a feverish chill.

The back of her leg was on fire. Muscles twitched and curled in her body.

She fought the urge to change into a beast. Every instinct was telling her she'd heal from the wound if she did, but making that mistake in view of the team would seal her fate with the Tribunal.

She kept hobbling along the sidewalk and chanced a quick look at Storm. He hadn't said another word after she'd forbidden him from using any majik to help her. His long fingers were balled into fists.

He must have felt her eyes, because his gaze cut over to her. "You don't have to be in this much pain. I could ease it before you get around the team."

"Thanks, but no." She didn't trust anyone to take control of her emotions or her sensory abilities. Not even someone she'd allowed to kiss her.

Did that make me a control freak? Damn straight.

Men who offered to *take care of her* were dangerous.

The doctor her aunt had worked for had visited Evalle in the basement from the time she was eight until she was fifteen. He'd been her only friend. He'd promised not to hurt her when he'd performed her first female physical exam.

He'd said he was there to take care of her.

And he hadn't hurt her. His touch had been clinical and his words had soothed her anxiety.

She hadn't found out he'd been lying all along until the next house call after that, a week later, when he'd wanted to talk to Evalle about her test results. Her aunt had given the thirty-four-year-old family doctor keys to her house and to Evalle's basement room so he could make a stop while her aunt had been working in his medical center.

He'd taken that private opportunity to give Evalle a hands-on lesson in his twisted fantasy.

"You have to get the Noirre venom out of your leg before you lose control," Storm said, breaking her free from reliving that nightmare again. "I can see you fighting it."

Her skin was clammy and cold in spite of the perspiration. She tightened her stomach muscles, anything to keep what was fighting to get out locked down. Cartilage along her forearms hardened and rippled beneath her skin. She gritted her teeth and clenched her fists until the ridges along her arms dropped back to normal skin and muscle. She'd explain the torn sleeves as having happened during battle, which was true.

"I can control myself," she gritted out. "Tzader will know what to do."

Tzader and Quinn were the only two she trusted not to say a word to Sen, who could use the Noirre majik infection as a way to put her into quarantine.

When she reached the walkway to the old Victorian house that Trey's wife and sister-in-law owned, Evalle searched the group of people clustered on the veranda stretching from corner to corner across the front.

Tzader must have sensed her coming, because he and Quinn both broke off from their conversation with Trey and hurried down the steps to meet Evalle on the sidewalk.

"What's wrong?" Tzader was staring at her, but that question had been directed at Storm.

"Not a big deal—," she started saying, but Storm cut her off.

"She was attacked by a possessed ghoul that stabbed her. She's got purple coming out of her leg with blood that smells like rotten oranges. Could be Noirre majik. We need to get that infection out now."

"Where were *you*?" Quinn asked Storm in a voice harboring vicious undertones.

"Chasing three more ghouls. When I realized they might have been sent just to split us up, I tried going back to where I'd left Evalle, but something was blocking me from reaching the south end of the park. Someone had spelled the area to prevent anyone from interfering. I tried calling you on the cell, but it wouldn't work. I don't know who she battled besides the ghoul. She wouldn't tell me that or let me touch her leg."

She didn't have to tell him a damn thing. "My leg's fine and I'm reporting to Trey, not you."

Storm turned a glare on her so hot it should have baked her face brown. "You're getting that venom out of your leg *first* before you do another thing if I have to hold you down myself."

She shoved close to him and paid for it with a sharp blade of pain up her leg. She croaked, "Try it and you'll die."

"You couldn't kick a snowman's ass right now."

Quinn piped up. "He has a point."

The chiding in his voice snapped her last straw. "Do not side with him."

"We're not taking sides," Tzader said, but before she could feel relief at that he added, "but he's right. We're getting that venom out of your leg."

She took a breath and dropped her voice. "I don't want to tell the others about being infected with Noirre majik. They might think I can't hold my human form."

Storm could have busted her then, but he didn't. She lifted her eyes to his, expecting more argument, but he actually looked . . . worried. How much of that was true and how much was him just doing what he'd been brought in to do?

Lucien was standing on the porch with his back to them. "We heard everything, Evalle. The only person on the team without exceptional hearing is Casper when he's not in his Highland warrior form, but he isn't even here right now."

She leaned passed Tzader to see the rest of the team and Trey's sister-in-law, Rowan, watching her from the veranda.

Oh, great, once again I'm the entertainment for the night.

"Nobody's turning you over to Sen," Tzader assured her.

252

"Not until *after* they find out what I know about the rock," she said, sensing defeat hanging around the corner waiting for her.

"Don't underestimate how much the team doesn't like Sen either," Quinn interjected.

"She thinks she's the *only* one with Sen problems," Storm interjected. "That everyone is her enemy except you two and she has to fight every battle alone to prove she's as capable as she is pigheaded."

His sarcastic dig jacked up her hackles again. She turned on him, but Tzader caught her by the arm. "Let's get up on the porch, killer, and see what we can do with that leg."

She hated handing control over to anyone.

"Don't make me use my majik," Storm warned her. "You've stretched the outer boundaries of my control by making me watch you limp in pain for a mile. Get up there or I *will* carry you." He walked ahead of her up to the porch.

Her mouth fell open. Was Storm really that worried about her being injured?

"My, my, that's interesting." Quinn's voice switched to mild curiosity. He looped his arm around her waist. "Lean on me, sweetheart."

When she reached the top landing, Quinn swung her to the left side of the porch and settled her on a wooden swing wide enough for three people.

Rowan came to squat down by Evalle's injured leg. "Been a long time since I've seen you. Sorry it isn't under better circumstances."

"Me, too. How's Sasha?"

"Sleeping. Ready to have the baby. Trey doesn't want her around any of this."

The last time Evalle had been around Rowan was before Trey had married her sister. Of the two witch sisters, Rowan was the more powerful of the two, but they were white witches. "Can you get the Noirre majik out of my leg, Rowan?"

"I don't know. We're not supposed to go near any form of black majik, but that might not apply to drawing it out of a wound. Let me try to touch it first." Rowan waited until Tzader gently lifted Evalle's leg, then turned her hand palm up beneath the gash in Evalle's jeans. She moved her hand up until her fingers were a half-inch away, then jerked her hand back with a hiss. "The Noirre is burning my skin."

Trey had been watching. "What about you, Lucien? Can you draw out the venom like you pulled the insanity out of Rowan that time she was possessed?"

Rowan had been possessed by an evil spirit two years ago when Trey had battled Vyan.

Lucien said, "No, I can't. That possession had originated with the Kujoo magician. I can't overturn something spelled by a witch."

Evalle didn't miss the intimate look that passed between Rowan and Lucien for a fleeting second. Word was he did not like witches, white, black or any other kind. But he liked something about Rowan.

Storm gave Lucien an assessing once-over. "How do you know it's spelled by a witch?"

Lucien's face barely changed when his lips turned up with an arrogant smile. "I just do."

Surprise lit several faces on the porch, Evalle's being one. She'd heard that Lucien had faced off with Rowan once when she'd been possessed and had gone airborne to attack. He'd stopped her by just putting his hand against her chest, then he'd drawn the dark energy out of her long enough for her to regain control.

Rowan lifted disappointed eyes to Evalle. "I'm sorry. But if I can't help you, maybe . . ." She looked across her shoulder, past the men on either side of her, toward the far end of the porch.

"Let me take a look." Adrianna stepped out of a black shadow where she'd been standing in a corner. Apart from the team.

Evalle spoke to Tzader mind-to-mind. *I don't want her touching me.*

I don't either, but we're out of choices unless you have an idea.

I haven't had a reaction yet. We could wait.

But what if you do have a reaction and start changing? I couldn't stop Trey or anyone else from contacting Sen at that point.

Fear over being touched by a Sterling witch caused Evalle to drop her vigilance against the change that still clawed the inside of her body. Her arms rippled with energy.

Rowan hadn't noticed when she'd stood up and backed out of the way, but Adrianna paused, eyeing the skin that moved along Evalle's arms beneath the ragged sleeves. The witch's gaze lifted to meet Evalle's, waiting for her to decide what she wanted to do.

Evalle licked her dry lips and came to a decision. "Fine. Take a look."

A shapely eyebrow swooped up on Adrianna's smooth forehead, but she didn't respond to the biting voice. "Stand up."

Tzader helped Evalle to her feet.

"Move over here," Adrianna said, directing Evalle away from the swing to the center of the porch, where everyone backed up to make a circle around her. "Face away from me."

Taking a moment to accept what she couldn't change, Evalle inched around on her leg, which felt twice its size even though she knew it hadn't actually swollen.

Adrianna dropped down behind her.

The back of Evalle's jeans ripped open. She didn't think Adrianna had touched the material or used a sharp object to rip the material. Only majik.

Adrianna's fingers spread across the back of Evalle's calf, and she started chanting, "Queen of dark and queen of hell, hearken to this witch's spell . . ."

The burning sensation tripled. Evalle's breaths were coming in fast pants. Her lungs were closing up.

Dots swam through her gaze.

When she looked for help in the crowd, everyone's eyes were on Adrianna but Storm's.

He vibrated with the effort it took him to stand in place.

Pain burst through Evalle's body. Her arms ruptured with cartilage exploding and changing into beast form. She couldn't stop it.

Tzader moved toward her, but Storm said, "I got her."

He stepped in front of Evalle and placed his hands on each side of her face. "Focus on me. You will not change. Breathe slowly."

His words mingled with Adrianna's chanting until the sound was one constant mantra that stood as a wall against the monster stomping inside her, waiting to break free.

Energy ripped through her, jarring her teeth when she shook. She lost contact with everything. Colors showered behind her eyes. Purple. Red. Orange. Green.

Had she shifted and insanity taken over?

The colors subsided until white blanketed her mind. Warm fingers touched her skin, sending gentle waves of white to wash away the heat and pain.

When she regained consciousness, Evalle was clutching someone's shirt. His arms were around her, supporting her weight against weak knees. She inhaled, trying to calm the trembling in her body.

Storm had her. She knew his scent. Warm, natural, earthy.

She opened her eyes and looked up at him.

He dropped his chin. "Okay now?"

"Did I change?"

His lack of quick answer and swallow told her she'd done something. "Why don't you sit down?"

She let him lower her to the swing. Her leg didn't throb anymore. Adrianna stood to the side, hands clasped in front of her. Tzader and Quinn exchanged worried expressions that made Evalle think they'd also spoken telepathically. But not to her.

"What happened?" Evalle had learned at an early age that avoiding the truth only delayed the consequences.

Rowan spoke up. "Adrianna drew the Noirre venom out of you."

Evalle didn't want to owe anyone for anything, especially a Sterling witch, but she had to give the woman her due for what she'd done. "Thank you."

Adrianna merely gave a little dip of her head.

"What else?" Evalle asked, directing her question to Tzader.

He heaved a long sigh and looked around at the team when he answered her. "The venom caused you to change into battle form. Nothing else."

Why had he hesitated? If anyone told a different story, Evalle would be out of time with the Tribunal and Tzader would have to stand trial right behind her for trying to suppress evidence against an Alterant.

Evalle's pulse thumped a rapid beat. She took in each expression on the porch, every calm and understanding demeanor matching the compassion she felt coming toward her in waves, until she faced Adrianna, who merely lifted a single taunting eyebrow.

Adrianna was the one person who would not sugarcoat the truth.

TWENTY-EIGHT

E valle would not ask anyone to support her, but she didn't want Tzader to go under the bus for defending her.

Storm spoke up. "That's what I saw—Evalle in battle form."

She swung around, lost for what to say. Storm had just backed Tzader's claim that she hadn't shifted into her Altcrant beast state.

Storm gave her a look that asked, *Surprised?* then passed a challenging glance at the rest of the team.

Quinn shrugged. "It was never in question."

Evalle smiled at him, letting Quinn know that she knew how he'd vote regardless.

"Looked like battle form to me," Trey concurred.

Lucien shifted his attention to the Sterling witch. "We're all in agreement, right, Adrianna?"

For the second time tonight, Evalle's fate rested with the same witch whose cherry red lips curled in a smile of mock innocence. "I'm not familiar with battle form."

There was a collective tensing.

Adrianna moved a dainty shoulder in a sexy shrug. "I only saw a reaction to the Noirre majik venom and Evalle is now healed. I see no threat. So let it be said, so let it be known."

Adrianna's smirk would normally have set Evalle off, but she couldn't take exception when the woman had just healed her leg and given her safe passage out of this situation.

One thing Evalle had heard about a Sterling witch was that once she said, "So let it be said, so let it be known," Adrianna could not recant or deny her words.

Honor among black majik witches? But this one had shown a side of consideration Evalle hadn't expected.

"Thank you," Evalle told her again and this time with true sincerity. Not enjoying being the center of attention, she changed the topic. "Let's talk about the Ngak Stone."

Trey spoke up. "I had a call from Sen. He said Shiva told him the stone had been located and would bind with its new master by Wednesday morning when sunlight strikes the spot where she found it. But Shiva still didn't say who the woman was."

Evalle stood and moved over to lean against the banister so that she wasn't lower than everyone on the porch. Her jeans flopped where Adrianna had torn the material, but other than feeling bruised, her leg was much better. "I don't know exactly where the stone is at this moment, but I think it's still in this area. I found the woman who has it. She was in the park with the stone, and that Kujoo Vyan showed up."

Quinn asked, "Who was the woman?"

Evalle heaved a tired sigh. "I don't know and doubt anyone else here will know her, because she's . . . human."

"What?" The single word rang out around the veranda.

Evalle shook her head. "I have no idea why she has it, but she *is* human."

"Was Vyan alone?" Lucien asked.

"No, but he was acting on his own. He stepped between the woman and another guy to protect her."

"So he wasn't trying to take the stone for himself?" Trey frowned, probably remembering the lonely warrior who had traveled forward eight hundred years to seek vengeance. Because of Trey's compassion for what the guy had lost, he'd allowed Vyan to walk away free.

"Not right then," Evalle clarified. "Vyan told her to drop the rock and run while he faced off with the other guy."

"Who was the other guy?"

Answering that was going to be tricky. "Someone Vyan knew, but no one I've met before."

Storm had been leaning against a wood support column for the porch, arms crossed, staring at the floor. His head lifted just enough

258

to draw Evalle's attention, and his eyes told her he knew she'd just colored the truth.

"Was the other guy after the rock?" Trey asked.

"Yes." Evalle welcomed the question to avoid Storm's silent censure. "But he wasn't Kujoo."

"What kind of power did he have?"

"Different than anything I've faced before." If she told the Beladors on the porch about Tristan they would call up a league of Beladors to go after him, which was exactly what she believed the Medb wanted, especially if it included Tzader and Brina. Brina could find Tristan immediately.

Or so Tristan had said.

Evalle couldn't risk any of them walking into a trap. If she told Brina that Tristan was an Alterant who had escaped his cage and that Brina should stay away from him, Brina would think Evalle was protecting an Alterant. She didn't know if anyone could really kill Brina, but she wasn't risking the future of the Beladors to find out.

If she told Tzader and Quinn that Tristan wanted to keep her, they wouldn't let her near Tristan.

But Tristan had given Evalle a chance to protect her tribe, and if that was her last option, she'd trade her life if that was the only way to save Tzader and Quinn. She would not, however, give Tristan the rock under any circumstances.

The team *did* need to know about the ghouls being altered.

"I think the guy I met in the park is changing Nightstalkers into crazed half-zombie-like things," Evalle told the group. "They can't hold their shape and they're aggressive. That's what stabbed me in the leg with a long fingernail. This strange guy has kinetics and can throw energy spikes like lightning bolts. Then he disappeared as though he teleported."

"He wields Noirre majik?" Adrianna asked. "Was he a witch?"

Evalle thought back on what had happened. "Not a witch, and I don't think he controls the majik. I had the feeling he was infected with the Noirre majik and passed that infection along to the Nightstalkers when he shook with them."

Tzader raked his hand over his head and walked around a minute. "A human female got the rock. How could that have happened?"

"I don't know, but I don't think she realized what she had," Evalle told the group. "When the other guy attacked Vyan, I stepped in as Vyan went down. I put up a shield for the woman and told her to drop the rock and run. She was rattled to the point I don't think she knew what she was doing and said she just wanted to go home. Poof. She disappeared with Vyan."

In his usual precise manner, Quinn summed up everything. "A human has the Ngak Stone, there's an unknown player in the mix and the Kujoo warrior Vyan is with the woman who has the stone. I suppose it could be worse, but I don't know how."

Evalle really hated to be the bearer of sucky news. "Here's how. My Nightstalker told me there's an ancient synergy in the city, and during our brief conversation I confirmed the strange guy I fought in the park is working with the Kujoo. Someone has brought more Kujoo warriors forward in time. Vyan isn't working alone, but I had the feeling he was in conflict with his warlord."

"We'll be ready for them this time," Trey said.

Evalle raised her hand. "Wait. This guy was arrogant and bragging about how the Medb had a plan for taking down the Beladors. From what I could figure out, the Medb are setting a trap and not preparing for a battle. If what he said was true, they're planning genocide of Beladors. We have to find out first what they're up to so Beladors don't rush into a slaughter."

"That makes sense," Quinn said. "Looks like we're still back to finding that rock, which might answer those questions. Shiva will give advice when he deems it necessary, but we can't call him or Macha into this until the Kujoo instigate a conflict."

"The strange guy said the Kujoo would *not* instigate a conflict," Evalle followed up. "I don't know what they have in mind, but this guy was confident about whatever the Medb were cooking up to use against the Beladors. They want us to show up en masse."

Storm watched her every time she spoke, and his eyes narrowed when she stepped all over the truth. Too bad. She had the Beladors' safety at heart.

Tzader swung around and addressed everyone. "Lucien and Adrianna—search for whoever is opening that portal for Kujoo.

Storm and Evalle will start shaking down Nightstalkers to see if any of them have a lead on a human female with a sentient power source. Also, you two find out how many Nightstalkers are missing that might have been changed by the Kujoo or this guy Evalle fought. If the Nightstalkers are being changed, the ones still here might lead us to this guy and the Kujoo."

Adrianna released a sigh that drew everyone's attention. "Where's Casper?"

Tzader addressed everyone again. "He's shaking down the trolls to find out if any of them know of a new powerful female in the city. Quinn and I will continue to track the Noirre majik and see if we can find the Medb source. Trey, you still on baby watch?"

Trey nodded. "Sasha's doing good, but the baby is due any day now and I don't want to leave her or Rowan alone if the Kujoo are here in force. Especially if there's a chance they brought Ekkbar with them."

"Who's Ekkbar?" Adrianna asked.

"The Kujoo magician." Trey's thick chest bunched when he crossed his arms. "He used dreams to possess Rowan two years ago. I don't think he can do it again, but I'm not taking that risk with her life, my wife's or my baby's."

Tzader nodded and told the team, "Keep reporting to Trey. He can alert the team if the situation changes. Let's head out."

Evalle tested her leg, walking to the steps. All systems were a go. She'd made it to the sidewalk along the street when Storm fell into step beside her. He didn't say a word until they were out of sight and earshot of the house.

"Why aren't you telling the team everything?" he asked.

"The same reason I'm not answering your question." She kept walking, not looking at him. "The less you all know, the safer you'll be."

He put his hand on her arm, but she didn't snarl at him this time. Why was it when he touched her she felt her insides go soft and gooey? "Don't push me, Storm."

"Would it be so awful to ask for my help?"

She considered her answer as she listened to the sounds of Atlanta. "Asking for help can sometimes be dangerous."

"I will not hurt you."

"I will not let you."

He breathed quietly for a moment, a quiet gathering of his thoughts. "If you won't ask for help for yourself, then think about the team and this rock we're after. We have to find it."

Evalle turned to him. "I *am* thinking of the team and that rock. Can you follow someone who has been teleported?"

"No."

"Did you sense a trail of any kind when you found me?" *Like Tristan's?*

"Only to the street and it disappeared."

"Then I don't think there's anything you can do that is more than we're already doing." She didn't snap at him because she sensed his sincerity.

"Tell me who the other guy was that you stopped from killing Vyan."

She didn't reply.

"I think you're afraid to tell me because you believe it's going to change your status with the Tribunal, but you're wrong. I'm not handing you over to Sen or them."

He was telling the truth. She sensed how important it was to him for her to believe that he meant her no harm. Her empathic ability reared its head at the strangest times. He'd been there for her tonight and hadn't hesitated to stand up for her with Tzader.

Would it cost her anything to give him an inch?

She lifted her hand but stopped short of touching his cheek. Maybe it was that same maturing empathic ability that was stir-frying her hormones. "I believe you, but I still can't tell you any more."

"You better be worth all the trouble I see ahead of me." He snagged her hand before she dropped it to her side, then kissed her scraped knuckles.

The touch of his lips stroked her heart rhythm into a gallop. She didn't want that hand back when touching him filled her with an unfamiliar happiness.

But he released her, so she folded her arms over her chest.

He kept nipping at her personal space, but he wasn't a lecherous doctor.

She'd try to remember that.

"Where're you going now?" he asked.

"To get my bike, swing by the morgue to see if the body came back on its own because we might be able to use that to track the Noirre majik, and I intend to hunt down some Nightstalkers. One in particular."

"Then let's get moving."

She kept pace with him all the way back to her motorcycle. He wasn't happy when she said she needed to work Nightstalkers on her own, but he didn't fight her and agreed his time was better spent seeing if he could pick up any trails. She agreed to meet him at the same entrance to the park at dusk, then hopped on her bike and cruised toward the interstate with a few hours left until daylight.

The morgue was in chaos. A gang fight had ended with four stiffs, and two more arrived from a tractor-trailer pileup. No mangled female body had been returned.

Evalle slipped out before anyone could yank her into service. After taking the Edgewood exit off the downtown interstate connector, she rode past Grady Hospital and parked in her usual place on a side street. She'd dumped her helmet and was putting on her sunshades when six men in black fatigues and all wearing night-vision monoculars emerged from the shadows with weapons trained on her.

Now what?

When they had her surrounded, the largest one said with a Southern drawl, "You're to come with us, ma'am."

Ma'am? "Who the hell are you?" She had a suspicion.

"I'm Laredo Jones. My boss wants to talk to you."

"Is this where I get to phone a friend?" She made a subtle move with her feet into a fighting position.

Must not have been that subtle, because the leader's gaze dipped to her feet, then rose back to her face, unconcerned.

She couldn't use her powers against a human, and he was the size of Texas. She thought about calling Tzader, but he couldn't get here fast enough if she did. And she wasn't sure what these weapons would do to Tzader and Quinn.

Her gaze stopped on one weapon to read the word engraved on the side. NYGHT.

Isak was kidnapping her.

TWENTY-NINE

"Shh, Brutus," Laurette whispered when she tiptoed down her hallway to take a look in on the sleeping man in the living room. The night-light she'd left on gave the room a pink glow, pushing the early morning dark away from his angular face.

Holding the stone in her hand, she could read the mantel clock that had belonged to her granddad. Not quite three in the morning yet.

Vyan was still there and more dangerous looking than earlier with his beard now starting to grow in. The pink cast was strangely beautiful on his Mediterranean-dark skin, which she wouldn't have been able to see if not for this magical rock she clutched in her fingers. The Sunday she'd found it seemed a long time ago, but today was only Tuesday.

Two days of having her vision back.

But now she had this man who actually knew about the rock.

And he'd stepped in front of her to protect her from that lightning-bolt-throwing guy. Why would he risk his life for her like that?

Being the brave dog he was, Brutus padded his way over to the inert man, circling him to sniff at his shoulder.

She squatted down and waved her hand to call Brutus back to her, but he had selective eyesight and ignored her. When she hissed at him to come back, the man's eyes opened and he turned his head to face her.

Dear Lord. He had two pupils in each eye.

Breathing became impossible.

She should have stayed in her room with the chair jammed under the knob.

"Hello." His dry voice had a funny accent. She'd noticed something Middle Eastern–sounding in the park, but now she also picked up warm and friendly.

She tried out her voice. "Hello."

Brutus had lain down next to the man's side and was currently getting his back rubbed.

The man continued to stare at her until she felt pressed to say something. "Who are you?"

"I am Vyan of the Kujoo."

Watching him for any signs of aggression, she asked, "How'd you end up here?"

His eyes smiled, as if he'd been asked an easy question she should have been able to answer. "You brought me here."

"No, I didn't."

"The stone you hold brought me here with you then."

That could have been the case. She'd been standing in Piedmont Park with this guy lying across Brutus's leash, which she'd been holding when she'd said she wanted to come home. Everything had blurred. She'd felt as though something had been sucking her down a wind tunnel, then all motion had stopped and she was sitting here with Brutus and this guy.

With an injured Vyan. She brushed her tongue over her parched lips. "Who was the guy that hurt you?"

"His name is Tristan."

"Why were you fighting him?"

"He wants the rock you have and will harm you to get it."

The thumping in her chest should be loud enough to wake the neighbors. She'd been searching the creek in the park to see if she could find any more glowing rocks when she'd encountered Vyan, Tristan and a strange woman, none of whom seemed to be friends. "Why does he want this rock?"

"You know the answer to that."

Okay, she did realize that *anyone* would want a magical rock, but she wasn't giving it up and losing her vision. She *was* happy to have someone she could talk to about this rock. "What does he plan to use the rock for?"

"For evil reasons that you may not believe."

She made a rude sound from deep in her throat. "If this had been two days ago, I might agree, but I'm holding a rock that gives me perfect vision and transported me home. This was *after* you pulled a sword on that Tristan guy, who had the power to throw lightning bolts at you. *And* a woman stepped in to stop him with some invisible power that made a force field of some sort. And your eyes aren't exactly normal. What makes you think I won't believe anything *you* have to tell me?"

He laughed, and the room filled with the pleasure of his happiness. "You are correct. I had not considered your experience with the Ngak Stone."

"Nak stone?"

"Yes, the Ngak Stone." He studied her eyes. "So you are blind?"

She flushed with self-conscious embarrassment. "Not yet, but I'm losing my eyesight."

"You must find another way to regain your sight. This stone is dangerous to keep. I will protect you as long as I can, but that time is limited and I will soon be outnumbered."

How many more people like Vyan were floating around Atlanta? She should have realized finding a magic stone would come with fine print. Standing up, she made a decision. "I guess you're not going to rape and murder me if you haven't yet." She almost laughed at the horrified look on his face until his expression changed to anger.

"I have *never* harmed a woman and *never* forced myself on one."

"I didn't mean to insult you." She lost her smile. "I was just thinking out loud. It's not smart for single women to bring strange men home."

His brow crinkled with thought. "I sometimes do not understand your language. You were joking, correct?"

"Yes, I was joking . . . as long as you really aren't here to harm me."

"I will not harm you."

The sincerity in his words touched her. He'd protected her earlier, and Brutus liked him. She ran out of ways to judge his character at that. "If we're going to talk, I'd like a cup of tea. Want some? I don't have anything stronger, like alcohol."

"Tea would be good, but I must find a place to wash my face first."

"Oh, yes." She pointed down the hall. "Last door on the right."

He pushed up to his elbows and gritted his teeth. His nice skin tone turned ashen.

She hurried over to help him before common sense jumped up to warn her about getting too close to the guy. "Take it easy. I'm not a doctor. I don't have a car or I'd take you to the hospital."

"No doctors or buildings. I will heal fine." He gained his feet, stood for a moment getting his balance, then took slow steps down the hallway. The worn jeans fit his body nicely.

It had been a long time since she'd noticed any man. Chuck the Thief hadn't interested her in a romantic way at all, but any woman would notice this Vyan in a crowd of men.

Especially bare-chested. Much as she hated to cover up that gorgeous body, she told him to wait a minute then ran to find one of her granddad's old T-shirts. "Here you go."

"Thank you for your kindness." He accepted the simple gift as if she'd handed him something of great value. Then he gifted her right back with a smile that would forever be framed in her mind.

Now, if she could just get her heart to stop beating as if she were still in her teens.

When the bathroom door clicked shut, she hurried to the kitchen to make tea. The pot of water was whistling by the time he stepped into the kitchen and dropped into one of four scarred chairs sitting around a small table. She'd planned to do more with this house when she'd moved in a few years ago, once she started growing her art sales. The house wasn't much to look at right now, but it had potential.

True potential if the rock allowed her to continue painting her giant pots and marketing them on her own. Since finding the rock, she'd been painting the last few pieces of pottery she had ready, but she needed to make more and needed two hands to handle the giant pots. Today's project was supposed to be figuring out how to do that while holding the rock.

Not entertaining a man with magical power.

But he'd put his life on the line for her . . . and was still trying to protect her.

267

She stepped over to the table and leaned down to pour tea in the cup next to him. He smelled of the outdoors, as though he slept under the stars at night.

He waited quietly while she placed a dish of oatmeal cookies on the table. What did you feed men who fought lightning bolts with a sword? "Want anything in your tea?"

"No. You have a fine home."

She looked around to see if she'd missed something about her home, then sat down. Maybe he saw the same potential. "Thank you. Now, explain to me about Tristan, his evil reasons for this Ngak Stone and how you fit into all this. Maybe I need to tell the police."

The twinkle returned to his eyes. "Your police can do nothing to help you."

She was afraid of that, but she sipped her tea so he could continue.

"Perhaps the best way to explain is to tell you where I come from."

"I didn't think you were from here, but we do have a large ethnic community, so I wasn't sure."

"I am from Tibet."

"I figured Middle Eastern," she said, having no clue where Tibet was.

"I don't know of this Middle Eastern, but did you *figure* that I came from eight hundred years ago?"

She put her tea down. Her head spun, so she grabbed the table.

"Are you sick?"

"Not yet, but that's probably coming next. Eight hundred years? As in you came forward in time?"

"Sort of. I have been living in immortal existence beneath Mount Meru for all these years."

She thought she was ready to accept anything this man said, but *he'd lived under a mountain for eight hundred years?* How had he ended up here? "Did Tristan come from the same place?"

Vyan's face tightened with a scowl. "No, that dog is of this era."

"How do you two know each other?"

"My warlord escaped Mount Meru two days ago with eight more soldiers, then we went to South America to free Tristan from a spell-bound cage."

She swallowed, trying to keep up with the story he was sharing and ask the right questions. "Why was he in a cage?"

"Because he changes into a beast that kills humans."

The tea churned in her stomach. "Why did you free something like him?"

"Because my warlord believes Tristan can get the Ngak Stone we need to send our tribe back eight hundred years to live in our time again."

"Why did you come forward in time if you want to go back?"

Vyan smiled. "It does sound strange. I will explain. Our entire tribe was cursed to live beneath Mount Meru as immortals eight hundred years ago after battling with the Beladors. We want to go home to our lands and live as natural men again, and the Ngak Stone is our only hope."

"Beladors. What are those?"

"That woman tonight is one. They are our enemy. In my time, the Beladors murdered our families. We have been forbidden to battle them by our god Shiva or we'll be further cursed."

"Okay, wait." She rubbed her temple to ward off the headache building. "You and your warlord and some of his men came to my time to find this rock, but you need Tristan to get the rock that he'll use to send your people back in time. Is that correct?"

"Yes."

"But the Beladors are here and they're your enemy, but you can't fight with them but Tristan can? Are the Beladors in this era evil people?"

Vyan broke his eye contact, letting his gaze sweep the room before coming back to her face. "They are my enemy."

She let that go to focus on the question that mattered most. "How does Tristan plan to get this rock?"

"You could give it to him."

"I hear an 'or' at the end of that."

"He can kill you and take it."

Fine print warnings had never been that dire in the past. What was she going to do? Then it hit her. "What if *I* send your tribe back eight hundred years?"

"I don't think you possess the power to control the rock at this point if you couldn't send me away earlier." He smiled.

"You heard that?"

His smile widened, so sexy it turned her mind to mush.

She'd be fanning herself soon if he kept that up. "Sorry, but I didn't know what to do with you."

Vyan's worried eyes met hers. "Tristan is not the greatest danger for you."

"You don't think getting killed by something that changes into a beast is bad enough?"

"You have until sunrise tomorrow morning to give up the stone or it will bond with you permanently as its master."

"That doesn't sound so bad. Maybe I *want* to be the stone's master."

"It is not so easy as it seems. This stone is as old as the earth itself. It has passed through the hands of many masters, all of whom are dead. The stone has always gone to a powerful being who could control the stone's powers. On Wednesday morning when the sun touches the spot where you found the rock, energy will fill you. This stone chooses its own destiny and may have chosen you because you are human."

This was as bad as listening to the evening news, full of death and disaster, except it would be *her* death and disaster. "What do you mean? Why is being human not a good thing?"

Vyan drew hard on a breath and took his time answering. "If the stone's energy does not kill you when the power hits your body, the stone may take over your mind and turn you into its slave to commit whatever actions it decides. It could choose for you to do good in this world . . . or to destroy everything and everyone in sight."

She released the stone she'd been clutching inside her pants pocket and suffered the loss of vision.

Live in a world of darkness forever or risk the future of humanity and her sanity?

THIRTY

The interior of the windowless panel truck bouncing over every bump on hard rear springs smelled of male perspiration and dedication. Evalle doubted she could say a thing to Laredo Jones, the mountain-size leader of these men, that would change their minds about delivering her to Isak.

And what about Isak, since he didn't think her aura was human? She kept her clammy hands clasped in front of her to keep from fidgeting.

She'd seen what his demon-killing megablaster could do.

Did these men have any idea she might be Alterant?

At least these guys hadn't stuck a sack over her head, but she had no idea where she was going.

The truck stopped. Then a groan of metal moving outside the van sounded next. That could be a garage-type metal door on a building. A really big one, based on how long it was taking to open. When the noise ceased, the truck drove forward about fifty feet and parked.

No one moved until the rear door opened. She waited for her cue to exit, then stepped out into a hangar that soared three stories high in the center.

She hadn't heard airplanes on her way here, so this might or might not be at an airport. The drive had taken half an hour. That would make the time around three in the morning, but she wasn't lifting her watch into view to check.

No sudden moves around men with megaweapons.

Laredo angled his head away from her. "Follow me."

She did as ordered, hiking through a building that could hold a

747, but all it contained right now was the panel van she'd arrived in, two dark green Hummers and a gold Dodge Ram 250 diesel pickup. At the far end of the structure, someone had built offices. Laredo opened a door and stepped aside, leaving her with simple instructions. "Continue down that hallway to the door at the end, ma'am."

She doubted escape would be realistic at this point, and the door was only three long strides away. She reached it and closed her fingers around the doorknob, pushing it open, when her sense of smell said *lasagna*.

Well at least Rambo liked Italian.

On the other side of the door was a large office space. Over to her left, a table had been set up with two place settings and chairs. She walked further inside until she saw a sideboard with food lined up.

Isak stood in front of the sideboard, preparing two plates. "Can't believe what it takes to eat a meal with you."

She sorted through her reactions, from trepidation to anger to annoyance to surprise, and settled on humor. She had, after all, stood him up twice. And he didn't seem ticked off with her or threatening. But he'd still snatched her off the street.

"Kidnapping me at gunpoint puts me in *such* an entertaining mood. Got a movie for later?"

He glanced her way, smiling at first, then did a double take, examining her from head to toe. His gaze turned murderous and he headed for the door. "Jones is dead."

"Jones?" She realized then that Isak had assumed his man had been the culprit behind her beat-to-hell look. "No, no, no." She pointed at herself. "He didn't do *this*."

Isak paused in midstride and turned to stop right in front of her. He touched her face with fingers so gentle it reminded her of the wind on her cheeks at night. "Did you wreck your bike?"

"Of course not." She'd hurt someone for scratching her baby. "Might say I had a bad day at the office."

His eyes held a thousand questions, none of which she could answer. Especially with him standing so close and with his fingertips grazing her bruised cheek. His fingers slipped under her chin and lifted slightly. "You're not going to tell me who did this to you, are you?"

272

"What would you do if I did?"

"Far worse than what happened to that Birrn demon."

He had to be the most charming kidnapper on earth. "No, I can't tell you. The smell of food is killing me. I'd like to wash up first."

"Bathroom's over there." He pointed to a door across the room.

She backed away from his fingers and went into the bathroom, which was clean and basic. A huge mirror told her just how bad the past twenty-four hours had been if her exhausted eyes, bruised skin and ratted-up hair were any indication. She scrubbed her face, arms and exposed chest skin, removing the mud that had dried from being slammed into the ground by Tristan at the park. She braided her hair again. Not much she could do about her ragged shirt.

Stepping back into the office-dining room, she sucked in the aroma of warm lasagna again. She should refuse to eat, talk or put up with being captured, but she hadn't eaten in so long she was getting shaky from low blood sugar.

Don't drool.

Music played softly in the background. Just enough sound to soften the quiet edges of the room. "Nice digs. Been using Martha Stewart's guide to kidnapping?"

The prick of smile at his lips was his only acknowledgment she'd spoken.

Maybe she should button down on the sarcasm. Best not to wake the demon-killing side of him.

"Wine?" Isak set a plate at each end of the table.

"Water, please." She was severely underdressed in her now filthy BDU shirt that had been new twenty years ago, the running top still gritty with mud, and jeans with a tear down one leg.

Isak's short-sleeved black dress shirt and clean black jeans fit him like a wicked whisper. She'd been right about his eyes. Blue as the ocean and set in a face that hinted of Norwegian ancestors. That would explain the genetics for a body built like a tank. He was as drool-worthy as the meal.

Those quick eyes that missed nothing met hers and saw the admiration she should have kept secret.

How many kinds of a fool was she going to be around this guy?

Get your head back into save-butt gear. She shifted her attention to a safe topic. "Smells delicious."

The smile lifting one side of his mouth should have worried her instead of kicking up her heartbeat. "Dig in."

She lifted a fork to stab salad in the glass bowl sitting to the side of her plate. She should address standing him up the second time. "Couldn't help missing our meeting again."

"Business, right?"

"Yes, actually. How'd you find me?" She might have to continue meeting him if he fed her like this.

"Remember? I have friends in low places."

"So . . . what? You have a complete file downloaded on me?"

"I have enough." He ate like a man should, no holding back, but she kept catching something in his movements that argued against his earthy personality. There. When he lifted the water goblet. It fit his hand as if he was as accustomed to crystal glass as he was to eating MREs—Meals Ready to Eat—in the field.

"In that case, what's in my file?" She pushed another mouthful of Italian deliciousness into her mouth.

"I know your name is E. Valerie Kincaid, but not what the E stands for."

"Me either. If you find out let me know." The aunt who'd raised her had never explained why Evalle only had the initial E and not a first name. Would Isak have found out who her father and mother were? Her aunt had never shared the name of either. She'd only told Evalle that her mother was trash and her father didn't want her.

"Why don't you know?"

She shrugged. "I've always had just E, which is why my nickname became Evalle. The woman who raised me called me E. Valerie for a while, then it morphed into E-val. You happen to find out who my father was while you were at it?"

His head canted to one side with an odd look of surprise on his face. "No. The records only show the woman listed as your adoptive mother."

So he didn't know the woman was her aunt? "What else do you know about me?"

274

"I know your aura is not human."

She paused with a forkful of lasagna at her lips. Go on offense when you have no defense. "That wasn't funny when you said it last night and it's not funny now, Isak."

Isak finished chewing and swallowing his last mouthful, then wiped his lips with the linen napkin. "Humans have a pale aqua and sometimes pinkish aura. Yours is silver."

She felt each heavy thump of her heart in the space between his last three words. She put her fork down and faced him, the muscles in her body tightening to face a possible threat even though Isak's tone had been one of curiosity more than challenge. "What are you accusing me of being? Something like that Birrn demon?"

He finally looked into her eyes—or seemed to look right through her glasses—then his gaze pulled back, studying her head and shoulders. "I'm not accusing you of anything. I'm curious to know why yours is different."

How to answer that question? "I don't know. I can't see auras. Are you sure about what you're seeing?"

Or had she misread his charm and he was toying with her?

"Yes, I'm good at reading auras."

No one had told her she had a silver one, but she lived around nonhumans all the time and couldn't see auras herself. Chances were they all had strange auras and thought nothing of hers. She had to either convince him she was not a threat or get the hell out of here quick.

But she needed information he had on the Birrn demon and possibly anything else he knew. Asking for that right now would not curb his suspicions. She turned the topic back to him. "I've always thought people like psychics saw auras. Are you psychic or something *else*?"

"Something else."

"Human?"

"Most definitely."

She tapped her fingers on the table. "This is pretty one-sided. You yank me in here like a captive and want me to answer questions, but you aren't sharing a thing. You want to know about me? Who are you? Where'd you come from? Who do you work for? Where'd you get that superblaster gun? How is it you're human and you can find nonhumans?"

He drew in a deep breath and leaned back as he expelled it. He propped an elbow on the table and rested his chin on his bent fingers, thinking on something. "I was raised in a military family, so I lived everywhere until I joined the army. I left the army last year. All my men are former military of some sort. They all work for Nyght, Inc. I can't discuss what we do, but we save lives that are threatened. I designed the weapon you saw the other night. And I guess you can say I have a natural gift for finding nonhumans."

Where was Storm when she needed the human lie detector? She pushed her plate away. "I can't help but think you brought me here because you think I'm not human."

He stood up and started clearing the dishes to the sideboard then sat down across from her again. "I haven't accused you of that. Just want to know a little more about you. Like where you grew up."

If he had her birth records he had to know some basics, but how much of the records was fabricated if her aunt was listed as an adoptive parent? She wouldn't tell him anything he didn't already know.

Since he was being reasonable and she still wanted information, she said, "I grew up in a little town in western Indiana."

"There's no school listing for you anywhere."

"That's because I didn't go to school."

"Your name would show up somewhere even being home schooled."

"I wasn't home schooled."

That stumped him for a moment.

She knew so little about where she came from she'd like to see the file he had on her, but that wasn't her first concern right now. "Why does my background matter to you?"

He sat down again, arm on the table, as relaxed as a tiger that could pounce at any moment. "I'll be honest with you. You were on site with that Birrn demon. There have been two more demons in the city besides that one. I'm following every lead on anything unusual. You're unusual."

"Unusual? In what way?"

"No one sees you during the day."

"Who do you mean when you say no one?"

Lifting his hands, he counted off fingers. "The morgue where you work has you listed as nights only, no exceptions. Your bike is only on traffic cameras at night."

She caught his look of *need I go on?* "What exactly do you think that makes me?"

"I'd say a vampire if not for your aura. The dead do not have auras." He'd said that in a joking manner, but she didn't think this man joked about things like that.

If she didn't give him a reason he could accept for her nocturnal behavior, he was going to become a problem for her. "I was born with a rare skin disease. Vitamin D is poison to my body. It's as simple as that."

"What about the silver aura?"

"I don't have an answer for you. What else have you encountered that has a silver aura?"

"Nothing."

Halle-freakin'-lujah. She allowed the trapped air to escape from her lungs but held her unconcerned façade. "Maybe the strange aura is just part of the whole allergy to the sun thing."

"Maybe."

He wasn't letting this go, not inside that iron-tight mind of his. She smiled in spite of her apprehension and said in a lighthearted tone, "You going to arrest me over suspicion of being unusual?"

"I don't arrest anything."

This conversation had taken a serious turn. "That's right. You shoot to kill and send your goon squad as limo drivers." Sometimes attitude was the best weapon handy. She stood up. "Dinner was wonderful. I really appreciate it and the curb service."

"I still have a question."

"I still have a busy schedule. Save it for our next clandestine dinner."

"How long have you been talking to Nightstalkers? None of them ever see you during the day either."

Crud. If she walked out now he'd take that as fear, and that wasn't happening. She sat down. "I already told you why I don't go out in daylight. What do you want, Isak?"

"The truth."

That wasn't going to happen. Tzader had warned her that Isak was after Alterants and to stay away. Coming here hadn't been *her* idea. What truth could she give Isak that might end his suspicions and open the door to finding out about his intel?

"One more time. The truth is that I was born with a severe reaction to the sun. It will kill me. I'm not a demon or a monster." Most days. "My parents were human. My mother died in childbirth. The woman who raised me was an aunt, if your definition of *being raised* is being kept in a basement twenty-four-seven for eighteen years, where I got fed every day."

He frowned at that but didn't interrupt her.

"She did teach me to read, write and speak so that I wouldn't require as much care. She hated my mother and told me my father didn't want some freak for a child. I do see spirits and can sometimes talk to them. I work at the morgue and do not harm humans, animals or aliens who don't harm me. What else?"

"Would you remove your glasses?"

If he knew what Alterant eyes looked like—which he probably did, since he'd killed one—seeing her pale green eyes would end all bluffing.

She'd been put on display and turned on a pedestal to be observed from all directions since escaping her aunt. He could kill her if he wanted, but she would not sit here and grovel. "You've reduced me to a specimen under a microscope and now you want me to risk my vision just to appease your curiosity. I've answered your questions and met my commitment for a meal. What's it going to be, Isak? You going to blow me to pieces to protect the world from a freak of nature or let me go?"

When he didn't answer, she rose and stepped away from the table, heading for the door. "I'm leaving unless you shoot me."

The rustle of clothes reached her ears before his voice did. "Wait, Evalle."

And his voice sounded different. Huskier.

Pausing a step from the door, she turned around to find Isak close. Very close. She could smell his freshly showered body. She expected to see the steely look of a man bent on protecting the world from monsters like her.

But when she raised her face to his, she was surprised to see the discomfort in his gaze. Standing close in this low light, he could see the shape and movement of her eyes through the protective glasses, but not the color.

He lifted his hand slowly, as though being very careful not to make the wrong move.

Don't touch my glasses. Her heart thumped wildly.

One of his fingers touched her cheek, then lifted a tiny strand of hair off her face. "I have a responsibility to protect humans every minute of every day, but I don't think you're a demon or a monster. I do think you're unusual. One of the most unusual women I've ever met."

He leaned forward and kissed her forehead, then her cheek.

She couldn't have moved if the building had been on fire.

Cupping her face with his massive hand, he leaned down and kissed her. Her heart raced out of control the longer his lips worked magic over hers. He had a persuasive mouth that convinced hers to kiss him back.

He tasted like the last sip of wine he'd had.

When he ended the kiss, she had her hand on his wrist, holding on for support.

What had she been thinking to kiss him? She let go of his wrist, dropping her hand to her side.

She hadn't been thinking. Her empathic side had been opening the door to emotions she'd never allowed to surface before. This was dangerous. First Storm, who was just as spectacular at kissing, and now Isak.

He ran a finger along her neck. "You're different and beautiful."

If she hadn't truly believed he was human, she'd have thought he was spinning a spell right now. Was she putting out pheromones to men these days? Did Alterant pheromones work on humans?

Or was she dealing with a hormone overload to feel a sizzle from standing this close to a man who'd threatened her entire world just a minute ago? Had to be her empathic sense maturing.

She needed to get that under control.

He gave her a long gaze. "I want to see you again."

When she was nervous, her sarcastic side came out. "You made that pretty clear by snatching me off the sidewalk. Do you grab all your dates that way?"

"Haven't actually dated in a long time. I knew you were too tough to be afraid, so I was hoping you'd go along with Jones out of curiosity."

His admission about no dating surprised her. She had to admit he'd pegged her right on being curious, but she had to find the Ngak Stone, and she might disappear any day if things didn't go well with the Tribunal. "I'll be honest with you, Isak. I've got a lot of things on my plate right now and some difficult people on my back. I may have to go away for a while, and I'm telling you this right up front so you don't think I'm avoiding you if that happens."

Worry stirred through his strong face. "I can help you with difficult people."

"I doubt it."

His lips curved in a smile that countered her words. "I don't just hunt demons, sweetheart. I'm good at making people disappear. Someone bothers you, just let me know."

She wasn't sure if it was the endearment or the vow to protect her that ramped up his charm factor, but her heart tingled over his concern. "I'll keep that in mind."

And she would. But right now her best plan of action was to see if he'd share information on the Birrn and get out of here while she still had her glasses on and Isak thought she was just another anomaly of nature. "If we're good, I'd love to know more about that Birrn you smoked the other night."

"Maybe next time. Much as I'd like to keep you here longer, you need to get to your bike before daylight, and I've got to find a Nightstalker and get some answers."

If Isak was human, then he couldn't cut a deal with a Nightstalker for a handshake, which meant he shouldn't be able to get any solid intel. She laughed to sell her next words. "You make it sound like Nightstalkers are informants."

"They are if they shake hands with someone who has power."

She reassessed Isak. "You said you were human."

"I am, but I have resources."

Ah, crap. "I'd be careful doing that if I were you. Most of the Nightstalkers are a half bubble off to begin with."

"Not the one I'm looking for."

"Who's that?"

"He's called Grady. I'm on my way to find him and get some answers."

She fought to keep her shoulders relaxed. Grady wouldn't tell Isak a thing about her, right? But then it hit her that Grady needed an hour of human form Wednesday night for something.

Would he trade her for that?

THIRTY-ONE

Evalle rode silently in the panel van with four Nyght Raiders and considered the clear skies growing lighter each minute as they reached downtown Atlanta. She had less than an hour until daylight only because she'd convinced Isak that Nightstalkers found her on occasion, not the other way around.

And he hadn't wanted her exposed to the sun.

He'd been very accommodating after that kiss.

She couldn't think about that right now, with a bigger worry looming. Grady. She had to find that old ghoul and make sure he didn't talk to Isak.

How was she going to do that and not agree to give Grady the hour he wanted tomorrow night?

Just once she'd like a simple problem to solve.

The van parked next to where they'd picked her up. Wet heat slapped her skin with the unwelcome rise in temperature after her chilly air-conditioned ride.

"Need anything before we depart?" Laredo said.

"Sure. How about one of those demon blasters?" She gave her GSX-R a quick once-over just to appease him, but she'd have known immediately if anyone had touched her bike.

Isak's man didn't crack a smile.

Save her from men with no sense of humor. "You're free to return to Yoda."

He climbed into the van, which rolled away.

Isak hadn't asked to see her eyes again, but he would eventually press that issue. If she ran out of time with the Tribunal, would he still offer to help her if he found out she was an Alterant? Or just rid the world of one more threat?

Lot of ifs and little time to spend on any of them.

Grady should have intel by now, but after an hour of stalking the old ghoul, she had a sick feeling something was very wrong. Where was he?

That hour he wanted on Wednesday night played loud in her mind. What was he willing to do to get that?

She'd have to head home soon or dig out her protective gear and ignore the heat already climbing into the nineties.

Nightstalkers normally gathered within minutes if someone with supernatural abilities stood in one spot and radiated a power field. She'd been doing that for the past hour. One wispy figure finally showed up, when Evalle would normally be engulfed in a crowd of them when Grady wasn't around.

With no other offers, Evalle cut a quick deal and traded a handshake with a scraggly woman who had to be in her eighties. She got right to the point. "Where are the other Nightstalkers?"

The old woman lifted a hand with paper-thin skin that showed every vein and used her scrawny fingers to brush at the delicate white hair tufted over her head. "They took the others."

"Who took the others and when?"

"Kujoo. They didn't act normal. Offered Nightstalkers a trade to stay in this form for more than ten minutes." She sniffed when a tear streaked along her wrinkled face.

"What's wrong?" Evalle put her arm around the woman. She would hunt down Tristan and make his bunch very sorry if they had hurt this woman when they'd been here.

"I was too slow," she mumbled again. "They swore we could stay this way, human, forever."

Evalle hated having to douse the hope in the old woman's voice, but she had to stop Nightstalkers from going with the Kujoo. "It's a lie. The Kujoo are turning Nightstalkers into something that can't hold a human form or a ghost form. Something evil. Pass the word around to hide from them."

Tears drizzled down the old woman's face and dripped off her chin at the stark disappointment in losing the glimmer of hope that she could return to her prior life. Evalle felt as though she'd taken a crayon from a child, but she wouldn't let the Kujoo trick any more of these poor souls.

Grady was a wily old guy who understood evil. Maybe he hadn't shown up here because he was hiding from the bad guys.

Maybe she'd convince herself that was the case in another lifetime, when in truth she had a sick feeling he'd been caught by Tristan and the Kujoo.

Daylight had pressed in close by the time Evalle made sure the old woman was safely back in her Nightstalker form and Evalle reached her underground garage.

She struggled to stay awake all the way to her apartment. Feenix thumped, thumped, thumped down the hallway, running to meet her. But he stopped short of flying at her.

He must have seen the desolation in her eyes that soaked through her bones. She forced a smile to her lips and made it real for him. "Hi, baby."

Clapping the sides of his body with his fat little hands, he waddled to her, grunting undecipherable words, then hugged her leg. She patted his head. "Let me get a shower and type a letter, then we'll play, okay?"

He danced around, chirping with happy sounds, before he landed on his beanbag, where he normally waited for her.

After a quick run through the shower, she pulled on a T-shirt and underwear, then plopped down on the bed with her laptop. Ignoring the possibility of being locked away by the Tribunal as a worst-case scenario or having to ask Isak to help her disappear as best-case scenario would be foolish. She opened a blank document and typed, "To Tzader and Quinn: If I lose my case with the Tribunal and don't return . . ."

Thumping and grunting noises reached her before Feenix showed up at her bedroom door. He was dragging his stuffed alligator and a pair of her dark sunshades. She had five pairs besides the one she was wearing.

He flapped his wings and flew to her bed, landing softly beside her. When he tucked his wings, she lifted her arm so he could crawl up against her. He put on the dark sunshades and settled against her chest with his alligator tucked under one arm.

She hugged him, her heart aching over the impossible thought of leaving Feenix, her apartment, Tzader, Quinn . . . and the rest of the team who had stood by her tonight.

And there was Storm, who knew she was an Alterant and had no issues with that.

She was beginning to think he might actually be telling her the truth about not helping Sen put her away. But he couldn't prevent Sen from carrying out a Tribunal decision.

Using one hand to type so she didn't have to give up any chance to hold Feenix, she pecked away. The pain of losing this little guy cramped her lungs when she tried to breathe, but she would make sure he was never left to depend on the world's mercy like she had been.

There was no mercy in this world for misfits.

Tristan had called that one right.

When she finished typing the letter, she attached it to an email set to send to Tzader and Quinn on Thursday by noon. If the Tribunal locked her up, the email would ensure Feenix's future was secure, but her baby would be lost without her.

People liked dogs and cats.

Not something that ate lug nuts and breathed fire. Only Tzader and Quinn would protect him.

He stopped muttering words and sounds when she closed her laptop. She should tell him she might not return, but she couldn't do it yet. "Let's go see what's in the kitchen utensil drawer for you."

Feenix turned and hugged her with one arm. "Mine."

She swallowed against the lump in her throat and hugged him back. "You're mine, too, baby."

For now.

There had to be something she could do, but what? The only Nightstalkers left in the city had no intel on the Kujoo. The human woman with the rock couldn't be tracked after teleporting. Vyan clearly did not like Tristan, but that didn't mean he wasn't going to hand the woman and the rock over to the Kujoo.

Sitting here with time disintegrating was driving her nuts. She had to do something.

She scrolled through emails while she groused mentally and stopped at one from Nicole with a subject line of IMPORTANT. It read:

Must see you soon. Even daytime.

Evalle lifted her phone and dialed Nicole, who answered on one ring. "Hi, Nic."

"Where have you been?"

"Butt deep in alligators. What's up?" Evalle shushed Feenix, whose eyes lit up with excitement when he realized she was talking to Nicole.

"You're in deep trouble."

"Tell me something I don't know, Nic."

"Come over and I will. Not on the phone. Sorry, but I don't trust it with the work you do and what I want to tell you."

Nic had a point. No telling what Isak could tap if he found her number. But going to see her friend now meant putting on gear to ride in the heat and she had no time tonight. Ugh. "Can you give me a hint?"

"You looking for a stone?"

Oh, shit. The heat be damned. "I'm heading your way."

"Ride." Feenix pushed away and stood up on the bed, bouncing as she ended the call. "Go ride. Go ride."

She'd taken him for a late-night ride on the bike once and he'd loved it, especially when she'd stopped by Nicole's to show Feenix to her. He loved Nic.

Nicole had never driven a vehicle, and she required someone to drive her wheelchair-accessible van when she did travel. For her, Evalle would make the ride in daytime. And to get a hand up on finding this stone. If traffic worked in her favor, she could make Avondale in fifteen minutes. Riding alone would be quicker, but she had little time left with Feenix if she lost her bid with the Tribunal. "Come on, baby. Let's get you dressed and go for a ride."

Feenix tossed his alligator up in the air and caught it, stomping back and forth on the bed. "Go ride, dammit."

"We're going to have to work on your vocabulary," she told him on the way to finding his T-shirt. "You'll need those sunshades, too. We'll be in midday sun."

But she was wrong. By the time she'd covered herself in a custom lightweight Aerostich riding suit she'd just received in the mail and wheeled her bike out of the elevator car, the skies were overcast, with temperatures in the eighties.

Not ideal, but a welcome break.

Putting the side stand down, she turned to Feenix, who hopped out of the elevator and landed next to her.

"Don't forget, you're a robot today," she told him.

Feenix immediately straightened up and pretended to move his hands and feet like a robot while he walked around in a circle.

"You're good." She put goggles on him to cover his eyes that glowed sometimes, and gloves, to keep him from using his power inadvertently. Then she lifted him up to the back of her bike seat. He gripped a looped strap on each side that gave him the look of a stuffed animal attached to the chassis.

The black T-shirt Nicole had given her for Feenix raised a smile to Evalle's lips. Just above his potbelly, it read EVL TOO. Nicole's idea of the perfect match for Evalle's vanity motorcycle tag, which read EVL ONE.

"Go fath, dammit." Feenix kept staring straight off the rear of the bike, but his mouth curved up.

"Will you stop saying 'dammit' if I get you a bucket of lug nuts?"

"Yeth. What ith bucket?"

"Never mind." Her gear was lightweight but hot standing still with no air moving. "Sit up straight and don't talk to anyone. Got it?"

He looked at her and pointed at his mouth, as in *you told me not to talk*.

She smiled. He had her there.

Climbing on, she cranked the engine and kinetically closed the elevator door.

The ride to Avondale, which was east of downtown Atlanta, took a few minutes longer than expected. A good little backseat rider, Feenix leaned with her through the curves and made a high-pitched whistling sound when she revved the RPMs.

Nicole lived in a remodeled warehouse near Main Street, not because living in a loft apartment was the style for a woman in her late twenties but because she liked the sense of community she found here.

Evalle used the security code to enter and parked in the secured garage beneath the four-story building.

Feenix hopped down and hurried over to the elevator, where he flapped his wings to reach the button.

"Feenix! Robot, remember?"

"Thorry." He dropped back down to the concrete and did his robotic circle walk.

Evalle reached the elevator as the door opened and two women walked out. They took one look at Feenix and stopped. Evalle lifted her key ring, which had a small black box on it, and pointed the box at Feenix. "Walk into the elevator."

He did a perfect imitation of a robotic gargoyle.

The women laughed and oohed over him.

Bless Feenix, because he managed not to smile when she could see how much he wanted to.

Thankfully, the fourth floor hallway was vacant of humans. Nicole's door opened before she knocked on it.

Beautiful. That word always jumped into Evalle's mind when she saw Nicole, with her caramel brown hair that flowed and curled around her brown sugar shoulders, but the woman wasn't the least bit vain. She wore a flowing sleeveless housedress that hid the crippled legs she'd been born with, and she leaned heavily on her rosewood cane.

"I've been waiting for you." Nicole inched forward to give a hug she knew Evalle didn't allow easily. When Nicole hobbled backward and opened the door wider, she saw Evalle wasn't alone. "Hello, Feenix. Oh! You're wearing the shirt I gave you."

Bouncing into the apartment, Feenix took Nicole's exclamation as a cue to be himself again. He stomped from foot to foot and pointed at his shirt. "Like it, dammit."

Nicole gave Evalle a sharp look at the curse word.

"Don't ask. It was an accident, and I haven't been able to fix it."

Evalle told Feenix, "'Dammit' is not a good word, so don't use it, okay?"

"Whereth my bucket?"

"What?" Nicole asked.

"That's another conversation. What's up?"

"You're in a lot of trouble."

"I don't need a witch with psychic ability to tell me that. I could have used my Magic Eight Ball."

"You need someone to clue you in on how bad it is." Nicole lifted her hands and murmured words, then the room fell dark as night. "Get out of that gear and start catching me up on the details while I fix our tea."

Nicole produced several colorful twirling toys that floated across the room. Feenix took up the chase, flying after them through the eleven-hundred-square-foot apartment while Evalle gave her the rundown. Tzader and Quinn had warned Evalle about discussing Belador or VIPER business with anyone outside the tribe and agency respectively, but Nicole knew both groups existed and, at times, details that surprised Evalle.

She'd met Nicole while patrolling Avondale for Southend warlocks her first week in Atlanta. Warlocks were male witches who walked on the dark side of life, and the trio terrorizing Avondale had been especially dangerous.

When Evalle had found the three supernatural goons, she'd thought Nicole was a lone wheelchair-bound woman in danger of being hurt. But Nicole had intentionally drawn the boys into a dead-end driveway at the rear of a shopping center after midnight. She'd revealed herself as a witch, then used her rare gift to show them what their future held where they would end up enslaved to a more powerful warlock with twisted sexual cravings.

Nicole had done more in sixty seconds than anyone had accomplished with the three boys in their entire lives. She'd given them a choice of going to a halfway coven house for rehabilitation or facing worse judgment by their peers for crimes committed against humans.

They'd made the smart choice.

When Nicole realized Evalle had witnessed the exchange, she'd warded Evalle against being seen by the warlocks when they'd walked away from the alley, protecting her from any repercussion down the road in case the rehab didn't work.

Evalle had never had a stranger act so selflessly on her behalf except for Tzader and Quinn.

Nicole was a rare witch, not because she was psychic.

Psi ability wasn't uncommon in witches, but Nicole could speak to spirits from the future and sometimes give that future a corporeal form. That might sound like a handy ability to have, except that opening up a channel for a spirit from the future also opened a pathway for that spirit to travel to the present day. With no way of knowing if the spirit was evil or not, Nicole risked being attacked or unleashing the spirit on someone she cared about.

And when Nicole's spirit traveled forward to search for answers, she risked being trapped in the pathway, which would leave her body an empty host.

But right now she was seated on a cozy chair in autumn colors across from where Evalle perched on a sofa. Nicole put her tea down on the glass end table at her left and clasped her hands in her lap while Evalle gave her a rundown on what had happened so far.

Nicole sighed quietly. "That explains some of my visions. You know of the ancient tribe who hunts the Ngak Stone, of the male being who is helping that tribe and about the human female whose life dangles in the midst of it all because she found the stone. But do you know why the female will not give up the stone?"

"She thinks it's like a genie's lamp that will grant her wishes?"

"That would have been my first guess, but when I asked the spirits for help all I got was that her world is a blur of fear."

"Fear of what? Is someone hurting her?"

Nicole frowned with deep thought. "Not yet. I think the blurry part is important, but I don't know what it means. Do you know anything about this woman?"

"I saw her."

"Really? Did you talk to her?"

"No, I was too busy fighting off the guy helping the Kujoo." Evalle rubbed her forehead, pushing back the ache from lack of sleep. "All I know is she's clueless about all this."

"What about the blurry part?" Nicole pressed.

Evalle ran back through last night in her mind until she hit on how the woman had been out in the dark with no flashlight and had felt with her hands at one point for her dog. But her eyes had been sharp and clear when she'd held the stone. "She might be blind."

"Ah, I hadn't considered that, since the woman was seeing something. It's wrong to assume blind means no vision at all. Fear of a blurry world would make sense. You think the rock is allowing her to see?"

"Maybe." Evalle sat up. "Do you know where she is?"

"No. Someone is blocking her face or shielding her."

Crap. "Could be the Kujoo Vyan. I think he's protective of her. If she is blind, she's got to be terrified, between losing her eyesight and witnessing all that she saw in the park last night."

"Hers was not the only fear I sensed. What is yours?"

The abrupt question caught Evalle off guard. "Nothing."

Nicole's pretty face stilled with disappointment at the lie.

Evalle sighed. "That's not true, but I don't want you searching my future."

"If you fear something that's coming, I can help."

"My future has always been a crapshoot, but the dice are stacked against me right now. If you go looking into my future you could run into anything and not make it back." Evalle considered what Nicole *could* do. "I need to know if I'm making the right decision on something. I have to find the Ngak Stone before another Alterant gets his hands on it."

"There's another Alterant free besides you?"

"Only because he escaped. He's the guy working with the Kujoo and he hates Beladors almost as much as the Kujoo do. He claims Brina locked him away even though he didn't turn into a beast or kill anyone before he was caged. I don't know if I should believe that or not, but I'm more concerned with finding out if the Alterant, the Kujoo or the Medb are setting a trap for the Beladors. If not, I should have told the team about this Alterant, but if he was telling the truth about *wanting* me to tell my tribe, I've got to find a way to stop them from walking into the trap."

"Do you know his name?"

"Tristan. Can you help me?"

"I'll try." Nodding, Nicole closed her eyes and leaned back. Several quiet minutes passed, then Nicole spoke a short prayer. Her eyelids started fluttering with rapid eye movement. "The Alterant Tristan . . . has a tortured past. He has lived as a beast in the jungle for five years."

But had he changed into a beast before being caged or not?

Nicole was silent a moment, then said, "This same man at nineteen . . . is frightened, standing in front of strangers, Beladors, who are talking to him about his strange green eyes . . . then he disappears from his job digging graves and is in a jungle, terrified . . . he changes into a beast. He is tormented and alone."

That sounds like Brina lied to me about Tristan. What about the other Alterants? Evalle's throat tightened. She wanted to yell in frustration, but she wouldn't distract Nicole.

"He does not have the stone yet. The Ngak Stone resides still with the female you met. She waits for . . . you. Follow the path from whence you last saw this stone. The trail will lead to the woman at her home, where you will find a sign of your next decision."

That wasn't a lot of help, since there was no way to track the woman after she'd teleported, and what did the "sign of her next decision" mean? Evalle kept quiet, watching Nicole's lips move as she spoke in a dainty voice.

"Trust will open the path for one who is born to the task."

Oh, great. Trust. One of my strengths. Why couldn't Nicole tell her kicking demon ass opened the path? She had plenty of credits for that.

Nicole's mouth puckered along with her brow with deep thought. "The path will lead to a choice one should not face."

Evalle thought her head would explode with holding back her questions. What choice? That path didn't sound promising.

"Your tribe's future depends on the choice you make . . . to trust or not."

What the heck did that mean? Evalle tapped her fingers on the fabric covering the sofa, waiting for a sign that Nicole was finished.

"You will be victorious—"

At that, Evalle gave up the breath she'd clutched in her lungs.

"—and you will lose."

"What?" The word popped out before Evalle could clamp her lips shut. "Sorry."

"It's okay." Nicole's eyes opened, drowsy at first, then lighting with the sharp intelligence that lived behind the hazel orbs. "The Kujoo do hold the future of your tribe in their hands."

"I didn't doubt that part. What did you mean about the choice to trust or not? To trust the Alterant Tristan?"

"Only you will know the answer to that one . . . unless you allow me to search your future."

"No. It's too dangerous. I'll figure out who I have to trust. What about the victorious and losing part? How does that work?"

"There is no absolute win in your future. You must lose something."

"Story of my life," Evalle quipped.

"I hope not. I want you to survive this."

"Me, too, but protecting my tribe comes first." The story of her life, which was shaping up to be a short story.

THIRTY-TWO

Laurette yawned, but she wouldn't end the conversation with this man called Vyan for the life of her. She'd lived alone so long that she'd forgotten how nice it was to have someone to share a meal with and talk to about things she would have once discussed with her granddad.

What would Granddad think of Vyan?

Where had that thought come from?

Vyan pulled her back to the conversation as he finished off the shepherd's pie Laurette had made for lunch, a Tuesday staple. "My wife shaped bowls and cups with her hands, too. She had skilled hands like yours to make such art from the earth."

She hadn't realized how much she missed hearing a compliment on her art. The last time had been her granddad's parting words before he'd left on a trip he wouldn't discuss and never returned.

Granddad had held her hands in his when he'd said, "You have a gift like no other with your hands. Promise me you'll always create pottery, especially the large ones, and mark them the way I taught you. Always have one of your planters outside each door to welcome visitors."

She'd never failed him, yet. Maybe if she'd made him promise to come back to her he'd be here now. He *had* returned to her in her dreams, where he'd told her he was sorry for not coming home, then assured her he'd always watch over her and send others if she ever needed help.

Now would be a good time for the cavalry, Granddad.

The dreams felt so real she believed he did watch over her.

Maybe he'd sent Vyan. That brought a smile to her lips until she realized the warrior had stopped talking about his dead wife. "I'm sorry for your loss."

"Thank you for that." His eyes seemed to gaze back through time, then dropped away, embarrassed. "I can no longer see her face."

That had to be hard. To not have a picture to remember someone by. "Will you find her when you go back?"

He shook his head. "I cannot go back to the time when she was alive, only the last day of my life before being sent to live beneath Mount Meru." Giving another little shake of his head as if wiping something from his mind, he said, "It was long ago and I am glad she did not have to live beneath Mount Meru. What of your family?"

"I have none now either." She could still see her granddad's face, but he hadn't been gone eight hundred years.

Lifting a hand scarred from battles, Vyan touched the small pottery vase she had on the table, which held fresh thyme and mint cuttings from her small garden out back. "I wish to toil the land, not fight with swords."

"Then don't fight."

"I fear that decision has been taken from me for now, but perhaps one day I will be able to lay down my sword." Pushing his plate away, he sat back. "Will you hand over the rock?"

"No. Will you try to take it from me?"

He shook his head. "I will not harm you nor allow anyone else to as long as I have breath in my body."

Her heart melted at his pledge. Why couldn't this man be from her time? She'd shared more time with him this morning than she had with any other man in many years.

She'd never turned the heads of men like other women. Not with a head of wild red hair and the pale features that went with it. Being an artist had turned her into even more of a recluse.

"I have realized my warlord and Tristan are planning revenge against the Beladors. They will need the Ngak Stone for this. I fear our people will be cursed further if we seek revenge, but even if we don't we still need the power of the stone. I want to send my people home or wherever each one wants to go."

"Where else would they go?"

"Some are tired of living and would rather cross over to be with family they have lost. If I held the power of the stone I would ask that their wishes be met."

"Do you want to cross over to be with your wife?" Laurette experienced a sting of regret over the idea of him leaving, which was absurd, since she'd only just met this man and he seemed so lonely. She would never want to keep him from finding peace.

"I do not wish to die yet, but I do not wish to live forever either. You would gift my people with the chance to go where they choose if you could?"

"Of course I'd do that." She couldn't imagine living in another world and not being able to return to everything she considered her life. But she wouldn't hand over the stone to anyone.

"I will talk to my warlord, Batuk, and see if I can change his mind. If I am not back by four hours past midnight, go to the Beladors for help. They will protect you."

Go to another bunch of people with powers? That might not be a good idea. "Why? Can't you come back?"

"I don't know. A powerful black witch is helping my warlord, and she bespelled me once yesterday already to use me to capture two young people for blood sacrifices."

Her look of fear, which must have registered at that, had to be the reason he quickly added, "I feigned a weakness to allow the two youths to escape and warned the Belador standing with them to be on guard against a witch. Go to the Beladors if I do not return in time."

Laurette couldn't believe how much worse this got by the minute. "How do I find them?"

"Ask the stone to bring a Belador to you. If that does not work, do not have that stone in your hand when the sun rises tomorrow."

"Thought you told me the Beladors were your enemies."

"That is true, but I believe they will not harm you, and I cannot say the same for my Kujoo warlord. If you meet the Beladors, that means I have lost, so I will give you a message for them. Tell them the Kujoo will return to their time as stronger immortal warriors and will leave no Belador standing."

What did that mean? "Will the Beladors try to take the stone from me?"

Vyan reached over and placed his hand over hers with a gentle touch. She held still, but not out of fear. The compassion that passed from him in that moment filled her with a sense of security and peace she hadn't experienced in a long time.

His sad voice matched his eyes. "I wish that you could keep the stone to regain your sight, but to do so would incur a curse you would never be free of."

She wanted to believe that was an empty threat intended to frighten her away from the stone, but after talking to this man for fourteen hours she could hear the truth in his words. "What curse?"

"The stone is selfish and dangerous. It teases you with power as one would tempt a child with sweets, tricking the child to follow them into danger. Once you are joined with the stone for the rest of your life, it will force you to do its bidding, whether you want to or not."

Vyan withdrew his hand, drawing his warmth and strength with it. She sighed like a teenager and didn't care. Life had been anything but normal for the past few days. If she could survive finding a magic rock, watching a man throw lightning bolts at a woman with invisible powers, and meeting a man who lived eight hundred years ago, she had no problem with being attracted to a stranger.

Vyan stood and walked into the living room, where he lifted his sword and slid the dangerous-looking blade into a sheath at his hip, then pulled on his coat. "I will say a special prayer to my god for your eyesight."

"What about your wounds?"

"Your kind hands and my immortal state have healed them. I am fit to battle."

She didn't care to hear that. "How do I find you again?"

"Do not look for me on your own," he ordered in such a fierce voice that she took a step back. His eyes closed for a moment, then he opened them and anguish flooded his gaze. "I did not mean to frighten you, but you must not come looking for me, or Batuk and Tristan will capture you. Understand?"

She understood that this man was trying to protect her from

dangerous people. "Yes. I will contact the Beladors if you're not back by four o'clock tomorrow morning."

Obviously pleased by her agreement, he smiled, then spent a long moment watching her.

When she rubbed the stone in her pocket, she could feel his thoughts, could feel something he wanted that he wouldn't ask. "What?"

Vyan walked back to her and put his hands on her shoulders. "Thank you for a day of peace like I have not enjoyed for many centuries. You have been a balm to my weary soul."

This man was stealing her heart one sliver at a time.

She lifted her hand to his arm. "I wish you wouldn't leave."

"As do I, but I cannot stay when each minute puts you further in danger."

The heck with normal. Life was never going to be the same, and she might never see this man again. He was far too much of a gentleman to make a forward move, but she wanted something to remember him by. She lifted up and touched her lips to his. He didn't move for a heartbeat, then he kissed her back.

And kissed her some more until she felt her feet lifting off the floor, which might be because he'd wrapped her in his arms. Good grief. No man kissed like that.

When he lowered her back to the floor and lifted his head, she was breathless at the affection in his eyes. "You have given me many gifts that I can never repay."

"Then come back alive and I'll make a payback list."

He smiled, but it did not hide the sadness in his eyes. He touched his lips to her forehead, then backed away and walked to the stairs that led to the second floor.

"Where are you going?"

"To leave by the rooftop so no one can track me back to your house."

Why couldn't she have met a man like him in *her* era? "Thank you for not taking the rock when you could have."

His face glowed with surprise and warmth, then he was gone.

Lifting the rock up to eye level, she stared into the molten depths. "I did not promise I wouldn't search for him on my own."

THIRTY-THREE

Waiting came as easily to Evalle as trusting, but for once she'd shown up twenty minutes early instead of late. She wouldn't have had to change her meeting with Storm at Piedmont Park to midnight if not for hunting Nightstalkers. She'd found six since dark had fallen over Atlanta.

Grady had not been one of them.

None of the ones she'd found had significant intel on the Ngak Stone, but every one of them had asked if she was also "offering a two-handed shake deal" like the Kujoo. Which meant that Tristan and the Kujoo might be turning hundreds of Nightstalkers into aggressive halflings like the one that had stabbed her.

Where were these Nightstalkers? Was Tristan, the Kujoo and/or the Medb amassing an army?

"Will wonders never cease," Storm said from behind her.

She stopped pacing along the sidewalk outside the entrance to Piedmont Park and swung around at his voice, almost colliding with a young couple pushing a baby stroller in the warm night air. "Sorry."

Giving her the keep-your-distance look, the couple scurried past Evalle.

"Scaring the natives?" Storm chuckled.

"I doubt there are many true native Atlantans here anymore."

He was too attractive for her peace of mind to begin with, but smiling amplified everything from his exotic eyes to his strong chin. His upper body flexed beneath his mocha brown T-shirt when he crossed his arms. The movement brushed a scent of virile male through the air, stirring her nerves into a scary dance of awareness.

What had gotten into her, noticing men like Storm and Isak?

She'd never taken an interest in men, not this way. The next time she saw Nicole she'd find out if her empathic ability was ramping up her emotions.

Because men were making her jumpy for a whole different reason than past fears. Storm in particular.

She had to shove this back to a business level. Angling a shoulder toward the gates, she said, "Tzader wants us to walk the park and see if we can pick up anything or if any of the Kujoo show up, since they'll be searching this area for the woman, too. What have you been up to today?"

Storm fell into step with her. "Found the woman's body from the morgue."

"Really? Where?"

"Adrianna and I tracked the Noirre majik to a house in Inman Park and found the body there. Looked like the family was out of town."

Evalle suffered a twinge of something she refused to call jealousy at Storm's working with Adrianna. "What prompted that trip?"

Storm studied her quietly, just long enough to let her know he'd heard the snippy sound in her reply. His lips twitched, just a little indication of a smile, as if he'd figured out something. "Adrianna suggested she could track the Noirre majik from your injury if she did it right away, so Trey contacted me and we gave it a shot."

Hopefully the dark surrounding her hid her mixed reaction. She had to admit that Storm's plan made sense and was glad they'd found the body, even if it had been Adrianna-the-sexy-witch who had spent the day with Storm doing it. On the other hand, this would be an opportune time to use Feenix's new curse word. "How'd you know it was the same body?"

"We didn't until we called in the death—"

"Who'd you call?" Snapping at him wasn't wise, but why did he and Adrianna have to find the body?

Storm paused long enough to take a breath that sounded burdened with patience on the exhale. "I called Trey, who contacted a Belador with Atlanta PD who investigated the *anonymous* phone tip on a dead body. When they got the remains to the morgue, the ME on duty recognized it."

Her shoulders slumped with relief. "Was the ME Beaulah?"

"That sounds like her name."

"I work with her. Did you tell Sen about the body?"

"Had to at that point."

Evalle tasted bitter disappointment in her next words. "Should I be watching out for Sen around the next corner?"

"I don't see why. We figured out the witch wasn't using the body for a blood sacrifice but hiding it in a deep freezer, because the minute Adrianna touched the remains the woman's ghost entered the room and told us how a Cresyl demon had killed her."

"You're kidding." Evalle couldn't believe something was working out in her favor for once. "That's great."

"No, I'm not kidding, and, yes, that is good news. I told Sen about the death and the Cresyl, so he has no reason to think an Alterant killed her."

Storm had come through for her again. "Thank you."

"You're welcome. But the trail stopped there, so we still aren't any closer to finding the rock."

Nicole had told her, *"Trust will open the path to one who is born to the task."* Wouldn't a Native American be "born to the task" of tracking? Wasn't that what Sen was using Storm for?

Storm moved through the unlit areas of Piedmont like he was on the hunt, every muscle flowing naturally.

"I did some work on my own today, too," she said, trying to figure out if he was the one who could find the rock if she extended some trust. "I was told that someone who was born to tracking could find the stone. I think that might be you."

"I don't think so. I came back earlier tonight to see if I could pick up a trail from where you found the girl with the rock and Vyan. The only energy I was able to sense was that of two powerful males." He paused, giving her a questioning look after referencing what had to be Vyan and Tristan's energy residue. When she didn't offer anything, he continued. "One trail just vanished and the other one ended in that same spot at Tenth Street next to the park where I lost it last night."

She didn't need to see his eyes to know he was waiting on her to tell him the truth about that encounter. "He shouldn't have disappeared so easily, but he did when he reached the street."

"Who and what is *he*?" Storm asked quietly, not demanding.

This whole trust thing felt like a severe case of food poisoning, but Nicole wouldn't have steered her wrong, and they were running out of time. "If I tell you, you can't tell anyone else without asking me first."

He strode along silently, long legs eating up ground like a big animal on the prowl. "Okay, you got it."

She wiped her clammy hands on each other, then stopped when she realized she was wringing her hands. "His name is Tristan and he's an Alterant who escaped a spellbound cage."

Storm cursed under his breath. "You faced him *and* two demented ghouls? Alone? He could have killed you."

His concern over her safety made her feel better about that bout of jealousy a moment ago. "I held my own."

"Why didn't you tell Tzader and Quinn about this?"

She'd wanted to more than he'd ever know. "It's a little complicated. First of all, Tristan swears that Brina put him in a cage even though he had never shifted or hurt anyone. I confirmed that through another source that I don't want to bring into this just yet, but it makes me question my faith in Brina. Even so, the minute I tell Tzader or Quinn about Tristan they'll have to tell VIPER *and* Brina. She has the ability to find Tristan immediately—"

"Why not tell her and recapture Tristan?"

"That's the problem. He said that's exactly what the Medb and Kujoo want Brina to do. They've set some trap and want her to call in the Beladors, which she would have to do in order to stop the Kujoo. But I have a feeling Tristan is not lying and the Belador tribe would be slaughtered and that he's holding back more than that."

Storm reached over and pushed a branch up she hadn't been watching with her eyes on the ground. She smiled her thanks.

After covering another ten steps, Storm asked, "Does Tristan think the Beladors won't hunt him to the ends of the earth?"

"That's where this gets worse, the part I think Tristan is leaving out. He said the Medb and Kujoo will wipe the Beladors from the earth, even their ancestors, but he didn't say how they would accomplish that. I don't understand how they could kill every Belador, but I don't want to risk that the Medb could be successful."

"He could be bluffing."

"True, but I've had someone else tell me the lives of the Beladors depend on what I decide to do and that the Kujoo hold the future of the Belador tribe in their hands. That sounds like what Tristan is saying."

"I don't get why you aren't telling Tzader and Quinn. Thought you three were good friends."

She swallowed. "We are. The best, but I'm afraid if I tell Tzader and Quinn everything they'll believe me. When Tzader tries to prevent Brina from going after Tristan she'll think I've convinced him to protect Alterants. I don't want him facing a Tribunal as a result, especially if I'm wrong about any of this. On the other hand, if I tell the Beladors everything, I know they'll think they can defeat the Kujoo and go into battle. No matter what I do, there's no good choice."

"What else aren't you telling me?" Storm's low voice rumbled with exasperation. "You're keeping something to yourself."

She walked quietly for a moment. "I can save the Beladors if I *don't* tell them about Tristan. He gave me a way."

"I'm not liking the sound of that."

Me either, but I never seem to get a vote when it comes to my future no matter who I deal with. She muttered, "I didn't say I'd do it."

"*What* did he offer?"

If she told Storm, she was pretty sure he'd interfere. "I want to wait until we find the rock to say more, because my options narrow if we don't find the rock first. The sooner we find out what the Medb and Kujoo are up to, the sooner the Beladors will know what to do and I may not have to make any choice."

"Why would you believe Tristan?"

"I didn't until I went to see a gifted friend of mine today who confirmed what he was saying, but in a different way." Fear welled up in her throat at the possibility of making a mistake and costing lives. "She indicated I could find what I look for."

When they reached the concrete steps that descended to the wide-open lawn area in the park, Storm stopped, eyes scanning the area. A handful of people jogged along the paths or walked dogs. "Won't Brina be angry when she finds out you didn't tell her about Tristan escaping?"

"I'm hoping that once she realizes I did it to protect the tribe, she'll understand I put the Beladors first. Doesn't matter. I'm not willing to risk Tzader and Quinn or any other Belador just to protect myself." She wrapped her arms around herself and stared over the open space, wishing the right answer would come to her.

His fingers touched her shoulder, sliding forward until his hand cupped the curve at the top of her arm. A small connection that let her know he was there. She let his hand rest there, testing how it felt. He had a way of knowing how much she'd allow, kept nipping away at her resistance with deft touches.

He had no idea he was chipping at a mountain with a toy hammer.

When Storm spoke, his voice was matter-of-fact. "Then we better get busy finding Tristan."

"That's not who I think we're supposed to track."

"Who then?"

"The woman with the rock."

"Already told you I can't follow a teleport."

"I know." Evalle unwrapped her arms from her chest and chewed on the corner of her thumb. "I just know that's the answer to locating the rock. You up for giving it another try?"

"Sure."

She moved away, letting his hand fall free. When they reached the area where she'd faced off with Tristan the previous evening, they found a couple walking a pair of dogs. Their sneakers glowed against the black night with each step.

Evalle waited until a group of teens with muffled music playing from their iPods passed them before she spoke. "Well? How does tracking work?"

"If it's majik, I can sense it on my skin and just continue moving in the direction the energy feels the strongest, but there's nothing new here besides the two trails I told you about."

"Vyan would be the one whose trail disappeared after he teleported with her. Tristan's was the one that vanished at the street." Evalle sat down cross-legged on the ground. "If you aren't picking up any energy signature, I don't know who would."

He sat down next to her companionably. "Now what?"

She started to shrug but stilled at the sight of an elderly man walking a mutt on a leash. That reminded her of the woman's mutt from this morning. "The woman with the rock had a dog." Evalle turned to Storm. "Can you track the *dog's* scent?"

This time he hesitated to answer.

He couldn't hold back on her now. "Storm?"

"Yes. I can track it."

When he didn't move, she said, "Well? Let's try it."

"I can't do it in . . . this form."

"What do you mean?"

He'd drawn his legs up and propped his arms on them, staring straight ahead. "I can't track as well in human form as I can in animal form."

It took her a minute to figure out what he was saying. "Are you lycanthrope?"

"No. I came from a line of shamans. One was a Spiritwalker and one was a Skinwalker. I can take the form of a jaguar."

She tapped her mouth with a finger. "Okay, that's going to be tough to pull off in Atlanta. A wolf would have been a lot easier to explain."

He dropped his head on his arms, laughing.

"What's so funny?"

Lifting his head, he faced her with disbelief. "I was worried about telling you that I can change into a jaguar and you're only concerned that it's the wrong species."

She'd just figured out how secretive he was being about this. "Why are you keeping this from the others? I'd think they'd be glad to know you had this capability. Does Sen know?"

"I've been keeping your secrets. You keep mine. I don't want *any* of them to know. It's a curse, not a gift. Where I come from, those who change into jaguars are considered demons. I haven't changed shape in a while, but I can track the tiniest bit of scent in animal form."

"Were you born that way?"

"I wasn't a Skinwalker until . . . something happened." The timbre of his voice altered in a way that meant he wouldn't discuss it further. "I can handle the change if I have to."

That meant she was asking him to do something he didn't want to do any more than she'd want to shift into her beast form. "Never mind. I didn't mean to put you on the spot."

"No, I'll do it. Makes sense that we could find her dog's trail, since he's been in the park and would have marked his territory all the time. If I can pick it up in a neighborhood around here, we'll find her."

"How do we do this without someone getting a little distressed over a jaguar roaming around downtown Atlanta?"

"A witch could ward me so no one but you saw me. Guess we could ask Adrianna."

Evalle opened her mouth to object. *Am I really going to say no to Adrianna's help?* That seemed petty.

Screw it. She'd been called worse.

THIRTY-FOUR

"Not Adrianna." Evalle wanted to pull those words back into her mouth.

"Really?" Storm's relief was immediate and tangible.

"What? You don't want the poster witch for black majik laying her hands on you?" Interesting. She refused to tell Storm that she didn't want the Sterling witch's hands touching him either, since he might read too much into that. Sterling witches were tainted. That was all. "I know someone else who can ward you from sight, plus she won't say a word and isn't with VIPER."

He considered it a moment. "That'd work."

"How far is your sport utility from here?" She hadn't seen his truck on the way to Piedmont Park after leaving her bike. "We'll need it to transport you once you've shifted."

"It's right up Tenth Street." He stood up and gave her a hand up to her feet.

The warmth in his eyes stole her breath. He wanted to kiss her. She knew it with every beat of her heart, and somewhere deep inside among all her confused feelings she wanted him to kiss her, too. But nothing good could come from allowing her empathic side to scramble her emotions. She broke away from him and set a fast pace to his vehicle.

The trip to Nicole's was more comfortable than the drive home from VIPER headquarters the first day she'd met Storm. She enjoyed eyeing Storm's profile and that he allowed an easy quiet to fill the time. She called Nicole to alert her they were coming and that she needed to do this warding in the garage, which Nicole assured her they could do.

When Storm pulled into the parking deck for Nicole's building, Evalle gave him Nicole's instructions on where to park in a corner that would give them privacy. That's where they found Nicole sitting in her wheelchair with a tall, physically fit female standing behind her, not smiling.

But then Olivia would not be happy about meeting Evalle any time, especially at one in the morning. Olivia "Red" Redwine had chopped-at-the-ear strawberry blonde hair, not red, and an athlete's body covered in gray-and-white warm-ups.

Evalle jumped out of the truck when he parked and addressed Nicole's life partner. "Hi, Red."

"Evalle." After speaking, Olivia cast a suspicious look at Storm, who waited in dark shadows at the front bumper of the car.

He was obviously not comfortable with any of this either, but he *was* willing to shift in order to help her, so Evalle asked Nicole, "Ready?"

She nodded. "I can do this, but it will only hold for maybe three hours. I put something quick together. To do more than three hours would take a stronger spell than I can effect here, and I'm not sure this one will prevent animals from sensing him." She looked up at Storm. "Can you control your jaguar?"

That might not have seemed so strange a question if Storm hadn't answered, "I won't harm Evalle."

What had Nicole noticed that Evalle had missed?

"Three hours should be enough time," Storm said for everyone's benefit. "If not, daylight will be our next challenge at that point."

Red leaned down next to Nicole's ear, but Evalle could hear every word. "What happens if the people they're hunting find out you helped them and come after you?"

Nicole smiled up at her. "I'm in no danger, love."

Standing upright, Red released a put-upon sigh and accepted what Nicole told her even though she didn't like it one bit. The glare she sent Evalle was to remind her how much Red didn't like her.

This favor would put a nice touch on the relationship. Sort of like a turd in a gourmet meal.

"Go ahead and change, Storm," Nicole directed him.

He stepped back around the sport utility. A door on the other side opened for a moment, then closed.

Was he stripping? Evalle stuck her head past the rear of the truck to check that no one was in the area, when in truth she wanted to scout all the way around the vehicle out of curiosity.

But that would be an invasion of privacy she wouldn't appreciate in his place.

She'd never been around lycanthropes or Skinwalkers. How long did it take to change? Barely a minute had passed when a sleek black jungle cat stepped around the front fender.

Looked like Ashaninka Skinwalkers were the plug-and-play version.

His eyes glowed like embers and didn't look the least bit friendly. He snarled low, a vicious sound.

Evalle's nerves rippled, lifting hairs everywhere.

Red's fingers clutched the handles of Nicole's chair so hard that her knuckles were white.

Nicole spoke softly to Storm, as if she saw a jaguar that had to weigh over two hundred pounds every day in Avondale. She held a hand out to Evalle with a silver disc in the center of her palm. A leather thong had been strung through a loop on the disc. "Tie this amulet around his neck."

Me? But Evalle didn't want to look like some wimp in front of Red, so she took the amulet and turned to Storm, whose lips curled back from his teeth.

She bent down slowly to her knees and waited quietly. Didn't seem wise to say "Here kitty, kitty" to a ginormous jaguar.

Storm padded over until her face was close enough to smell the warm animal scent of his fur. He stared hard into her eyes, then lifted his head so she could reach his neck. As she tied the amulet, she realized he was exposing his most vulnerable spot to her.

But he'd said he wouldn't hurt *her,* so did this mean he trusted her not to hurt him?

She grabbed his head, bringing his eyes back level with hers, then kissed his nose. "You're the best."

He nuzzled her face, then turned to Nicole.

Evalle stood up and backed away as Nicole chanted softly in a voice that should be singing lullabies. When she finished, Nicole looked at Evalle. "No one except you will see him unless he chooses to reveal himself. Three hours isn't an exact time, so don't push it any longer than you have to. It's already one o'clock. You should go."

Evalle would have hugged Nicole if not for Red standing guard. Red was the jealous type to begin with. "Thanks, Nicole. I owe you one for sure."

"I'll hold you to that if it means you'll be here to pay up." She smiled, then patted Red's hand. "Let's go back up."

After loading Storm into the backseat, where he'd have more room, Evalle drove back to Tenth Street and parked along the curb in a neighborhood close to Piedmont Park. She held her breath when Storm jumped out of the truck and prowled along the sidewalk.

At the corner, two men jogged past Storm. One had a Labrador on a leash. Neither human noticed the jaguar who stepped out of their path and onto a front yard.

But the dog jerked around, sniffing, until his leash tightened.

Storm watched them pass, then looked up at her. This time, when he pulled his lips back, he exposed razor-sharp teeth in what she thought might be a smile.

"Let's beat feet and see what we can find at the park," she said, catching up to him.

When she reached the spot where she'd last seen the woman with the rock, Storm put his head down to the ground and turned into a predator on the hunt.

She was glad not to be his prey.

He spent almost two minutes there, then spun around and headed for Tenth Street, where he dashed across the highway without going to a crosswalk where a streetlight would stop traffic.

Running to keep up with him, she waved her hands at cars trying to mow her down when she crossed right behind him.

Evalle, where are you? Tzader asked in her mind.

Back at Piedmont Park. Storm thinks he may have picked up a scent. Literally. *Where are you two?*

Sen decided there was nothing to be risked at this point by bringing

310

in recruits since the stone is going to bond with the new master by day-light. We've been tied up all day calling in more Beladors to flood the city to search for the Kujoo.

No. That's just what the Medb wanted. *I don't think that's a good idea, Z. Not until we know what they meant about wiping out all the Beladors.*

We've got strength in numbers once we link. I'll put a wall of Beladors up against any Medb or Kujoo at any time.

What if the Medb had a plan to kill Brina when the Beladors linked? Massive slaughter. But that wouldn't wipe out all the generations.

Got to go, Tzader said. *Call us if you find anything and we'll get warriors to you.*

Will do. The lump in her throat was getting thicker by the minute. She'd put her trust in Storm, which was what she believed Nicole's vision meant. *Don't let me be wrong.*

Storm wove through streets, hesitating occasionally to sniff a mailbox post or a car tire. This area was packed with animals, which had to be hampering his tracking.

Or the young woman with the rock walked everywhere. If she was blind and unable to drive, that could be the case. Or if she carried her dog some of the time, she'd have broken the scent trail.

Two hours later, Evalle's legs burned from jogging up and down a couple inclines without slowing. She only had two legs, but she wasn't going to complain, dammit.

She hunched her shoulders in defense right after cursing mentally, sometimes anticipating an air slap to her head from Brina, but it never happened.

Tzader said Brina heard all cursing, but maybe she only listened to the rest of her tribe, not Alterants.

Storm bumped Evalle when he swung around, intent on something. Had he picked up an especially promising scent?

When he slowed and crept up to a house, Evalle cast a glance all around to check for animals. The last dog they'd encountered had followed them for a while. Was Storm's protection ward beginning to fail?

He padded across the street to the driveway of a cottage-style wooden house painted blue and white. The yard was neat and filled with flowers. Storm paced several feet back and forth across the driveway, then lifted his head to her.

Evalle walked past him, over to a window on the side of the house, and peered in.

The woman she'd been hunting was curled up on her sofa with her mutt next to her. Bingo.

Hurrying back to Storm, Evalle squatted down and brushed her hand over the soft fur on his head, considering what to do next. "This is the girl's house. I don't want to scare her, so I'm going in alone."

He growled and nipped at her arm with his lips.

"No arguing. That dog we passed on the last block sensed you. You're close to being out of time with the ward. Go back and change into the clothes I left in the bushes for you. I'll meet you at the park with the girl."

He didn't move.

"Storm, I need you to do this. You can't go in with me, and if someone sees you when the ward wears off they'll call animal control. I don't want Sen coming after you for doing this around humans without authorization." She stood up.

He rubbed his wide head along her leg, then took a step, but paused, reluctance to leave in every move he made.

"I'm fine. I can call Trey, Quinn and Tzader telepathically if I get into any trouble. Trey is superfast and lives maybe a mile or two away at the most. He can be here in a minute. But I'm not calling anyone until I know what's going on with this girl, the rock and Vyan." She leaned over and kissed his head. "This might save my tribe. Thank you."

He licked her cheek, then trotted away, looking back every fifty feet until he disappeared into the night.

When she climbed the wooden steps to the cute porch, she took a close look at the pottery planter next to the door that came up to her waist. She'd been studying ancient languages at night on her computer. She'd seen those letters before and made a mental note of the

312

bold inscription across the top, but she put it aside for now and knocked on the door. When it opened, Evalle faced the young woman from the park. "I need a minute to talk to you. It's important."

The woman gasped. "I saw you in the park early this morning."

Finally. Something would be easy. "Yes, you did."

"Are you a Belador?"

Not a question Evalle expected. "Yes, I am."

"Are the Kujoo your enemies?"

That's when she noticed the rock in the woman's hand and reconsidered the first response that came to mind, since there could be a wrong answer to that question.

Easy never stayed in her vocabulary long.

THIRTY-FIVE

"Can I come in?" Evalle asked the woman holding the Ngak Stone, which could wreak devastation on the entire world.

"You didn't answer my question. Are the Kujoo your enemies?"

Evalle considered a couple things quickly, like the fact that this woman had only met Vyan, not all the Kujoo. "I don't have an issue with Vyan."

Wariness crossed the woman's pale face, but the blue eyes concentrated hard on whatever she was deciding. Her hair fell in flaming red waves to her shoulders.

A dog's bark made them both jump.

Her mutt scampered through the open door and danced around Evalle's legs. She instinctively reached down to pet the dog.

"Okay, Brutus, you win." The woman extended her free hand. "I'm Laurette Barrett."

"I'm Evalle Kincaid, and I'm here because you're in grave danger."

"I know." Laurette said that with simple acceptance and backed away, opening the door for Evalle to enter.

The interior had a cozy feel, with sheers over the windows and flowery pillows tossed on a cream-colored sofa. All the secondhand furniture had been kept clean and given TLC along the way. Something with meat had been cooked recently, filling the house with a wonderful lived-in smell.

Now Evalle felt justified in suffering a moment of jealousy over someone living in a real house that had a lived-in feel.

Laurette stopped in the middle of the room and faced her. "Vyan said to find a Belador if he didn't come back to my house by four this morning, and that was five minutes ago. I think somebody's going to hurt him."

"We need to talk about that rock in your hand first."

"I'm not talking to you unless you're going to help me trade *this* rock for Vyan."

Saving a Kujoo was counterproductive to saving the Beladors and civilization. Evalle wasn't sure if she could talk this woman out of the rock or take it from her, but she was not handing it over to the Kujoo or Tristan. "Why don't we sit down and work through this?"

Laurette heaved a long breath as though the world rested on her shoulders, which wasn't far from the truth as long as she held tight to the rock. She sat down on the sofa and her little dog curled across her feet. Her fingers never stopped stroking the Ngak Stone in her hand. "How do I know you're a Belador?"

Evalle never had a good answer for that one. "I have no way to prove it to you, but I know Vyan. I met him two years ago when he first arrived in Atlanta."

Laurette nodded. "He said that's when he met you. What are the Beladors?"

"The short story is that we're sort of a special group that protects national security, which is why we need to talk about the Ngak Stone you're holding."

"But you're Vyan's enemy?"

Add him to the list, but let's move this along. "The Beladors and the Kujoo have a lot of difficult history from eight hundred years ago, but none of today's Beladors are responsible for that. Where did Vyan go?"

"I don't know. I asked the rock to take me to him, but it wouldn't. He left by the roof instead of the front door so no one would pick up his trail."

No one from the street, but someone could track him *back* to Laurette's house. Evalle asked, "Did he tell you anything about that rock?"

"Yes."

"Then you know we're working on a tight schedule or you could end up bound to the Ngak Stone forever . . . if you survive being bound to it."

315

"I have to keep this rock."

"Are you blind, Laurette?"

"Not yet, but soon. I can see when I hold it."

"The rock is seducing you. It's meant for a different kind of person than you."

"One like you or that guy Tristan, because I don't throw around lightning bolts?"

"That's right. You're human." Evalle wanted to tell her not to feel disappointed or hurt about her human status. Being nonhuman was no joyride. "Some of the most powerful sorcerers and wizards have gone mad after bonding with the stone. The stone has been around forever. Every time the stone takes a new master its power builds upon the previous power gained. I doubt a human would even survive the bonding, and even if you did, the stone would control you, not the other way around."

Laurette's eyes glistened with tears. "Vyan told me not to ask the stone for my eyesight. Is that too much to ask?"

"It's dangerous to seek any gain from something powerful. If you ask for your eyesight, someone else might lose theirs in exchange."

She gasped. "I would never take someone else's."

"I didn't think you'd want that." What would it take to get her to part with the stone besides saving Vyan? He must not be cooperating with the Kujoo and Tristan. "You have to decide soon, Laurette, or the choice won't be yours to make at daylight."

Laurette fought tears, struggling to do the right thing. "I'll give it up, but not until I know Vyan is safe."

"Why do you think he's in any danger?"

"Because he doesn't agree with what his warlord is planning and has gone against the Kujoo by not handing me and the rock over to them."

"What is the warlord planning?"

"Vyan gave me a message for the Beladors if he didn't return. He said his warlord wants Tristan to use the Ngak Stone to turn the Kujoo warriors that are here now into superwarriors, then Tristan will send them back eight hundred years. Those warriors will kill all the Beladors so that your race ends. Vyan said some witch assured Tristan that something called an Alterant will be safe from the genocide."

Oh, dear goddess. Evalle's heart shook with possible consequences of that happening. That's what Tristan had been talking about and why he had said she'd be safe. In this time period, Beladors lived as sleeper cells for the good, scattered all over the world in every position, from mothers to pilots to doctors to bus drivers to maybe even those in the highest levels of government.

If they all disappeared at one time, the result would be devastating to more than just the non-Belador members of the families that survived. The world could go into chaos. There would be no way to prepare for the immediate disappearance of over a million Beladors worldwide.

And she'd lose Tzader and Quinn.

Laurette's voice turned thin and desperate. "Vyan is helping your Beladors. Please help him."

Now to make the right choices that Nicole had warned her were imperative to protecting the Beladors' past and future. Evalle forced her words to be calm, though she wanted to shout at Laurette to hand over the stone. "If I promise to free Vyan, will you hand over the stone to people I know?"

Laurette got up and walked across the room to look out her window. She gripped the stone in both hands. "Who are these people you're talking about?"

The less Evalle shared with this woman about the Beladors the better, but VIPER had one person with the ability to ease Laurette's worries. "His name is Storm. He'll take you to a place that is safe to leave the rock and I'll take a team to help Vyan."

Laurette's dog jumped off the sofa and ran around her feet, growling. "I can't think. Give me a minute." She frowned at her little dog. "Okay, Brutus. Let's go out back."

Evalle had to sit on her hands to keep from jumping up and shaking Laurette to make her hurry, but the woman was coming around. Just the fact that she hadn't said no meant she planned to say yes.

This was almost too easy.

Storm should be close to changing by now. Once Evalle called him to pick up Laurette and the stone, she'd contact Tzader and Quinn to meet her at Trey's house, then they'd call in every Belador in the city to hunt the Kujoo. The minute VIPER had control of the stone, Tzader would have to convince Sen to ask the stone for help with containing the Kujoo, Tristan and the zombielike beings the Nightstalkers had been changed into.

Sen might be a miserable SOB and a mystery, but there was no more powerful operative within VIPER.

This could work.

When Laurette returned, she stopped at the door to the kitchen, acceptance clear on her face. "I guess I really don't have any choice."

"Not really, but I give you my word we will save Vyan if we can get to him in time. Let me call Storm, one of our agents, to come escort us. The sooner we get moving, the sooner we'll find him." Evalle pulled out her cell phone as she stood up.

The front door burst open and Tristan strode in. "I should have expected to find you here."

Laurette clutched the stone to her chest. "Where's Vyan?"

"Waiting on you." Tristan extended his hand. "Give me the stone and I'll take you to him."

Evalle jumped in front of Laurette and threw up a forcefield to stop Tristan's advance. She yelled at Laurette, "Go to Storm."

Laurette squeaked out something Evalle couldn't decipher.

Tristan's face erupted with rage. He raised his hand and shoved it toward Evalle, knocking her backward . . . into an empty kitchen, where she slammed into the cabinets.

That rung her bell. She reached up and rubbed her head. Had a new lump on the back. Tristan must be getting stronger.

Evalle glanced around, clearing her vision.

Laurette was gone.

But had she gone to Vyan or to Storm?

Tristan barged into the kitchen. "You should have done what I told you and come to me with the rock."

"Do I *look* like June Cleaver following Ward's orders?" Evalle sat up. "I don't dance to anyone's music but my own."

"If you had come through I could have saved you."

"But killed all the Beladors," Evalle countered. "They won't come. I didn't tell any of them about you."

"They'll come. They're all over the city already. Don't bet on the girl going anywhere with that rock but to Vyan."

I hope you're wrong. If Laurette did go to Storm, he could come back and track from this house.

"Get moving, Evalle." Tristan stepped back so she could push to her feet. "You screwed up big time by not coming to me first."

She ignored his words, planning to contact Tzader as soon as she figured out where Tristan was taking her. If she risked it now and Tristan had the ability to pick up her telepathy, she'd blow her only chance. He'd said he wanted her, so she should be safe for now, at least until he got the rock. She held hope close to her chest until she stepped outside the house with Tristan.

Her hands slapped together in front of her as if locked.

Tristan hadn't done that.

Evalle looked past him to find a Medb priestess hovering above the grass in the front yard. "Ah, Sleeping Beauty returns."

Kizira's robes glowed in the night and billowed around her as if there was a breath of wind in the middle of summer. "Where is the stone?"

"The girl disappeared with it to . . . someplace." Tristan could have said that Evalle knew where, but he was sure Laurette had gone to Vyan.

Or he'd been protecting Evalle.

No way.

Kizira's eyes beamed like two tiny yellow suns when she smiled. "You may have escaped me two years ago in Utah, Alterant, but not this time. You will tell me where the girl is."

"She's traveling first class on the Ngak Rock Airlines. If I could tell you where she went I'd play the lottery." Evalle struggled to free her hands or use her kinetics mentally, but she was locked up tight. She could only hope that wherever they were taking her would eat up enough time for Storm to find her, if he could track them.

But she had to alert Tzader to the Kujoo's plan now.

Tzader, where are . . . Pain shot through Evalle's head. Her knees folded, but Tristan caught her arm to keep her upright.

"What're you doing to her?" Tristan demanded of Kizira.

"Stopping her from contacting other Beladors until we're ready for her to send a message. I'll enjoy making you pay for killing my brother, Alterant," Kizira said to Evalle.

I'll enjoy making you eat my boot heels, bitch.

The priestess lifted her arms and spoke words Evalle couldn't understand until everything swirled into darkness.

Ah, no, not teleporting.

Storm would never find her now.

THIRTY-SIX

Pain seared her neck, her back and her legs. Evalle hung from her wrists, bound by invisible threads to the ceiling of an old downtown Atlanta school auditorium that hadn't been used for years. With all the windows broken, the night air she breathed should have been fresh and not clogged with the sickening smell of Medb evil.

Blood covered the walls. This placed looked like a Freddy Krueger horror flick stuck on replay. Whatever the Medb had been doing had backfired a few times, exploding bodies. Hideous creatures that had probably once been Nightstalkers crouched everywhere on the walls, floor and ceiling with various parts of their bodies in solid form and the rest translucent.

Sweat poured down her face and stung the cuts on her neck and shoulders. One eye was swollen from where a Nightstalker she used to take gummy bear candy to had backhanded her.

She forgave the poor creature with soulless eyes who hadn't recognized her.

As if life wasn't enjoyable enough, daylight would hit in less than an hour, and the wall of broken windows faced east.

Tristan stood at the side of the cavernous room with the Medb priestess and a group of warriors that had to be the Kujoo Mount Meru escapees.

Tristan had shocked her by intervening when Evalle had taken the first blow to her head, but Kizira had locked him in place with majik.

Kizira had her head close to Tristan's, speaking to him as though coaching her number one player. Her sharp fingernails were still extended, trailing along the floor next to her as thin razor-sharp strips she'd used as a cat-'o-nine-tails.

Where had Kizira gotten *that* nail job?

Evalle's skin burned from where those nails had left strips of Noirre majik eating into her body. She'd doubted anyone would find her here, not even Storm. She tried to shift once, hoping to fight her way out even if it meant exposing her beast side to the world.

Kizira kiboshed that with a spell.

"They wait for you to call your Beladors with your mind," a feeble male voice said on her left.

Evalle turned her head to where Vyan hung near her. At least he was on the side with the eye she could still see out of. Her glasses were gone, but the candles burning below were far enough away that they were not blinding her. "They waste their time. I will not call the Beladors into a trap. I am not a traitor. Why didn't you come to *us*, Vyan?"

"Beladors want only the Ngak Stone. I want my people to be free of their cursed lives."

She couldn't really argue with that and noticed he hadn't included himself in that wish.

"Evalle?"

She heard her name called softly from below her where captive Nightstalkers were clustered inside a circle of power.

"Grady?" She whispered to keep from drawing the attention of their captors. He *was* here. Just as she'd feared. "Why'd you do this?"

His weary eyes had never sagged as much as they did now. "I wanted an hour of human form tonight."

Grace be to Macha. Evalle couldn't have given him an hour, but she might have stopped him from being caught by the Kujoo if Isak hadn't kidnapped her.

We're coming, Evalle, she heard in her mind.

Trey? Is that you?

I've been trying to reach you for a half hour but I had to find a way through a barrier.

A witch spell. She's not paying me any attention right now. Must be how you got through.

Nah. I'm just that good.

322

She rolled her eyes.

Trey said, *We're outside. Tzader and Quinn are with me.*

She didn't know how they'd found her, but she couldn't let them march in here to save her. *It's a trap. Don't come in and don't let Brina show up. They're waiting for her.*

Tzader's got an ace to play when we come in. He won't lead our tribe into a slaughter or let anything happen to Brina. You have to learn to trust us. You can't save the tribe alone.

I hear you. She let out a raw breath. Thanks be to Macha. Tzader had found her and had this under control. *Did he get the stone put somewhere safe?*

It's safe enough.

It has to be absolutely secure. Tell Tzader the Kujoo plan to send super-warriors back in time to wipe out the entire Belador race. All of you would die.

All of us would die, Trey repeated, emphasizing "us." *We're prepared for them.*

She swallowed at the show of support from a fellow Belador. She wouldn't die in vain. Her tribe would continue.

The grotesque Nightstalker halflings started howling.

Down below, Tristan's head jerked up. Kizira swung around. The one Evalle now knew as Batuk roared and his men drew swords, then spread out around the room.

Heavy double doors hanging at the end of the building appeared to be new. Kizira had taken time to do a little remodeling, eh? The doors burst inward. Tzader and Quinn marched in first with Trey, Storm, Casper and twelve more men who were Beladors.

Evalle could feel her body welcome their power.

Then Laurette stepped up next to Tzader.

With the Ngak Stone in her hand.

Oh, no. That's how they found me.

Tristan laughed. "I knew they'd come for you, Evalle."

What are you doing, Z? Evalle yelled telepathically at Tzader. *Get Laurette and that stone out of here.*

She wouldn't leave or hand over the stone until you and Vyan were free.

"This is how you take care of the innocent?" Vyan snarled at Evalle.

"I didn't bring her here, dammit. This is the witch's fault—" Then Evalle yelled at Quinn, *Sleeping Beauty's here.*

Purple smoke boiled behind Tristan as the priestess disappeared. Tristan and the Kujoo leader exchanged worried glances.

"Release Evalle and Vyan if you want to live," Tzader ordered.

Now free to move, Tristan stepped forward. "Hand over the stone and I'll give you those two."

"You will not!" the warlord shouted.

Tristan leveled the Kujoo leader with a vile look of contempt. "You lied about what you were going to do with Evalle. I will do as I say."

"Do not hand over that stone!" Evalle caught Laurette looking up at Vyan, who was murmuring words as if in prayer.

Wouldn't do him much good if he was talking to Shiva. The Hindu god had refused to intervene.

Storm made a move forward and Tzader stopped him. Evalle sent Storm a small smile to thank him for coming through. She called to Laurette. "Free me and Vyan."

Laurette's gaze shot up and down between Evalle and the rock in her hand. The young woman said something to the rock and Evalle fell to the floor, but Vyan still hung above her.

Evalle stood up and asked Tristan, "You still want a throw down?"

Tristan released a growl of disgust. "Don't make me do this, Evalle. You'll lose."

"I don't think so. We have the rock on our side."

That pulled a wry laugh out of the male Alterant. "You going to take the rock from her?"

"No. But once I link with her I'll have that power on top of being an Alterant. Don't make me use it on you."

"You *can't* link with a human who isn't Belador." Lack of conviction lay beneath his challenge.

Evalle turned to Laurette. "Where did you learn to put those Gaelic words on your pottery?"

"From my granddad."

"Do you know what they say?"

"No."

"I do." Evalle glanced at Tzader and the rest of the Beladors when she spoke. "The words say, 'This is the home of a Belador descendant. Care for my grandchild as I would.'" She turned to Tristan, whose lips parted in surprise. "We *can* link with her, and you will lose."

Way to go, Evalle, Tzader murmured in her mind.

Yeah, but I really don't know if it will harm Laurette or not if we try to link with her.

Tristan opened his mouth to speak, but the warlord screamed at his men and the Nightstalker creatures, "Kill them!"

Evalle swung into the battle as all the Beladors poured into the room except for two left to guard Laurette.

Vyan called to Evalle. "My sword! In the corner."

She looked where his head had angled and saw the weapon she yanked to her hand kinetically just before a crazed Nightstalker flew at her. She swung the blade, slashing him in half.

Triquetra blades flew from Quinn's hands as fast as bullets from a rifle.

Spinning as she moved, Evalle brought the sword up, swinging it at the warlord, who turned in time to block with his sword, which broke hers in half.

How'd that happen if Vyan is immortal, too?

Brina appeared in the corner and lifted her hands, chanting.

Every Belador in the room instantly held a gleaming sword with their triquetra emblem on the hilt and Celtic scrolling engraved in the metal. Even Evalle. Storm and Casper were gifted with a pair of swords as well but not Belador weapons.

Tzader spun his sentient blades at a Kujoo, slicing off his enemy's head. Immortals were hard to kill, but cutting off their heads usually worked.

Blood spewed across Evalle's neck and shoulder from the arm Casper slashed off a ghoul that flew away screaming. Casper became a blur of cowboy and Highland warrior, wielding a sword like a man born to it. Storm swung his sword with equal fervor, looking deadly if not skilled.

A Belador went down beneath a wad of clawing Nightstalker creatures.

Evalle blasted a wave of power at them, scattering the creatures.

This might not be enough Beladors to win the fight against immortal warriors the Medb had infused with Noirre majik.

Evalle looked at Laurette, who stood shaking in a corner behind the two men who would protect her with their lives. The young woman was terrified. Evalle yelled, "Laurette, look at me!" When she had the girl's attention, she shouted, "You're a Belador. This is your tribe."

Before she could say more, a Kujoo attacked. Evalle fought back, meeting his sword blow for blow until she struck across his body, cutting it in half. She yelled at Laurette, "Order the rock to end the bloodshed."

Laurette looked down at the Ngak Stone in her trembling hands and cried out, "Make everybody stop!"

Evalle's body froze. Crud. She should have been more specific.

Laurette raised panicked eyes to sweep the room then park on Evalle. "What now?"

Evalle tried to talk but could only make noises.

Laurette lifted the stone. "Free Evalle to move and speak."

Evalle's muscles loosened at once. "Good girl. Step out from behind the men, because they can't move." When she had Laurette standing in the open, Evalle told her, "You're almost out of time."

"I want to send the Kujoo home. I told Vyan I would do that."

"I'm not sure you can do it with them frozen, but I don't want you to free the Kujoo so they can kill the Beladors." Evalle turned to Brina, surprised she hadn't spoken. "What do you want her to do?"

"I can't direct her to ask that rock anything. It carries Noirre majik deep within its powers."

"The Ngak Stone?" Evalle hadn't figured that, but it made sense. Maybe that was how the Medb had known about it. Evalle had assumed the stone was only Hindu in origin, but something that had survived since the beginning of time would have gained a lot of different powers.

Laurette took a gulp of breath. "I understand. I have to decide."

She gave the stone a new order. "Free everyone, but make them stay where they are and don't let them attack each other."

All the bodies in the room took a breath at once, but no one left their spot or tried to strike an enemy.

Tristan called out to Laurette. "Give me the stone and I'll free the Kujoo . . . and I'll give you your eyesight. I heard you were going blind. I'll have the power to heal your eyes."

The hope in Laurette's face hurt Evalle's heart, but she shook her head. "You can't do that."

Laurette nodded, her eyes red. "I know."

Brina spoke up. "I have no say over the stone, but the Kujoo cannot leave here yet. They have broken the truce and must be punished."

"No!" Laurette shouted at Brina, who merely cocked her head as if she were looking at an addled child. "I will give the rock to Tristan if you don't swear to free the Kujoo."

Tzader sent Evalle a worried look. "Do something."

Me? "Like *what?*"

"Yeah, Evalle," Tristan chimed in. "What about your offer to help the other Alterants? To see all of us free?"

Evalle took in the quick look of disbelief on Tzader's and Quinn's faces. "Shut up, Tristan."

Brina forgot about Laurette and zeroed in on Evalle with a look that promised all her good deals had just run out. Then she struck Tristan with a piercing glare, studying his face. "Tristan? As in the Alterant that was sent away? You *knew* he escaped and offered to help the others escape?"

"No," Evalle argued. ". . . I didn't say that exactly."

Frustration at things not turning out the way he'd expected started winding Tristan's voice into a tight ball of deadly anger when he spoke to Evalle. "I did as you wished and had the Medb free all of them. You owe me."

Evalle turned to Brina. "Let me explain."

"We don't have time for this." Brina swung her gaze to Laurette. "You have eighteen minutes, young lady. What are you going to do?"

"The rock doesn't always do what I ask." Laurette glanced from Brina to Evalle with eyes begging for help.

Evalle took mercy on her and started giving her direction. "Send the Nightstalkers that are half changed to the other side of death so they can rest in peace."

Laurette spoke to the rock and the creatures disappeared.

"Send the Kujoo . . ." Evalle paused, feeling Brina's glare bearing down on her. The Kujoo had not become superwarriors yet. If they were not immortal, she had faith in the ability of the Beladors who lived eight hundred years ago to protect themselves. "Send them to their original time, but without their powers."

"No! We end this fight today!" the Kujoo warlord screamed.

Vyan still dangled overhead and had been quiet until now. His wrists bled and his skin was a sickly gray, but his voice was strong when he spoke. "Yes, we do end this today." He shifted his gaze to Laurette. "All will be right. Do as I asked of you."

Laurette gave Vyan one long look that was filled with pain Evalle didn't understand but sympathized with nonetheless. When the young woman lifted the rock this time, there were tears in her eyes. She put the stone close to her lips and whispered words even Evalle couldn't hear.

All the Kujoo vanished, including Vyan.

Laurette turned her watery gaze to Evalle. "Now what?"

"Free the Nightstalkers that were not changed so they can return to their places in Atlanta." In the next instant, Evalle watched ghouls whip out the windows, all except for Grady, who came to hover by her.

Laurette squeaked a sound of pain. "The rock's getting hot. I can't hold it." She started juggling the rock between her hands, then pitched it at Evalle, who caught the stone against her stomach.

The stone was warm, but not too hot to hold. Was that because she was a powerful female?

Grace be to Macha. She held the power to do anything, even save herself from a Tribunal decision.

The room went deathly quiet.

THIRTY-SEVEN

E valle closed her fingers around the stone and colors burst in her mind. The surge of energy was unbelievable. Even her bruised eye opened up.

Everyone left inside the derelict school auditorium was icy still. Were they afraid of her or what she'd do?

"Tristan must return to his cage," Brina ordered.

"Nooo!" Veins stuck out on Tristan's neck as he made an aggressive move, but his feet were glued to the floor from when Laurette had ordered the stone to stop everyone from attacking each other. "Evalle, you said you cared about the Alterants, that you'd help me. Help all of us."

Every word he spoke fell like a ring of death between Evalle and Brina. This was not the moment to make a wrong decision.

Brina spoke in a quiet tone that carried the strength of a general's order. "Hand the stone over to Tzader to be placed in the VIPER vault."

"No. Keep it, Evalle," Tristan yelled. "You'll be safe forever. You can live free of persecution and the threat of being caged. Come with me and we'll go far away from all the Beladors."

Mesmerized at the connection she felt, Evalle stared at the rock that glowed like a molten rainbow. *Live. Safe. Free.* Her mind was lost in a haze of colors and words. She felt drugged.

"Evalle, do not do this!" Brina's voice held a dire threat if she was not obeyed. "That rock puts every Belador's future at risk if it is not put somewhere safe. The Kujoo could find a way to return to this time and destroy the entire tribe the next time. You must always put the tribe first."

"Like the tribe put me first?" Tristan shot back at Brina. "A tribe shouldn't turn their backs on each other. You locked me away for *no* reason. Evalle, ask Brina if I did anything before she sent me away to purgatory. Ask her!"

Tristan's question got through to Evalle. She shook her head to clear the cobwebs and raised her gaze to Brina. "Did Tristan commit any offense or shift into a beast?"

"Do not think to question me," Brina warned.

Turning to Tzader, Evalle considered asking him telepathically, then changed her mind. Everyone needed to hear this answer. "Do *you* know the truth?"

Tzader cut his eyes at Brina, then back to Evalle. "Yes, but I wasn't a part of sending him away. He's telling the truth."

"Tzader!" Brina's hologram blazed with light. Sparks shot off the edges. She gave him a quelling look before shoving her glare at Evalle. "I do whatever is necessary to keep the Beladors safe from danger."

The drugged feeling had to be the reason Evalle pursued her point. "Please, Brina. I need to know the truth. I've stood alongside Beladors since I was eighteen, and I need to know you acted with honor."

Tzader made a noise Evalle took as a crushed curse.

When Brina spoke it was in a reverent tone. "I am bound by an oath as well. Many oaths, in fact. There are things I cannot share with anyone. You are not the only one who has to perform difficult tasks, but in your case you have the gift of making choices along the way. I have been given one task above all others and that is to oversee and protect my tribe. Protection comes in all forms. Beyond that I will only say that I did act in honor."

For the first time since taking her oath as a Belador warrior, Evalle wondered what it would be like to be Brina. To live away from everyone, holding the power of the Beladors by her presence on an island. To exist solely to serve and to have no choice in the matter.

Maybe she hadn't given Brina enough credit.

But she still didn't know where she stood with Brina.

"What about me?" Evalle asked quietly. "Am I a danger to be locked away, too?"

330

Brina didn't hesitate. "If you were you would not be here now."

Evalle noted that Brina did not really answer her question.

Heat pulsed from the rock, sending waves of energy up Evalle's arm. She swallowed, trying to think clearly.

Quinn asked Evalle, "Are you ready to turn your back on the Beladors? If you do not obey Brina, that's what you're doing."

Indecision hovered over her. She knew to do the right thing, but there was that tiny part of her that wanted desperately to be safe and secure. To know she could live without a cloud of doubt always hanging over her.

To know who you are is the greatest power of all.

There was that strange voice in Evalle's mind again. The same one that had told her when the rock had been found.

Who was it?

Tristan pleaded, "Bring the rock and come with me. I'll take care of you, Evalle."

"I'll take care of you." The doctor who'd raped her when she was a teen had spoken those same words.

That flushed her mind clear of the fog that the rock had been weaving through her thoughts. The Beladors had rescued her from being locked away in a basement, at the mercy of the world. Tzader had said she had to give trust to get it in return.

Keeping this Ngak Stone meant she'd forever be safe from being caged, but at the risk of walking away from who she was and everything she held dear. "I. Am. A. Belador."

Brina's face softened in a way Evalle had never seen. In a gentler voice, she said, "Yes, you are. We take care of our own. It's time to finish this."

"Don't do this, Evalle," Tristan begged. "Brina will listen to you. Send me to another continent. Don't put me back in that cage."

"I'm sorry, Tristan." And she was. Evalle lifted the rock toward him.

"No! Kill. Me. Now."

Even with all the trouble he'd caused, she felt his agony. She, too, would rather die than be caged. She would not forsake him and the other Alterants, but she had to protect the world and her tribe first.

331

She spoke to the Ngak Stone. "Send Tristan back to his South American cage."

Tristan's blood-curdling scream thrashed through the room, then squeezed down to silence when he disappeared.

Evalle squeezed her eyes shut and swallowed. She asked the stone to keep him safe until she could help him. With her next breath she said, "Release all the Beladors."

Tzader strode over to the hologram, speaking low to Brina. "Keep in mind that Evalle found the rock and put her life on the line to prevent harm to any Belador."

Brina's gaze was crabby with annoyance. "I'm not sending her away, so you don't have to beg me for her life."

Evalle stepped over to Brina. "I didn't tell you about Tristan because I believed that's what the Medb wanted me to do so they could trap you. Tristan said the witch had a plan that would ensure destroying you and Tzader." She cut her eyes at Tzader for a moment, glad she didn't see condemnation in his. "I couldn't risk either of you being harmed. I did what I thought was honorable."

"I understand." Brina crossed her arms and tilted her head. "And I'm proud of you."

Evalle was speechless at hearing words she'd never expected to be said to her. A swirl of warmth brushed Evalle's skin when Brina smiled at her.

The warrior queen's gaze took in the room before returning to Evalle. "I will be with you tomorrow when you meet the Tribunal, and I will give testimony to the fact that *my* Belador protected the world."

"My Belador." Evalle played that over and over in her head until Tzader's hand touched her shoulder. She turned to him and smiled. "You told me . . ." . . . *to trust Brina,* she finished telepathically. *I'll do a better job of it from now on.*

The grin he gave her was answer enough. *You're running out of time before daylight.*

I've got seven minutes. Sen can ward one of the vehicles to get me home.

Storm stood to the side, watching her and the exchange. Evalle gave him a quick wink to let him know she'd see him soon.

Brina closed her eyes, speaking in a tone of request. "Sen, please come forth to retrieve the Ngak Stone."

A vapor spun at the side of Brina, then Sen appeared with a container the size of a cigar box carved of white marble the color of mother-of-pearl. "Where's the Ngak Stone?"

"Here." Evalle held it up and fought not to smile at his shock over her possessing the dangerous treasure. She waited for him to come to her, then placed the stone in the box sitting open on his two palms. The lid shut immediately and the seam between lid and bottom disappeared.

Her bruised eye swelled shut again and the lashes on her back burned like the devil.

"I need some help getting home." Laurette whispered the words as if afraid to speak up. Her eyes were milky with impaired vision.

Evalle owed this young woman so much. "I'll take her."

"No." Brina shook her head, eyes searching the room of Beladors and VIPER agents moving toward them. "Quinn can take her."

Laurette once again ignored Brina and edged over to Evalle, who took the young woman's hand when she spoke to her. "Thank you for doing the right thing and for being willing to face all this to save me and Vyan. After seeing those words on that planter outside your door, I'm pretty sure your grandfather was a Belador. He'd have been very proud of you."

Laurette tried to smile past the deep hurt lining her face.

"Her grandfather *was* one of our warriors." Brina made that announcement. "Macha has just informed me that prior to going into a battle he did not expect to survive, Laurette's grandfather asked Macha to spare his granddaughter from taking up the sword, because Laurette was born a Belador as well. He knew she'd spend her life alone once he left and wanted her to be free to follow her heart and be an artist. Macha agreed. You are indeed part of the Belador tribe, Laurette."

Evalle squeezed Laurette's hand. "That makes you family if you need anything. Quinn is wonderful and will escort you safely home."

Laurette nodded silently. Tears hung at the corners of her eyes.

Quinn appeared at Evalle's side and placed his hand over Laurette's shoulder. "This won't take long." He turned to Sen. "Why don't you teleport us?"

Sen nodded, then instructed Laurette, "Take Quinn's hand, envision your home and say when you're ready."

Evalle gave Sen a narrowed look. He never gave *her* that much warning.

The minute Laurette reached for Quinn's hand, she said, "Ready," and the pair vanished.

Evalle would check on Laurette later this week. She turned to Brina, wanting to discuss the Tribunal meeting, but the warrior queen beat her to it.

"The Tribunal will send someone to escort you after midnight tonight, Evalle. Make sure you're above ground at that time. Do not be late."

Evalle answered Brina, ignoring how Sen was close enough to hear her. "I'll wait for my escort in Woodruff Park."

Brina sent an arched-eyebrow look at Sen, who angled his chin in acknowledgment. Apparently finished with everything here, Brina disappeared.

The swords vanished at the same moment.

Crud. Evalle had meant to have Brina ask Sen to ward a vehicle to get her home. Tzader would ask him.

Sen looked over in Trey's direction. "Tell Adrianna to come in and clean up this mess. She's outside cloaking the building from civilians."

Trey swung around from where he was debriefing VIPER agents and Beladors. "I look like your lackey?"

Sen shrugged. "Evalle can do it . . . with her hands."

"I'll get Adrianna," Tzader called out to Trey, then slowed by Sen on his way out. "You ever take a day off from being an asshole?"

Sen let his glare speak for him.

Once Tzader was out of hearing range, Sen's narrowed gaze hardened even further. He tucked the box with the stone under his arm and strode forward.

She didn't see a warded vehicle in her future.

Sen stopped close to Evalle and leaned down. "Be on time for your

Tribunal hearing and don't make me hunt you. If I can't find you, Tzader will be held responsible. If you're not there for the Tribunal meeting, Tzader will have to take your place and accept the consequences of the ruling."

"Somebody pee in your crispy-doodles this morning?" She couldn't leave Tzader to face the Tribunal and Sen knew it.

But Brina had said she'd be there. Time for another dose of trust.

Storm had finished talking to one of the Beladors and moved closer to where she stood with Sen, his body flexing as if he intended to protect her.

But she didn't need saving or protecting. She was a Belador. She jutted her chin at Sen. "I'll be there, but don't hold your breath that the Tribunal is going to make your day and send me away."

His smirk spoke volumes before he teleported away with the Ngak Stone.

Asshole. Evalle felt a pop against the back of her head the minute she swore. *Sorry, Brina.* But Evalle smiled at the reprimand that meant she was one of Brina's family.

"Is that the one who wants your ass?" Grady asked.

"Yes." The Tribunal was a bigger problem than Sen, but she couldn't discuss that here with Grady. She'd forgotten the Nightstalker was still here. "How'd you get caught in the Kujoo trap?"

His eyes shifted away from her guiltily. "I got sucked in when I heard about the double handshakes."

Tzader walked back inside just in time to hear what Grady had said. "You know none of us can do that, and look what happened when the Kujoo shook with those poor Nightstalkers."

Grady's image wavered in and out, eyes shooting angry darts at Tzader. "I had a reason."

Adrianna came into the room, took one look at Evalle and turned toward the windows, where daylight was coming on fast. Adrianna's lips moved as she raised her hands. The windows turned into a solid wall. She ignored Evalle after that, directing her attention to Tzader. "I have a question for you."

Tzader walked over to the Sterling witch Evalle was starting to reevaluate after all that Adrianna had done. Sterling witches didn't give without expecting something in trade. That Adrianna hadn't asked for a thing—yet—was reason enough to remain vigilant around her.

With everyone busy, Evalle took the opportunity to find out what was going on with Grady. "What's the reason you need an hour tonight?"

A sad smile shifted his face. "I have a granddaughter getting married in Atlanta. I don't want to meet her, but I wanted to hear her words. When I'm in this *half-alive* form, my hearing and sense of smell are dulled. Not crisp like a human's senses. I want to hear the organ music play her wedding march and hear her say her vows. I want to smell the fresh flowers." His eyes strayed from her face, turning watery. "I want to soak up a memory I can hold on to for eternity."

Her heart might split from breaking. She had to get out of here before she lost the shaky grip she had on her emotions after all that had gone down tonight. "I understand." She took a breath and cleared her throat. "You should go—" She started to say *home,* but Grady didn't have a home. "I'll see you later, okay?"

Grady stared at her so long that she thought he was stuck in that spot. He finally shimmered toward the exit, then vanished.

The room was far darker with the windows gone, but the glass skylights still intact allowed enough light to see. Storm finished closing the distance to her, clearly not caring what anyone thought when he put the back of his hand against her cheek. "That's some shiner."

Her heart tripped over itself at his touch. Guessed she had to reevaluate how she thought of him, too. "You told them how to find us and brought Laurette with the stone. She must have found you okay."

Storm gazed at her for a few seconds. "I was buckling my belt behind a hedge in the park when she popped into view holding that rock."

"You were supposed to put Laurette and *that rock* somewhere safe, not bring it around this place."

"I don't see the world in shambles, and that stone wasn't going anywhere until you were safe."

Okay, that just earned him more points than he'd know how to use. "Thanks, but what if Tristan had gotten the stone?"

"He'd have had to kill me to do that, and I'm not so easy to kill." Storm reached behind his neck and untied a leather cord, lifting the amulet from inside his shirt. "Give this back to Nicole when you see her."

Evalle stood still while he leaned forward to tie the cord at the back of her neck. His lips brushed her cheek before he lifted away. He ran his hand down to her shoulder, and she flinched when his fingers touched the slash cuts from Kizira's bullwhip nails.

To keep from moaning, she gritted her teeth.

Storm moved around behind her. "Your back's a mess. We need to get Adrianna to draw out the Noirre venom again."

"I'd be happier to owe a loan shark," Evalle muttered.

Storm sighed. "Don't move, and I'll ease the burn." He waited until she nodded to put his hands on her back.

Heat, then a wonderful numbing sensation, raced across the nerves just beneath her skin.

When he finished, Storm kissed her neck this time.

In spite of worrying that someone might have seen the intimate touch, she smiled.

Heavy footsteps pounded in her direction. Tzader strode up to her, but his glare blasted Storm, who returned it with a look of *what's-your-problem?*

Before anything erupted between them, Evalle intervened. "I need to grab a shower, get some sleep and take care of a few errands before I meet with the Tribunal."

Tzader broke off from the visual posturing with Storm and addressed her. "Think you can stay out of trouble between now and midnight?"

Evalle considered what she'd just decided a moment ago. She didn't want to lie to Tzader, but neither did she want to share what she was planning to do. Trouble was a mild way to describe it. "What, and give up the only thing I'm good at?"

THIRTY-EIGHT

The world swirled and blurred in Laurette's milky vision the minute she took the hand of the man Evalle had called Quinn. He squeezed Laurette's fingers and said, "We're almost there."

She expected to wake up any minute and find out that she'd fallen in Piedmont Park and hit her head and that all of this had been a bad nightmare. But when her feet touched solid ground next, she was wide awake and still clinging desperately to some guy she'd bet would answer to the name Quinn. "Are we there yet?"

"If you live in a charming cottage with blue shutters and a large pottery vase next to the front door, I'd say we are."

She could only see blurry light. "It's my home, but I may need some help getting inside."

The sound of him moving around was followed by the familiar squeak of her front door opening. He took her arm with gentle fingers and led her slowly inside. "How impaired is your vision?"

He had a kind voice full of understanding, but Evalle had already told her no one could fix her eyesight. Laurette wouldn't whine. "It's manageable now that I'm inside."

"Take this." He pressed a cell phone into her palm. "I know this has been a harrowing experience, but you are part of the Belador family now. Can you find the number five in the middle of the keypad?"

"Yes."

"Press that to call me when you're ready to talk about a companion dog and adapting to the changes you'll be facing. We won't leave you to face them alone."

"Thank you." She needed him to go now or she was going to break down in front of him. The rock had certainly seduced her, because she felt the loss of her vision as acutely as when she'd lost her granddad. On top of that, she couldn't quiet the urge to see Vyan again, but he was where he wanted to be.

She would be happy for him and remember the way he'd made her smile. Remember the way he'd stepped between her and danger.

Remember his kiss.

"Thank you for bringing me home, but . . ." *Go away.*

"I sense that you're ready to be alone. I'll leave, but I'll expect your call soon. And know that you can call any time, day or night."

She just nodded because she couldn't push any words out of her tight throat. When the door closed, she gave in to the pain expanding in her chest. A sob broke free over everything she'd lost. But she'd found out why her granddad had never come home. He'd been a Belador. They spoke of him as if he was a hero. He used to tell her the Barrett women were strong, that her ancestors were warriors. Warriors!

She was a Belador.

A blind one.

And Granddad would have been frowning at her right now for giving in to despair. She sniffed and wiped her nose with the back of her hand.

Suck it up and act like my granddaughter. She could almost hear him saying that.

Having practiced recently, in anticipation of her vision being all but gone, she stuck the cell phone in her pocket and felt her way across the room. She might not be able to create her signature designs on the large pottery anymore, but right now she needed to sink her fingers into the clay and feel her granddad's spirit surround her again.

At the door to the basement, she put a hand on the rail along the stairs and worked her way down. She'd reached the bottom landing and had taken two steps into the room when she heard someone's sharp intake of breath.

Her own breathing was suddenly short and frantic. "Who's there?"

"'Tis I."

Fear pumped with the blood slamming her heart. "Who?"

"Vyan."

Impossible. "What are you doing here?" Her heart raced for an entirely different reason now.

"I don't know." He sounded lost, which cut through her thrill of happiness over finding him here.

"I'm so sorry. You weren't supposed to get stuck in this time period."

"What did you tell the rock when you sent the Kujoo away?" His footsteps moved toward her.

She thought back on her exact words, the ones she'd chosen based on what Vyan had told her. "I asked the rock to send all the Kujoo tribe wherever their hearts desired. I thought you would go home with the others."

Had she condemned him to this world by not being more specific?

He chuckled and touched her hands, folding them inside his. His scent met her next breath. "I knew you were a wise woman, and my heart is wiser than my head some days. I did not know where I wanted to go, but I did not want to return with Batuk to war, nor did I like leaving you alone either. It seems my heart chose to stay here."

"You're happy about this?"

"I believe I will find happiness here I have not felt for many years."

She wouldn't have been able to see through her tears even if she had unimpaired vision. "You are a gift I never expected to receive." Getting used to being blind was not going to be easy, but now she didn't fear the darkness with Vyan staying in this world. She couldn't believe he was really here.

He took her hand in his. "I asked for a gift as well but was denied."

A deep voice boomed into the room. *"No, my faithful Vyan, you were not denied. I merely waited to see if you were truly content to remain in this time and still wished to give up your immortality before I granted your request."*

Vyan was silent for a moment. "If I return to my home with the other Kujoo, I will be expected to pick up a sword again. My family would still be dead. What would be the reason to continue life there? None that I can think of. But I have managed for two years and know I can survive here. More than that, I can start anew here."

Laurette wiped at her wet eyes. "You really don't want to go home?"

"My heart would miss you." He lifted his voice. "I am ready to trade, Shiva."

"To trade what—" Her words were cut off in a gasp when bright light flashed through the room. She covered her eyes with her hands. Warm fingers clasped hers and pulled them away from her eyes.

Crisp details of everything in her studio flooded her vision. Vyan's happy face was completely in focus. "What happened? My eyes . . . I can see. Oh, Vyan, I can see!"

His warm eyes—warm brown *human* eyes—crinkled with happiness. He cupped her face with his hand. "When I could not escape Tristan and Batuk to come back to you and make sure you would be safe, I told my god Shiva I wished to offer my immortality in trade for your eyesight. I did not want to leave you alone and blind. I expected to die at the battle with the Beladors, but I still survived. I do not wish to live another eight hundred years—only as long as you live."

Tears streamed down her face. "I'm a Belador descendant. You're sure you want to stay here with your enemy?"

"You will never be *my* enemy." He leaned in and kissed her softly, a tentative touch that gave her the confidence to kiss him back.

She could feel her granddad's blessing flood over her.

THIRTY-NINE

Evalle hadn't worn dress clothes for anyone, but tonight was important. She had to look her best. Wanted to look her best. The simple brown pants and jacket probably looked better on the chipped-up mannequin in the used-clothing store, but she couldn't have come in here wearing her battle gear.

Cool air swam around her face and arms, a welcome change from the heat bombarding Atlanta outside.

Murmurs drifted to her ears, nothing specific. Chatting littered the serene air in the church below the balcony where she hid. The small group gathered in the main vestibule waited with reverence. She'd never been one to pray, but she sometimes wondered if those who did were heard.

She cut her eyes sideways at the dashing elderly man on her left. Was she good or what? Just look at that rockin' cleanup job she'd done.

Grady wore a gently used black suit she'd gotten from the same secondhand store. He sat as straight as a general waiting to meet the president, but he was holding himself erect in anticipation of a wedding march.

She'd brought his clothes and a shaving kit she'd pieced together to the upstairs bathroom that served the balcony of this church on busy Sundays. Not much traffic up here at a small Wednesday night wedding.

Watching the clock down to the minute, she'd laid out everything for Grady in the bathroom, shaken his hand, then shut the door.

He turned his clean-shaven face toward her. The smile he

bestowed on her was worth the sanction she'd face for this if she got caught shaking hands with a Nightstalker for personal reasons, but she was feeling pretty good about her position among the Beladors.

Why not make someone else's dream come true?

Grady leaned toward her. "You must always believe, no matter what. Tzader and Quinn won't let anything happen to you. Neither will that Injun."

She smiled at Grady's newest slight. Storm was not an "Injun," but Grady wanted to get a rise out of her to keep her mind off the Tribunal. She smiled at him. "I'm not worried."

Much.

His granddaughter's wedding would start any minute now. The minute they were done she'd make the eight-mile ride back to downtown with him clinging to her bike. He'd gotten lost after being freed from the Kujoo this morning and spent hours finding his block around Grady Hospital.

All the shaving and changing to clean clothes would go away as soon as he glimmered back into his ghoul form.

But he'd have the memory for as many decades as he remained a Nightstalker, which could be a very long time. Her heart pinched at the waves of happiness she felt coming off him.

After she made sure he was safe back near the hospital, she'd have two hours to spend with Feenix. She'd take her little darling on a bike ride out where he could squeal in delight as much as he wanted and no one would hear.

Grady's fault. He'd got her thinking about making good memories.

Then, she'd have to get past Go with the Tribunal, but Brina had said she'd be there.

The room below quieted when the piano music stopped and Grady leaned forward, anxious to look over the edge of the balcony where his granddaughter had planned an intimate affair.

He started to fade. He stared at his hands, then turned panicked eyes to her.

The last thing she wanted to do was hurt Grady or risk his half-life in any way. Evalle opened her mouth to speak, but the wedding march struck up.

It was the look of anguish on Grady's face that ended all debate. She couldn't live with that as the last memory of him if there was a chance that she would get sent away tomorrow by the Tribunal.

Hoping this would not harm him, she reached over and grasped his hand.

Relief and gratitude poured from his body. He squeezed her fingers and leaned over to whisper, "I prayed for a miracle and God sent me you. I'll talk to him about the Tribunal."

Emotion she had never felt clogged her throat. Lifting her chin, she smiled at the old ghoul, who grinned back.

She'd fought the Kujoo, an Alterant and demons this week. She'd protected her tribe and upheld her oaths.

If the Tribunal wanted to lock her away, they'd have a fight on their hands. Bring it on.